Redemption

DeJay

Regal Crest

Port Arthur, Texas

ISBN 978-1-935053-95-8

First Printing 2011

9 8 7 6 5 4 3 2 1

Cover design by Donna Pawlowski

Published by:

Regal Crest Enterprises, LLC
4700 Highway 365, Suite A, PMB 210
Port Arthur, Texas 77642

Find us on the World Wide Web at
http://www.regalcrest.biz

Published in the United States of America

Acknowledgments

A big thank you to L-J Baker for letting me participate in the Lesbian Fiction Forum, (www.lesbianfiction.org) when I knew absolutely nothing about on-line protocols, or the craft of writing. You've taught me so much. Most importantly L-J, thank you for your friendship. To all the ladies of the Private Workshop, thank you for dealing with my feeble attempts at writing. I learned so much and owe so much to you all. To the many first readers, your input was invaluable and I thank you. Thank you to the following: Andi Marquette, for naming this story and giving me insight into characterization, to Barb Clanton, for introducing me to Self Editing for Fiction Writers. To Lisa Boeving and Elaine Burnes for being diligent Beta readers and helping me to shape the story that I so desperately wanted to tell. Elaine Burnes, I hope I've finally learned to provide adequate description. To Fran Walker, there are no words that can ever express my gratitude for your kindness and patience when I simply didn't get it. For teaching me POV, tense and most importantly Show vs Tell, all things I had never heard of. You truly are a saint. I hope you know how special you really are.

Thank you to Cathy LeNoir for taking on this book in spite of the subject matter, and being brave enough to publish it. Thanks to Pat Cronin, who always patiently answered my numerous questions and to Brenda Adcock, editor extraordinaire. You made the entire process pain free while keeping this nervous newbie calm and I thank you for that.

Lastly many, many people helped me along the way to make this story what it is today. If you enjoy the book they should all get the credit, however if there are any mistakes they are mine and mine alone.

To Lee, for taking a chance on me when no one else ever had.
I love you with all my heart and soul — and more than life itself.
Happy thirty-third anniversary, sweetheart.

Prologue

I BRUSHED MY unruly hair for the fifth time, staring hollow-eyed at my reflection.

I hate you.

Revulsion filled me. The white pinstripe shirt I had picked up from the cleaners lay on the floor taunting me. The plastic bag shredded during a fit of anger and despair. I yanked the wrinkled top on and buttoned it slowly, observing my jerky movements in the mirror as if watching a horror show that wouldn't switch off. The cufflinks I had set out earlier lay on the nightstand where I had left them. Izzy had given them to me on our wedding day. I hesitated before reaching for them.

You never deserved her. Never.

It took three tries to push the gold-initialed studs through the buttonholes due to my trembling fingers. The new three-piece suit that Isabella insisted I needed for business hung on the closet door.

Business. Always the fucking business.

A knock at the door jarred me.

"Mac?"

"One minute." I pulled the pants off the hanger and tugged them on, tucking the shirt in as I went. "Okay."

The bedroom door opened and Sarah stood there clutching a hankie, her eyes red-rimmed from crying. "It's time, sweetie."

I removed the vest from the hanger and slipped it on. "This look okay?"

"You look fine," she said as she waddled closer and straightened my collar. Her hands were icy cold, and quivered against my skin, her eyes reflecting my pain. The tenuous third trimester of her pregnancy was being made more difficult by the events of the past week and today's tribulations were compounding the issue further.

"Why don't you stay home with Mikey," I suggested. "He's going to be scared and you—"

"I loved them too, damn it," she answered, her voice raspy. Her tears started anew; her bottom lip trembled. "I'm going." She shook her head and dabbed her eyes. "That's final."

I acceded. Sarah could be stubborn at times. The shoes I had spent an hour polishing lay by the dresser. I stepped into them and plucked my suit jacket from the hanger. "All ready."

"Will you be warm enough?" she asked.

"Not today Sarah, please."

She took my arm as we walked down the hall of the ranch-style home she shared with her husband and two-year-old son. We entered the living room, neither of us speaking, everything already expressed. Sarah's husband, Michael, stood before the picture window. When he glanced at us his eyes were bloodshot from lack of sleep and spent tears. "We have a problem. The news vans are out front."

I went to the window. The entire street was lined with their damn vehicles, satellite dishes reaching into the sky assuring their ability to transmit the latest up-to-the minute news. Commentators clamored in the road, microphones in hand, interviewing anyone who would let them, anyone who wanted their ten minutes of fame. Cameramen jockeyed for a better angle and photographers lined up their shots. A neighbor crying, a mother calling her children in from the chaos or whatever would translate into tonight's glaring headline. Male and female television personalities vied for interviews, hoping for some big scoop. "How do you want to do this?" I asked.

"The judge sent two officers over to escort us. I say we let them help block the path," Michael responded.

"Okay, but let's keep Sarah in the middle," I said. "I don't want her jostled around."

"Thank you, I agree." Michael picked up Sarah's coat and helped her into it while I scanned the street a second time. A famous blonde from Fox News was questioning the neighbor on the left. The perpetually animated reporter tossed her blonde tresses and flashed her beautiful smile. The fact she'd never done any real investigative work was evident every time she opened her damn mouth. A police car pulled into the drive and all cameras immediately focused on the occupants. I could almost hear the clicking as the eager photographers competed for the money shot. I was determined they wouldn't get one of me. "Ready?" I asked.

"Ready." Sarah tipped her head once as she clasped Michael's hand.

I proceeded to the door, glancing back one last time before opening it. We all knew it would become a mob scene. It was better that I lead the charge and let Sarah and Michael bring up the rear. Two officers were waiting on the front walk as I opened the door and they rushed quickly to the stoop in anticipation of the crowd. Television, newspapers, and various AP services were covering my family's story and all surged forward as I walked onto the porch.

"Ms. Taylor, we're here to assist you." The small silver name tag read Pete Jenkins, but I already knew that. I had gone to school with his older brother.

"Thank you, Pete. Please make sure my friends are safe. Sarah's pregnant."

He motioned to the other officer as two more leapt from the second cruiser and we made a circle around Sarah before we trekked down the path to the waiting limousine. The driver held the rear door open for easy access. I kept my eyes averted as we maneuvered through the crowds of reporters screaming questions at me.

"Ms. Taylor, can you tell us how you feel?"

Like I'd been run through the planer in my shop, repeatedly...until there was nothing left but the sawdust of my soul. That's how I feel you prick, like there's nothing left, but that wasn't the answer he wanted. He wanted to know about my misery, about the emptiness I felt inside. He wanted to know what it was like to see my wife and child dead on a cold slab in the morgue. If I ached at their loss. He wanted me to describe the horror of seeing bullet holes in their bodies, or evidence of the torture they had both suffered. He wanted to see me bleed. They all wanted the fucking gory details to boost their ratings. Well, they could all go to hell.

"Ms. Taylor, are you angry with how this all played out? Will you be suing the police department?"

Angry? How could I be angry? It was my fault. I gritted my teeth to keep from responding.

"Ms. Taylor, any idea when the crime scene will be released?"

No fucking idea you asshole. Fortunately I never responded. It wouldn't change the circumstances and I never wanted this kind of notoriety. Next to the car, I waited for Sarah and Michael to enter first, then followed them. The driver closed the door and shut out the melee.

Once we were moving I stared out the blackened window not seeing, merely anesthetized by my grief, my mind struggling to deal with the events that had transpired over the last five days.

"Sweetie, look."

I gazed at Sarah, then the direction she was pointing. The drive to the funeral home was a mere ten blocks, about half the size of the entire town, but today it would take at least twenty minutes due to the number of men, women and children lining the streets crying or waving as we passed. Isabella was beloved by many and valued by all who knew her and they had come out to pay their respects — hopefully not in pursuit of the macabre. I felt the tears form and blinked furiously to stop them. I would not cry. I would not break down. I would accept this punishment as their final retribution.

At the funeral home, I detoured into the bathroom for a moment to myself before I faced the crowds. I entered the viewing room only to find it packed solid with friends, neighbors, and fellow citizens. I had ordered the casket be closed. There would be no gawking by curious looky-loos. No one searching for injuries. No comments about how peaceful they looked. They were not peaceful. They were dead. I especially didn't want pictures showing up in the tabloids as so often happened in cases like this.

It appeared the entire town had come out. Sarah and Michael greeted each and every mourner, while I sat numbly waiting for it all to be over. Initially I prayed it was a nightmare, one I'd wake up from. Now I accepted this was my reality, my life for eternity. My hell on earth.

Church doctrine wouldn't allow the bodies of sinners to be admitted into the cathedral for the usual Requiem Mass. Instead the priest would accompany us to the cemetery for a small graveside service at a not so small nominal fee. My anger made me choke on the hypocrisy, but I would tolerate anything to make sure Isabella and Bella received absolution through the priest's prayers.

The trip to the cemetery took us past the same people we'd seen earlier. Though the skies were clear, bitter winds driving down off the Rocky Mountains dropped the temperatures into single digits and frost bite became a real concern. Still, people willingly lined the streets to show their respect for my wife and child.

"It was a lovely turn out, don't you think?"

The priest addressed his question to me. I knew he didn't care about my opinion and I refused to disgrace Izzy by spouting it.

"Mac, how about some water?" Sarah gripped my hand and squeezed it tightly. I shook my head, unable to speak.

The limo glided through the gates of the cemetery and parked while the hearse and flower car drove ahead. I knew it was standard procedure, but I didn't want Izzy or Bella out of my sight. I felt the separation pulling them farther and farther from me. My chest constricted and my heart felt like it was tearing in two. "I need air," I rasped. I opened the limo door and quickly slammed it shut again. The media was waiting for us. *Fuck!*

"Michael, I thought the police were going to keep them outside the gates?" Sarah's quiet words belied her anger and pain.

"I'll check with our escorts." Michael hastily climbed out of the car, but not before one photographer managed to push his camera lens inside to get a shot of the occupants. Shortly, Michael re-entered the vehicle. "They've been ordered to stay outside the fence or chance arrest."

"With those lenses it doesn't matter." I scrubbed my hands over my face and through my hair. "They'll get their damn pictures in the end. The tabloids always do."

"Child—"

"I am not your child, Father, no disrespect meant, and honestly there's nothing you can say that I want to hear.

"Mac, he's only trying to comfort us." Sarah squeezed my hand.

"Let him comfort you then."

She twisted to face the priest. "You must understand the strain and shock of everything we've been through."

"I do, I truly do. I—"

I leaned forward, my fury exploding, "You understand? Have you loved a woman with all your heart only to have her murdered? Have you lost a child to a homicidal maniac's malicious and demented acts of violence? Don't *you* ever tell me you understand, not until you have your life snatched out from under you and you sit here, right here, waiting to bury your family, like I am today."

Michael slid next to me and placed his hand on my shoulder. "It's not Father Reilly's fault, Mac."

"I need air," I said again. I pushed past Sarah, opened the door, and lurched out onto the blacktop.

"Mac, please—" Sarah leaned out the door.

I gazed back at her. "It's okay. I'm gonna start walking up the path. I need to move." What I really needed was to be closer to my family.

"I'll come with you—"

"No Sarah, I have to do this alone."

The service was short once it got started. People huddled together, sharing warmth against the blast of arctic air. Sarah sat in a chair with a blanket over her lap while the priest droned on. People cried, some sobbed. Even Michael sported tears on his cheeks. I remained stoic, waiting for the moment when I could be alone with my family. Baby Bella was in the coffin with Izzy. I had her placed in Isabella's loving embrace. Mother and child would share eternity, as they had life. Some suggested separate interment, but I had angrily objected. My only wish was that I could join them.

After the service, after the mourners paid their last respects, I asked Sarah and Michael to give me a moment alone. I willed words to come. I wanted to beg Izzy to forgive me. To hold them both one more time. To tell Isabella how much I loved her and our child. Words failed me, just as I had failed them.

The hardest thing I had ever done was leaving my family's gravesite. Michael, Sarah, and I walked arm-in-arm down the path toward the waiting limo. A television crew had breached security and they stood equipped as we approached. The videographer was filming our descent and the newsman waited with his mike in hand, a smile on his face. The closer we got, the more I pulled away from Sarah, trusting that Michael would protect her.

"Ms. Taylor, how do you feel?"

I motioned toward the open car door to indicate Sarah should enter first.

"Ms. Taylor do you think Ms. Sanchez is dead because her ex found out about your illicit relationship?"

Michael stilled, but I gestured for him to follow Sarah into the limo.

"Ms. Taylor, some people are suggesting that Isabella and her child are being punished by God because of your homosexual liaison with her. What do you have to say to that?"

I took one step and delivered my heartfelt response.

Chapter One

THEY WERE THERE again, standing behind the backstop, he excitedly enjoying the game while she nervously shifted from foot to foot. His eyes were eager as a small smile tugged the corner of his mouth. I was on the pitcher's mound sweltering under the late afternoon sun, beads of sweat forming on my upper lip. Concentration was futile. All I could think about was the two of them. He measured about thirty-inches tall, small for what I estimated as his age. She impatiently waited next to him, not much larger, holding his hand tightly. Watching. Her eyes were guarded and her stance restless. Anytime he managed to pull a hand free she grasped it back while continually scanning her perimeter. She apparently took her job of guardian seriously and I was curious to know why. My past efforts to approach them scared them both off and they stayed away for days. I wasn't sure what to do then, any more than I was now.

The sun beat on my back, perspiration trickled between my shoulder blades and along the curve of my spine. As I prepared to toss the ball to the child in the batter's box, my temper flared. My mind wasn't on the game or the batter. Those two kids were too frigging young to be out on their own and yet there they were. Something wasn't right. Instinct told me they were in trouble.

The batter, Janice, studied me, anticipating the pitch. She's eager, taunting me. I cast my eyes toward first base and winked at Patrick. Then I began my wind up for what was sure to be a low velocity pitch. Janice swung and made contact. The ball rolled past me as she took off hobbling toward first base before anyone attempted to field the grounder. The boy behind the backstop clutched the fence with his hand while I made a grand show of preparing to throw the ball. He silently cheered for the girl stumbling her way to first. He jumped in place, his eyes shining with hope, his smile brilliant. But then most of my kids have had that same look at one point or another.

All the children on Team Bella were special. Some dealt with physical disabilities, some were special needs kids, some were victims, but all twenty of them belonged to me every day while we played ball. The players knew we didn't have losers on the team. I wouldn't allow it. Everyone participated and everyone was cheered for. Those were the rules. Some of the parents helped me from time to time and there were volunteers from the local gym and fire department. Weather permitting, we gathered every afternoon so these children could play ball like their so-called "normal" counterparts.

Janice grinned triumphantly when she touched first base even before the ball left my hand. The braces on her legs hadn't prevented her from being safe or from doing her happy dance once there. The sheer joy in her eyes sent ripples through me. It always did. This was why I did this, for all the Janices who would never get the chance to play ball if not for Team Bella.

Andy, the first baseman, tossed the ball to Jim Collins who was catching for us. Jim got ready to lob the ball to me when I saw my mystery girl tug on the boy's hand. They were leaving. I motioned for Jim to hold up and called Patrick, my assistant, to replace me on the mound. I sauntered casually over to the sidelines, not wanting to scare them. After snatching a bottle of water I squatted down to her level, keeping the fence, her safety net, between us and smiled. "Hey, you two. It's only the third inning. You're not leaving already, are you?"

She tugged his hand harder trying to pull him along. I made sure not to advance. She was one mistrustful little girl. One wrong shift from me would make her bolt and I didn't want that. He peered at me closely. I sensed he wanted to say something, even as he allowed her to drag him away.

I stood up and witnessed their departure. He glanced back sorrowfully as they began to wander off. He wavered and I took a chance. "Well, you have a good day and maybe I'll see you back here soon," I called out. "Better yet, maybe you'll want to play. Whaddaya think?"

He smiled and bobbed his head. *Progress at last.* I tracked them until they were out of sight, hoping to see an adult in the vicinity, but there were none. Previously, I'd asked them to join the team, but the girl had refused. The second time I tried, she yanked him away before he could respond. He didn't appear happy, but didn't argue with her. Another time I attempted to follow them. That had only frightened her and they ran. My temper simmered. Where were the parents of those two kids? Why were they walking the streets alone?

MY ATTENTION RETURNED to the game as the team finished up. However, the boy and girl were never far from my thoughts. Connie Collins, Patrick's mother, approached as I came off the field. "Mac, great game today," she said.

I smiled. "Thanks, beautiful."

"Patrick did well, don't you think?"

"Absolutely," I agreed. Connie was proud of her son, and she credited the team for building his confidence. "Patrick's a natural."

Janice's mother, Noreen Thomas, was handing out refreshments and offered me a bottle of water. "Mac, you okay? You look tired."

Noreen's a pretty young thing with red hair and blue eyes. Her daughter was born with a form of muscular dystrophy that had affected her legs. Mercifully, the progression of the disease was slow. "I'm fine, sunshine. How are things with you?" I opened the water and took a swig.

"Frank's due home Tuesday." Noreen's eyes revealed her loneliness. "We're both excited," she beamed, a smile radiating across her freckled face. "He'll be home for a whole week this time, the truck needs servicing."

Frank Thomas was an independent truck driver with no medical insurance. He was on the road for weeks at a time. They had a ton of medical bills and he was desperate to keep ahead of them. He'd been known to stay out for two months straight, hauling freight in an attempt to make ends meet. "Tell me you're not planning to put sugar in the gas tank to keep him home a little longer." I teased.

"Mac, you know me better than that." Noreen blushed.

I strode away, chuckling as I jotted a note in my Blackberry to talk with Mary, my assistant, later. The parents and the kids slowly filed off the field and back to their other lives while I reflected on the afternoon's action. Little Tommy got a base hit and was ecstatic. His father clearly felt the same. I'm really proud how quickly Patrick has learned the rules of being an assistant coach. Down's Syndrome didn't mean he couldn't. It just meant extra care was required to teach him. My real concern was for Denise. She was having a hard time breathing and I wondered if the excitement was too much for her. Her asthma often required that she stop playing in order to use her inhaler or the portable oxygen tank. The frequency was increasing, along with my anxiety. I added a note in my Blackberry to speak with her dad the next time I saw him.

Sweet little Tracey got a home run today. She bravely ran the bases and finished by scrambling into the bleachers where her mother waited with open arms, bringing tears to my eyes. She's still a frightened little girl, but she was trying. Her mother, Andrea, attended the games daily, helping her daughter's healing process. Tracey was the victim of molestation, something I know a little bit about. I shook my head, trying to block out the images. I packed up the equipment, helped Noreen with the garbage, and started out. It had been a good day all around.

WEEKS LATER I was on my way back to the hospital. I had left
just over an hour previous, to take a shower, get a change of clothes
and grab the mail from my office when I heard someone call my
name. "Hey Mac, hold up. Where you going?"

I whirled in the direction of the voice and saw Sarah running
across the street. She had been sun bathing again. Her tan was
nicely set off by her blonde curls and beautiful blue eyes. "Hi,
what's up?"

"Let me buy you some breakfast and we'll discuss it. How's
that sound?" Sarah asked, entwining her arm with mine and pulling
me toward the diner. Her offer to pay told me she was up to
something.

"I don't have time," I said. "I need to get back to the hospital.
Dani's waiting." Dani was a patient brought into the emergency
room last week, another child-victim of domestic violence.

"Honey, you need to eat. Come on."

After we were seated and Maggi, the waitress had taken our
orders, I gazed at my companion. "Okay, out with it, what's
wrong?"

Sarah grimaced. She knew how I was. I often ignored the social
graces she relied on when delivering awful news. And I knew it
was bad because she was making a production of unfolding her
napkin and placing it just so in her lap. She gazed up and smiled
sadly. My stomach clutched.

"Dani died about thirty minutes ago." Sarah's eyes were wet as
she reached for my hand. "I'm sorry, Mac."

The news hit me hard. My chest felt as if it had been struck by
a sledgehammer. The doctor had assured me she was progressing. I
schooled my response, not wanting to give away any outward signs
of how much I cared. I didn't want Sarah to see how much it hurt or
that it brought everything back. "What happened?" My voice was
raspy, my throat tight.

"She had massive internal injuries. The surgery took its toll on
her little body." Sarah wiped away a tear. "By the time we got to her
the damage was beyond repair."

"The mother?" I asked.

Sarah stared out the window for a moment and appeared to be
struggling for an answer. Finally she shook her head and said, "We
don't know."

"Sonofabitch!"

"Mac, don't. Please don't."

My hands were fisted in my lap, my anger quickly spiking.

Sarah rose and sat next to me in the booth. She took my hand in hers and rested her head on my shoulder. "We do what we can, honey. You *know* that better than anyone. Last week we saved those two women, remember?" She asked. "Let's concentrate on that. We need to celebrate the wins or we'll *never* survive," she said while rubbing my knuckles with her thumb.

Sarah's a doctor in the local ER. She sees most of the victims. The hospital staff does what it can medically, then they call the police. Next, they contact me. I'm a full time architect, but I also run the crisis center in town. It's a vicious cycle that tears a little piece from everyone involved each time we lose someone. Even worse, the supply of victims is endless. I tried to smile but failed.

Maggi approached with our order. She gazed at Sarah's face then mine. "Dios mio! Is everything okay? Lo que ha sucedido?" She'd known us for ages. We were one year behind her in school. I stared out the window, blinking back tears.

"The Henderson girl died this morning. Mac's...upset." Sarah responded. "We all are."

Maggi blinked back tears. "Querido Dios." She made the sign of the cross, put her hand on Sarah's shoulder, and squeezed before withdrawing without another word. Sarah sat quietly, offering her support.

I pulled my hand free as gently as I could and motioned for her to go back to her seat. "We don't want the rumor mill running amok now, do we?" I said.

"I seriously doubt we have to worry about that after all these years."

"We always have to worry about that and you know it." I grasped my coffee cup and gazed into her eyes. The same beautiful eyes I had a crush on almost thirty years ago. The same eyes that told me then, as well as now, it could never be.

We first met the day her folks transferred in across the street from my foster parents. We were both seven at the time. I taught her to climb trees and she helped me with science. I taught her how to make and throw snowballs and she taught me to bandage limbs on her dolls. I helped her pass driver's ed and she helped me accept who and what I am.

Sarah picked up her bagel and spread jelly on it. "Honey, we did everything we could. You did everything you could. Let this go."

The tears escaped, unwanted and pointless. It was too late. Another child was dead. Another mother was fighting for her life. I scrubbed at the drops on my cheeks before they could fall. I rose quickly and dug in my pocket. "Thanks for breakfast. I gotta go. I'll see you around." I threw some bills on the table for the tip, as was our custom. I grasped her hand, but no words would come. My throat was constricted, choking me with anger and despair.

Pain was clawing at me from all directions. Oblivious, I stormed down the street, hands fisted at my sides, vision blurred by the red haze of my frustration. My mind was ablaze with fury. Where the fuck was our benevolent God while these kids were being beaten? When children were born with diseases? When babies were created with damaged chromosomes or missing ones? When adults abused beautiful, innocent little kids?

I barreled around the corner blindly. Packages flew everywhere before I realized I'd hit someone. Too late to avert the collision, I pulled the woman against me to prevent her fall. My body absorbed the force of the impact as we slammed against the wall of the building and she landed against my midsection with a thud, knocking the wind out of me.

After a few moments she lifted her head. I stared into the most incredible brown eyes I'd ever seen. Her long black hair, generously sprinkled with silver, draped around parts of her face. "What the hell?" she grumbled.

"I'm sorry," I uttered. "I wasn't paying attention. Are you hurt?"

She unwittingly thrust her hips against mine as she attempted to push herself away. A groan rumbled in my throat at the intimate contact. She paused to assess herself. "No, I don't think so," she said. "You appear to have taken the brunt of it." She grasped my forearms, regained her balance, and backed away.

I gazed at her full form, and had the presence of mind to extend my hand. "Mac...uhh...Mackenzie Taylor, clumsy ox, at your service."

"Emily O'Brien," she said as she took my hand

"Here, let me get these boxes for you." I offered and began to gather them, thankful my carelessness didn't seem to have broken anything.

Emily reached for the packages, but I told her I had them. She whirled back to the pickup beside us and removed more parcels. "Follow me," she directed.

A flashback of Isabella saying the same thing emerged. I remembered thinking, *As if that had ever been a question.* I jerked myself back to the present and the woman before me.

We rounded the corner and entered an abandoned store front. At least it had been the week before. In more of a statement than a question I said, "You're new here." I knew almost everyone in town and I didn't know her.

"Yes, I'm opening a bookstore. This is some of my initial stock." Emily walked around a long table and into the back of the workspace to place the boxes on the counter. "If you could put them there, I'll get to them later. I want to get the rest of the supplies from the truck," she said.

"Why don't I unload the truck? It's the least I can do after nearly trampling you." I pivoted to begin the process.

"You don't need to do that. It was an accident."

I glanced over my shoulder and said, "I don't need to do a lot of things. You'll find I do them anyway."

Emily furrowed her brow. By the time the last box was unloaded, she was at the back of the store pouring a cup of coffee. "Can I tempt you?"

"Please."

"I've got creamer substitute and sugar. Sorry, no real cream as yet."

"Black's good for me, thanks."

She handed me a mug, then picked up her own and started to prepare it with two sugars and one scoop of creamer. She was only an inch or two shorter than me, which would put her at five-foot-five or six. I was guessing she was in her mid-to-late-forties and, thankfully, not one of those women who believed that anorexia nervosa was attractive. She was dressed in well-worn jeans, a short-sleeved, scoop neck T-shirt, and work boots. Overall, she was an enticing package for sure until I noticed the wedding band on her left hand.

I caught her staring at me and became uncomfortable. *Crap.*

"So, where were you going in such a hurry?" Emily asked. Her eyes twinkled with merriment.

"I apologize. My mind was elsewhere, obviously." For a moment the pain caught up with me, but I quickly pushed it aside. There would be time for that later.

She appeared to study me and an unfamiliar feeling started in the pit of my stomach.

"What about you?" I asked, changing the subject. "A bookstore—will your husband be part of it or is he employed elsewhere?"

Emily's eyes grew dark, a flash of pain slipped through. She turned away and started to open a carton with the box cutter she had removed from her back pocket. "My husband died three years ago. This was always *my* dream. I decided to follow it." Emily's voice was low and husky. Sadness seemed to be floating on the air currents between us.

"I'm sorry for your loss," I said. I meant it, too. I placed my empty coffee cup on the counter next to hers. "So, how soon do you open?"

"There's a lot of work to do before that can happen. I need to paint this place and find someone to build bookshelves...cheap. More stock will need to be ordered." Emily scanned the room. Her eyes seemed to be envisioning the store as it would be, and not as the barren structure it was.

"Do you have anyone in mind for the carpentry work?"

A frown transformed her features. "I'm thinking I'll do most of it myself. Money is tight and I need to pinch every penny." She returned to her task and emptied the box on which she had been working.

"What are you going to make the shelving out of?"

Her curiosity was apparently peaked and she asked. "Why?"

"Well, I'm a pretty fair carpenter on the side. I can make the shelves for you, if you tell me what you want them made out of." Her skeptical gaze made me smile. It happened a lot.

"I couldn't ask you to do that and I'm sure I couldn't afford your services if you're any good." Emily continued her task.

"Why don't you tell me what you want them made out of and how. You pay for the supplies and we'll work something out for the labor. Okay?"

Her head dropped and her shoulders stiffened. She whirled back toward me, her eyes blazing. "And what would be acceptable payment for your labor, Ms. Taylor? Hmm?" She said it quietly, no anger in her tone, but she was brimming with it. And I had caused it.

"Whoa." I put my hands up. "Sorry. I thought maybe you could order some books that I normally go to Denver for. You'd be saving me a trip, one I hate making." I stepped back, giving her space. "I was being neighborly. I thought we could work out an exchange— that's all. I swear it."

She finally seemed to relax although her suspicion lingered. "I drew up plans for the shelves. They're upstairs. Let me get them and I'll show you." A short time later she was back with the dimensions and specs neatly detailed on two sheets of paper.

I took her drawings and reviewed them. They were comprehensive and I was damned impressed. "I see that you noted oak for the work. Do you intend to stain the shelves?"

Emily contemplated with a crease between her brows. "I'm going to paint them. I intend to paint everything...in bright colors." She swept her arm in an arc. "I want people to enjoy coming here and spending time browsing." A smile lit her face. She was naturally attractive, but her smile...wow...her smile was stunning.

I found myself mesmerized by her enthusiasm—by her. *A long forgotten feeling stirred deep within me. Desire? Ridiculous, I was married.* After a moment I shook myself and got back to the task at hand. *Shelves. Think about the shelves.* "Can I make a suggestion? We could use MDF — medium density fiberboard. It will hold up to the weight of the books — "

"Don't I need the strength of wood to carry the load?"

"Not if we put another upright in the middle." I drew in the extra brace and showed her the design. "It will take paint easier and I can build them at about sixty percent of the cost of the oak." The plan came together in my mind. I could precut, predrill, sand and paint everything before I even returned to the store.

Emily appeared pensive, her brows furrowed. She grabbed my pen and pointed to the plans. "Can we extend the length of the shelves to accommodate the extra upright? I've got them measured to hold a certain number of paperbacks." She tapped the pen against the counter. "Sorry, I'm thinking about the extra savings." She dropped the pen, her eyes bright with speculation.

I watched from the corner of my eye as she surveyed the room. Then quickly brought my focus back to the plans and made notes to extend each shelf to account for the extra width of the support. "Do you know what color you want the shelves? I could get them painted for you so the day they're installed they'll be ready for the books."

Her back was to me and she appeared not to have heard me. "How long do you suppose this will take you?" She suddenly twisted around, excitement glowing in her eyes. "Could we build a window seat here?" she asked gesturing toward the oversized window at the front of the room.

I laughed out loud, surprising even myself. "I don't see why not. It's your store." I didn't know this woman, yet I found myself excited by her energy, something I rarely allowed myself to feel.

We agreed I would get started the coming weekend. Between my job and my afternoon activities, I speculated it would take me a couple hours a night in my workshop over the next two weeks to complete the project. Installation would take one day with help, two if I worked alone. I gave her my business card with my cell, office, and home phone numbers. She advised me her phone hadn't been installed yet.

LATER THAT AFTERNOON I sat in my office, thinking about the events of the morning. I had been so distressed by Sarah's news that my anger blocked all rationality, an all-too-frequent occurrence with me. The results could have caused serious injury to Emily. I absently rubbed the back of my left shoulder, which I was sure was going to be stiff for a few days. Thankfully, she had come away unscathed.

After my discussion with Emily, I stopped at the hardware store to order the MDF and made arrangements to pick it up the following day. The paint colors would have to wait though. Emily said she needed to check with her design consultants.

A hesitant knock at the office door announced my assistant, Mary. "Mac, you okay? Want some coffee?"

"I'm fine, don't worry about me. Did you make those arrangements yet?" I sensed what she was up to.

Mary inclined her head. She knew when she could push me and when she couldn't, still I could see her foot tapping while she lingered in the doorway. It was the sigh that broke me.

"Okay, okay…coffee, but no meaningful talks. I wanna go over that information." I glared, but she couldn't have cared less.

She returned moments later with my cup filled to the top. She placed it on the desk, sat, and opened her steno pad. She began her report without further fuss. "I spoke with Sam at Murphy's Garage and took care of the bill on the Thomas tractor, fifty percent like last time."

Mary paused as I checked the item off my list.

"Donaldson's Mortuary will hold the viewing tomorrow at one. You can bring the mother over anytime after eleven—if she's strong enough." She paused to examine her notes and adjusted her glasses higher on the bridge of her nose.

Mary was in her late fifties, married, a mother and grandmother, but she could also be tough as nails when needed. She had been my assistant for over twelve years. I wouldn't be able to run my firm without her, and she knew it. She also knew my past, my secrets, and my grief. She wanted to protect me whenever she could. It had to be the maternal thing. Today though, I didn't need her protection. It already hurt and nothing would change that.

She continued on, jarring me from my thoughts. "The plot is under a tree like you requested and a small headstone's been ordered. The minister will hold a graveside service at three, burial to follow, as you instructed." She studied me, trying to steel her expression, but I saw the anguish in her eyes.

I grunted in lieu of an answer, my throat tight with grief. I had stopped by the hospital earlier and spoken with Dani's mother. The woman was devastated. She feared her daughter would be buried in a pauper's grave due to her financial circumstances. I assured her the crisis center would absorb the costs. All we needed was her input on what arrangements she wanted. My stomach knotted at the memory of her suffering. I have lived with that anguish every fucking day for the last five years. I swiveled my chair toward the window, my fingers steepled while I gazed at the panoramic view of the town and snow-capped Rocky Mountains beyond it. Centrally located between Grand Junction and Denver, this sleepy town was just a spit in the road, not even worthy of sign posts. The population was just under eight hundred people, but the surrounding communities and farm land justified the small hospital that witnessed so much misery.

Mary waited patiently. Finally she stood and circled behind me. She placed her hands on my shoulders and squeezed gently. "You need to let it go, Mac, otherwise it will eat you alive." She waited for my response; none was forthcoming.

I STOPPED AT the hospital on my way to the ball field. An earlier meeting had been cancelled and I wanted to update Dani's mother about the arrangements we'd made. Lynnette Henderson was appreciative and also ashamed that the crisis center would absorb the funeral costs. She was humiliated for needing charity. Money should have been the last of her concerns. She was already dealing with enough crap.

As I approached the ward, a nurse scurried out and rushed into the locked medicine room. I waited off to the side as another nurse raced past me with a crash cart. I sensed what was coming. *Fuck.*

Sarah dashed off the elevator, her stethoscope wrapped around her neck. She saw me and put her hand out. I'd been around enough emergencies to know that all this activity meant Lynnette was in trouble. Sarah knew it would affect me, but I didn't need her empathy. I didn't want it.

Fifty minutes later Sarah, covered in sweat, exited the room and approached me. "We did every—"

I raised my hand to stop her. I didn't need the empty words. I'd heard them all before. In fact, I was probably an expert on them. I retreated down the hall to the safety of the elevator, buying a little time during the trip to the first floor. The elevator doors parted and I took off running. I burst through the front entrance, out into the bright sunshine. I gulped air into my lungs, desperately needing to escape from it all.

It was late. I had a ball game to go to. Inside my truck I put the transmission in gear, nabbed my cell, and hit the speed dial for my office.

Mary answered. "What's up, boss? I thought you'd be pitching by now?"

I took a calming breath. "Call Donaldson's and change the arrangements. We're going to do a two for one. See if they can put it off a day. I want Lynnette Henderson placed in the same plot as her daughter." I punched the disconnect button. There was nothing more to be said.

AT THE BALL field little Tommy Jenkins hit the ball with the aid of Patrick. He jerked in his wheelchair expectantly. Patrick gripped the handles and started pushing him toward first base while Tommy's face lit up. Patrick's dad was pitching in my absence and grinned as his son maneuvered the wheelchair like a pro.

I strolled toward the bleachers and stopped cold. My waifs were back, watching the game from behind the fence. My mystery boy was laughing as Tommy's wheelchair touched the white rubber base. His arm shot in the air; his fist pumped proudly. I extracted two ball caps from the team locker and wound my way beside them. We silently observed the next play. Leonard Atkins, who is legally blind, and ironically, one of our best hitters, was on deck. Once again Patrick stood ready to aid his teammate. The connection between bat and ball echoed and the two boys clasped hands and started running. One of the rescue volunteers pushed Tommy's wheelchair toward second. Everyone was safe.

The girl stole a glance at me as I squatted down and rotated slowly toward her. She was so pretty, but so fragile-looking too. Her hair was long, black, and curly. Her eyes big and brown, warning me off with a glance.

"Hi. Since you two make such a good cheering section, I thought maybe you'd like to have a team cap. What do you say?" I held them at arm's length and waited.

The boy reached for them but she jerked his arm back. He was blond and blue-eyed, still it was clear they were siblings. Although their coloring differed, they could have been twins. He stared for a moment before whispering, "Ith's okay Kaithlin, sthe's not gonna hurth uth." There was a front tooth missing that caused his lisp. I smiled at his silly grin.

She flinched as he seized the two hats and handed her one. He tightened his with the plastic snaps on the back and plopped it on his head. He modeled it proudly, pleased with his new adornment. Little Kaitlin held the hat loosely in her hand. It was clear she wasn't sure and didn't trust me. I stood slowly, turned back, and walked toward the bleachers, giving her the space she so desperately sought. The children appeared to be cared for and clean. They were well-nourished and polite. So why were they at the ball field without supervision? They couldn't be more than six or seven, if that. They were too young to be on their own each day, yet there they were. Why?

The boy and girl remained until the end of the game, wide-eyed and grinning as the players came off the field. She was beaming this afternoon and seemed to have relaxed a bit. As they turned to leave, I called out, "We have soda and chips if you're interested."

He fixed his eyes expectantly on his sister. Her momentary vacillation was all he needed. He pulled free and ran to where the volunteers were handing out the goodies. I stayed where I was since it appeared I was the one she didn't trust. He came running back with snacks for each of them. She took his hand and began pulling him toward the street, back the way they had come, back to who knew what. I watched their departure, pleased with the progress I was making. Instinct told me to follow them, but logic told me not to.

Patrick galloped toward me and threw himself into my arms. "Mac, did you see me? I did it," he enthused, his words screaming with pride. "I helped Michael and Tommy today, did you see?" I embraced the boy tightly, picked him up off the ground, and swung him up in my arms.

"I'm so proud of you, Patrick. I knew you could do it. Didn't I tell you?" I placed a kiss atop his head.

Jim strode over. "Hey, Mac. Everything okay?"

I had called him earlier from the hospital and explained the situation. I bobbed my head, suddenly unable to form words.

He clapped me on the back. Team Bella had won today. I smiled at the pride on Patrick's face and remembered why I did this. Why we all did.

THAT NIGHT SLEEP was elusive. In my workshop I pulled out Emily's plans and tried to figure out the best way to build the shelves at minimal cost. While I analyzed her figures and specs, it became clear something was off. I took her plans again and reworked all the information. The plank sizes were correct and, based on her sketch, there would be nine sets of bookshelves back-to-back, each no taller than five feet. She said she wanted to use the natural light from the windows to cheer the place up. She also wanted to afford herself a clear view of the store. As I reviewed the specs — wood lengths times the bookcases to be built — times the height and width I discovered her error. Somewhere along the way, she had picked up an extra ten linear feet per shelf, per bookcase. I revised everything, checked to be sure of my math, and entered the numbers into an Excel spreadsheet that confirmed my calculations. Yep. She'd made an error. That would also save her nicely. I intended to drop by the next morning and get her approval to be sure.

With the plans for the bookcases completed, my laptop and I were done for another night. The files I brought home went into my briefcase. My ire had settled and my body was relaxed. All that remained was a decision about where to sleep. Truth be told, I slept in my workshop more often than the house. I groaned and stretched my back. It ached from bending over my drafting board, but my mind was finally tranquil. It always got this way any time I was entrenched in a project. I took a quick look-see at the clock. Two in the morning. Definitely time to hit the sack.

Chapter Two

MY CELL RANG as I exited of the shower. I wrapped the towel around my midsection and went to the nightstand to pick it up. "Hello."

"Hi, it's me. I didn't wake you did I?"

I grinned to myself. She knew better than that. It was well past seven. "What do you want, Sarah?"

"What if I told you I wanted *you*?" she giggled. "Well? What do you say, hot shot?"

For a moment my heart skipped a beat. I couldn't help myself. She'd been my fantasy for as long as I could remember. I used to compare the women I met to her to see how they measured up. All too often they hadn't. That was until Isabella. "I'd say it's about time you came to your damn senses."

"Oh honey, if only you came with the plumbing I crave." Sarah's voice was sad, a little wistful.

"Funny thing. You have the exact bits I'm looking for. Maybe you're wrong, huh?" I started laughing as I pictured her blushing. Sarah had always known about my crush. We often laughed and teased each other about it, but it had never gotten in the way of our friendship.

"Honey, I'm worried about you," Sarah continued. "The way you ran out of the hospital yesterday, and you didn't return my calls last night. Mary told me you hung up on her and never answered your pager."

I pictured Sarah biting her lip, a habit since our teens. Whenever she was worried she chewed on them, sometimes drawing blood. "I'm fine," I sighed. "I didn't need your platitudes and I certainly didn't want Mary hovering over me. I had a game to get to. Life goes on." The statement came out harsher than I intended, but it was too late to take it back.

Sarah gasped.

Shit. "Hey, I just got out of the shower. How about I get dressed and we hit the diner for some breakfast...my treat?"

"Okay. How long will you be?"

"'Bout half an hour. That work for you?" It would take that long to get dressed and down the mountain.

"I'll meet you there," she chuckled. "I'll be the one ordering one of everything on the menu. You *did* say you're buying. Bye."

Knowing Sarah, she probably would. I'd swear the woman had

a tape worm.

I tossed the towel into the hamper, removed a pair of jeans from the closet, and plucked a white T-shirt from the dresser. Underwear was optional and I rarely opted. My naturally wavy hair was unruly and refused to be tamed. It would do what it always did—appear tousled. It didn't help that I needed a hair cut. I pocketed my wallet and hooked my cell on my belt. Then I snatched the keys to the truck from the night stand and shrugged into my leather jacket before heading down the stairs and out the back door. The post-and-beam structured house sat high up on the mountain, obscured by tall timbers in an isolated area outside of town. The road leading to it was little more than a dirt path hidden by thick native shrubbery. The drive into town would take me twenty minutes by which time Sarah would have my breakfast waiting.

MY EIGHTH GRADE teacher, Mrs. Baxter, was approaching the entrance as I arrived and I held the door for her to enter ahead of me. She patted my face. "You always were so thoughtful, Mackenzie. Thank you."

She and her daughter met at the diner every morning for breakfast. I took her arm and escorted her to their usual booth by the window. "You have a good day, Mrs. B, and say hi to Annie for me." I spotted Sarah at the back of the diner, attacking her pancakes with gusto. I slipped into the booth shaking my head. She could eat like a horse and never gained an ounce.

"I have a high metabolism," she said with a smile as if she could read my mind. Her eyes sparkled as she chewed a mouthful of food.

Maggi approached the table with a plate of bacon and eggs for me and a full coffee pot. I flipped the cup over, allowing her to pour it after she set the plate down. "Thanks Mags, appreciate it." She touched my shoulder and walked to the next customer.

While reaching for a napkin I spied Emily striding into the diner. After placing an order with the waitress, she turned around, leaned back against the counter, and casually surveyed the room. I dropped my eyes to focus on breakfast instead of the way the morning sun caught the highlights in her hair or the way the curve of her hip caused my pulse to speed up.

Sarah was in the middle of a story when I felt Emily's presence and jumped up. "Emily. Hi," I said. Positive Sarah was watching us I added, "Emily, this is my friend, Sarah Downs—err Doctor Downs, actually." Sarah paused from her eating long enough to shake hands and make nice.

"Would you like to join us?" I asked. A part of me hoped she would while another part told me to stay clear of this woman. I wasn't sure why, but she unnerved me.

"No, I don't want to intrude. Sit, eat." Emily motioned to the booth. "I only wanted to say hi. I'm getting some breakfast before heading to the hardware store. I'm going to start painting today."

When she changed course to return to the counter, I put my hand out, not quite touching her, but catching her attention. "I was going over the plans last night and I think I found an error that could save you even more money." The rest came out in a rush of mumbled words. "Could I stop by later and go over it with you?"

Little laugh lines appeared at the corners of her mouth when she smiled and her eyes glimmered. Her face was open with smooth, clear, make-up free skin. Her dimples grew more pronounced, deep creases reached almost to her jaw. "I'll be there. Behold the spilled paint can, I'll probably be under it." Emily laughed as she started to rush away but paused to say, "It was nice meeting you, Sarah. I hope we see each other again."

Emily jogged to the front counter as Maggi called out her order was ready and she paid her bill. I remained standing, my eyes riveted on her and feeling foolish. She paused at the door, casting a wave and a smile my way as she exited the diner. That was the moment that thing happened in the pit of my stomach. I was grinning as I sat back down and started on my eggs which were no longer hot. I was about to bite into my toast when I noticed Sarah watching me. "What?" I asked.

"She's very attractive."

I refused the bait.

"She seemed nice and I heard you say you're doing some work for her, so I thought —"

I set my fork down and stared directly into Sarah's impish eyes. "Look, I damn near crushed that woman yesterday after I left here." I took a sip of my coffee, trying for calm before I continued. "I offered to help her with some shelving. She's opening a book emporium where the ammo place used to be. It's *known* as the barter system, Sarah. Labor on the bookcases in return for her ordering books for me. You know I hate the trip into Denver." Satisfied that the conversation was over, I picked up my fork again.

Sarah seemed to mull over what I'd said. "But she is pretty, right?" she finally asked.

"And straight, Sarah. She's widowed." My stomach did that thing again and I was sure I was coming down with something.

"Sorry, she seemed nice and you *were* smiling." Sarah tucked her hair behind her ears, another of her nervous tics. "I want you to be happy. I love you, you know. You're my best friend and I worry about you."

There was no answer for that.

We finished eating in silence, the comfortable kind, where two friends didn't need to talk. They simply enjoyed the company. That was Sarah and me. We *got* each other. We'd always been there for one another and always would be. I paid our check, she left the tip and we strolled out of the diner, sated and ready to face another day.

BEFORE I HIT the hardware store, I wanted to stop and see Emily. As I strolled down the street, the wave Emily gave me right before she left the diner flashed through my mind. My insides fluttered now as they had then and a warm feeling filled me. The doors to the bookstore stood open and I paused a moment, taking in the sight before me. Emily was on a ladder, painting the ceiling a bright sky blue. She was using a paint roller without a splatter guard. Her T-shirt stretched tautly across her full breasts as she reached up and out with the roller. Her jeans hugged her well-rounded hips, completing the picture of her full, lush figure. *Oh yeah, I was enjoying this view waaayyyyy too much.* A small cough covered my errant thoughts as I greeted her. Her welcoming grin sent a pleasant vibration through my body. I couldn't help but laugh when paint dripped down her cheek.

"You're getting an awful lot of pleasure from my mishap." She climbed down from the ladder and thrust the roller toward me menacingly. "It would be a shame to get that nice white T-shirt of yours all full of paint." She placed the roller back in the pan, still chuckling.

I hooked a rag from the counter and inched closer. Her dark penetrating eyes set my stomach flipping as I dabbed at the paint on her cheek. A nervous smile was all I could manage as I quickly handed over the cloth. I'd overstepped and retreated to the safety of the counter while my innards struggled to settle. I pulled the papers from my jacket's inside pocket and began the explanation. "So, I've reworked your numbers and I'd like to show you where you made a mistake." I spread the papers out, including the spreadsheet, for her review, still feeling a little off-balance.

Emily wandered closer, wiping at the paint on her hands. "Mac?"

I glanced up from the paperwork and immediately fell into the depths of her eyes, two swirling chocolate fountains that opened into her soul. With great effort, I refocused on the papers and pointed to the revisions I'd made. My voice was gruff once I managed to speak. "Here's where the error occurred, but review the info and let me know." I needed space and took a step back. The desire to flee overwhelmed me and the words tumbled from my lips. "I'm gonna head out. I still need to pick up some supplies and should get to work sooner rather than later. If everything checks out, call me and I'll start on them tonight." *My need to get away from both her and the sensation she caused within me was overpowering.*

As I turned to leave Emily put her hand on my arm, her touch soft, and warm even through the sleeve of my jacket. "Mac. Are you okay?"

"Yeah, fine. I've got a lot to do is all." My throat was tight, my words strained.

"If this is an inconvenience, I would understand." Emily dropped her hand and the feeling of loss was instantaneous. *Ridiculous.*

"No, I love doing projects like this, and it keeps me out of trouble. I just have a lot to do today." I lifted my arm, motioning toward the walls. "As do you. You've got all this to paint, right?" I forced a smile to hide my frayed nerves.

"Can I ask you something?" Emily questioned as she rubbed her hands on the paint cloth.

"Uh sure, what?"

"It's none of my business. I'm new here, but I was wondering — you know — trying to get the lay of the land." She studied me. "Are you and Sarah, well...is she your girlfriend?" Emily averted her eyes and I waited her out. The ensuing silence was deafening.

"I'm sorry," she said, taking a step closer. "It's none of my business. I...I'm not sure what I...I'm sorry." She took another step closer.

Her intentions were unclear and I backed up, pissed. My response was measured as I picked my words, trying to control my voice. "Sarah and I have known each other since grammar school. She's my best friend. For the record, she's married and has two kids." With that I pivoted and exited the building.

"Mac, wait," Emily called out, but I kept going. *Fuck.*

THREE O'CLOCK FOUND me at my desk playing with a slide rule and getting absolutely nothing accomplished. I hated days like this. I couldn't stop thinking about Emily and the episode in the bookstore. Why did it always come down to my sexuality? Why must I always be judged by that? It was never Mac the architect, or Mac the coach, or even Mac the bitch. It was always Mac the dyke. It wasn't as if I flaunted my lifestyle. I hadn't been with a woman in five years. And why was it anyone's business?

Then there were my well-meaning friends who all wanted me

to meet someone new. As if it was that easy. As if I could forget what I'd lost simply because time had elapsed.

Mary had been in my office three times. If she brought me any more coffee, I'd float away. She meant well, but I didn't need mothering. The phone rang, two sharp blasts, and I knew it was her. I grabbed the receiver. "Yeah?"

"Jim Collins is on line one."

"Okay."

I hit the button. "Hey Jim, what can I do for you?"

"Mac, I called to see if you needed me to—well, to cover for you tomorrow—for the game?"

At first my mind was blank and then it wasn't. *Crap*. "Uhm, yeah that would be great. If it's not an inconvenience." My eyes slammed shut as I leaned my head back against my chair. God I hated this. I hated everything about it. Children abused, tortured, dying. Deep breathing was suppose to help calm me, *it didn't*.

Jim agreed to cover the game and handle the refreshments.

The afternoon had been a total waste of time and I headed home. My workshop was calling to me. The distraction exactly what I needed.

THERE'S SOMETHING INHERENTLY gratifying about working with my hands. I could take a raw piece of material, and shape and mold it into a useful, hopefully beautiful, end product. Projects such as Emily's bookcases had kept me sane during my formative years. Working with my hands seemed to center me and on more than one occasion it had facilitated the redirection of my erstwhile tendencies. Sarah's dad introduced me to woodworking when I was a kid. I spent many days in his workshop building things and working through my anger.

Three hours later the MDF had been run across the table saw, cut into the proper shelf widths and lengths. Next, I guided the uprights across my router table, cutting the grooves at twelve-inch intervals and angled downward at a quarter-inch grade. The cross shelving would slide into these slots and create a tighter, more durable fit. After I'd finished the vertical pieces, fifty-four in all, I changed the bit and started the process of rounding over the edges on the shelving. My inner turmoil settled as I lost myself in the creation, the noise of the machines the only distraction.

My mind focused and I forced myself to prepare for the next day and the thought of burying little two-year-old Dani and her twenty-three-year-old mother, both victims of senseless abuse, assuming any mistreatment could be considered sensible. They were dead at the hands of Mrs. Henderson's husband, and Dani's father. The bastard came home drunk and dinner wasn't ready. He'd beaten them before, but she had refused to press charges, always too afraid of what he would do in retaliation. Now it was a moot issue. Two innocent victims were dead and that rat bastard sat in a jail cell, getting three squares a day and his rights protected. The legal system did nothing to protect victims and everything to ensure that the guilty party's rights were safeguarded. Fury erupted inside me at the idea that a murdering scumbag like Darrell Henderson was alive while his wife and baby girl would never experience the life that should have been theirs. I finished off the last piece of MDF and shut the machine down before my anger made me careless and I ruined one of the pieces.

After a short break, I carried the sections to the drill press and prepared to pre-drill the holes required for assembly. The project was going better than I had anticipated and I'd probably have them ready for installation by the weekend. Only the paint colors remained undetermined. Too bad I had stormed out of Emily's shop before I asked her. Self-loathing welled up inside. My temper always got the best of me.

I set the first board on the drill press and wondered about the fairness in life. About the injustice that let predators like Darrel Henderson live. About a parole board that had put a stalker back on the street because he conned them or his psychiatrist into believing he was cured. Why were laws made that couldn't protect a woman from a violent husband until he had already followed through with his threats in a heinous fashion. The memory of Isabella's lifeless body filled my vision. Her blood-splattered form and sightless eyes haunted me. Baby Bella was three and had never hurt anyone, yet that bastard ruthlessly murdered them both. My mind was raging. My wrath normally simmered just below the surface, ready to rise up at the slightest provocation. Thinking about Dani and her mother, amid thoughts of Izzy and Bella, pushed it to its limits. Fortunately, there was more work to do on the shelves. I needed to channel my anger into something good, something productive.

The next couple of hours were spent hand sanding everything smooth on the individual parts to remove any roughened edges from the various processes I'd conducted on the boards. At long last, everything was ready for paint and installation.

As I prepared to close the shop for the night, I was startled to see the sun coming up over the meadow outside the window. I glanced at the clock, sure there was a mistake. It was four-forty and dawn was indeed breaking. I had totally misjudged the time needed to complete the project. Though my body was tired, my mind was relaxed and I felt ready to face the new day's trials.

Ready to put Dani Henderson and her mother, Lynnette, to rest. God knew they deserved it.

I ARRIVED AT my office and hung the garment bag on the door of the small bathroom located in the corner. There was a shower stall, pedestal sink and toilet. The room was barely large enough for me to clean up in and dress when called upon. My normal attire for work was boots, jeans, and a T-shirt and today was no different. The suit was for the funeral scheduled for later in the day. I knew it didn't matter, but I believed in showing respect. Somewhere along the way I'd learned you dressed for these things. You prayed even though you didn't believe and cried because you didn't know how not to. The only consolation was that I'd be alone with the minister and the gravediggers. My tears would go unnoticed.

I shuffled behind my desk to check my planner. There were four appointments scheduled for the morning. Three concerned on-going projects, all of which were very near completion. I anticipated those meetings should go smoothly. The last appointment was to design a home up in the mountains east of town. The owner said he wanted to build green, but time would tell if they were really willing to do it. The initial cost factor scared most people off, although the long-term savings more than made up for it. It was a type of construction that's near and dear to my heart. Sadly, not many people were prepared to pay for it.

My stomach rumbled, a reminder that I hadn't eaten since noon the previous day. It was early, only six-fifteen, plenty of time before everyone came in and I decided to run to the diner. I'd be skipping lunch; therefore, a hearty breakfast was a must.

I WAS SITTING at the counter sipping my coffee when the hair on the back of my neck prickled. My head snapped up and I saw Emily standing next to me in the reflection of the mirror along the back wall.

"Mac, can we talk...please?" she asked.

I spun on the stool, puzzled by the concern in her eyes. She was wearing what I had come to understand was her casual look. The packaging made my chest constrict, but I knew when something was off limits. When I raised my eyes to hers, she didn't appear pleased.

Though there was no point for further dialogue, I couldn't very well refuse with so many of our fellow diners within ear shot. I shrugged, loathe to create a scene. "What would you like to talk about?" I asked.

She motioned with her head. "Could we share a booth? It's a little more private."

My brow furrowed. I would have thought private would be the last thing she wanted. I indicated a booth in the back, snatched my coffee cup and juice, and took them with me. Maggi would find me; she always did. Emily chose her seat first and I slid in across from her. Before either of us could say anything, Maggi magically appeared with the coffee pot. I flipped Emily's cup over so it could be filled, pushing my own within easy reach to be capped off. Maggi took Emily's order and left. I pushed the sugar and creamer toward Emily. She made a production out of fixing her coffee, the set of her shoulders telling me she was tense.

"So, I had some time and I finished the bookshelves," I said to break the silence. "If you've decided on the colors, I'd like to get them painted before we install them." I placed a napkin in my lap. "How's the painting going at the store?"

Emily gazed up, the relief in her eyes evident. "Thank you," she said.

I shrugged.

"Thank you." Emily restated.

"For what?"

"For not making this harder than it already is. For not making me more uncomfortable than I am." She reached across the table and placed her hand on mine.

I was conscious of the other diners who might misinterpret her action, but I was also warmed by the gesture.

"I made a terrible mistake yesterday," Emily said.

Before I could say anything Maggi arrived with our orders. She smirked at me when she saw Emily's hand covering mine. *Shit.* I didn't need this kind of problem and I certainly didn't need the local gossips talking about me and the straight lady from the bookstore. Maggi set our plates down and departed.

"Mac, I'm sorry I made you angry. It wasn't my intention, I swear." Emily said as her eyes met mine.

I shrugged again. "Not a problem. Everyone wants to know who the dyke is dating. I'm used to it. Really." I knew my response was trite, but I couldn't help myself. My anger at the questions people asked me hadn't dissipated over the years. If the tables were reversed I'd be called a pervert. Hell, some called me that anyway. I picked up my fork, assuming we were done, that is until I glanced at my companion.

Emily's head snapped back. She slammed her fork down on the table and gripped her coffee cup. "I was not trying to find out the latest gossip on the *town dyke*," she whispered angrily. "I wanted to learn something about you. Try to get to know you." She was pissed and her hand was trembling. "I'm sorry, maybe my question seemed inappropriate," she continued. "We don't know each other, but it was strictly curiosity. I wasn't being malicious." She put the cup down, her hand shaking so hard the coffee sloshed over the top.

I surveyed her closely, surprised by the irrefutable distress in her eyes. "Okay."

She cocked her head to the side and stared at me. "Okay?" She shook her head. "You're either a woman of few words, or you're not sure you believe me."

I put my fork down and sipped my coffee. I needed to choose my words carefully or our budding friendship would collapse before it began. "I've been the town oddity all my life. It's a sore subject. I might have overreacted, but like I said, it's a sensitive issue."

Tears gathered in Emily's eyes. "Melanie, my daughter, was gay. I know *some* of what you feel and have gone through. I agonized seeing her struggle to live her life. I saw some of the things people do even when it's not intentional. I experienced her pain firsthand and I hated it." Emily kept her eyes trained on me the entire time.

I set my cup down, surprised it was empty. A glance out the window provided me the time needed to absorb this information. I'm always astounded at what the human population does to itself in the guise of tolerance, or intolerance as the case may be, and the anguish caused under the excuse of good intentions.

"You said *was*." I refused to look at her. I didn't want to see her pain. "What happened? If that's not too personal."

Maggi appeared with a fresh pot of coffee and refilled our cups. Emily struggled with her emotions while I waited, giving her the time she needed.

"She died—was killed, in a car accident a year ago, January." Emily swiped at the tears on her cheeks, but they kept coming. "She—she left behind two small children. They're with *me* now." She lost her emotional battle while quiet sobs wracked her body.

I handed her my napkin and got up to get replacements, along with a glass of water. "I'm sorry," I mumbled.

Another moment passed and she was in control again. "I didn't tell you for your sympathy. I want you to know...well, to understand I wasn't judging you. I'm sorry it came out that way." Emily wiped her eyes and smiled, but her pain was still raw, bleeding, and all encompassing.

"You've had a rough time the past couple years." I smiled sadly, acknowledging the loss of her husband as well as her daughter. My respect for her went up a couple notches. Even through her loss, she was trying to move on, to make a new life for herself and two children left without their mother.

I steered the conversation in another direction. "Have you consulted the decorator yet? Do we have paint colors?"

She appeared puzzled at first. "My decorator?" Then chuckled. "It's the children, my grandchildren. I promised they could help choose the colors. Why?"

I laughed deeply, touched that she would trust the decorating of her livelihood to her grandchildren. "Well, the shelves are cut and ready to go. I thought I'd paint them in the workshop. That way the mess would be contained."

She frowned. "Oh, I sort of promised the kids they could help me paint them. I'll figure something else out." Emily seemed to be plotting a different course of action.

I couldn't believe I was going to say this, but what the hell. "Why don't you bring the kids to my place over the weekend? We can get the shelves painted in the workshop and control the mess. That way, I'll get to meet them and we can complete the project. How's that sound?"

Emily gaped at me. "Do you have any idea how much trouble a five-year-old boy and his six-and-a-half-year-old sister can be?" She chuckled.

"Actually I do. I coach baseball in the afternoons for some kids out at Bella's Ball Park. Maybe you'll bring the kids sometime and catch a game. I promise it's like none you've ever seen."

We finished our breakfast and made loose plans for Emily to call me Saturday morning to firm up a schedule. I paid the bill and walked her back to her store. It occurred to me she had been with me over an hour and it was early in the morning. "Where are the kids?" I asked.

"Oh, they made friends with the Tompkins' children. They're on an official sleep over." She paused. "Do you know the family?" Emily glanced at me from the corner of her eye, as we strolled along.

"In fact, I do. They're good people. Their next door neighbor is my assistant coach for the ball team."

Reminded of the day I had asked Patrick if he wanted the job made me grin. He got so excited he ran home without answering me—he wanted his father's permission first. By the time he got home, he was crying. Dan told me later that he wanted to kill me, until he realized what really happened.

Emily nudged me from my musings. "You don't mean Patrick? He's...well, he's—"

"Yes. Patrick has Down's Syndrome. All the kids on the team

are challenged in one way or another. That's what makes the team special." Emily tripped as she hopped onto the curb and I grasped her arm to prevent her from falling.

"Thank you," she said as she righted herself and stopped to study me. "You run a baseball team for special needs children?"

"Yes."

"Really?"

"Yeah. Why not?"

Emily walked on, shaking her head.

"Why not?" I asked again.

"I don't know you very well. Hell, I don't know you at all." She stopped outside the bookstore and brushed a loose strand of hair off her cheek. "You don't reveal much, but what you do say sure leaves an impact."

I hesitated trying to understand her point, not sure I did. With no time to ponder, I let it go. I had to get to my meetings and I still had to bury what was left of the Henderson family that afternoon.

Chapter Three

MY LAST MEETING of the morning was taking longer than expected. The couple, Tom and Penny Wilson, argued about paint colors and furniture styles. The house hadn't been designed yet and frankly I'd had enough. "Listen folks, while this may be important to you, it's got nothing to do with me." I smiled tightly. With my hands folded on my desk, I continued, "First things first, you need to review the materials I've given you about building green and what that encompasses. You need to examine the cost factor and decide if you're willing to absorb the extra expenses. We can sort out the architectural aspects of your needs later." I peered from one to the other and they seemed to be in agreement.

I stood, effectively putting a quick end to our meeting. My upcoming duty was more important than their decorating choices, and I wouldn't allow them to get ahead of themselves on my time. After extending my hand to each of them, I escorted them to the door. "Read over the materials I've supplied you. If you have questions give me a call. Once you make your decision to proceed, make an appointment with Mary and we can discuss the designs and your specific wishes." I waited while they wandered past me and gently closed the door behind them, shaking my head. *Thank God that was over.*

I grabbed two folders from the pile of paperwork on my desk and dropped them into my briefcase so I could work from home over the weekend. Next I synced my Blackberry for the following week's projects and set it to vibrate.

There was a knock at the door. "Come in Mare." I wasn't in the mood for her hovering, but I expected it.

"Mac, I wanted you to know I'm on my way to the bank to make the deposit and get lunch afterward. Do you need me for anything first?" Mary leaned on the door, her navy blue dress a stark contrast to her alabaster skin and silver hair. Arresting, steely blue eyes gazed at me intently. She was pleasantly plump and grandmotherly. I should have been so lucky growing up. She pushed her glasses up on the bridge of her nose, waiting.

I was mildly surprised but secretly relieved by her demeanor. I was already dreading the afternoon. She must have realized that. "Go ahead, Mare," I said. "Hey, why don't you take the afternoon off? It's quiet. Close the office. Just make sure you put the answering machine on." I continued packing my briefcase. A last-minute check of my desk and the credenza behind it assured me I hadn't forgotten anything.

Mary's voice caught me mid-thought. "Are you sure, boss?"

"Hey, don't argue. Go home and give Harry a thrill. A little afternoon delight, ya know?" I laughed and thankfully her hands were empty. Otherwise I would have been ducking.

"You take care of yourself today, hear me?" Mary said as she paused to see if I was listening. "Mac, please. It's no one's fault. You did what you could. Hell, everyone did."

"And yet a small child and her mother are dead." I gritted my teeth as the words tumbled from my mouth. My temper flared. This time it was a good thing. It would get me through the afternoon. It would guard me from the pain of reliving my past. It would comfort me when there was no one else there. I glanced at Mary. "Go on, get out of here before I change my mind," I growled.

She left the office and I thought back to that fateful night I had received the call from the crisis center. Heath, the manager had been desperate to find me. The hospital needed someone from the center immediately. Once I arrived, Sarah tried to send me home, knowing I would have trouble dealing with the case. She had begged me to call Lily, my backup in, but I refused. I ended up spending five days by Dani's bedside, talking with her, holding her little hand, willing her to get better. They assured me she was stabilized, otherwise I would never have left the hospital. All her vital signs looked good, the doctor said. Meanwhile, a small blood clot had traveled through her system and she died before they even realized what was happening. In hindsight, the decision to grab a shower and change of clothes, followed by a quick check of things at the office, like getting the mail, seemed imprudent. While I took care of trivial matters, Dani slipped away, alone. That was the second time I had left someone in need for absurd reasons. Acknowledging the flaw in my internal structure nauseated me. I had failed loved ones before and it had cost them their lives. A painful gasp caught in my throat as I tried to shake myself free of those memories, if only for awhile. There were things to do, places to go, people to tend to.

The bathroom door stood ajar, reminding me of the need for a quick shower. I would then have only ten minutes to dress before I left to bury these latest victims.

THE DRIVE DOWN the street toward Donaldson's Mortuary surprised me. Cars crowded both sides of the roadway the entire length of the block, narrowing the already thin strip of blacktop to a barely navigable single lane. Malta was a small town and I didn't recall reading of another death. I parked my truck beneath a giant oak tree, its foliage shading the front lawn of the mortuary. Dappled sunlight filtered through the leaves offering a bit of a respite on the warm, sunny afternoon. A deep breath fortified me to begin the trek up the path and ascend the stairs in front of the building. The smell of flower arrangements assaulted me at the door. The sweet fragrance of roses, petunias, and gladiolas that would normally bring visions of sunshine and the outdoors coalesced into a sickening reminder of death and decay inside this tomb of a building. I heard the murmurs, voices lowered in respect for the dead. My insides tightened. I'd been there before to bury the blameless. My heart started to pound in my chest; my knees began to tremble as a moan escaped my lips. *I could do this. I would.*

"Hey, sweetie. Here, take my hand." Sarah appeared out of nowhere, wrapped her left arm around me, and took my right hand in hers. She whispered in my ear, "It's okay. I'm here." She was wearing a long-sleeved black dress with black pumps to match. Her blonde hair was pulled back into a bun. I knew she could feel me trembling and I was powerless to stop as she tightened her arm around me in a hug. "I'm here, Mac. It's going to be all right. We'll do this together," she said softly and soothingly.

I nodded, unable to speak. My throat was closing on me. I wanted to scream, cry, rant. I wanted to kill the bastard for doing this to his wife and child. After a deep settling breath, I squared my shoulders and allowed Sarah to lead me into the viewing area. A small shock went through me when I saw the entire ball team and most of their parents inside. Janice Thomas and her mother, Noreen, were seated in the back, next to Dan Jenkins. Little Tommy's wheelchair was parked in the aisle with him in it. Connie and Jim Collins sat one row up, next to Patrick who was proudly wearing his assistant coach shirt. Leonard Atkins sat with his mom, Helen. His father had skipped town years ago. Now Helen struggled trying to make a home for the two of them. Tracey and Denise sat together with Denise's mother, Bette Peters. Mary was up front with her husband, Harry. Maggi from the diner, along with many other friends, had all come to pay their respects. They had come to say good-bye to an innocent child who had never really had a chance, to bid farewell to a mother too afraid to believe that help existed outside her four walls of hell.

Sarah guided me up the aisle to the closed caskets. Dani's picture reflected her chubby face and adorable smile. Little wisps of her blonde hair curled around her ears. Her eyes were the same blue color as my computer screen, her cheeks rosy. She was so pretty. At least no one would see the damage, the broken pieces that were left within the sealed box. I tried to console myself with that, but tears started to form anyway and I shook my head trying to push them away. The picture of Dani's mom, Lynnette Henderson, called for my attention. There was a strong resemblance between mother and daughter. The only difference was that Lynnette's eyes were haunted, full of fear and hopelessness. Lynnette stood five-feet, two-inches tall and weighed ninety-eight pounds when she was killed. Her husband, Darrell, was six-feet, five-inches tall and weighed two-hundred-and-sixty-two pounds. The doctors told me about the burn marks across her breasts and arms, probably from cigarettes. She had a broken arm and a fractured skull when she was brought into the hospital, but that didn't include her previous fractures and injuries. The bastard had the balls to complain about the scratches she had inflicted in her feeble attempt to fight him off. My hands curled into fists as anger pushed up from my depths. Sarah tightened her arm around me and directed me to seats in front. She murmured softly, but the words escaped me, silenced by my roiling fury. I fixed my gaze on the coffins through the storm-raged fog of my anguish.

I unbuttoned my suit jacket and sat. Sarah took my hand in hers trying to soothe my malice. Mary grasped my other hand and held it tightly. They had to know what being here was doing to me. They had to remember the last time we had been here like this. They surely realized I might not get through it. The minister arrived and we waited for him to begin.

The service was short per my request. I had no idea there would be such a turnout, or that every person would insist on going to the cemetery. I had expected the interment to be private. Instead the sudden outpouring of support gave me the tiniest spark of hope for humanity.

As the caskets were loaded into the hearses, I stood next to Sarah, my insides quaking. I prayed I wouldn't humiliate myself as my memories surged to the surface and the pain threatened to engulf me.

"I've got you," Sarah assured me. "I'm right here, sweetie." She steered me to her car and opened the passenger door. I climbed in without thought.

The drive took less than five minutes. The cemetery was on the west side of town, mere blocks away. We sat in Sarah's car waiting for the caskets to be transported to the burial plot. Finally she exited and came around the front and opened the passenger door. I stared into her eyes as I sidled out. I saw the love she had always offered and her recognition of my pain. Somehow, that helped.

"Come on Mac. Let's give this family the dignity they deserve." She took my arm and we made our way up the slope to the grave site. The minister waited until everyone was in place and settled.

It was a beautiful afternoon. The sun was sitting high in the sky and I could feel the warm rays reaching down to caress my skin. There was a light breeze and the flowers offered up their bouquet. The open grave lay beneath a majestic elm with low dipping branches that seemed to embrace the mourners, offering both shade and comfort. It was an odd complement to our current task as the prayers began. The minister spoke of God's lessons, God's love, and God's sacrifices. He spoke about Lynnette's life and her pain, of Dani's life, and the fact they were taken from us too soon.

He didn't mention the motherfucker sitting in his jail cell or that he was already claiming it as an accident. How the hell could anyone hit a two-year-old child — their own daughter–with a hammer and call it an accident? Forget about the burn marks, the broken bones, and the contusions. How could he have intentionally destroyed another human being? One he helped bring into the world? How could he club his wife with the claw end of that same hammer and claim it was an accident? The rest of the minister's sermon was lost, obliterated by my anger. Nothing would change. Dani and Lynnette were still dead. I couldn't bring them back and God surely hadn't protected them. He must've been busy that day.

The kids and their parents filed past, each placing a flower on the caskets, waiting as they paused to pay their respects to two victims they only knew in passing.

Mary was at my side and gave me a long squeeze. "I love you, Mac," she said. "I'll see you Monday. Okay?" She was crying. She was such a softy. Harry took her arm and guided her back to their car.

Maggi came up next and clasped me close. "*Mi estimada amiga. Mis sinceras condolencias en este momento tan triste. Me siento apenada por tu gran perdida. Estoy disponible si necesitas alguna ayuda.*" Roughly translated it meant – "My friend. My sincere condolences on this sad moment. I feel pain for your great loss. I am available if you need some help." Clearly I needed more than help.

"*Si gracias,*" I said.

She dabbed at her eyes and meandered away. The rest of the mourners had departed, leaving only me and Sarah. The grave workers were off to the side, waiting for us to leave, waiting to lower the caskets and close the gravesite.

"Mac, we can go now. They're at peace, honey. No one can hurt them ever again." Sarah pulled me close, trying to absorb some of my pain. I pushed away from her. I wouldn't let her do that. I couldn't. We silently made our way back to the car.

"Why don't you come home with me tonight?" Sarah offered. "We'll order pizza. The kids would love to see you and Michael is

out of town until the tomorrow." Sarah started the engine and
slowly drove away.

My lack of an answer wouldn't surprise her. Instead I stared
out the side window watching as the caskets were lowered.

WE PULLED UP next to my truck and I leaned over to kiss
Sarah on the cheek. I grasped her hand. I wanted to thank her for
coming, for helping me, and for caring, but I couldn't get the words
past my throat. Her eyes told me she understood. In any case she
didn't press. I slipped out of the car and glanced back in, clearing
my throat. "Maybe another time. I can't...I...not tonight." My voice
cracked. The need to escape was unbearable. Sarah tipped her head
and gave me a reassuring smile. She knew I didn't share that part of
me. Not now. Not then. Maybe not ever.

I climbed into my truck and drove to the florist to pick up a
small bouquet. Then I returned to the cemetery, back to where it all
began. The new graves, not even an hour old were already covered
over, with flowers decorating the mound. I wondered about little
Dani. My concern for their safety was immediate, even without
prior knowledge of their history, the pain and fear resonated on
their faces the night they had been brought into the emergency
room over a year ago. That was the first of several trips to the ER,
all ending with Lynnette going back to her abuser, afraid not to.
Once I saw them, I knew everything. I recognized what they'd been
through. I understood their pain and that it would *never* go away
without accepting help. Time slipped by as I thought about the
sonofabitch sitting in a jail cell, fat and happy, while I stood over
the graves of his wife and child. I lingered, wanting to avenge their
deaths and knowing I would never have the chance.

As the sun started to dip in the sky, I straightened my
shoulders, took a deep breath, and changed course. I trudged
further up the hill toward the real purpose of my return visit. The
ebony grave marker called to me and I stumbled toward it. I
cleaned dried leaves from around the base of the stone before
placing the flowers in front. This grave contained my family, my
life. Isabella, my wife, loved white daisies and I'd brought her some
today. I paused a moment to remember before the pain, as fresh
now as when it first happened, swallowed me. My tears started to
flow. Slowly at first, then heavier, turning to sobs. Soon I heard
guttural, pain-filled howling. It was me. I couldn't seem to stop. My
life had ended the day they died, the moment they were wrenched
from me. I clenched my jaw in a vain attempt to control my wailing,
but to no avail. My heart was broken and I couldn't breathe.
Isabella was thirty-seven the day she died. Our Bella was only

three. Two innocent lives had been destroyed by a fucking maniac intent on brutalizing his victims. I fell to my knees unable to stop crying. I wanted to crawl into the grave with them to stop my pain. I wanted to end the emptiness I felt every single day without them. I sat back, my elbows on my knees and put my head in my hands, weeping for the way of life that was taken from me. I cried for my wife and my daughter. I bawled because I was nothing without them. I screamed because of all we lost. My body was rocking back and forth, but the tears kept coming. I couldn't staunch the flow. I finally lay down and curled up into the fetal position, sobbing. My tears watering the lush green grass beneath me. I cried until there were no more tears, and still my heart bled. My pain was as sharp as a finely honed chisel and it hadn't dulled in five years time.

I heard the footsteps, but I didn't care. I needed to be with my family. I wanted to see Isabella's smiling face. I wanted to hear her laughter just one more time. I wanted to hold her in my arms. I wanted her to smirk at me when I flirted with her. I wanted to watch Bella as she ran into my waiting arms. I wanted to laugh at her silly smile. I wanted to feel her sloppy kisses on my cheek. I. Wanted. My. Family. Back. My sobs grew louder as the pain cut deeper.

"Mac? Mac, is that you?" a familiar-sounding voice asked.

I rolled onto my back and saw Emily standing before me, the fading sunlight casting a soft orange halo around her. I managed to sit up and wiped my eyes on the sleeve of my jacket. "Yeah, it's me." My voice was raspy and raw with pain.

Emily knelt beside me and took my hand. She'd read the inscriptions and now she'd become a kindred soul of sorts. "Oh Mac, I'm so sorry." She held my hand in hers, offering comfort and solace. For a moment I felt it, the warmth spreading through me like a soothing balm for my ravaged heart.

Guilt forced me to yank my hand back. I didn't want to share this pain, this emptiness — she had her own to deal with.

"Mac, please let me help you." Her hand was on my arm.

"You want to help me? You want to ease my pain?" My heart was breaking anew. How could she help me with that?

"Yes." Emily said, tears glistening in her eyes.

"Then bring them back to me. Give me my family, my life, back. I want my wife and child alive. If you can't do that, get out of here," I snapped, jerking my arm away. "Just get the *hell* out of here."

She gasped at my abrupt withdrawal and explosive anger.

I struggled to my feet and stood with my back to her, staring at the inscription on the marker.

Isabella Sanchez
Beloved Wife of Mackenzie Taylor
Bella Sanchez Taylor
Precious Daughter of Both

Emily stepped beside me, her hand in the small of my back offering strength. Warmth spread through my body and some of my pain receded.

"I didn't know, Mac. I'm sorry. So sorry, for your loss." The tremor in her voice told me she understood. We had each suffered under different circumstances. However, loss was loss.

She waited quietly beside me, placidly offering support in the unwavering strength that emanated from her. She shivered. The sun had gone down and the breeze had picked up. I slipped my suit jacket off and placed it around her shoulders. Without a word, I stepped back and walked down the path, away from the only place I felt whole. Away from my family.

Emily followed me down the walkway to where our vehicles were parked. I opened the door to her truck to let her slide into the driver's seat. She took my hand and searched my eyes in the dimming light. "Come home with me. We'll order take out or I'll cook something. The kids would love to meet you." She stared out the windshield before she continued. "You shouldn't be alone. Not tonight."

She was still holding my hand. I raised hers to kiss the back of it and smiled gently. "I'm okay. Don't worry. You drive safely and don't forget about painting the shelves this weekend." I took a step back and closed the door to her truck. She reached to return my jacket, but I held up my hands. "Keep it until you come over."

Emily started the engine, glancing back one more time, and put the truck in gear.

I lingered in the roadway witnessing her taillights vanish around the bend before I made my way over to my own truck and got in. I was cold from lying on the wet grass and exhausted from my emotional ordeal. A flick of the switch brought the heater to life and a roll of the dial increased the volume on the CD, both providing relief to my aching body and tortured soul. Lucy Blue Tremblay blasted through the six speakers to keep me company on my trip back up the mountain to home. The structure I had once shared with my now deceased family had become my living tomb.

THE RED LIGHT on the answering machine blinked at me insistently as I entered through the back door. I crossed the room and hit the play button. There were five messages. *Fuck*. I went into the kitchen and took a beer from the fridge, then twisted off the cap and took a deep pull while the machine kicked on.

Sarah was first, of course. "Mac. Are you there, honey? Please call me. I love you. I'm not going to sleep until I hear from you. Call me."

"Hey Boss. We're doing burgers on the grill if you're interested. Come by anytime. We'd love to have you." Mary doing her nurturing thing again.

"Mac, call me, please." Sarah pushed, wanting me to talk. She knew how hard that would be for me. I smiled sadly. She understood but couldn't let it go.

"Mac, it's Emily. I wish you had come with me. I'm worried about you. If it helps, I know what you're going through. Call me. Please." Emily left her new number. I didn't bother to write it down. She had her own problems, her own grief.

"Dammit, don't make me pack the kids in the car and drive out there. Call me, please. I love you." Sarah knew which buttons to push, what threats would get my attention.

She answered on the first ring. "I'm home and safe, Mommy," I said. "Now go to bed and I'll talk to you sometime over the weekend."

"Mac. Please...tell me you're all right. Tell me...talk to me, please." Sarah's voice stopped me before I could hang up.

I sighed. There was no point in lying. Of course I had gone to their grave. Of course it had hurt, and of course I was angry. "It's okay, Sarah. I'm home...safe and sound. I made it through. I put some flowers on the grave and came straight back here. Okay?" She knew there was more. I knew she knew it, but why go into it?

"Mac, Izzy wouldn't want you suffering like this. She loved you too much for that."

"I have to go," I said quickly and hung up before she could say more. Before she would say Isabella's name again, forcing me to rehash all the times we'd all spent laughing together right here in this house.

Sarah, her husband, Mike, Izzy, and I had been the four musketeers, always joking and sharing our lives. We celebrated our victories, worked through our difficulties, and gave strength through our shared miseries. I stood up for Sarah the day she married Mike, and even agreed to wear a tux. Izzy helped Michael establish his law office by working for free with him until he could afford a secretary. We took vacations together until Sarah's son was born. Sarah delivered Bella and placed her in my arms for the first time. Izzy and I were godparents to their son, she and Michael for our Bella. We had done everything together until the fateful day that bastard ripped it out from under us.

I stumbled into the den, placed the beer bottle on the end table, and lay down on the cushiony leather couch. I wouldn't sleep in our bed tonight. I missed Isabella with all my heart, but those memories were too painful. I hated passing Bella's room. I hadn't cleaned it out. Any of it. Everything in that part of the house was just as Izzy had left it. I didn't need a fresh reminder of what was missing from my life. I lay back and covered my eyes with my arm, shutting everything out. I hoped sleep would come and prayed for no dreams because it was the good ones that hurt the most.

Chapter Four

THE INCESSENT RINGING of the phone clamored for my attention. The fog of sleep dissipated with the chronic, annoying noise. My hand flailed, reaching for the elusive nightstand, and then I came fully awake when the answering machine kicked on. It all came rushing back—I had slept in the den, away from my nightmares, away from the bed Isabella and I had once shared. Away from Bella's room where her princess bed still sat in the corner, her pink floppy-eared bunny lounging on the pillow waiting for her. The voice on the recorder startled me and a queasy feeling settled in my stomach.

"Mac, are you there? We've got an emergency. Mac, do you hear me? It's Heath." Heath managed the crisis center. "I need to know if you can cover this? Mac?" I snatched the receiver before he could hang up.

"I'm here," I said, still groggy from sleep.

"Mac, good. I'm glad I caught you. There's a pregnant woman in the emergency room. She needs our help." Heath was reading from his notes. I heard him shuffling through papers. "Okay, here it is. See Nancy. The police asked her to call us. They want a counselor." I sat a moment with my head back against the couch, my eyes closed, my mind screaming...*not already...not so soon?* I shook my head.

"Mac?"

"Where's Lily?"

"She's been on the last three nights."

Lily, Heath, and I shared the workload. Actually, Lily and I shared the calls while Heath ran the center and our two safe houses. He dealt with any in-house residents by himself, manned the phones, and handled all of the paperwork.

"Mac?" Heath repeated.

A sigh escaped. "Yeah, Heath, I'll be there in forty minutes. Let 'em know." I slammed the phone down and ran upstairs to change into clean jeans and a T-shirt. I splashed water on my face in the bathroom and brushed my teeth before checking my reflection in the mirror. My eyes were swollen and red, but it didn't matter. The patient wouldn't even notice. On the way downstairs I felt for my keys as I slipped into my leather jacket and strolled out the front door, already on autopilot. I patted another pocket and felt the reassuring weight of my cell phone. I had everything I needed.

Now if I could just provide relief for the victim as easily, it would be a good night.

THE EMERGENCY ROOM parking lot was jammed with cars and I was thankful the medical center provided a space for counselors. The sliding glass doors of the entrance opened automatically as I approached. My ID tag was a matter of security and I looped it around my neck as I walked. Basically a formality since nearly everyone at the hospital knew me. An empty gurney sat idle at the door, a janitor worked to buff the faded linoleum back to a shine, and a nurse rushed past me with a bag of blood and tubing in her hands. The waiting room was quiet for a Friday night. One man snoozed in a chair while a woman knitted, her fingers working furiously in time with the clacking of the needles. The smell of disinfectant filled the air, reminding me to get some rubber gloves from the supply area before meeting my patient. Nancy, the head nurse, was talking with a police officer as I approached. I needed her to give me the specifics.

"Lord in heaven the human race baffles me, Mac," Nancy said. "For the record we're filled to capacity down here." She pulled a chart and glanced at me. "Hey, you okay? You look like shit. What's going on?"

A quick pivot removed me from further scrutiny. "I'm fine. I was sleeping when the call came. You remember sleep? What most people do at night?" I shook my head. "So where's my patient?"

Nancy tilted her head toward the left. "Room three. She was severely beaten and she's pregnant. Mac—it's bad, maybe—"

"What?" I snapped. My need to help these women was what gave me the strength to go on, but sometimes it was difficult.

Nancy closed the chart. "Nothing."

"I'm sorry." My hand captured hers, gently squeezing. "I'll be okay."

Nancy had been the head nurse in the ER for as long as I could remember and there was nothing she hadn't seen or handled. If she said it was bad, it must be worse. I knew she was concerned and wanted to protect me. I also knew the drill. At the door marked *Exam Room Three*, I paused. *I can do this...I will do this.* A deep breath braced me before I knocked.

A murmured reply. "Yes?"

I pushed the door open slowly and saw a young woman lying upright on a bed inside the dimly lit room. She was crying and I took some tissues from the nightstand and handed them to her. "Hi," I said. "I'm Mackenzie Taylor from the local crisis center. I'm here to see if you need some help?" I paused briefly to look at her injuries. Both of her eyes were blackened and a deep gash over her left brow had been sutured. Her jaw was discolored and swollen. Her bottom lip was split in two places and the imprints of finger marks were easily visible around her throat. The new bruises would fully develop by the next day in sharp contrast to older ones which were already fading. Sadly, there was a term for that. It was called rainbow-effect bruising, where the various shades indicated regular beatings and different stages of healing. This was *not* her first attack.

I took a deep, calming breath before I asked, "What's your name, miss?"

There was no answer. Her left arm was in a sling and her fingers protruding from the wrap were swollen, with dried blood still caked in the crevices and around her nails. She twisted her head away and I saw a shaved area running into her hair line that sported more stitches. A thin line of blue sutures about two inches long snaked up the back of her skull.

She was cautious, unsure if she could trust me, or if she wanted to. The fear in her eyes was tangible. "Patti," she whispered. I might not have heard her if I hadn't been paying attention.

"Okay, Patti, can I call someone for you? What do you need? I'm here to help in any way I can." I placed my hand lightly over hers to offer support, if she would accept it. All too often the victim felt guilty, as if their assault had been deserved.

Her eyes stayed fixed on me while her right hand covered and rubbed her stomach protectively, sliding her hand up, over and around the outline of her pregnancy. "My baby, is he...will he be okay?" The tears started anew. Her concern was for the child she loved. That would be half the battle.

"I don't know, but we're gonna find out for you."

Patti started to cry harder.

I smoothed back her hair. "Shush, it's gonna be okay."

Her face was tear-stained as she spoke again. "You're going to think I'm awful."

"I'm not here to judge you. I'm here to help."

"My husband...he's not the father. He said he didn't care. He said he'd love us both. He did this. He tried to kill my baby."

"Well, we won't let that happen. Hear me? You rest here and try to remain calm. I'll go find a doctor who can tell us the extent of your injuries. Okay?" She acquiesced and offered up a small smile through her tears. I patted her hand and strode out the door.

At the nurses' station Nancy was writing in a chart, a large pile next to her awaiting her attention. "Who's working tonight, Nan?" I asked.

She studied me, clearly gauging my reactions. "Jeffries. You're in luck. She's finishing up reading an EKG. Should be out in a minute, but if you feel the need for privacy, she's in Room Six." Nancy smirked and cocked her brow at me.

"Don't start," I warned.

The subject of our conversation appeared through an open door at the end of the corridor. Doctor Jeffries walked toward the desk, immersed in a chart. She glanced up as she approached and smiled. "Hi Mac. How's my favorite architect?" she asked with a wink. "I'll be with you in a minute."

"Evening, gorgeous," I responded with a smile. Cindy was a friend, and we went way back. Cindy Jeffries, Doctor Jeffries, was tall, blonde, blue-eyed, and beautiful. She had a great sense of humor and a wonderfully warm, compassionate manner. As an added bonus she was gay—something she didn't hide. Anyone in their right mind would want to get to know her better or ask her out on a date, just to see about the possibilities.

She had let me know in a million ways she was interested in me and would like to explore the prospect of what-ifs. I couldn't. I might be a flirt, but I could never cheat on Isabella.

"Mac, are you okay?"

Cindy knew my story firsthand. The night they brought my family in, she was on duty. It fell to her to tell me that both were gone, murdered, and that my entire life as I knew it was over. Despite not agreeing and strongly advising otherwise, Cindy supported me when I insisted on viewing their battered bodies.

Her hand on my arm pulled me back to the present. "Mac?"

I shook my head and blinked away the tears. "I'm okay." I cleared my throat, my voice hoarse. "The patient, Patti, she's concerned about her baby. She's scared and needs to know what the status is."

"Nancy, can you give me the chart on—" Cindy smiled when Nancy handed her the appropriate binder already opened for her review. Cindy slid her hand up and down the length of my forearm. "Okay. Let me finish the notes on my charts. Five minutes, alright?"

"Yeah, good." Hospitals had unnerved me since my adolescence, the smells, the sounds, the helplessness. Now, with my recent history, they had become synonymous with loss. The constant beeping of the monitors pounded in my head, and the fear of the unknown fed my anxiety. I acceded and shoved my hands in my pockets. I sucked air into my lungs as everything seemed to be closing in around me. "I'm gonna go back to her room," I said.

The short trip across the hall to Exam Room Three was a mere four steps, but it packed a surprise. I entered and saw a man standing next to the bed talking to Patti. I could see her eyes and almost smelled her fear.

"Excuse me. Can I help you?" I advanced on the intruder, cutting the distance between us as I spoke. A quick assessment gauged his height at six feet. He was skinny though, probably only about one hundred seventy pounds. My physical presence might not have been intimidating, but I would fight for this woman and her unborn child, if necessary.

"I'm Patti's brother, John Chester," he said as he gazed down at his sister and smiled softly. "Is he in jail? Is the bastard behind bars or can I go find him?"

The breath I was holding expelled as the muscles in my neck relaxed with relief. He wasn't there to hurt Patti or her baby. "That won't settle anything and Patti needs you here."

His sister's body trembled as her eyes shifted between John and me.

"Let the law deal with him." I shrugged my shoulders. "Honestly, I really don't know his status. I haven't had time to get into all that yet."

Patti concurred and gripped her brother's hand tighter. Her concern about what he might do was clear. I, however, was sympathetic with his desire for revenge. "Hey, can I get either of you some juice or coffee?" I asked. "Something to eat? It's going to be a long night. Patti will likely be admitted for observation. The ER doctor will be in shortly to talk to you." I patted her sheet-covered foot.

Patti's eyes went wide. She glanced from her brother to me, and back again. "John, I can't stay here. I can't afford it. I don't have insurance." She attempted to rise, but I put my hand up.

"Whoa, relax. We have government agencies to help with the medical bills and the crisis center will pick up the balance. Someday when you hit the lottery you can make a donation. In the meantime, worry about getting better." I cringed inwardly, certain the center's accountant would smack me for that one. What the hell, it was only money — mostly *my* money.

There was a chair on the other side of the bed and I dragged it around for Patti's brother. "Why don't you sit with your sister until I get back? I'll go see what I can scrounge up from the nurses' station and the break room." My hand was on the doorknob when Patti called to me.

When I returned to her side, she asked, "He...can he...will my husband be able find me here?" Her fear was real and I stole a glance at her brother.

"Absolutely not," I assured them both. "Tell you what, I'm going to get us some food and something to drink. After the doctor comes in and talks to you, we're going to lock that door. The three of us will wait together until morning and *no one* is going to hurt you. You have my word." I squeezed her hand — determined no one would harm her on my watch.

I started out to see what, if anything, Nancy could help me find in the way of food and drink.

HOURS LATER, THE sound of angry voices pulled me from my slumber and I bolted upright in the chair. The commotion in the hall set my heart to thumping, and the hair on the back of neck to stand on end as John and Patti continued to sleep. I shifted in the chair to nudge John awake. I brought my finger to my lips for him to be quiet and cupped my ear to signal for him to listen to the ruckus outside the room. I went to the door to ensure it was locked.

The nurses station was just a few feet away and the loud voices just kept getting louder.

"Where the fuck is she?" A man's voice asked.

"Who? Who are you looking for?" It was Nancy that asked.

"My wife, you stupid bitch." He responded.

"A name, I need a name." Nancy's voice quivered.

"Allison, Patti Allison. I dropped that fat cow off here hours ago and she hasn't come home yet?"

"We don't have a Patti Allison here?" Nancy shouted back.

"Don't fucking lie to me."

"Mr. Allison, you need to leave here immediately! Security is on their way." Cindy's voice carried an authoritative force.

I turned and signaled for John to wake Patti.

An idea was coming together in my head as the yelling from the nurses' area continued. Someone screamed and there was a thunderous crash. I snatched the phone from its cradle and punched zero for the hospital operator, hastily relating the details of what was happening. Security and police were expected momentarily. We only needed to protect Patti until they arrived in the ER. A plan formed in my mind, I whispered to John and his sister.

"Patti can you hide on the floor over there?" I pointed to the far side of the bed.

Her entire body was visibly trembling but she nodded bravely.

"Good, come on we'll help you down." With Patti in place I turned to John and motioned to the corner where the door would swing in. "I need you to wait there. Let him think I'm the patient, hopefully it will buy us the time we need."

I stashed my coat on the chair, kicked off my boots, and pulled up the legs of my jeans. One of the nondescript hospital gowns covered my remaining clothes while I lay waiting on the bed with the sheet pulled over me. I knew it wouldn't be long before he came searching for Patti.

Sure enough, the door handle rattled and I heard cursing on the other side. I lay on the high hospital bed pretending to sleep, but every nerve in my body was alert and ready to spring into action. The door splintered as it was kicked in. I sat up trying to appear disoriented and distressed, when, in fact, I was pissed and poised to strike if necessary.

"Who the fuck are you?" he snarled. He stood at least six foot, with a lanky frame except for the beer belly hanging over his belt. His hair was greasy, and his eyes dark and beady.

I peered at him through partially open lids, my peripheral vision taking in the gun he was holding. "Mac. W…who are you?"

He lurched closer, almost close enough to touch. As any good soldier would tell you, avoiding conflict was always preferable, but having a strategy was imperative. The intruder cast a furtive glance around the tiny room. The only illumination was an up light above the bed that cast the space in shadows and made it appear empty. Confused, he swung back, staggered closer, snatched my wrist and twisted. "Where's your name tag, bitch?"

Two security guards rushed in. He turned, his gun raised chest high. He never knew what hit him. Paul Smithers cracked the assailant's head with his night stick. The sound was almost sickening. *Almost.* Patti's brother, John, jumped from behind the door and watched as his brother-in-law went down like a rock. I leapt from the bed while the security guards took control and John and I helped Patti up from her hiding space. They cuffed him and secured his weapon.

"Hey guys, the police are on the way. They should be here shortly." I said.

"Good enough. We'll need your statement," Smithers said.

"I'll be here." John and I watched the guards remove Geoffrey Allison from the room. "John, stay with your sister. I need to check on everyone else." I pulled the hospital gown off and slipped into my boots, then ran to the nurses' station. It was empty, but I heard voices calling for help. The door to the medicine room down the hall was closed and the deadbolt engaged. Someone was jerking the handle furiously as I raced down the hallway. "Nancy?"

"Mac, is that you? Get us the hell out of here. Cindy's hurt."

"Where's the key?"

"At the desk last time I looked. Hurry!" Nancy's voice betrayed her distress.

More security guards appeared as I reached the nurses' station. I hijacked one to assist me.

My hands were shaking. *Fuck.* "Okay Nancy. We're coming in," I said.

The lock turned and the door opened. Cindy lay on the floor, blood pooling on the right side of her head. JoAnne was kneeling at her head, hands on both sides securing its position to prevent a neck injury as Nancy pressed a stethoscope to Cindy's chest checking her vitals. Stacey held fresh gauze against the open wound applying pressure. Athena, the Candy Striper, chewed on her lower lip. My insides knotted as I rushed in to pick Cindy up.

"Don't." Nancy stopped me. "We need to secure her neck." She ordered Athena to get a cervical collar and a back board. Once those were in place we gently lifted Cindy onto a gurney. I pushed it out the door as Nancy followed, yelling instructions to the staff. "JoAnne, call Doctor Downs and get her in here—apprise her of what's happened. Stacey, give security the details and make sure someone calls the police. Call radiology stat. I'm going to need help after you're both done."

I rolled Cindy into an open exam room and updated Nancy. "He's in custody. He broke into Patti's room, but her brother and I hid her. Security apprehended him. Her brother is with her now to keep her calm and safe."

"Good." Nancy shined a light in Cindy's eyes.

"How long has she been unconscious?"

Nancy glanced up. "Since he hit her."

The gash on Cindy's forehead was minor compared to her unconsciousness. I gently brushed her hair out of the way, leaning down to whisper in her ear. "I'm here, darlin'. Don't get any ideas about checking out. 'Cause I'm not letting you go." I held her hand like she had held mine all those years ago, helpless to do more.

Nancy took Cindy's blood pressure and re-checked the rest of her vitals.

"What can I do? I can help until Sarah gets here," I pleaded. "Please—let me."

"Stay with her. Talk to her. I've gotta get the x-ray tech in here." Nancy reeled around to go in search of him.

I was murmuring to Cindy when Nancy interrupted. "Mac?"

When I glanced up, she said, "He wanted to kill Cindy because she fought him. Said he was gonna kill his wife, too. We all heard him."

My temper simmered. "He's not going to kill anyone tonight." I said. "They cold-cocked him." I gazed down at Cindy, caressing her cheek and imagining the terror she must have felt. "Come on, cutie pie. Time to open them baby blues and smile at me. Come on, Cindy, please, open your eyes. Talk to me, honey."

Minutes later I was still encouraging Cindy when Nancy reappeared with the x-ray tech. "Mac," she said as she pulled the curtain around the bed. "I need you to step out while we prepare her."

My urge to protect Cindy was strong, but Nancy had more important things to do than argue with me. "What should I do?"

"Call Administration. Someone needs to get in touch with Cindy's next of kin."

My stomach clenched, but it had to be done.

THE ONLY USEFUL thing I could do was sit at the nurses' station with JoAnne while she answered phones and wrote out her statement for the police. Sarah rushed in carrying Taylor on her arm, Mikey Jr. holding her free hand. The kids were in their pajamas. I took the sleeping girl and briefly explained things. Sarah aimed for the exam room and I settled the kids in the lounge. I covered them with blankets and let them sleep.

Screams erupted down the hall and I stiffened and waited. The police had arrived and were dragging the bastard, cuffed and cursing, from the security area. Patti's husband was ranting that he'd been assaulted, that his rights were being denied. John Chester watched from the doorway and saluted before going back to his sister's bedside.

Arrangements needed to be made for her and the child, but I hadn't had a chance to discuss her options. A doctor needed to check on her after the excitement settled down.

Stacey called me. "Cindy's conscious and asking for you."

"Can you find Athena and have her stay with the kids while I check on Cindy? Please? I don't want to leave them alone." She agreed and I ran to Cindy's room.

I strolled to the top of the gurney and took Cindy's hand. "You trying to scare me, darlin'?" I asked with a smile. "Let's make a deal. Don't do that again, ever?" I kissed her forehead.

Sarah smiled. "She's gonna be fine. A big headache, but she's got a thick skull. Dr. Wolber is pretty sure there's no neurological damage, but she's ordered a CT scan to be sure. She's waiting around to personally read it."

"Can I go with her?" My question surprised me as well as Sarah. She hesitated before consenting.

Cindy's hand was encased in mine, neither of us wanting to let go. The need for her to be okay filled me. She squeezed my hand to get my attention. "It's not your fault, Mac. He's an evil person."

"I'm sorry I let you down," I whispered as tears filled my eyes and I leaned down and kissed her cheek.

IT WAS FOUR-THIRTY Saturday morning when I finally tiptoed back into Patti's room. It had been a long fuckin' night.

Sarah called in two interns and one had examined Patti a couple hours earlier. The good news was the baby was fine and Patti would be, too.

The intern, Doctor Reynolds, examined Patti in my presence. Her brother had stepped out of the room to give her some privacy. I had attempted to follow, but she asked that I stay and I complied.

"Aside from the multiple contusions, and the seventeen stitches it took to close your scalp wound, you were fortunate Mrs. Allison, there's no permanent damage to your larynx. In a couple days the discomfort will ease considerably." The doctor said. "We've set your elbow and with the proper physical therapy, you should be good as new in six to eight weeks."

Patti smiled tremulously at that.

The doctor stepped closer and listened to her heart a moment. Next he shone a light in her eyes. "You have a slight concussion, I don't anticipate any problems, but we're going to keep you overnight just to be sure. You're a smart woman, it's clear you took most of the abuse from behind, including the rape and sodomy. That saved your baby's life." The doctor stepped back. "The sonogram confirms your child is healthy, and we'll continue to observe his heartbeat but as you can see," he pointed to a monitor at the head of the bed "it's loud and strong."

Patti turned to the unit and back. "That's his heartbeat?"

The doctor grinned. "Yup, he's doing fine. One last thing, we've ordered a psych evaluation, it's standard for all rape victims. Any questions?"

I thought experience had inured me to this type of brutality, but I was wrong. Though his bedside manner needed work, at least the news had been good with regards to Patti and the baby. I glanced at Patti then the doctor. "When can she be released?"

"If psyche clears her, tomorrow morning." He walked to the door. "Have a good day ladies."

I turned to Patti shaking my head.. "What an ass."

"I thought it was me." She giggled softly.

"No, it wasn't. But at least we know you and junior there are both going to be okay. I'll get John for you and be back in a little while, you take care."

"Thank you, Mac."

I grinned at her. "No thanks needed, you just take care of yourself and that precious baby."

IT TOOK TWO hours to answer the questions the police posed and thirty minutes to write out my statement. It took another two hours for Cindy's tests to be completed and reviewed. John was asleep in the chair, his hand resting on Patti's arm. She was staring out the window, rubbing her stomach and humming to herself — or the baby — as dawn began to break on the horizon. I veered over to the right side of the bed and touched her foot. "I'm sorry for abandoning you last night," I said.

She squinted up at me and her lip started to quiver. "Is that doctor...is she okay? She's not dead is she?" she asked as tears rolled down her cheek.

I shook my head and smiled. "Nah, she's gonna be fine. A little headache, but other than that all the tests came back clear. She'll be released later this morning like you." I squeezed Patti's hand to reassure her. "What about you?" I tilted my head toward her brother. "I know he wants to help. What can I do?"

Patti glanced at John and smiled softy. "He told me to come home with him. To stay with him and his family until the baby is born. We can go from there, but it won't work." Tears rained harder. "He and Missy have a newborn at home. I won't take a chance that Geoffrey will show up searching for me and hurt them. I can't let that happen." Patti sobbed as tears flowed freely.

I tapped the back of her hand. "We can make some arrangements for you. If staying close to family is important, we can get you a lawyer and an RO. Work with some agencies to help you financially."

"Geoffrey will never let it rest. He's determined to kill me and my baby." Patti's hand rested on her stomach.

"Well, the center works with a network of people across the country. We can relocate you. Once we do though, there's no coming back. No contact with family, no contact with friends. That includes no calls, no emails, no nothing."

"How would that work?"

"We make arrangements to change your name and transport you away from here," I said. "Help you get set up with a job and day care after the baby is born. We'll help you get some counseling. If you want, legal aide will assist with a divorce. All you have to do is say the word and we can start the paperwork." I stole a glance at John who was starting to stir. "We can have you in a safe house upon discharge and no one will ever hurt you again."

She looked at John, who was now listening intently. "Yes, please. I have to protect my baby. He's the most important thing in the world to me. I want him to be safe.

I smiled, pleased with her decisive answer. "I'll make some phone calls right away. You'll go directly to the safe house and from there Patti Allison and her baby will virtually disappear off the face of the earth."

"You can do that? You can keep us safe? Really?"

"We work with an extensive network of people driven to protect women from their attackers. If you do as they tell you, you'll be safe. You'll have a job, a home, and a new life. It won't be easy. You'll go through two weeks of instructions, learning to respond to the new identity and counseling. It's not an easy transition, but it's necessary if you truly want to remain safe."

John and Patti were talking quietly as I left the room. It gave me great pleasure that the crisis center could help her get out of the mess she was in. I wished more women were as brave as Patti. As Sarah always said, we needed to celebrate the wins. That night we had two.

BY SIX-THIRTY all the arrangements for Patti and her new beginning were in the works. The OB-GYN on duty had cleared her for release and the psych evaluation was positive. Patti and the baby could be transferred as soon as the paperwork was signed. Heath would pick her up shortly after ten and she would be whisked to the safe house. From there she would be processed and moved to a location of her choice, within reason. I made a quick stop to say good-bye and wished her well. As I walked down the hall, I was satisfied with the outcome and pleased that she and her baby would be safe from her asshole husband.

Cindy's room was dark as I tiptoed in a little after seven and sat in the chair next to her bed. The curtains were pulled shut to block any sunlight. I took her hand in mine, needing to touch her. Needing to know she was okay. I rested my head on the bed rail and closed my eyes. It had been an arduous night and I was exhausted. Geoffrey Allison was in jail, at least until bail could be set. With luck no one would post it. Felony charges were pending because of the gun. Another few hours and Patti and her baby would be out of his life and out of his reach permanently.

A gentle tug on my hand made me smile. "Hi," I whispered.

"Hi yourself." Cindy was staring at me, her eyes worried. "Now go home."

"Hey," I said as I leaned over the rail. "I'm not the one who got cracked on the noggin last night. How you feeling, sexy?" My hand brushed her cheek.

"Oh, Mac."

"What's wrong?" I asked when tears dripped from Cindy's eyes. "Are you in pain? I'll get Nancy." Fear caused me to panic, but before I could find help Cindy squeezed my hand.

"Do you have any idea how long I've waited for you to notice me?" she asked. "To see me as more than a friend? To look at me the way you used to gaze at Izzy?"

I froze at the mention of Isabella's name. I couldn't help it; the pain cut deep. "Cindy, I—"

"I know, Mac. It's okay. You still love her. I get that. You don't think of me that way." She pulled my hand to her cheek and held it there. "Go home. Don't promise me more than you're capable of."

She was right and we both knew it. I would be cheating her. I would never love another as I had Isabella and our daughter. Tears blurred my vision as I bent over and kissed Cindy's cheek. "I'm sorry. Sorrier than you'll ever know." I whispered

I staggered out of her room and walked to the nurses' station. Nancy glanced up as I approached.

"Is she awake yet?"

"Yes." I coughed, trying to disguise my distress. "Can you stay with her for a while? I think she could use a friend. Her mom's due about nine. She's driving straight through."

Nancy studied me. "I'll stay with her, but what she wants is you. She's in love with you, ya know."

What could I say to that? I took a deep breath and let out a sigh.

Nancy shook her head. "You know last night should be a lesson for all of us. Life is too short. That bastard truly makes me question the concept of redemption, but I need to believe everyone obtains it...eventually."

I stared, numbed to the possibility.

"Cindy's loved you for a long time," Nancy added. "And you could do a lot worse."

I conceded. "But the point is *Cindy* deserves more, Nancy, and that's the crux of it. I'm only a shell. She deserves the whole package." My voice cracked. I exited the ER, into the morning air and away from any chance at my own redemption.

Chapter Five

THE ORDEAL AT the hospital left me too hyped for sleep and too exhausted to work. Desperately in need of staples, I made a quick trip to the market before heading up the mountain. My cell rang while I was loading the last of the grocery sacks into my truck. I checked the readout, pleased to see Emily's new number. A fluttery feeling shifted through my chest as I answered the phone. "Good morning. You're up bright and early."

"Mac, did I wake you?" Her voice sounded apprehensive.

"No, I've been up for hours." Not exactly a lie. I climbed into the truck with the cell to my ear and started the engine.

"I was worried. I couldn't stop thinking...well, you know. I thought about all you've lost. I'm so sorry." Emily cursed softly and I heard something fall in the background.

"Everything okay?" My stomach tightened.

A sigh of exasperation came through the phone. "Yeah fine. I dropped a plate," Emily muttered, obviously distracted. "Sorry about that. I called to see if you're still up for company today? The children are excited about painting the book cases, but if you're not up to it, I'd understand."

"I'm not only up to it I'm actually looking forward to it." I was too. Spending the day with Emily and her two grandchildren was exactly the medicine I needed. Suddenly I felt invigorated. "So what time can I expect the three of you?"

She chuckled. "Only one problem. I don't know where you live."

Duh. I slapped the steering wheel. "Hey, I'm right around the corner from you. How about I pick you up and we'll go together? I'll bring you back later this afternoon. There's a game scheduled and I'm coming back into town anyway."

She laughed easily. "I'll need a few minutes to get the kids ready. There is a fresh pot of coffee on that should keep you occupied while you wait."

Coffee sounded good right about then, especially home-brewed. I'd had all the vending machine crap I could handle for one night. "I'll be there in five minutes." I hung up and pulled into the right lane. Emily's street was at the next corner. A glance in the rearview mirror revealed an unexpected smile on my face.

THE ALLEY BEHIND the bookstore provided ample parking for shoppers and tenants. I utilized one of the empty spaces, then climbed the steps at the back of the building. Emily and the kids lived in the apartment above the book store. It was a large space, seventeen hundred square feet of oversized rooms with an open floor plan and I was very familiar with the layout. My management company owned the newly renovated structure, most of which fell to me. I checked my reflection in the window pane. My eyes were no longer swollen. The dark circles remained, but were nothing new. I knocked on the door.

Emily opened it, a smile reaching her brown eyes, making me feel welcome. She was dressed in her usual attire with her black hair spilling down her shoulders. There was something so damned appealing about the way she filled out the T-shirt. It was snug enough to outline the soft swell of her breasts while the sleeves revealed the definition of her arms. Her jeans sculpted her butt and strong legs, making mine weak. *Stop staring, you idiot.*

"Hi, come on in. I'm excited for you to meet the children." She backed up and as I walked past her I could smell her shampoo, something floral. Her toothpaste was minty. On her it was a visceral combination. I stepped back and waited.

We passed through the mud room and into the twenty-two by fifteen foot kitchen. My eyes were immediately drawn to the changes made since my last visit. At that time, I had installed new pine cabinets, which were topped off with cream-colored granite countertops and new white appliances. The renovations created a work space. Emily had transformed it from an ordinary kitchen into a family hearth. A candle — vanilla — burned on the counter top, but it did little to erase the heavenly aroma of blueberry pancakes and bacon that still lingered in the air. A long-forgotten memory of Isabella preparing a similar breakfast made me smile. Freshly brewed coffee dripped into a carafe on the kitchen island. A large, plank-style oak table sat perpendicular to the hub of the work station. School books were stacked on one corner, homework partially completed. Curtains with matching placemats and seat cushions brought a dash of color to match the newly painted red accent wall. A bowl of fruit was set on the counter along with a wooden block that housed cutlery. The refrigerator was covered with drawings, presumably done by her grandchildren. A calendar hung on the wall near the table and I noted a number of days marked with appointments. Memories of Izzy's hastily scribbled notes scattered on the fridge flooded my mind as I scanned the warm and welcoming room.

"Kids, come on. We have company," Emily called into the empty space, the sound floating through the expansive rooms.

Suddenly the quiet was broken by the sound of feet running through the living area.

They barreled into the kitchen and stopped short when they saw me. Surprise and fear flashed in their eyes. Shock and a quick rush of temper flared within me. *These are Emily's grandchildren?* I hid my initial response as I bent down to Kaitlin's height and put my hand out. "Hi, Kaitlin, I'm Mac."

She peeked at her grandmother and tentatively stepped forward to take my hand. "Hello," she said before she backed up quickly. The boy seemed filled with uncertainty, but stepped up dutifully after a glance at Emily.

A squat put me at his level. "Hi. I never did learn your name, but I'm Mac."

His grin revealed the gap from his missing tooth. "I'm Kylie." He giggled and returned to his sister's side, clutching her hand.

Mild shock filled Emily's face as she looked from me to the children. "Am I missing something here? You three know each other?" The question was valid and I had a couple of my own. The truth was a good place to start.

"Your grandchildren are the cheering section for my ball team. They even have official team caps for the great job they do."

Kylie produced his hat from his back pocket and started to put it on.

"Ah, ah, ah." He stopped at his grandmother's admonition.

"Am I to presume that's where they are afternoons despite the fact they have chores at the store?" With her hands on her hips, Emily glared at the children. I studied the effect to detect if she was serious. She wasn't. The breath I held whooshed out of me. Her eyes shined with love for the kids and they smiled back without hesitation. Whatever secrets they were hiding, I was relieved it wasn't due to Emily. A huge weight lifted from my shoulders.

"One question does come to mind. Why do they arrive at the ball field alone and leave afterward without any supervision?" I asked.

Emily gaped at me, but focused on Kaitlin. "Honey, what does Mac mean *alone*?"

Kaitlin hung her head. "We're not alone. Mommy Renee is there."

To say I was on tenuous ground here was putting it mildly. Kaitlin clearly didn't trust me, but there had never been a Mommy Renee within sight. I shrugged. "I've never seen her."

Emily placed her hands on her granddaughter's shoulders. "Kaitlin, *where* is Mommy Renee?"

"In the car," Kaitlin mumbled, her chin touching her chest. I was more than a little curious about this Mommy Renee. *What the fuck?*

Emily seemed to absorb the information while Kylie glanced nervously up at his sister. Whatever was going on, or was wrong, they were mightily protective of one other. Their grandmother wasn't happy and I felt slightly more justified by my concern.

"I'll have a chat with Renee on Monday." Emily shook her head and passed me a cup of coffee. "Did the fish get fed?" She addressed her question to the kids and at their affirmative response she continued. "And the rooms have been tidied?" Kaitlin signaled in the affirmative, but her brother hesitated.

Kylie was busy studying the floor. "I didn't clean up, Gram. I waff playing." He tilted his face up to peer at Emily and tears threatened.

Before Emily could say anything, I moved toward Kylie and put my hand on his shoulder. "Hey, Emily, how about I help him clean up quick? I'm here earlier than he expected. It's not his fault, right? You finish whatever you need to do, then we can head out."

She folded her arms and studied Kylie with a stern face, pretending to ponder my offer with great deliberation. Finally she winked. "I suppose since you arrived early, there was no way to judge time. Go on. Go straighten up the room while I clear the dishes."

Kylie tilted his head up and smiled.

"Lead the way, little man."

I followed him through the living area to his room and was surprised how neat it actually was. Kylie's attempt to make the bed exposed a rumpled blanket and sheets hanging out from under the Spider Man bedspread. A collection of Transformers sat on top. Maybe not as tidy as an adult would have done, but a very good attempt for a five-year-old. The dirty clothes were crammed mostly in a hamper in the corner. The major part of the mess was composed of cars and trucks strewn around the floor thus making the task pretty easy. My own room didn't show this well now, never mind when I was a kid. An armful of toys later I asked, "Where do these go?" Kylie pointed to one of three baskets in the corner and I dumped them in the designated spot. I turned back only to find he was behind me with another handful that I also placed in the basket. He observed me with round eyes and a crease between his brows.

A Nintendo DSi sat on a small, orderly desk in the corner of the room. A lamp, mat, and small pencil box shared the space with the electronic toy. A chair was placed within the appropriate slot. "So what kind of video games do you play?"

"Motor Thstorm." Kylie was a boy of few words. I laughed, realizing I had never heard of the game. It was a little intimidating to know a five-year-old was more knowledgeable about certain things than I was. We shuffled to the other corner of the room and picked up the remaining toys. Fear of failing his grandmother's inevitable inspection drove us to be thorough. A bookcase opposite the bed had a collection of children's books, two stuffed animals, one a dinosaur, the other a floppy-eared dog. A picture in the center showed a younger, taller version of Emily holding Kylie as a toddler.

"Thath's my Mom," he said quietly.

Even though he didn't share her coloring, he had inherited her expressive eyes and engaging smile. "She's very pretty. You must miss her a lot."

Before Kylie could answer, Kaitlin rushed into the room, her arms crossed over her chest, her eyes blazing. She was a miniature of her grandmother in that pose. "Our mother was beautiful, and you stay away from the picture." She grabbed the frame and rushed out of the room.

I was left stunned, wondering what I'd done. What was it about me that scared her? Or was it all adults?

Kylie fixated on me, waiting for a reaction. It was vital I did the right thing or I would lose his fledging trust. I inched closer and squatted down. "Should I go say I'm sorry? Will that make it better?"

He seemed to brood over my question, then simply shook his head. "Sthe missthes mommy, but sthe don't thsay it."

The opportunity availed itself and I took advantage. "What about Mommy Renee, do you miss her, too?" My hope was that Kylie would talk. He stared at his feet instead. I patted his shoulder. "It's okay, kiddo. Let's finish up."

His quick hug warmed my heart. We shared a smile then carried on picking up the room. When the last items were in place, Emily came to the door. Kylie trooped in front of me and I put my hands on his shoulders.

Emily's eyes twinkled. She strode in and made a show of appraising our work. At last she smiled. "Very good job. Did you have to teach Mac how to help?"

Kylie gazed up at me, his grin toothless and wide. "Sthe learned good and ith's all done, and nofthing under the bed, sthee." He ran and pulled up the spread to show the underneath was clear of debris.

Emily put her arms out and Kylie climbed into them. She clasped him tight and kissed him, making him giggle.

Embarrassed for intruding on this private moment, I slipped out of the room. There was an ache in my chest that reminded me of what was missing in my own life. Back in the kitchen, my coffee had turned cold, but it still tasted better than the dregs of the night before.

Emily and the children approached and I heard her ask, "Kaitlin, what about you? Did you help clean your brother's room?"

The girl glanced from her grandmother to me and down at the floor. It didn't take a rocket scientist to know she was afraid I would tell Emily about our encounter. Before I could say anything, Kylie interjected. "Kaitlin took Mommy's picture into her room to fix it." I smiled at the small boy so well-trained to shield his sister. My question was what had created this need. What triggered their protectiveness? Who was frightening these kids?

"That's my fault," I said. "I, ahh...picked the picture up to study it and smudged the glass. Kaitlin was kind enough to take it and clean it for Kylie." Kaitlin looked at me wide-eyed. "Thank you. It was very careless of me. I'm sorry."

Kaitlin regarded me cautiously. She obviously had never expected an apology or for me to withhold our conflict from Emily. I rinsed my empty coffee cup in the sink and placed it in the drainer. "So, anyone here ready to go paint some bookshelves?"

Kylie jumped and yelled. "*Me!*" Kaitlin giggled at her brother along with Emily, who laughed out loud at his exuberance. The light-heartedness flowed through me, soothing some of the raw places left by the brutal images of the last twenty-four hours.

"Well okay. Let's hit the road, people." Once down at the truck, Kylie came to my side. I strapped him into his car seat which we had removed from Emily's truck. Kylie giggled as I tested the tightness of the straps. I tickled his belly and he giggled more. He proudly wore his team cap and laughed when I pushed the bill down on his face. Kaitlin watched our interaction anxiously, apparently ready to leap at me if I hurt him.

I walked around the truck and opened the passenger door. "Here, let me help you." I put my arm out for Emily to balance herself as she climbed up on the outer rail. I closed the door gently, walked around and slipped into the driver's seat. Emily's eyes were glued to me the entire while. With the engine started, we were off for our adventure in painting.

THE STEPS WERE reversed when we reached my house. I strolled around as Emily opened her door, offering my arm as she climbed out of the truck.

"What?" I asked when I saw her expression.

She grinned and shook her head. "Nothing."

"Is something wrong?"

"No, just the opposite."

Confused, I walked back to the driver's side and opened the back door to unstrap and lift Kylie down. Emily and Kaitlin joined us while Kylie gawked at the surroundings.

"Let's go through the house," I said. "I want to unload the groceries and put them away. We'll get started on the painting right after."

Kylie stomped his feet as he trudged behind me and waited with his arms out. I eyeballed him with a grin, then handed him the largest bag. It held paper towels and I was confident he'd be fine with it. Kaitlin was next and that surprised me, especially as it appeared she didn't trust me. I handed her a bag with boxes of tissues and other small items. Emily stood beside me and nudged my arm. "Think I can get a light one, too?" Her delicate brown eyes were locked onto mine. There was a mini eruption within my chest and I was held captive by her gaze. Their swirling vortexes threatened to pull me down and under. In a flash of memory, I saw Isabella's smiling face, the image so crystal clear I ached for her.

"Mac?"

I was jarred back to reality and could see Emily's concern when I looked into her eyes again. Unable to speak, I gripped two sacks and handed them to her. I grasped the remaining bags and guided the three of them to the back door. Once the groceries were put away, I questioned my intrepid helpers. "So what does everyone want to snack on while we're working?"

After a brief discussion I brought in a cooler from the back deck and loaded it with water bottles, juice, and soda while Emily filled a shopping sack with fruit, cheese, and crackers.

ISABELLA AND I had chosen this acreage when house hunting because of the old sixteen-bay horse barn at the back of the property. I immediately transformed the building into my workshop, incorporating a small office space and bathroom during the renovations. My hand tools were aligned on a peg board on the far wall and beneath that was a work table approximately twenty feet long. Various hand-held power tools sat on a shelf underneath. Larger woodworking equipment, router, drill press, table saw, and planer sat near the back wall where the dust collection system was easily attainable. That configuration allowed me a large prep area in the middle of the room for actual projects.

Once in the shop, I addressed the crew. "Okay, ladies and gentleman, I picked up the paint yesterday. The exact colors you requested. Do we know how everything is going to be painted?"

Emily smiled at the children. "Well, we've decided that we want to paint the bookshelves in groups of colors." She shifted to me. "Each set of two bookshelves will depict a genre."

Kaitlin frowned and Emily caught the look. "What I mean is

each section will be a different color according to the variety of book displayed, right sweetie?" Kaitlin smiled, love reflected in her eyes. It was such an innocent and adoring look it took my breath away. Could something so simple really create such happiness for this little girl? Once again I wondered what made the two children so cautious and fearful.

"All righty," I said as I proceeded to the storage area in the corner where several sets of sawhorses were stacked. "We have a plan. Let's get the work tables set up in rows. We'll set the paints next to them and can get to work." With two sawhorses down, I put one in front of Kylie and Kaitlin. "Can you two pull this over in front of the first overhead light?" I pointed. They eagerly agreed and dragged the stand with them.

Emily snatched the next one and followed suit. Once everything was setup, I opened the paint cans. An examination of my helpers presented a problem. "Hold on one minute. I'll be right back."

I ran to the house to snag a bunch of old T-shirts and some cheap rubber gloves. Upon my return, Kylie was waiting with his bottom lip jutting out and his arms crossed. A glance at his sister told me nothing. "Okay, each of you put one of these on so you don't get your clothes paint splattered."

We soon discovered that my shirt came to Kylie's ankles. It was unlikely anything could touch his skin. He and I giggled.

Kaitlin tentatively held the shirt out. "What if we get paint on these?"

To prove to her the shirts were dispensable, I dipped my finger in the nearest paint can. I ran it down Kylie's front, smearing the paint on the tattered old shirt. "Nothing happens. That's why I'm giving them to you."

Kylie squealed in delight and ran to dip his entire hand in the paint. He came back and placed it directly in the center of my newer, clean T-shirt.

Emily gasped, realizing the mistake. All I could do was glance down and laugh. Kylie's eyes alternated between me and his grandmother. I leaned over and whispered in his ear loudly, "This is still my good T-shirt, you knucklehead." Kylie put his hand over his mouth and managed to smear the rest of the paint on his face. I picked him up and threw him over my shoulder, tickling him. "You, young man, are going to work with me." He giggled as he struggled to be put down.

"Put him down!" The onslaught blindsided me as Kaitlin kicked me in the shin, hard. "Put him down!" She was crying and hitting me over and over again with her fists. In my zeal to prevent Kylie from making a bigger mess, I had frightened her.

"Kaitlin!" Emily admonished her granddaughter and grasped her from behind.

I swung Kylie down and captured Kaitlin's hand as she swung again. "Kaitlin. I'm not hurting him." I tilted my head. "Look, he's laughing. See!" I smiled. "I would never hurt him—or you." Her hands were secured as I tried to stress my point. She struggled to get free. I knew I wasn't hurting her. "Kaitlin. Do you trust your grandmother?"

She bowed her head, tears running down her face.

I released her. "Your grandmother would never let me hurt you or Kylie. You should know that."

Kaitlin turned to her grandmother for reassurance. Emily agreed, but the girl still appeared skeptical.

"You could hit her, too," Kaitlin said as she sniffled and wiped the tears falling from her eyes.

And there it was. I had seen this mistrust from Kaitlin ever since I first saw her at the ball field. This was her greatest fear. I stole a glance at Emily, expecting shock. Instead I saw sadness. My gaze returned to Kaitlin. "You know what? I promise you I would never do that. Ever. But if anyone scares you, including me, you have my permission to kick hard. Deal?"

Emily squeezed Kaitlin's shoulder and added, "You kick them as hard as you can and make sure you scream really loud."

The girl listened to her grandmother and stared at me, guardedly. "Okay."

She didn't believe me. She was still wary, but I thought she *wanted* to trust me and *that* was a step in the right direction.

My fingers gently cupped her chin. "So, are you ready to paint now?"

A small smile tugged at her mouth and she acceded. Kylie slunk up and took my hand. "I will paint wifth you. I don'th do so good." I nodded at him knowing exactly how he felt and tiptoed away with him, grateful for his faith, no matter how flimsy.

For the next three hours we laughed, we spilled paint, and while waiting for the first coat to dry, the kids decided that the door to my work shop should be painted in the same neon colors. Kylie used the day-glo-yellow on the four flat panels of the oversized door while Kaitlin dipped her brush into the fluorescent blue for the outer planks. They had already used the hot pink on the trim. I managed to get a genuine smile out of Kaitlin when I lifted Kylie up so he could reach the top of the door frame. Kaitlin was poised on a ladder, Emily holding her from behind while she painted. Kylie sat on my shoulders so he could reach the top panel of the door. I felt the first drip as Kaitlin's eyes grew big.

Emily burst out laughing. "Oh, Mac. You are a mess."

Kaitlin giggled so hard she dripped paint on Emily.

I reached up and took the paint brush from Kylie's hand. "Okay you two. This is war." I acted as if I was going to paint them. Emily yelped and threw her hand up, making Kaitlin laugh even harder.

"Grandma, watch out." Kaitlin swung her paintbrush at me and we dueled. She finally jabbed me with it, leaving her triumphant. I was not only painted but in Technicolor. It was all worth it though to be graced with a real smile from Kaitlin.

Hours later the second coat was done. We were a mess as we slogged back to the house. It had been a terrific day and I'd had a wonderful time. Even Kaitlin's mistrust comforted me in some small manner. I hated to see the day end and wasn't ready to take them home. "Hey crew, I have an idea. How would you like it if we all went to the ball game together and afterward, if Grandma says it's okay, I could take you out for dinner?" I looked over the kid's heads and searched out Emily's eyes.

"Mac, aren't you sick of us yet?" she asked. "I'm sure you have other things —"

The disappointment I felt must have shown on my face. She stopped abruptly and shifted her eyes from me to the kids who were watching her expectantly. She laughed and shook her head. "I know when I'm beat. Okay. Baseball and dinner, but next time I'll cook."

"Deal." My heart burst with joy. The kids high-fived with me and I caught myself stealing a glance at Emily a number of times just to make sure she was real. There was something about her I found comforting, like an old friend whose company I enjoyed, but didn't need to be *on* for. A friend with whom silence between us was easy and soothing. My rationalization was we had both faced grief and survived it.

It took a half hour for us to clean up. I still had multiple colors in my hair, but I figured it would become a new trend. We weren't clean enough for church so it was a good thing it was only a ball game and dinner at Stella's. Kaitlin and I reached the truck at the same time. She let me lift her into the back seat. Next I lifted her brother in. Once Emily and I had them settled, I held the passenger door and assisted Emily.

As I climbed behind the wheel I heard Kaitlin ask, "Gramma, why does Mac have to help you get in the truck?"

The flush started at my neck and in no time was burning my ears. It had never occurred to me. It was something I'd always done for women. All women. I apologetically looked over at Emily. She smiled at Kaitlin. "Because honey, Mac, is a gentlewoman and she believes in being chivalrous."

"Whatths chivalrouth, Gramma?"

"It means Mac has good manners." She reached across the expanse of the front seat and gripped my hand. "I know you don't mean anything by it, it's okay."

She was right...*Right?* I sat for a moment longer wondering, *was she?*

Chapter Six

WE ARRIVED AT the ball field a little early. It was past two-thirty when I pulled up to park behind the bleachers and scooted around the truck. Unconsciously, I reached to open the passenger door and quickly caught myself. Uncertain of what to do, I shoved my hands in my pockets. My stomach spasmed at the thought that I enjoyed assisting Emily. An image of Izzy flickered in my mind's eye. I worried about what she would think of this budding friendship? The attraction was secondary in spite of my baser instincts. My main interest was the children, my need to shield them impelled from within. I couldn't sit idly by and do nothing if something or someone was scaring them. My primal urge was to safeguard them. I prayed Isabella would understand if she was watching.

Emily opened the door and said, "Mac, give me your hand, please." Not complying never occurred to me. She grinned as she climbed out of the truck and squeezed my hand. "Hey, you are who you are. I don't mind it," she said.

Was that good or bad? At least she wasn't offended. We helped the kids from their safety seats and I went to the back of the truck to unload the equipment.

Kylie ran back and started to pull on the bats. "Do you know where they go?" I asked. He smiled. Evidently he had been paying attention.

Kaitlin approached me timidly. I leaned back on the tailgate and focused on her. "Ya know, we're gonna be short some players today. Any chance you and Kylie want to fill in?"

For a split second her eyes grew wide with excitement. She glanced at her grandmother, then back at me hesitantly. "I don't know how. We never played baseball."

"That doesn't mean you can't learn. I could teach you. Would you like that?" Past experience told me not to push her; she was too emotionally fragile. What or who had frightened this little girl so badly? An image of an older Bella surfaced. Would she be fearful and distrusting as well if she had lived?

Kaitlin sought her grandmother's approval and grinned shyly at me. "Okay."

I smiled, grateful for that small show of trust as Kaitlin ran to help Kylie with the gear.

Emily pulled one of the heavy coolers filled with refreshments off the tailgate. I caught the other end in time to prevent a crash. "Damn, that's heavier than it looks," Emily grunted.

Her muscles were straining against the weight and her shirt was drawn taut across her breasts. My eyes felt like they were glued to the gentle swell of cleavage. *Fuck.* I was ogling her. I yanked the ice chest from her hands and carried it to the small table we used for refreshments. *What's wrong with me?* I felt like a lech, but Emily intrigued me. I understood that, but what I found surprising was I wanted to know everything about her. Why? What was this infatuation with her? I silently chastised myself.

Emily placed her hands on her hips. "Why won't you let me help you?" she asked.

Our eyes locked and my heart thumped so loudly in my chest I was sure she could hear it. Before I could answer, Sarah showed up and her kids came bounding out of her car. I hugged and kissed them while Sarah approached, smiling smugly.

After the introductions were made, the kids continued to pull equipment out of the truck and set it in place. Sarah watched with a glint in her eye.

Emily engaged her in conversation, oblivious to Sarah's self-satisfied grin. I unloaded the second cooler, refusing to feed Sarah's need for gossip or speculation. I knew she was reading way too much into my friendship with Emily. I was married.

TWENTY MINUTES LATER, Kaitlin was up at bat. I handed the pitching over to Jim Collins and approached her slowly. "Still okay if I help you?"

She studied me carefully, and agreed.

"Good. Here's what we're going to do. You'll stand here and I'll be behind you with my hands on top of yours. When the ball approaches we'll swing together until you learn the timing. Okay?"

She scanned the viewing stands to find her grandmother. Sarah and Emily were sitting on the third tier waving at us. Emily called out, "Come on Kaitlin. You can do it."

The girl grinned at Emily and moved into position, but I stopped her. I thought I remembered her using her left hand to paint. "Kaitlin are you left-handed or right-handed?" She blinked at me quizzically. "Which hand do you write with in school, kiddo?" She smiled and lifted the left one. I thought so; I was left-handed myself. I placed my hand lightly on her shoulder and shifted her to the other side of the batter's box. "We lefties bat from here," I said.

She bobbed her head. She was excited and I was pleased.

"Keep your eye on the ball. Make sure you swing once the ball is close enough to make contact." I whispered the next part. "Most importantly, have fun sweetie."

Kaitlin nodded vigorously.

Jim tossed the ball right over home plate. We pulled the bat back slowly with my hands covering Kaitlin's as we swung. The bat connected and Kaitlin watched the ball sail into the outfield, a smile spreading across her face. I murmured in her ear, "Run fast, sweetie."

Cheering could be heard from the bleachers and Emily screamed as Kaitlin took off toward first. The wheel of Tommy's chair got stuck in a rut and he missed the ball completely. Patrick urged Kaitlin on to second. As her foot touched the base she jumped with joy. My chest filled with pride.

Kylie was up next and I leaned down to his level. "You ready to do this?" He giggled, his crooked grin melting my heart. "Okay little man, which hand is the crayon in when you draw? He lifted his right arm. I guided him to home plate and stood behind him with my hands over his. Kylie was not fearful and I spoke to him while we waited. "Don't swing too soon. Wait for the ball to come to you and swing with all your might."

He licked his lips in anticipation. Jim tossed the ball and I murmured, "Wait...wait...wait...now." We swung and missed for strike one. I rubbed his shoulders and instructed him to wait the next time and watch the ball closely. Jim tossed the next pitch. "Wait...not yet...*YES*." Kylie swung and hit the ball with all his might, knocking it into right field over that player's head. He might have been small for his age, but he was powerful.

"Run, little man, run." Kylie took off for first while Kaitlin rounded third. The third base coach waved her in and I waited at home plate with my arms open wide. It seemed like the most natural thing when she leapt into them. I swung her up, holding her to me and kissed the top of her head. "You did it! You scored, Kaitlin. I'm so proud of you." She squeezed me back and giggled. My heart swelled with an emotion I didn't deserve. She ran to her grandmother, who also waited with open arms. Emily spied me over Kaitlin's head and our eyes locked. Time stood still and, for that instant, we shared a real connection, one I had missed over the last five years. Emily winked at me before she directed her attentions to Kaitlin. The connection and feeling were lost in a nanosecond and I felt bereft.

Kylie was screaming at the top of his lungs as he ran toward me full force. He had continued running around the bases and was going to score. I caught him in my arms as he crossed home base and laughed when he lifted his cap high and waved it. I kissed his baby soft cheek and nuzzled him. He was such a beautiful little boy. I was thrilled for him.

An hour later the game was over and our team had won. Kaitlin scored one more time. Kylie struck out, but most importantly everyone had fun. I strolled over to the bleachers where Sarah was waiting for me.

She nudged my shoulder. "So? This was a surprise."

A quick search found Emily with the kids. "It's not what you think," I said with a shrug. "Remember, she's straight, but the kids, well." I glanced at Sarah. "There's something wrong, but I'm not sure what."

Sarah watched the exchange between Emily and her grandchildren. "You don't think she's responsible do you?"

"No."

"But you're convinced something's wrong?"

I expelled a deep breath. "Oh yeah."

"Well, it's a good thing you're on top of it." Her eyes were playful and I knew what she was thinking.

"Don't Sarah," I warned.

"Now *Taylor*, don't get your panties all twisted up in a knot."

"I hate when you call me that."

Sarah grinned evilly. "Well, it is *your* name and we both know it." She elbowed my ribcage and giggled.

"Knock it off." Years ago, Child Protective Services, CPS had a mix-up in my paperwork, with half of my file getting lost between agencies. Instead of Taylor Mackenzie on the label, it had been reversed to Mackenzie Taylor. I liked it and never looked back, much like my biological parents hadn't.

"So, how close are you with the grandmother?"

"*Sarah, don't!*"

"Don't what? Don't tell you how cute you are with the kids? Don't tell you I see the way you look at her when you think no one's watching? Or don't tell you I want you to be happy?" She looped her arm through mine and leaned her head on my shoulder. "It's okay to live, ya know. After all this time, Isabella would want you to move on."

"Jesus, Sarah, what's it going to take for you to understand? She's straight and she was married. She had a daughter, for cripes sake." I stared at Emily and a small part of me thought Sarah could be right. I shook my head. *Lord, there's no fool like an old fool.*

Sarah leaned in and rubbed her cheek against mine. "I can tell you like her. I've *seen* that look before." She smiled sadly. "If she is straight, please be careful. Don't get hurt."

"And how do I do that, huh?"

"Oh, honey. I don't know...talk to her, be honest. She seems like a wonderful person. Let her know you have feelings. See what happens." Sarah kissed my cheek and put her head on my shoulder.

I rested my head on hers. She was right, but the thought of any woman saying no was more than I cared to contemplate. The thought that Emily would reject me made my stomach flip-flop.

Emily twirled, and I unwittingly caught her eye. It was as if an electric current was passing between us. I couldn't seem to glance away and my heart tumbled. There was no preventing it and somewhere deep down inside I felt the prospect of happiness lurking.

Later, after the refreshments, after we had loaded the truck up and secured the kids in the back, I automatically helped Emily into the cab. I shrugged sheepishly as realization dawned. "Sorry. Habit."

She laughed, a full, deep, and hearty guffaw. "I'd think something was wrong if you didn't, Mac. I've come to understand it's who you are. For the record, I wouldn't change a thing about it."

Traffic migrated slowly out of the ballpark and Emily must have spied the sign. "Bella's Ball Field," she read out loud and smiled sadly. "It's a wonderful tribute and a great place for the kids."

The compliment hung in the air. The ball field had originally been Isabella's idea. I had only been the instrument who saw it through. I wouldn't take credit away from Izzy. As I pulled out onto the street, Emily let out a small gasp. The street sign read "Isabella Drive." The names had been my only contribution. Well, that and the fact I had bought the properties on the entire block where they had died to build the ball field.

"Mac, I'm so sorry. I don't know what to say."

Peace settled in me. Emily understood. She had dealt with her own pain and loss. Somehow it helped to know she truly comprehended the emptiness I felt and I patted her hand. "Thank you."

I caught her glancing at me periodically while I was driving. "What?"

She laughed. "You really hate talking about yourself, don't you?"

My shrug was automatic, but insufficient. "I'm probably one of the most boring people you'll ever meet." I wondered if I could chance it, if I dared to share parts of myself with anyone again. "If there's something specific, ask."

Kylie piped up from the back seat. "What's boring?"

My laugh was spontaneous. "Yeah, grandma, what's boring?"

The explanation was made, then we relived the exciting events of the afternoon right up until we pulled into the parking lot at Stella's Diner. We shuffled up the front steps and it occurred to me that the entire population of the town — or at least a good portion —

was most likely inside. It was Saturday night and Stella's was the only venue in town.

Emily saw me hesitate. "What's wrong?"

I shook my head as we waited inside the entrance to be seated. The hostess, Teresa, saw me and picked up four menus. "A booth, Mac?" she asked. I answered yes and we followed her to the back of the diner. Various townspeople and friends glimpsed our small group during the short trip and they all made sure to say hello. Once we were seated and the drink orders placed, I surveyed the room.

"Are you going to tell me what's bothering you?" Emily was intent and there was no ignoring her question.

"I didn't think about this dinner invitation's repercussions. Some people might get the wrong idea—about you and me." She seemed amused, but I was worried she didn't understand and groaned inwardly.

"Is that a problem?" Emily stared at me keenly.

"Hell," I muttered, then cringed and quickly glanced to see if either Kaitlin or Kylie were paying attention. They were each busy coloring on their place mats and I lowered my voice. "No, but...I'm worried for you."

Emily placed her hand on mine and smiled. My chest constricted at the warmth in her eyes and the feel of her touch. "I'm not worried about it," she said.

I sputtered incredulously. "You do understand what I'm saying, right? They're gonna think that you and I are..." I glanced at the kids. "They're gonna think we're a couple," I hissed.

Emily cackled. "I knew what you meant." Her laughter curled my toes. It was hearty and deep and her eyes crinkled. A warm feeling filled me.

The waitress appeared to take our order. It was Lorraine, Nancy's sister. "Hey Mac, crazy one last night, huh. That poor woman and being pregnant, too. Nancy was whipped when she got home, let me tell ya. I hope they lock that nut-job up and throw away the key, don't you? Thank goodness Cindy's okay."

My glare was deadly. We weren't supposed to talk about it. HIPAA required all medical practitioners to guard a patient's privacy and the whole purpose of the crisis center demanded *confidentiality*.

"Sorry, Mac." Lorraine did appear contrite and it wasn't my place to chastise her.

I tipped my chin at Emily. "Do you know what you want?" I asked.

She ordered a Reuben for herself, hotdogs and one order of fries for the kids. I ordered a cheeseburger and steak fries and asked for more coffee. Once Lorraine strode away Emily asked, "Last night?"

Crap. "I volunteer for the women's center. Mercy had an emergency last night."

"And?"

I scouted the dining area. It was mostly a stall tactic, but Emily would find out the truth as soon as she read the newspaper. "A pregnant woman came into the ER. She had been beaten. The husband showed up and one of the female doctors was hurt in the shuffle, but the basta...ahhh, he's in custody now." Kaitlin was listening. *Crap.*

"Sounds dreadful."

"Yup. Abuse usually is." I didn't mention ugly. It was always ugly.

"What time did you get home?"

"Good evening, Mac," a male voice interrupted. Heath appeared upset. I introduced him to Emily and the kids. With the pleasantries over, he got right to the point. "Our newest client is settled in, but I received a call from the police. They want an interview."

"Can this wait?" My eyes darted to my companions. Emily was monitoring us with growing alarm, and Kaitlin had stopped drawing. "Can we discuss this tomorrow. I'm out with friends."

"But, Mac—"

"Call the judge. Explain things."

"Thank you. I'll do that," he said before making his good-byes. In addition to managing the crisis center, Heath was a good friend. I was lucky to have him.

The meal capped off a delightful day. Emily had proven to be a great conversationalist, full of wit and charm. She told anecdotes about her career in corporate America, stories about her daughter growing up, and about her grandchildren being born. I envied her resilience and I loved listening to her. She was so vibrant and animated about certain subjects, the kids being one. When I pulled up behind the bookstore, we discovered Kylie was asleep in the back. I carried him upstairs and Kaitlin appeared exhausted as well. It had been a long and exciting day for both of them. I settled Kylie on his bed and took off his shoes while Emily helped Kaitlin.

Back in the kitchen it was suddenly just us. My pulse started to race and I realized that I didn't belong there. "Hey, I had a great time today. Thank you for coming to the game and dinner. The three of you made it special." And it had been. It had been a long time since I had relaxed and enjoyed a day off.

"You never answered my question," Emily said. She pulled out a chair from the kitchen table and motioned for me to do the same.

"Can I get you something to drink?"

"Water, please." The opportunity to spend more time with Emily was something I was reluctant to squander, even if common sense said otherwise. I pulled out the nearest chair and sat sideways to enjoy the view. I studied Emily's efficient steps as she maneuvered around the kitchen and found the sight beyond pleasurable. There was something so extremely feminine about her, yet there was an inner strength that was undeniable. It didn't hurt that her butt was caressed by her well-worn jeans or that her full hips swayed seductively from side to side as she paced.

"What question was that?" I finally managed to ask.

Emily caught me staring and advanced closer to set my glass on the table. "When did you get the call?"

I sipped from the glass, wondering if I should tell her. The fact that I was even considering it was astonishing. I didn't usually share that side of myself. I studied her face, taking in every detail and committing each one to memory. She had fine lines around her mouth. Even without smiling, her dimples were etched into her cheeks. She watched me and I made my decision. "The call came in around midnight, give or take a few minutes," I began.

"And your friend, Heath. He's somehow involved?"

A simple smile was her response.

"Please tell me you managed some sleep."

I glanced up at the clock. "Probably in about an hour from now, give or take."

She stared for a long moment. "Why didn't you say *no* this morning? We could have rescheduled." Emily placed her hand over mine for the second time that night.

Desire, so strong I barely recognized it gripped me as our fingers linked together. A yearning to hold her hand in mine and never let go overpowered me. I missed the warmth of other human beings, the casual touch of friends who weren't doing it out of pity. I missed the shared caresses and intimacies of being part of a duo. And because I wanted so badly, because I was craving human contact more than I had any right to, I gently extricated my hand and stood up.

"Well, because I was too wound up to sleep and I was eager to meet your grandchildren," I continued. "Never doubt what a great time I had today. It was a treat for me. Thank you." I placed my glass in the sink and swiveled back toward Emily. "I would trade every night's sleep to have the adventure we shared today." My keys were on the table and I reached for them. "Thanks, it really meant a lot to me." The time I had spent with Emily and the kids was a glaring reminder of what I was missing.

"It was for us, too. The kids loved painting and both of them were thrilled to play ball."

"You should think about letting them join the team." I wanted to know them better. Maybe discover what it was they were afraid of. I needed solid facts before I could discuss it with Emily. I needed to know who they were afraid of, why they were afraid, and if it was justified. There was no reason to alarm Emily if I was wrong.

"They'd like that. I'm not sure Renee can pick them up every day though, she works at a bar in Leadville and with the bookstore I sure can't."

"Not a problem. I almost always come back to the office in the afternoons. I can drop them off for you."

"Are you sure?" Emily's eyes lit up. "They'd love that."

"I look forward to it. We can start Monday, okay?"

Emily followed me out, I assumed to lock up. As I glanced back to say good night, she reached up and pulled me toward her to kiss my cheek. "Thank you, Mac. We all had a great time today. Drive carefully. I'll talk to you soon."

Stunned, I left, unable to speak. My emotions were ricocheting all over the place and I felt like a damn teenager. *Shit*. All the way home I thought about that kiss. My cheek was warm where her lips had grazed my skin. My heart hammered in my chest. For the first time in years I was interested in a woman and she was fuckin' straight. *Double shit.*

Chapter Seven

TUESDAY MORNING THE phone in my office rang two short blasts. "Yeah, Mare?"

"Emily O'Brien is on line one," my assistant said.

My stomach flipped. Joy filled me as I closed the office door. Wherever this conversation went, I didn't want it overheard. I took a deep breath and picked up the phone. "Hi, how are you?" My voice was low, my throat tight.

I had seen her the day before when I dropped the kids off. They had both joined the team and Kaitlin made fast friends with all the players. She even deigned to talk to me afterward. There was a trust issue for her, so I was careful not to push. Kylie was the reverse. He was completely comfortable and talked my head off. Still, when upset he would rush to his sister's side for support. Although I knew patience was needed, it just wasn't my strong suit. "Mac, am I interrupting?" Emily asked.

"Never. What's on your mind?"

"Well, the painting will be done by the weekend and I was wondering if you could come by with the shelves and install them. I need to get things moving."

"That's great. How's Saturday morning around eight sound?" The anticipation of spending the day with her had me grinning. "Hey, did you give any more thought to the bench seat?"

She hesitated. "I don't want to impose."

"You're not. I asked you. I need to stop by before Saturday so I can measure the area. Will you be around?"

"Don't be silly. If I'm not in the store, I'm upstairs. Come get me. In fact, why don't you come for dinner?"

As tempting as her offer was, I wasn't sure it was a good idea. I didn't want to intrude or give the town gossips more fodder. I had already heard comments about the new woman in my life. It wasn't fair to Emily and wasn't respectful to Isabella. "Not necessary, but thanks. I'll stop by, probably tomorrow. Okay?"

"Mac, dinner will be at seven. Don't be late," Emily ordered. "I'll feed the kids early so it will be just us adults."

My eyes slammed shut. Was it so wrong? Would I be setting myself and Emily up for hurt?

"Mac?"

"Okay, if you're sure it's not a problem?"

"Problem? Not at all. I'm serving peanut butter and jelly

sandwiches. How hard can that be?" she chuckled.

I laughed out loud. "You're on, but the jelly better be grape. I don't like any other kind."

"Seven sharp. I'll be waiting. Bye," she said before she hung up.

Sweet Jesus, did she say she'd be waiting? I hung up and took a moment to think about our conversation. It was like she got me. We shared a shorthand that worked. I wished, well, it didn't matter what I wished. She was a nice lady and was becoming a good friend. You could never have too many of those — especially non-judgmental ones.

Izzy and I had worked so hard to be accepted, to blend into the fold. People knew about us. Some didn't care, others accepted us. Of course, there were those who felt Izzy got what she deserved for going against God's word, that our love was wrong and immoral. No matter what the pundits thought or said, I missed her more than I ever thought possible. Izzy and Bella were in my thoughts daily. I ached for them.

I SPENT THE rest of the day at various building sites. A few problems had cropped up and the GMs needed input from me. I traipsed from site to site managing the issues and returned to the office at nine that evening. Mary had left me a pile of messages, which I shuffled through. Sarah had called twice, Emily once, and Heath once.

I pressed the speed dial for the crisis center and the call was answered on the first ring. "Crisis center, this is Heath, how—"

"Heath it's me. What's up?"

"Mac, I wanted to let you know. Patti Allison gave birth to a healthy baby boy this morning. He weighed in at eight-pounds three-ounces, and is twenty-one inches long. She especially wanted to make sure you knew she named him Mackenzie."

I was overwhelmed. She didn't even know me, but her son would carry my name. A bubble of pride rushed up before I could quell it.

"Mac?"

"Yeah."

"This is good news, enjoy it. Good night."

"Thanks. Night, Heath."

I called Sarah next and her machine picked up. I hated voice mail. "Hi, it's me. I'm back and got your messages. I'm in range if you need me. Otherwise, I'll talk with you soon. Love you, Sarah." She had been the one constant in my life, my longest relationship. I didn't know what I would do without her.

I left Emily for last and was giddy with anticipation. She

picked up on the second ring.

"Hello."

"Hi, it's me, ahhh Mac."

"I recognize your voice. How are you?"

A warm current ran through my system. "I'm good. What's up?"

"Are you getting a cold? Your voice sounds raspy."

"Nah, I'm fine. Been out in the wind all day. How are you?"

"I need a favor."

"Anything."

"Be careful, I might hold you to it." Her chuckle vibrated though me. "Renee can't watch the kids Saturday. Maybe we could do it next week sometime, or—"

"It never occurred to me they wouldn't be there. I fully expected them to help us. So Saturday's still good with me. Is it okay with you?"

"Oh Mac, are you sure? I mean you know how rambunctious they can get. I don't want you to try to work around that."

"Emily, I love the kids. I love working with kids. Don't worry about it." And that was the problem. I did love kids. Especially those kids. They were sweet and wonderful and frail. I wanted to shield them from harm. Of course, I couldn't discount Emily. She was such a warm and loving woman, with absolutely no clue the effect she was having on me.

"Come early. I'll make breakfast."

"You're cooking tomorrow. Let me buy you breakfast. It'll be fun. Say yes, please."

She laughed deeply. "You're a glutton for punishment, Mac Taylor."

"So it's a date?" *Fuck.* "Shit, Emily I didn't mean that, I just—"

"Mac. I'll see you tomorrow night. And yes, it's a date for Saturday breakfast. The children will be thrilled. Goodnight," Emily said, her voice soft and warm.

"Night Emily." I sat in my chair thinking about our conversation and my *faux pas*. I hadn't meant it like that, but once the words had been spoken, all kinds of images filled my head. A candlelit dinner. Emily in my arms slow dancing. Long hikes through the mountains. Snuggling in front of a fire on a cold night. Breakfast in bed on Sunday mornings. All the things I used to have with Isabella. When had Emily slipped in? When had I decided I wasn't married anymore? When did I choose to cheat on Izzy? My heart ached at my betrayal. Isabella deserved so much more.

THE DOORS WERE open when I pulled up in front of the bookstore. I called inside to let Emily know I was there. She had phoned earlier to tell me that Kylie had an upset stomach and she didn't think breakfast out would agree with him.

I had begun removing the painted planks from the rear of my truck when Emily arrived and picked up the first set. "The kids are finishing breakfast," she said. "They'll be right down."

We strode through the open door and I pointed to where we should set up a workspace. I stared in amazement at the completed paint job. Emily had painted clouds and a sun on the ceiling. The bare, overly large windows made the artwork come to life. Each wall was painted a different color and accented with murals. The finished effect gave the appearance that an artist had created it. Most noteworthy were the famous quotes taken from the classics that were strategically placed at various points around the room. All of the quotes providing words of inspiration. "This is incredible."

Emily smiled. "Thank you. I'm pleased with the way it came out."

"You should be. It looks wonderful."

"Yeah, yeah. Let's get to work." Her face had acquired a pink tinge.

Emily and I made our second trip out to the truck. She looked wonderful that morning. Her hair was pulled back in a ponytail and I thought she could easily pass for ten years younger. The mint-green T-shirt favored her skin tone, giving her a healthy glow. I was left tongue-tied.

"A couple more trips and we can get started, right?" she asked.

I answered with a nod.

The kids charged into store from the rear entrance and Emily chastised them for running. I plucked three pair of protective goggles from my tool kit. "Helpers need to wear these at all times, understood?" They bobbed their heads in unison.

"Okay put 'em on and do not take them off. We'll split up into two teams. Who wants to build a window seat and who wants to put the bookcases together?"

Kylie yelled first. He wanted to construct the bookcases, which worked out well because Kaitlin chose to build the window seat.

"Kylie, you're going to help Grandma," I said. A quick demonstration on how to erect the bookcases gave Emily an example to work with. I left her with the supplies and tools she would need. While she and Kylie set up the shelves, Kaitlin and I would build the window seat. It would be complete — hopefully — at the same time Emily finished the shelving, in three to four hours.

After setting up the saw horses, Kaitlin and I gathered the tools we would need. I began by measuring for the frame of the window seat. "And how many things have you built young lady?"

Kaitlin giggled. "None silly, I'm too little."

"Actually, I was your age the first time I started to work with wood." I ruffled her hair. "Let's get going."

She seemed excited, which pleased me immensely.

Kaitlin was an excellent student and helper. She followed instructions and listened carefully as I explained things. I showed her how to measure the space between the walls. "Okay little lady, let's take those measurements and mark them on the wood. We'll use a speed square and a measuring tape to transfer the dimensions so we know where to cut."

I explained the importance of keeping the pencil finely sharpened so that all the lines were the same depth for cutting purposes. I taught her to re-check her measurements and we did. "Is that the same number from before?" I asked. Her answer was a grin and a vigorous nod.

I knew she didn't understand the importance of measuring twice and cutting once, but I hoped the concept would sink in for future reference and other life lessons as she grew. We carried the pieces of wood to the compound miter saw. I showed her how to adjust the blade and how to align the laser-trac with the measurement. "Now remember you always want to cut on the left side of the pencil mark, which is the garbage side of the wood. That way you make allowances for the width of the blade." Kaitlin listened attentively and I thought she really understood. We placed the board to be cut on the saw. She stood on an old milk crate I found in the back of the truck to watch. "You're too young to use the power tools, but you can observe, okay?" I began the cuts, and she monitored each one. Kaitlin waited quietly and beamed with pride once all the pieces were sawn.

The next step was to pre-drill the holes for the fasteners.

"Why are we making holes first?" she asked.

I explained that by pre-drilling, the wood was less likely to split or splinter. She had a mind for detail and asked intelligent questions.

Two hours into our project Emily appeared with fresh coffee, and milk and cookies for the kids. We gathered around the counter at the back of the store to enjoy our snacks.

Kaitlin and I returned to our build. We set the framing in place and I let Kaitlin use the cordless drill to secure the fasteners under my guidance. I showed her how to use the level, ensuring plumb and even work. Next we cut the MDF and covered the fascia of the frame. For the seat we used birch wood. I showed Kaitlin how to measure for the piano hinge and let her apply it, adding storage for Emily under the seat. We labored for the next hour and a half and were cleaning up the workspace when Emily approached. She threw her arms around my neck and pulled me close, taking my breath away. I remained with my arms at my sides, afraid to embrace her, afraid of wanting more.

Emily was thrilled with the finished product. She smiled broadly, when she tested the seat. She told Kaitlin she was very impressed with her handiwork and the girl glowed under her grandmother's praise. Kaitlin pointed out the storage underneath and Emily happily concurred there was no such thing as too much storage.

"I can paint it for you while you brace the bookcases," I said. The plans called for securing the bookcases back-to-back and then to the floor to prevent tipping. I needed Emily to decide which colors to paint the window seat.

She smiled and shook her head. "We've done enough for one day. Help me finish the bookcases. I need to get the children bathed, lunch on the table, and figure out something for dinner."

"Why not let me buy you dinner, especially since we didn't get together for breakfast."

"I should be buying you dinner for all the work you've done."

"Kaitlin did most of it." The girl smiled proudly. "You paid for the supplies, and I've already got a list of books I'd like you to order once the store opens."

"That's our deal. Fair enough," She said.

"I'll finish up. Take the kids upstairs and get cleaned up. The bookcases will only take a minute to secure. I'll sweep up down here and run to the office to shower. I'll be back by six to pick you up, okay?"

"You better have a long list of books you want," Emily said with a grin. "Kids, come on. We're gonna wash up and go out to dinner with Mac tonight." Kylie and Kaitlin erupted into cheers. Kaitlin shocked me by kissing my cheek.

"Thank you! What was that for?" I asked.

"I liked working with you. It was fun."

"Good, we'll do it again."

"Promise?"

"Absolutely."

THE FOLLOWING SATURDAY morning Emily and I took the kids to the Denver zoo. We spent the day eating junk food and learning about the animals. The next week we went bowling. Kaitlin continued to impress me with her natural athleticism, and Kylie with his tenacity. Sports didn't come easily for him, but he didn't give up.

The week after that, the county fair opened and the kids

convinced Emily and me it would require two trips to experience it all. We ran into Sarah, Michael, and their kids the first night. Kylie screeched on each ride, his love of speed evident on his face. Little Mikey squealed as well. Kaitlin excelled at the games of chance, winning numerous times, taking home multiple stuffed animals and two goldfish. She gave a pink teddy bear to Taylor, making her a very happy little girl.

Sarah and Emily had hit it off and Sarah had even recommended a dentist for the children. Emily told me they had done lunch and that Sarah had joined the new book club at the store. Hopefully, Sarah would see her worries were for naught.

Emily, the children, and I had become closer with each outing. The kids were at ease with me and I baby-sat on nights the book store was open late. Emily and I had grown closer as well, our friendship deepening. One Friday night we took in a Disney movie. Emily and I shared a tub of popcorn while Kaitlin and Kylie were too engrossed to eat. On Saturday night the four of us drove to Bailey to eat at the Canyon Grill. Afterward we walked through town exploring the sights. Later, after she put the kids to bed, Emily and I shared coffee and talked. Mostly she talked. I loved hearing her stories, which never failed to make me smile.

TWO WEEKS LATER I was in the kitchen pouring a cup of coffee when the phone rang. "Hello."

"Hi, it's me," Sarah stated the obvious. "How was your dinner date?"

I walked into the living room and sat in my leather chair in front of the crackling fire I had started earlier to take the chill out of the house. I glanced around and realized it was time to clean. Dust bunnies gathered in the corners and cobwebs clung to the ceiling. Isabella would have been so disappointed if she saw the way I was tending to our home. She had always been so meticulous about things, never to the point of being neurotic, but always prepared for company. The furniture shined, the floors and ceilings were dusted, and the fridge fully stocked with enough food to feed an army should friends stop by.

"Mac?"

A groan forced an answer from my mouth. "Yes, Sarah. Good morning."

"Last night?"

"It was *not* a date." She was like a dog with a bone, determined and annoying. She wouldn't let it go. "Emily, the kids, and I had dinner in Bailey. No biggie. Afterward I dropped them off and I came home to get some sleep. End of story." I wouldn't tell her that sleep was the last thing on my mind by the time I got home. That all I had wanted to do was turn around and go back to spend more time with Emily. Sarah didn't need to know that. She also didn't need to know I had awakened from an erotic dream that morning. Emily was sitting astride me naked as the day she was born, thrusting her wetness across my hips as I caressed her dark erect nipples. In my dream I had stroked the slick black hair between her legs right before my fingers sank effortlessly into her silky wetness and she threw her head back in surrender as I gently stroked her clitoris. Sarah didn't need to know how Emily had screamed as she collapsed into my arms, her orgasm rippling through her for long minutes afterward. She didn't need to know any of this, or that I had climaxed myself upon awakening. It was my first orgasm since the night before Isabella had died.

"Mac, are you listening—"

Distracting images of a naked Emily flickered before my eyes like vintage black and white, reel-to-reel videos filmed in shadows. "What? I'm sorry...what were you saying?" I stammered.

"Honey, if she's straight you need to shield yourself from getting hurt. You need to keep your distance."

"Sarah, *I'm not looking*. Emily and I are friends. Stop worrying about this, will ya?" I walked back into the kitchen, needing another cup of coffee. "Did you have a reason for this call or are you trying to aggravate me today?" I loved Sarah, but she worried too much. She was constantly hovering, trying to shield me. Nothing had protected me when I most needed it, just as nothing protected my family.

"I wanted to see if you're free for lunch?"

"Work is crazy. I brought home six files I need to work on today."

"Mac, I—"

"Hold on. I've got another call coming in." I hit the button and made the new connection. "Hello?"

"Mac, good morning. How are you today?"

"Emily." I caught myself smiling at the sound of her voice. That was so *not* good. "Fine. Good. What's up?"

"I'm making a roast for dinner and was wondering if I could tempt you to join us. That is, if you don't already have other plans."

"No, I don't. It...sounds great."

The last time I had accepted an invitation for a home cooked meal was weeks ago and that happened because I allowed Sarah to drag me to her place after work. Michael was barbequing and I stayed the obligatory hour before running away from the happy family. *This* dinner invitation had me vibrating with anticipation. This time there would be no pitying stares or awkward silences and no glances at the empty seats around the table.

"What can I bring?" I asked, quickly calculating how I would get everything accomplished and still be able to join Emily.

"Just yourself. The kids and I are going to the video store to pick up some movies. I can't guarantee they'll hold you captive, but I did promise the children." She was laughing and in my mind I could almost see her face. Her eyes twinkled when she laughed and there was a mischievous characteristic always lurking.

"Why don't I come pick the kids up and I'll take them for the videos? You can relax or finish up cooking." Tendrils of happiness surged through my body. It was caused by Emily and the kids and was something I hadn't allowed myself to feel in some time.

"Mac, I can take them."

"I know. I want to. What time do you want me there?"

She laughed on the other end of the line and I imagined her shaking her head. "Come whenever you want. They're all ready. I'll hop in the shower now and be ready by the time you get here."

"I'll be there in an hour, and thank you for thinking of me." My heart was racing as the image of Emily as she appeared in my dream the night before filled my mind...eyes glazed over, naked, sensual. She was all that and more. Then I reminded myself that we were only friends and not to forget I had taken a vow to love another.

The beep in my ear signaled me I had another call. I hit the button and was reconnected with Sarah. "Sorry, that was the crisis center. Heath needed some info about a client." The lie was bitter in my mouth and it went against everything I believed in, but I didn't want Sarah nagging me, or worse, pushing me. "I'll call you later in the week to catch up."

"Okay. I'll let you go. Call me if you're free or if you want to talk."

"Bye Sarah. I love you."

The house cleaning would wait. An opportunity to play with the kids far outweighed a chore I hated. I banked the fire to allow it to die down while I ran upstairs to take a shower and pull on some clean clothes.

THE KIDS AND I strolled around the video store searching for something age appropriate. Emily had given me strict instructions there was to be no violence in the movies we picked out, a tall task from what I could see. I was amazed that even cartoons could be rated as violent. I was so out of the loop. Kylie brought me *Cars*. After reading everything on the case, I told him yes. It appeared to meet his grandmother's criteria. Kaitlin chose *Hannah Montana, The Living Rock Star* and *Mary Poppins*. I knew at least one was safe. A glance at the cover of Hannah's video told me it was as well. Kaitlin was thrilled. As a surprise I picked up some movies for Emily and me. We were in the check out line waiting, when Sarah strolled in with Taylor and Mikey. *Fuck.*

"Hello Mac. How's the workload?" Sarah asked sarcastically. She was hurt and I felt like a piece of crap. I hadn't meant to lie to her and this was precisely what I had wanted to avoid.

"Sarah, I'm sorry. It's that—" I never meant to hurt her; she was my best friend. "Emily called and invited me to dinner. I...err...the kids wanted some videos."

Sarah sidled a little closer so that only I could hear her words. "Be careful. I love you," she whispered. She touched my cheek, a light caress, then disappeared. I sighed and knew I would have a lot to make up for. Sarah was not the kind of friend to let something rest. I loved her like crazy, but I wasn't ready to discuss everything I was feeling. There was something about Emily that stirred me. The kids were better with me, but still had moments. I wanted to help them and didn't know how. Guilt welled up when I saw Sarah across the store and I made a mental note to call her later in the week and invite her to lunch. Emily and I weren't hurting anyone, and yet I knew the gossip mills continued to spew their garbage. Sarah had been on my case to back off. It wasn't fair and I resented it. Hopefully I would have a handle on everything I was feeling and how to explain it at lunch.

KYLIE GIGGLED AS I tightened the strap of his safety seat, clearly ticklish. I leaned over to make sure Kaitlin's belt was also secure. "Okay, we're all set. Let's hit the road, you two." I climbed into the driver's seat and started the engine.

"Mac, is Sarah your girlfriend?" I stared in the rearview mirror at Kaitlin before twisting around. She reminded me so much of her grandmother.

"No Kaitlin, Sarah's my best friend. We've known each other since we were your age." I watched her absorb the information.

"You mean like Janice and me."

I was impressed by her quick analysis. "Yep, like you and Janice." I waited to see if there would be more questions. If she had them, she didn't voice them. I wondered about her interest, and speculated why she would care. I couldn't push her. Instead we headed home.

EARLIER I HAD presented Emily with a nice bottle of wine. Currently, she and I were enjoying a second glass while cleaning up the kitchen after a delicious and enjoyable meal. She settled the kids in front of the TV with one of the videos, which would tie them up for an hour at least. I listened to Emily converse as she washed the dishes and I dried. Such a simple chore was made more pleasurable simply by Emily's company. She had kept up a torrent of small talk about the kids, her life, and her hopes for the bookstore. I asked questions from time to time, but basically enjoyed listening to her and being in her company. She moved with an economy of steps, but fluidly and sensually. Everything about Emily exuded femininity. As I dried the last dish I was sorry to see our chore completed.

"Mac?"

The sound of Emily's voice pulled me from my doldrums. Her eyes showed concern and maybe a bit of curiosity. I smiled. There was a small wisp of hair escaping the clip holding her tresses high on her head. I wanted so badly to remove it and let her hair hang free, to run my hands through her curls. I shivered at the thought, then saw her reaction. It was as if she had read my mind. "Yeah?"

She watched me over the rim of her glass as she sipped the wine. "Why are you still single?"

I hadn't expected that. Her question was so direct, so personal and so much more than I was ready to reveal. I looked around the kitchen searching for some small chore I hadn't completed, something to avoid her penetrating gaze. I reached to pick up my glass, but instead faced her. "Isabella and I were married." Tears gathered in my eyes, but I staved them off. "Just because someone dies—a partner—doesn't mean you're not still married or that you're not half of a couple. I don't make promises lightly."

Until very recently that was how I felt. Marriage was forever, simple. I was married and therefore not free to date or free to get on with my life as my friends were always telling me to do. Until recently I hadn't felt lonely. But until recently I hadn't known Emily.

She studied me, "Is that what Isabella would want?"

Her question paralyzed me. A wave of pain tore through me. It was as if she had read my mind. Isabella and I were soul mates from the very beginning. The first time I saw her I knew she was the one and she always asserted it was mutual. That first night we talked into the wee hours of the morning. We rarely separated after that except for our respective jobs. We moved in together within three days. I asked her to marry me on our four-week anniversary. She said that in her heart we already were married. Isabella was pragmatic and I knew if she could see what had transpired she would not be pleased. Izzy believed in the principle that balance was necessary in all matters. Work, play, and love, and she practiced that daily. She would probably shake the shit out of me if she were privy to my choices.

Emily's hand on my arm jarred me from my reflections.

"Sorry, I was thinking." I said, shaking my head. "And to answer your question, I think Isabella would be very disappointed in me." I shrugged because my throat had closed when I said her name out loud.

Emily saw my struggle and rubbed my arm. "Come on, it's almost time for the kids to go to bed. We'll watch the end of this video with them. Then we can choose one of the others you brought." Emily stepped away, giving me a moment to gather myself.

I STROLLED INTO the living room unobtrusively and sat on the sofa. Kylie was laughing at something on the TV when he spotted me. He climbed into my lap and I wrapped my arm around his belly. We stayed like that until the end of the film. Once the DVD was ejected, Emily announced bedtime. I anticipated an argument, but there was none. Kylie kissed me on the cheek and wandered to his room. Kaitlin hesitated only a moment. I held my arms out and she let me hug her. I kissed the top of her head and said goodnight.

Emily helped the children with their nightly routines while I cleaned up their popcorn bowl and juice boxes. By the time everything was put away, Emily was back in the living room ready to choose a movie. I'd brought three. *You've Got Mail*, *Sabrina*, and *An Affair to Remember*, the second rendition of the film with Deborah Kerr and Cary Grant. I always thought they had given the best performance.

Emily picked up the three cases and selected my favorite. She popped the disk in the DVD player and sat down next to me. She wasn't touching me, but my body was entirely alert to her every nuance. My senses shot into overdrive.

She grabbed the remote and hit play. "I love this movie," she said. "But I'm warning you, I always cry at the end."

Her glass of wine was on the end table and I handed it to her. Her nearness was wonderful and excruciating at the same time and I knew I was in for a long evening. The movie was a favorite that I'd seen many times. Emily pointed out things I had never paid attention to before, like the loveliness of the villa where the aunt lived, the gentle way Nicky/Cary was protective of her. Or the way Terry/Deborah refused help after her accident. As the final credits rolled Emily *was* crying, her head resting on my shoulder. Love had conquered all in the movie, but, as we all knew, real life wasn't a film.

Emily pulled away and I handed her a tissue. "I told you," she said with a laugh as she wiped her eyes.

"Yes, you did." It was late and time for me to leave. I didn't want the neighbors to see my truck there after dark. That would only fuel the fires. "I better go."

I took our empty wine glasses into the kitchen and placed them in the sink. Emily stood in the doorway studying me. I picked up my keys from the table and my jacket from the back of the kitchen chair. "Thank you for today," I said. My voice hitched and I added, "It—I mean—it's been wonderful. Thanks." I wanted to say so much more, but I was afraid I'd make a fool of myself.

She came closer, then closer still, and placed a kiss on my cheek. This time, even though I expected it, the kiss sent a jolt through me.

"Good night, Mac. You drive safely," she said, her hand resting on my arm.

"Night."

THE KNOCK ON the door startled me until I recognized the hulking form lurking in the shadow of the hallway. At six-foot four-inches tall and approximately two-hundred-fifty pounds, the familiar face made me smile. "Michael. What are you doing here?" I hopped up and strode across the room to greet my visitor.

"I was going to ask you the same thing. Isn't eleven a little late to be designing homes of the future?"

I motioned for my friend to sit, and did the same before leaning back in my chair. "Maybe. And what's your excuse?"

"An early court case tomorrow. I stopped to pick up the file on the way home. When I saw the light on upstairs, I knew it was you. Mary would never leave one burning."

"That's the truth," I said with a grin. "When did you get back?"

"A little while ago. I wanted to surprise Sarah. Got anything to drink around here?"

I opened the small refrigerator in the corner. "Let's see what we've got, juice, sip-its, beer, or water?"

"Beer."

I snagged a water for myself and handed him the bottle. "What's new? How long's it been?"

"It's been over a month and what's new with you is the reason I'm here."

"What? A month— Why? Nothing is new here."

He took a swig of the beer, his eyes never leaving mine. "I hear there's a new lady in your life."

"There is no woman in my life, new or otherwise. Sarah is a

pain in my ass."

Michael grinned. "Yes she is, but you already knew that."

I shook my head in disgust and glared at him.

"Tell me something about Emily," he said.

"We're friends. I did some work for her. She runs the bookstore. You've met her, she's a nice woman. The end."

"Okay."

"There's nothing going on. I'm married, remember?"

Long minutes ticked by without either of us speaking. "Actually, my friend, you're not," Michael finally said. "You're a widow."

"Fuck. You."

Michael peeled some of the paper label off the bottle he was holding. "I loved Isabella, you know that, and I miss her every day. But it's time to let go, buddy."

"You miss your *friend*. I lost my wife and child. There's a big fucking difference."

"Yes, there is." Michael stared at me. "I haven't put her on a pedestal and pledged the rest of my life to her memory. Izzy was wonderful, but she wasn't a saint and wouldn't want to be treated as one."

"Get out,"

Michael's eyes filled with tears. "Mac, I've watched you immerse yourself in causes close to Izzy's heart. The center, the ball field, the domestic violence lectures. You've damn near killed yourself working to make her dreams come true. I had hoped you were ready to slow down and have a life of your own."

"She's straight." The words tumbled out.

"Her loss. There're other women. Gay women."

"It's not like that Michael. We're friends. I'm not interested in anything more."

His eyes compelled me to explain further, or was it the lawyer in him? "I've been out of sorts lately. I don't know how to explain it," I said with a shrug.

"I'll explain it. You've locked everyone out. Hell, we used to go out once a week for beers or hang out in the shop. I don't have to tell you how close you and Sarah were. I can't remember the last time we talked or the last time you were at the house."

I gazed down at my hands clenched in my lap. "Nothing's changed, Sarah's still my best friend."

"Really? When was the last time you two spent time together?"

"What the hell is this all about? Why do you care if I spend time with Sarah or not?"

"Because you're hurting her by shutting her out. Because she misses you."

"Go home to your wife, Michael, and leave me alone."

"Are you drinking again?"

My head snapped up. "What?"

"Are you?"

Guilt rolled over me like fog on a warm rainy morning. "No. I gave you my word."

Michael stared at me for a long time. "Nothing?"

"The most I have is a beer once in a while. Maybe a glass of wine with dinner, but never more than two of either."

"Good enough. So tell me about Emily."

"There's nothing to tell."

"Sarah—"

"*Sarah* is letting her imagination run away with her. Emily's a good person. She's a widow raising her two grandchildren. We enjoy each other's company and the kids play on the team."

"Why?"

I blinked at him, confused. "Why what?"

"Why do her kids play on the team?"

I crossed my arms over my chest and stared back at him. "Because something or someone is scaring them, *okay*?"

"Okay."

"Go home. Tell you wife you tried and then let it go, will ya?"

"She wants me to invite you to dinner. What's a good time for you?"

"I'll call her."

"In other words, you're not coming."

My temper snapped. "So I can sit with you, Sarah, and the kids and see what I'm missing? Watch you two make eyes at each other in your perfect little world with your perfect little family? See the pity in your eyes every time either of you dares glance at me? No, thanks. I'd rather drill my own teeth."

Michael stood up, put the empty bottle on my desk, and walked to the door. "You're part of our perfect little family. I'm sorry you forgot that."

"I have nothing to offer anymore, don't you get that? I'm angry all the time, and I can't forget about it. It's not good for your kids, and it only upsets Sarah."

"Have you talked to anyone?"

"Go home, Michael. Please leave me alone."

He closed the door behind him and I heard the steps creak under his weight as he left the building. *Fuck.* I banged my head on the desk wondering how everything had gotten so fucking complicated.

Chapter Eight

THE NEXT MORNING I met with the green-project couple at their future construction site. "Morning Tom. Penny."

"Good morning. Isn't it beautiful up here?" Penny gushed. "Look at that scenery."

Tom grumbled. "Yeah, yeah, but will this site work for the house we're gonna build?"

"What's the acreage?"

"Five acres, and they back up to a state forest."

"Well, the good news is the valley below is the north side, so we'll be able to incorporate that view in the design for you."

"Wonderful, I knew it." Penny paced off an area. "I want a big porch right here so I can sit out evenings and enjoy it."

"Can we concentrate on the energy aspect? That's the crucial issue," Tom said.

"All I can say is there's no perfect building method, but I guarantee we will get as close as possible with today's available technology." I glanced between husband and wife.

"I want this house to be self-sufficient. How are you going to accomplish that?" Tom asked.

We paced the perimeter of their site, discussing layout and sun direction. One major hurdle would be the removal of fifteen mature cottonwoods that grew smack in the middle of the southern exposure. "Well you'll be starting out with a crap load of fire wood once it's cut-up and split for you," I said. "Your house should be about eighty-seven percent self-sufficient upon completion. That's in comparison to the standard forty-six to fifty-four percent of homes built in the typical manner."

"That doesn't really sound all that efficient," Tom said.

"It's thirty-three percent better than anything else currently being built."

"Well, you're the expert. Convince me," Tom lamented.

"Okay. We'll place the house to make the most of its southern exposure." I pointed in the direction for him to get a visual. "On that side of the roofline we're going to install six photovoltaic or PV arrays that convert sunlight to energy. That'll provide up to eighty-five percent of your electric needs. During off-peak hours and sunny conditions, those units will produce more electricity than the house requires."

Tom perked up. "What happens to the excess?"

"The overage is sold back to the local utility through a two-way power meter on the side of your house and credited to the home's account for your future use. The utility company supplies basic power meters. For this home they'll install one that is capable of running backward while the home's system is *feeding* power into the grid and runs forward if you call for power. So the meter itself keeps track of the energy used."

"For what we're paying for this construction, there better be a credit each month." Tom wanted more information on the technology I would be integrating.

"You can check with the AIA, American Institute of Architects, the BCA, Building Commissions Association, and NAHB, National Association of Home Builders. Visit their web sites and see for yourself. They're all up on the latest technology and provide question and answer forums. You should be able to find any information you want."

He wrote down the acronyms I'd given him. "Thanks Mac. It's not that I don't trust you, but this is a lot of money."

"The more you know, the easier my job is."

"Can you explain about the construction again?" Penny opened a binder to take notes.

"Absolutely. The walls and roofline will be built off-site as structurally insulated panels. That creates whole-wall R-value and air tightness over ninety-five percent of the home." I took a breath. "It will save as much as forty-five percent of a home's energy use for heating and cooling that normally escapes through the wall cavities via light fixtures or wall sockets. Joints between panels will be sealed with insulated splines and SIP sealing mastic and polyurethane foam at every edge. Even the interior joists of the roof trusses will be sealed to prevent the intrusion of air leaking into panel joints."

"What about the mechanical parts of the house?" Penny questioned.

"We'll use high-efficiency windows and doors, HVAC, Energy Star appliances and the latest energy efficient lighting."

Penny glanced at her husband and smiled.

"A geothermal heat pump will provide hot water to the home and be large enough to handle the radiant floor heating." I continued. "The underground piping system will keep the driveway free of ice in the winter. The well will be five hundred feet deep, assuring plenty of water. The septic system is designed to be autonomous and will outlast the lifetime of this home. Once construction is completed, the home's energy costs should be less than three-hundred dollars a year, or a mere eight-two cents a day, which is the best the industry offers." I grinned. "Of course, that will depend on me doing my job correctly."

Tom piped in. "Won't the radiant floor heat increase the electric costs?"

"Normally I would say yes, but with the use of the thermal heat pump, the water is already warmed at inception. Keep in mind that the fireplace we're designing comes with a Replenum heat recovery ventilator at the heart of it. The system brings in outside air through an exterior vent, which is immediately heated by the fire, and delivered into your home. That way, only the stale air from inside goes up the chimney. No heat is lost, and the energy of the fire is maximized."

"You'll cover up the steel box, right?" Penny asked.

"Absolutely, the firebox will be installed flush with the masonry and create the appearance of a solid hand-crafted fireplace. And because it's centrally located, it will radiate heat for the entire home, which means the floors will require less power to sustain set temperatures."

"And our electric bills will really be under three hundred dollars a year?" Penny questioned.

"Yup."

"They better be." Tom checked his watch. "We need to get going, I don't trust Eric to open on time, and Vail is an hour from here."

"Stop it. He's a hard worker and has always been on time." Penny admonished him.

"He's a faggot and lucky I keep him on."

Penny slapped his arm. "You know I don't approve of that. Eric's a good worker, now stop."

Tom mumbled something unintelligent and I made more notes in my file. I cringed inwardly from his caustic remarks but it wasn't anything I hadn't heard before.

"Thank you for everything, Mac. Come on grumpy lets take one more look." Penny embraced Tom and dragged him off to reexamine the view from their future front porch.

The Wilson couple were really open to the green concept and appeared willing to forego minor design features to attain it. Tom was leery, but I was sure the end result would more than please him. The meeting lasted three hours, after which I was off to another site for a final walk-through with the new owner. With any luck I would make it back to the office by five, after our ball game. My desk needed cleaning, then I would have dinner with Emily.

THE BALL GAME was refreshing as usual. Janice fell once, but was fine. In truth, she handled it better than I did. I worried about the kids, all the kids. Denise was on a new asthma medicine and it seemed to be working. She played the entire game without needing to stop. The highlight for me though was when Tracey ran for home and jumped into my arms. If I lived to be a hundred I would never forget the moment she whispered, "I love you, Mac." I kissed her cheek and put her down. She ran to her mother and threw herself into her arms. She was healing nicely thanks to a great therapist and a doting mother. Afterward on the way to drop Kaitlin and Kylie off at the bookstore, Kaitlin talked about school, her teachers, and her friends.

"Mac, do you like us?" she asked.

Our eyes met in the rearview mirror and I smiled broadly. "I love you guys."

She peered at me intently. "Do you like Gramma?"

"You know it. We're good friends." Friendship with Emily was all I could handle. It was useless to want more. I had nothing to offer a woman like her and I couldn't cheat on Izzy.

A sad expression crossed Kaitlin's face. When I glanced up there were tears in her eyes.

"Hey, why the tears?" I asked.

"Mommy Renee is Gramma's friend, too."

"Why does that upset you?"

Kaitlin didn't respond. When I pulled up in front of the store I asked, "Do you want to talk some more?"

She shook her head and started to unclip her seatbelt. My frustration continued to build. It had been months and I had yet to see Mommy Renee. I helped Kylie out of the truck and they ran inside. I waved to Emily as she greeted the kids, then headed back to the office where there was a pile of paperwork waiting to be dealt with.

MARY PLACED A neat stack of files on my desk. She sat and waited as I went through each one, signing the appropriate paperwork and approving the necessary documents. She was efficient, and anal, when it came to our permits and contracts, but I always checked. It was my signature and reputation on the line. She had come to expect it and if she thought I wasn't paying close enough attention she pointed it out to me. I was halfway through the stack before I sensed her eyeing me and glanced up. "What, I'm not reading fast enough?" I asked. "You and Harry got a hot date tonight?" I started laughing at my own joke, but the look she gave me made me come up short. "*What?*"

"I'm not sure what. Are you all right?" She leaned forward in her chair.

"Yeah, why? Don't I seem all right?" I laughed, embarrassed.

"I don't know what's different, but something is." She adjusted her glasses and continued to gaze at me.

"I don't know what you mean." I went back to my paperwork while Mary persisted in her examination. As I closed the jacket on the last folder, I smiled and passed it to her.

She released a small gasp.

"What? What is wrong with you today?"

"You're peaceful. That tranquility, it's back in your eyes." Tears flooded hers. "Something or someone is making you happy." She dabbed her eyes with a tissue. "I'm sorry. It's just so wonderful to see again."

I ignored the implications and started cleaning my desk, pulling out the files I wanted to take home. There were only three because I refused to allow time constraints to hamper my dinner with Emily.

Mary waited. "Mac, I love you like my own daughter. If you've found someone to make you smile, to make you laugh, then I say go for it. I don't care who you sleep with. I *care* if you're happy."

Tears threatened and guilt flooded me.

"We all learned life is too short. Don't be foolish," Mary continued before she strolled out of my office.

Fuck. I remained seated, twisting my wedding band, reminded of the day Isabella became my wife. We held an outdoor ceremony in the meadow off the back of the house. She wore a white lace, billowy-type dress and was barefooted. Her hair hung past her waist. A simple gold necklace was her only jewelry, a gift that morning for marrying me. I wore black pants and a white shirt. Sarah and Michael were our witnesses and heard our vows. When I slipped the matching band on Isabella's finger I felt light-headed. I had never been so happy in my life. Every dream came true that afternoon and it only got better with time.

Isabella was my life — my everything. Four years later she came to me and asked about children. I stared at her dumb-founded. "You do know I would love to try and gladly will, but I'm pretty sure it's physically impossible, honey."

Izzy smiled seductively and climbed onto my lap. "Well, knowing you, anything is possible." She nuzzled my neck and kissed me. By then, she had me. I would have died trying to give her anything she wanted. When the kiss ended she handed me two pamphlets, one about artificial insemination and the other about choosing sperm donors. She was serious. A little over a year later, we welcomed Bella into our hearts and our lives. It was the second most joyous day of my life. Our world was ideal and complete.

Always beware of perfection.

Three years later Izzy's ex found us and decided he would teach her a lesson. Teach both of us a lesson. I should have protected her. It was my job to take care of her and Bella. That sick motherfucker brutalized them. My insides started to churn. Every time I thought about those lost days, seventy-two long horrific hours that she and the baby were missing, I became incapacitated. I remembered the call and my elation that they had been found. The instant it became clear we had been too late followed soon after. My hands gripped the armrests of my chair and nearly tore the padding off. *Shit.* Don't go there, I thought, not tonight.

Tears streaked my face. I ached everywhere and missed my family. At times the pain swallowed me and now was definitely one of those times. I grabbed my briefcase and checked my planner. I needed to get out of there.

AN HOUR LATER I climbed the back stairs to Emily's apartment feeling drained and excited at the same time. The door opened as I reached the small deck and I handed Emily a bottle of wine. At the flower stand next door to the liquor outlet I had picked a bouquet on a whim.

When I presented them, Emily appeared startled. I realized how it looked. *Crap.* "Em, I'm sorry. I wanted to thank you for cooking. Jesus, what was I thinking?" I snatched the flowers back, my heart thudding in my chest. How could I have been so stupid? "I swear they weren't meant that way."

"It's fine," she said. "You just surprised me."

"Let me—" I wheeled to retreat down the stairs.

She gripped my arm. "Give them to me."

I gazed back at her and felt sick inside. Bringing flowers was something I had done for Izzy. My earlier trip down memory lane had blindsided me—*fuck.* "Please let me throw them away—"

Emily snatched the flowers, lifting them to her nose with a smile. "They're lovely. Thank you." She leaned up and kissed my cheek.

I wanted to crawl into a hole and never climb out.

"I hope you're hungry. I made lasagna." She was cheerful as she went in search of a vase.

Wonderful aromas surrounded me as I followed her into the apartment, recognizing more than lasagna. Garlic bread, sausage, and meatballs sat in chafing dishes on the counter. The enticing smells reminded me how hungry I was. "Can I do anything?" I asked.

"Why don't you go inside and say hi to the kids." I wondered if Emily was concerned about my distress. It was either that or she was upset, too.

I took my leave and visited with my two favorite munchkins. When I entered the living room, Kylie spotted me first and sprung up. He rushed into my arms. "Mac, I misthed you."

A quick glance confirmed another tooth was missing and his lisp was even more pronounced. I laughed and cuddled him. "I missed you too, little man, even if it was only a couple hours. Can I have a kiss?" He wrapped his arms around my neck and kissed my cheek. He was such a generous boy. I put him down and shifted toward Kaitlin. "And how are you tonight, little lady?" She smiled and I opened my arms. She let me hug her. I kissed the top of her head and rubbed my cheek on her hair. "Thank you. I really needed that."

"Why?" she asked.

Why indeed. Why *had I* become so needy lately? Why was I craving human contact? Why couldn't I get enough of this family? I blinked at Kaitlin and shook my head. "I don't know, sweetie. I just do."

Kylie came to where I was seated and rubbed my hand. "Don'th be thad." The next thing I knew tears were running down my face. An internal dam had broken and Kaitlin went in search of her grandmother.

Emily sent the kids to their rooms. "Mac, what is it?" she asked as she sat next to me.

I was rocking back and forth, my arms wrapped around my sides. I ached so badly all over and didn't know how to make it stop. When it did, for even a moment, guilt overwhelmed me because I was alive and my family wasn't.

"Oh honey, come here." Emily gathered me in her arms and held me while I cried. Deep sobs tore through my body; I couldn't seem to stop. I didn't know how long we stayed like that. I only knew how good it felt. Too good. I pulled back and swiped at my eyes. "I'm sorry. I don't think I'm going to be very good company tonight. I'm gonna go."

"Wait Mac, talk to me. What's wrong?"

I staggered into the kitchen, needing air and some space. Whatever was happening was scaring the hell out of me and I didn't want to burden Emily. My selfish outburst had already frightened the kids.

"Mac, please."

I gazed at Emily. "I don't know what's wrong, I don't understand any of this. I'm sorry." I started to leave, but saw Emily still in the doorway. "I'm really sorry about the flowers...I...I didn't mean." I hung my head. *What the fuck was I thinking?* "I don't know what I'm doing anymore, forgive me." I said as I walked out the door. She was calling me, but I couldn't go back. I had to go see Isabella. I needed to talk to her, to explain things. I needed her to help me.

MY LEGS WERE stiff and cold from sitting on the hard, damp ground. I had been stroking the solid granite headstone, caressing it, needing to feel closer to my family. I knew every inch of the stonework by heart. I had been talking to Isabella for what felt like hours, begging for her forgiveness—for guidance. I ached with emptiness and I didn't understand why it was worse now than before. It was consuming me whole. I was so ashamed of myself for failing Izzy and Bella, for wanting more when they didn't have the same opportunity. I was ashamed that there were actually moments when I could be happy without them. Tears tracked silently down my face, dripping onto the frost-hardened grass. I didn't think I had any tears left after my episode with Emily, but it appeared there was no end to my torment. I rested my head in one hand as the other stroked the marker.

Unexpected but familiar arms wrapped around me and I turned into her embrace. "Oh God why, Sarah? Why did this happen?" Sobs erupted, the pain shredding what was left of my heart. I wrapped my arms around her and held on as never before. I needed her to anchor me, or I thought I would die.

She rocked me, murmuring words I didn't even hear, holding me tight, as though afraid to let go. After my tears were spent, Sarah pulled back to wipe my face with the sleeve of her sweatshirt. She tipped my head up. "Sweetie, let's go home," she said.

"How did you know?"

"Emily called. She's very worried. She told me what happened. This is where you come when you're grieving." She shrugged. "It wasn't that hard to figure out." Sarah pushed my hair out of my eyes and wiped at my tears again. "Honey, what happened?"

I put my head down. I couldn't bear for her to witness my humiliation. "I brought her flowers."

"And?"

I squinted into Sarah's eyes. "Sarah, I brought flowers for Emily."

"I heard you. Did she get mad? Did she overreact? Did she slap you? What?" She snapped.

My chest was tight with emotion. I crawled from within Sarah's arms and stood up, then reached out to help her rise as well. "Sarah, I think—I mean—crap. I..." I raised my eyes and stared into the space where I thought hers were. "I realized Isabella's never coming back to me. That I'm always going to be alone. I'm never going to wake up from this nightmare."

She wrapped her arms around me again and pulled me to her. "Honey, I think you're finally healing and its scaring the bejesus out of you."

I whispered softly, for fear of Isabella overhearing. "I don't feel married anymore." My tears started to fall again. "Why is this happening? Why now?"

"Oh honey." Sarah kissed my cheek and held me. "You're always going to love Izzy and Bella, but there's room in your heart for more. There's room to love again." She kissed my forehead. "Izzy would want you to live life to the fullest. She would never have wanted you to suffer, to lock yourself away."

Sarah pulled me down the walk toward the exit. Our vehicles were parked outside the fence, one in front of the other. We had both scaled the wall in order to enter the cemetery. We would do the same to exit.

"I'll call you tomorrow, Sarah, okay."

She hesitated. "Mac, come home with me, please."

"I can't. I love you, but I need to be alone. I need to think. Can you understand that? Please?"

She cradled me close and kissed my cheek. "I love you, sweetie. I'll always be here for you."

I hugged her a little tighter, afraid to let go. "Thank you for coming to find me."

HOURS LATER I'D visited three job sites, checking on their progress and that the construction trailers were secure. Afterward I stopped in at the crisis center to see Heath and catch up on paperwork. As I climbed back into my truck, I still had no better understanding of all that I was feeling, or why my perfectly constructed cocoon was collapsing from the inside out. Something drastic had changed within me and I was no longer content to simply exist. I wanted to get back to living and realized Emily was at the root of it.

I liked spending time with her. I felt like I could be myself with her without trying to hide my pain. Ironically, the one person who made me feel safe was also the person who made me want more. There was a hunger in the pit of my stomach and it got stronger every time I was near her, thought about her, or dreamed about her.

Suddenly I found myself parked in the alley behind the bookstore. I wasn't sure why I'd come back there. Emily had weakened my structured existence. No matter how wrong it was, no matter that I knew it could never be; I was drawn to her. For the first time in five years I was feeling something besides pain and I had picked a woman who could never be interested. As I sat with my head against the headrest, my thoughts chaotic, the passenger door opened and Emily climbed in. She placed two baby monitors on my dash and shifted toward me, her arms open. They offered warmth, comfort, and momentary relief. My defenses disintegrated. I slid across the seat and into her waiting arms.

"I was so worried about you," she said.

I buried my face in her neck, relishing the scent of her lavender soap. She was soft and smelled exquisite. I wrapped my arms around her middle, absorbing her kindness and strength.

"Can you tell me about it?" Her soft voice vibrated against my skin.

I pulled away from her, the distance making me shiver. I grasped her hand, needing to feel a connection. I sighed because I needed to be honest. Because this would probably be the last time I would have this chance. "I'm experiencing a meltdown," I said quietly. I rubbed my thumb across her knuckles. "Why did you call Sarah?"

"I was frightened. I didn't want you to be alone." She reached out and caressed my cheek. "Sarah seemed to think she knew where you were." Emily searched my eyes. "You went to the cemetery. Is that what this is about? Isabella?"

"Yes—No—It's hard to explain." I put my head back and closed my eyes. I was suddenly tired. Tired of being alone. Tired of hurting. Tired of loving a woman who was dead.

"Mac, look at me. Please."

I opened my eyes. The chocolaty depths of hers seemed to offer promise.

"Your wife is gone. I know that hurts, but she is." She patted my hand. "I can't imagine she would want you hurting like this. Grieving for her and your child and forsaking your own life and happiness."

It was essential that I be honest, with her and myself. "No. She wouldn't. The problem is I felt married and that was enough. We had a good life. We were happy. Hell, that's more than some people have in a lifetime." Emily's expression showed her concern and I surrendered to the warmth of her friendship, a camaraderie that had come to mean so much. "Lately that's changed and I've been craving more. I've been experiencing emotions again and I feel guilty because of it. Isn't that crazy?"

"No, sweetheart, that's normal. We deal with our pain in our own time and we bow to the changes that have been forced upon us. It's taken you longer than some." Her hand rubbed gentle circles on my forearm. Emily didn't mean for the touch to be arousing, for it to set me on fire, and I needed to make sure she never found out.

"I'm sorry about dinner tonight, and I'm really sorry about the flowers. That was stupid. I wasn't thinking. It's been a crazy day. I hope I didn't offend you. I...that was never my intention."

"Oh honey, you didn't offend me. I loved the flowers. I was touched by them. You misunderstood my reaction." She paused. "To be honest, I can't remember the last time someone brought me flowers. I thought it was very sweet of you." She kissed my cheek and there was sadness in her eyes.

"I guess I should go and let you get some sleep. I really am sorry about dinner."

She withdrew and I felt the separation deep in my soul. She had given me hope when all was lost, offered life where there was none, happiness where only devastation existed. "Are we still on for the movies Saturday?" I waited for her reaction, promising myself I would accept whatever decision she made.

Emily wavered, biting her lip. *Oh God, she was going to say no.* "Mac, I—"

I put my finger to her lips. "Shhhhh. It's okay, I understand." My heart was hemorrhaging, but I steeled myself against the pain. I would remain in control. I would not make this wonderful woman feel culpable. "I better get out of here. You need to get some sleep. I'll talk to you soon?"

She paused, as if she wanted to say something, but changed her mind. She picked up the baby monitors and slid from the truck. "Goodbye, Mac."

Goodbye instead of goodnight. I took that as my cue and my withdrawal from Emily began.

Chapter Nine

THE FOLLOWING WEEK was spent reconciling myself to the necessity of stepping back from Emily and our budding friendship. It became clear to me that I wasn't capable of controlling myself in spite of good intentions. Everything went straight to hell the minute I was near her.

I didn't deserve more. The decision to throw myself into my work was an easy one. I visited each site a couple hours a day, concentrating my efforts on my work instead of daydreaming about the impossible.

ONE AFTERNOON THE ball game was in full swing before Kaitlin and Kylie arrived. A recorded message that morning had advised me not to pick them up. I made a point of searching for the elusive Mommy Renee, but she was nowhere to be found. I drifted over to them and bent down. "Hey, you two gonna play for me today?"

Kaitlin dipped her head and smiled. "Only for a little while 'cause she's coming back soon." She glanced cautiously over her shoulder. "Why is she taking us home today?"

The question cut deep, but it was my own fault. "You two better go get in line. You'll be up after Stevie." I was determined that Mommy Renee was going to make an actual appearance or those kids weren't leaving the ball park.

Twenty-five minutes later a woman lurched onto the field. Neither Kaitlin nor Kylie noticed her approach. They were on base and too excited about playing. As the woman got closer I really scrutinized her. She was dressed in ratty jeans and a dirty T-shirt that had seen better days. I estimated her to be in her thirties, but it was purely conjecture. Her hair was mousy and unkempt, her complexion seemed pasty, and her mouth was twisted in a permanent scowl. The nearer she came the more I wondered about her unsteady gait. She arrived at the fence and bellowed for Kaitlin.

Once Kaitlin saw her, she came off her base and called for Kylie to do the same. The game came to an abrupt standstill.

I lingered by the fence as the kids approached. "Who's that?"

Kaitlin leaned in and whispered. "Mommy Renee."

"You know, the game is still going and you're both on base. You can't just leave like this." I said it softly with a smile. Kaitlin glanced at her stepmother and looked uneasy, Kylie, clearly was too.

I turned toward their absentee-parent. "You don't mind if they finish this inning, do you?" I asked.

"Yeah, I do. Come on you two. I don't have time for this shit," Renee said as she motioned with her arm.

Kaitlin gripped Kylie's hand and dragged him along. She glanced back at me, but doggedly kept going.

I signaled Jim to continue the game.

Though I didn't hear the initial exchange between Kaitlin and her stepmother, I was horrified as Renee's hand lashed out. I watched in shock as Kaitlin landed hard in the grass, the result of being back-handed.

Renee screamed, "Get up, ya little brat. I mean it."

I ran over to Kaitlin and cradled her in my arms. She was crying and her lip was bleeding.

"Hey, you. Put her down," Renee ordered. "Stay out of this."

My lethal glance shut Renee up momentarily as I carried Kaitlin to the bleachers. Connie was manning the refreshment stand and handed me a napkin with a bit of ice. "Put this on your lip, honey. It'll help the swelling." I said. Kylie came to stand by his sister, his eyes darting between me, Kaitlin, and Mommy Renee. "Can you watch them a minute, please?" I asked Connie.

Renee lurched toward me as I stormed in her direction. "What the hell is the matter with you? You *do not* batter kids like that. I don't care what they did."

"Fuck you," Renee retorted. "Kaitlin, Kylie, let's go. Now." Renee glared at the children.

That was when I smelled it. The odor of alcohol permeated the air around us. She was drunk. "They're not going anywhere with you," I said, glancing back to make sure the kids couldn't hear me. "You're plastered. You shouldn't be driving and you sure as hell are not taking them in the car."

Renee swung at me, clipping my cheek, and I erupted.

I hooked handfuls of her T-shirt and snarled, "You will *never* hurt those kids again, do you understand me, you lousy drunk?" I shook her hard.

Jim tackled me from behind. "No. Mac, don't."

I propelled Renee away from me and she fell flat on her back. It all seemed to happen in slow motion. She struggled to get up and screamed anew for the kids to join her.

My arm shot out toward the kids. "Stay." I swiveled back toward Renee. "You're drunk and you are *not* transporting these kids anywhere. If you try, I'll call the police and have you charged with child endangerment. Your choice."

"I could have you arrested for assault," she seethed.

I unclipped my cell and held it out to her. "Go ahead, call the police. There are easily thirty witnesses who saw you slap Kaitlin and take a swing at me."

She smacked my hand away and struggled back up, staggering as she turned to leave. I had witnessed the results of drunken accidents in the past. I ran after her, knowing her condition. "Wait, let me take you home. You shouldn't be driving."

"Leave me alone." She flipped me the bird and kept going.

After I chased her a couple more yards I plucked the keys dangling from her hand. "You can let me drive you, or you can crawl for all I care, but you're not going to jeopardize anyone else's life.

"Give me my fucking keys."

I crossed my arms over my chest..

Renee took another swing, but I ducked. "You bitch," she spat as she stomped off in the direction of a side street. I followed and scouted as she continued up the block and into a small apartment complex.

When I returned to the field, Jim approached and whispered in my ear. I turned to discover Kylie had wet himself. He was crying and Kaitlin was now trying to comfort him. Connie had joined them on the bleachers. I spoke with Jim for a moment, then approached the kids. "How about we head home and get you two cleaned up."

I picked Kylie up and offered my hand to Kaitlin. The boy whimpered and rubbed his eyes. Kaitlin joined with me thoughtfully. As I settled them in my truck, Kylie wiped his face on his sleeve. "I'm sthorry Mac. I wet myself."

"Hey, there's nothing to be upset about, stop crying. I'm not mad. Okay?" I tightened the seatbelt on Kaitlin and examined her mouth. "You all right, honey? Does it hurt?"

Kaitlin surprised me by asking. "Does it hurt where she hit you?"

I reached up and gingerly touched my cheek. It was slightly swollen. "Yeah, a little bit."

"She's gonna punish you for knocking her down." she said.

I cupped her chin and searched her eyes. "Does she punish you for stuff, Kaitlin? Things you didn't do?"

A visible shudder ran through the girl's body.

"I want to help you, but you have to trust me," I pressed.

"Is that why you knocked her down?"

"Yeah, because she hit you and it made me angry." I shrugged. "Are you mad at me?"

She shook her head, leaned over and kissed my cheek.

I never expected the kiss. "Okay, good. Let's go home and get cleaned up."

AT THE BOOKSTORE we exited the truck and I realized Emily would still be working. I carried Kylie while Kaitlin grasped my hand as we headed that way. They both seemed unnecessarily anxious. I had to admit I was too. Inside the store we spotted Emily in the back signing some paperwork for a driver. A delivery of cartons sat next to his dolly.

She smiled when she saw us. "What's going on? Why do you have the children?" That was when she saw Kaitlin's lip. "Oh honey, did you get hurt playing ball?" Kaitlin started to cry and buried her face in my side.

"Can I take them upstairs and get them cleaned up? We'll come down afterward and tell you about it, okay?"

"Why aren't they with Renee?" Emily asked.

"There was an incident at the park. Let me clean them up and I'll explain everything. Please?"

Emily's body stiffened. "As soon as I get this delivery squared away, I'll be up and I expect some answers."

I began filling the tub in the upstairs bathroom with warm water. I helped Kylie out of his wet clothes and put him in the bathtub before handing him a washcloth and soap. I tossed his wet clothes into the hamper and turned to Kaitlin.

An exploration of Emily's medicine cabinet produced peroxide. I dabbed some onto a clean washcloth. "Don't worry, this won't hurt," I said when Kaitlin started to sniffle a bit. "I'm sorry, honey. I'll be gentle, okay?" She agreed and let me apply it.

Emily entered the bathroom as I finished. She gazed from Kaitlin to Kylie and back to me. The questions were swirling in her eyes, but she opted to address Kylie. "So was it time for your yearly bath?" He giggled.

"What happened to Kaitlin's mouth?"

"Mommy Renee hith her." Kylie delivered the news before I could respond.

Emily froze, then took the washcloth from his hand. "What happened?"

Kylie became a boy on a mission. "Mac goth mad and Mommy Renee fell'd down." Kylie used his arms to demonstrate. He grinned proudly and I slammed my eyes shut.

"She did, did she?"

"Mac wasth mad and sthaid bad words."

"I can explain," I said.

She glanced my way, but at Kaitlin's lip, not me. "Does it hurt, honey?" Her voice was sympathetic.

Kaitlin held the instant ice pack I had found in the bottom cabinet against her lip. "A little. Mac put medicine on it."

"She's been a trooper," I said. Actually she had been strong through the entire episode and that made me wonder exactly how often this had been going on with Mommy Renee.

"You and I need to talk," Emily said, looking at me. She lifted Kylie up and wrapped him in a towel. "Where are his dirty clothes?"

I pointed to the hamper and she shook her head. "They're going to smell in there. Put them in the washer for me, while I get him dressed."

I nodded, grateful for the task.

I POURED DETERGENT into the machine and dropped the clothes in as Emily appeared behind me. "Do you want to enlighten me?"

"I know it seems bad, but—"

"Why would you confront Renee? And how could you use physical force?" Emily planted her hands her on hips.

I exhaled a breath. "I didn't hit her—but I wanted to. She showed up at the game drunk. I didn't realize it at first. She called to the kids. I didn't hear their exchange. The next thing I knew she slapped Kaitlin and the kid *fell* from the blow." I took a breath. "I confronted her for hitting Kaitlin and we had words. That's when I realized she was intoxicated."

Emily's eyes closed. When they opened anger simmered in their depths.

"I told her she wasn't taking them anywhere. She told me to butt out. I told her it wasn't going to happen. She swung first."

"And she clearly connected." Emily's hand reached to touch my cheek, but I jerked my head away.

"I lost it and shook her good. I was furious."

"And?" Emily asked.

"Then I offered to drive her home. I didn't want her to get behind the wheel. She refused. I took her keys and she staggered away."

"How drunk do you think she was?" Emily brushed me aside to put fabric softener in the washer.

"I didn't exactly have her do a breathalyzer test. She was staggering and smelled like a brewery," I said with disgust.

Emily glared at me. "Dammit Mac. She could press charges for assault."

"She hit me first, remember that. Besides, she already threatened to. I reminded her there were witnesses to her assault on Kaitlin and me. I also stressed the wisdom of not getting behind the wheel in her drunken state."

Before Emily could respond, Kaitlin and Kylie walked into the area. "Gramma, are you mad at Mac for hitting Mommy Renee?" Kaitlin asked quietly. Kylie imitated an imaginary punch.

Emily smiled despite herself. "I don't believe in violence, but I don't want Mommy Renee hitting you either."

"Mac wasth mad." Kylie grasped his hands together as if he was strangling someone.

Emily laughed out loud. "Yes, you said that." She embraced the two kids. Her daughter, Melanie, would have been proud. "Why don't you go play? Mac and I need to talk. Later we can get some ice cream."

The kids ran off together.

I'D BEEN RELEGATED to waiting in the kitchen while Emily settled them.

She returned to find me rolling a soda can between my hands. "Renee is a recovering alcoholic," she stated

"Not anymore she's not."

She frowned. "No, it would appear not. I hesitate to limit her access to the children, but I guess I'll have to."

"Aren't they biologically Melanie's?"

"Yes. But they were a couple when the kids were born. Renee's been part of the family from the beginning. There were problems in the relationship but Melanie loved Renee. The children had lost so much. I didn't want them to lose her, too." Emily explained with a frown.

"Who has legal custody?"

"I do, of course." She rubbed at her face. "Melanie didn't trust Renee because of the drinking. They had split up a couple times and always went back to each other. I believe Renee loved Melanie, but she loved the bottle more. My daughter was adamant that Renee not be cut out of the children's lives. I've tried to honor her request."

"So Renee pays child support?"

"No, of course not." Emily glared at me.

"Why not?"

"I don't need it. I'm perfectly capable of taking care of them." Emily was peeved.

"If they're her children, if that's how she feels, she's responsible to help support them. More importantly they're afraid of her."

Emily sighed. "You don't understand. They're not afraid of her. They know a drunk driver killed their mother. They probably fear losing her."

"They most definitely *are* afraid of Renee. I don't know why, and they won't say, but I'm telling you there's a problem there and obviously Melanie thought so as well."

Emily stared at me. "Why are you so sure?"

"Experience."

Long minutes went by without conversation. "Melanie was a good mother," Emily said. "She wanted the best for the children." She stood up and strode around the kitchen. "She made her will out two weeks before she was killed. It felt like fate, like she knew." Tears tracked down her cheeks.

"Maybe she did or maybe she wanted to make sure *her* wishes were documented."

"Maybe." Emily shook her head. "I'll never know."

"Well if it'll help, I'll apologize to Renee. I didn't mean, well — she pissed me off, but I'll apologize."

"No, she probably won't remember anyway. Thanks for keeping the kids safe — and for the offer." Emily held her glass, wiping at the condensation, and studying me from the corner of her eye.

I sensed she was preparing to say more, but I wasn't up to it. "Well, I'm gonna head out. I'll see you around." I pulled my jacket off the back of the chair and strode out the door without another word. I had paperwork back at the office that needed to be completed.

Chapter Ten

WEEKS LATER I was in the office going over some documentation for permits and supply orders when Sarah made an appearance.

"Hi, handsome, come on. We're going to lunch." She stood in the doorway, dressed in scrubs, her hair draping her shoulders, a frown on her sun-kissed face.

"Can't."

She sauntered to the desk and stole the pen out of my hand. "We're having lunch." The file I was working on was closed and cast aside. "You look like crap and everyone, *even you,* has to eat." The challenge in her voice defied me to argue.

I leaned back in my chair to study her face. Something was on her mind and I was pretty sure I didn't want to know what it was. "I can't," I repeated. "There's tons of work to do. I'll call you next week. We can do lunch then." I grabbed a different pen and reopened the file.

Sarah leaned over the desk and planted her hands on the paperwork before me. "*We are* going to have lunch. *You are* going to eat, and *you are* going to talk to me. Mary says you're not eating, that you work all hours of the day and night. Michael has seen you here long after normal hours and it has to stop. I'm worried about you. A lot of people are."

I threw the pen down on my desk and stood, leaning in face-to-face with her. "I don't have time for this bullshit. *Mary* needs to stop gossiping or look elsewhere for a job. Now go away, Sarah."

She teared up and turned for the door. I dropped into my chair and lowered my head into my hands. *Fuck.* The door slammed and I sat there a minute, trying to figure out how everything had gone so wrong. The answer was obvious. Simple. Everything had changed when I started to want more.

Then I heard the sound of rubber-soled shoes on the hardwood floor. My head snapped up to see Sarah watching me. I felt like a piece of crap.

She came closer and picked up the phone. "Mary, could you please order two sandwiches and some soup from the deli." She eased her hip onto my desk and listened, a smile spreading across her face as she hung up the phone. "Lunch will be here shortly," she announced sweetly. "Mary said to tell you her resignation will be on your desk at the close of business. In the meantime, you're to shut up and listen to people who care about you. It's for your own good."

I sighed and ran my hand through my hair. "Sarah please. Let's not do this. I'm begging you."

She walked around the desk and tugged me out of my chair. "Honey, we need to talk. Whatever is wrong is eating you up. Look at yourself: you've lost weight, you're constantly grumpy, and you're fighting with the people who love you." She enveloped me. "I do love you. You can tell me anything."

I held her close, savoring the contact. Suddenly I remembered that she belonged to another lifetime. She was straight, like Emily, and I needed to get some work done. I eased her out of my arms. "I'm fine. You don't need to worry about me. You know this is the busy season. We're having a good year and that means more money for the crisis center." I started packing my briefcase. "I'm okay. You don't need to fret."

"Emily isn't."

The folder slipped from my hand and my heart thudded in my chest. "What do you mean? What's wrong with Emily?"

"She's lost her friend and doesn't understand why." Sarah's eyes zeroed in.

I shook my head and returned to packing up my files. I would work on them at home, probably in the quiet of my workshop. "She's better off."

"She misses you."

"Don't."

"Help me understand. Tell me what the hell happened."

My temper blew. I was sick and tired of everyone butting into my business. "You already know what the fuck happened. You warned me. Does that make you feel better?" I slammed my desk drawer shut and opened another one which held my business cards and extra blank work orders so I could replenish my stash.

Sarah absorbed my words. "You've fallen for her." Her voice was reverent, soft, like a whisper in the night.

I tried to ignore the comment, but couldn't stop myself. "Yes. Okay?"

"Did you tell her?"

My head snapped up. "She's straight. You know what that is. Lord knows it's been your excuse for thirty years." My hands fisted at my sides.

"Talk to her," Sarah said. Before I could respond she put her hands up. "At least clear the air between you. Try to salvage the friendship...we did."

"This is different," I hissed. I corralled my leather jacket off the sofa.

"Why? Why is this any different?"

The irony that she, of all people, couldn't let the situation go and leave well enough alone pulsed through me. Fine. "Why? I'll tell you why. Because from the first moment I met her something clicked. I'm drawn to her. There's a connection I can't explain. I can't be around her without wanting her. I can't see her without aching. I can't talk to her without imagining her and the kids in my life. She takes my breath away." I snatched up my briefcase and strode to the door. "Of course, there's the little issue of Isabella, remember her? I made an oath to her and look at me, I can't even keep that promise. Oh, and there's the trivial little matter that once I realized I wanted more, I made the mistake of falling for a woman who's not available—*again*. A woman who's straight, *again*. See a pattern here?"

As I swung the door open, Mary was standing on the other side with lunch. I glanced from one to the other. "Enjoy ladies. It's on me." I marched out of the office listening to Sarah call my name. I didn't stop. There were a couple of problems at job sites that needed my attention.

TWO HOURS LATER, I was at Cove Canyon with one of my GMs when my cell rang. I excused myself to take the call. "Hello."

"Mac, can you hear me? It's a really bad connection."

"I'm here Mary. What's up?

"The contractor for the Wilson project called. He says there's a problem and he needs your input."

"What kind of problem?"

"Something to do with changes to the design."

I rubbed my brow, thinking. "Ahh, okay I remember. We made two structural changes. He needs the updated plans. Can you print them up and get them delivered to him."

"Which pages?"

"If you open the file it's the two with last Friday's date on them."

I heard Mary tapping the keys. "Got 'em."

"Good. Publish them and that should take care of him. Thanks."

"What about the subcontractors?"

"They don't need this update. It doesn't affect them. Anything else?"

"Nope. I'll call you if there is." Mary ended the connection.

I returned to my discussion with the GM, Anthony Higgins. He had been complaining about an erosion issue at the job site, one of our largest projects.

"Thanks for coming out so quickly, Mac. I knew you'd want to see this."

"I'm not sure what we can accomplish, but yeah, I need to understand the issue."

Tony felt sure that if we didn't address the problem now, it would come back to bite us in the butt later. Foundations were the backbone of any building and I didn't tolerate haphazard work. I climbed down into the trench with him to study his finding.

Tony and I stood at the base for the structure. "See right here," he said, "and you can follow it down all the way to the edge."

We were standing on a thirty-six-inch-deep slab of ledge, but a two-inch crack running perpendicular revealed there was a significant erosion situation happening that stretched approximately thirty-five-feet through the middle.

"Crap," I breathed.

Tony responded. "That's what I'm saying. I don't want to pour cement and hope for the best."

"This is beyond my expertise. I need to call in an outside engineer. One who specializes in this type of situation." When we climbed out, we were covered in mud. It was agreed that all further construction would stop until we had an answer. This could turn out to be a dead issue or it could be an underground spring at work. Either way I wouldn't put anyone in danger. We closed down the operation and notified the owners. They weren't happy, but understood it couldn't be helped.

Next, a call to Mary was in order. "What's up, boss?" she answered.

"We need an engineer who can do a study on the Jenkins job. We've got an erosion issue that's gonna require a certified specialist. I shut it down. See if you can get Bill Korman to take a look, or if not him try Manny Rios." I climbed into my truck and waited to see if she needed anything else.

"Okay, where you going?"

"I'm off to see about some plans in Blue River. I'm gonna stop home first. I need to clean up. If you want to reach me I'll be in range the rest of the day." I placed my clipboard on the passenger seat and buckled up. "You have anything urgent?"

"A couple calls. Nothing important."

"Okay, I'll talk to you late or in the morning."

THREE WEEKS PASSED with no word from Sarah. I'd only seen Emily through the window of the bookstore when dropping the kids off. Our relationship had been reduced to a simple nod from time to time, nothing more.

I was at the drafting board in my office when Mary arrived with a cup of coffee. "How about some lunch?"

I smiled, but shook my head. I wasn't really hungry and needed to file the final blueprints for the Wilson project. "How late are the reprographers open tonight?" We were hoping to break ground in two weeks and I needed to ensure that all the permits and plans were in place before that could happen. Eighteen-hour days weren't enough time to keep up.

"They close at six. Do you need me to drop something off?"

"Yeah, give me about an hour. I'll have these finished and we can get the copies out to the GM, subcontractors, and the county clerk. Thanks."

Mary breezed back into the office late that afternoon. "I'll put your mail over here," she said and dropped everything on my desk. "Mac—please don't work late tonight." She hesitated.

I had been abrupt and rude for the last couple of weeks and was surprised she had put up with it that long, especially after she had submitted her resignation. I accepted it without comment, but tore it up as soon as she left the office. "I'm okay. I have a lot of stuff going on."

She made a show of smoothing down her blouse. I could tell by her stance that she was ticked off. "Don't lie to me," she snapped. "At least respect me enough not to do that." With that, she slammed out of my office.

Great. Now I was three for three. Absolutely no one was talking to me. I hadn't heard a word from Sarah since we had gotten into it. Michael told me it was because she didn't approve of the way I was treating Emily. Emily hadn't spoken to me since the incident with Renee.

Hours later as I turned out the light over my drafting board I noticed the mail sitting on my desk. I decided to open it rather than waiting until the next morning. While reviewing the various correspondence, separating what Mary and I would respond to and what was to be filed, I saw an envelope marked personal. The logo in the corner told me all I needed to know. "KK's Book Emporium." I held it in my hands, shocked to see they were trembling. After all the time that had passed, what had prompted this now?

Kaitlin and Kylie came to the games most days. Sometimes they played, sometimes they didn't. Kaitlin wanted to be angry, but didn't seem able to maintain it once she was engaged in the game. I took them home two or four afternoons a week. On the other days I made sure they didn't leave alone. Renee had been parked, sitting in her car waiting for them.

"Hey, you two. How are you?" I ruffled Kylie's hair. "I miss you." Kaitlin whirled away from me. She was mad and, in my heart,

I knew I deserved it. She probably thought I had abandoned her. Even on the days I drove them home, it had been a struggle to get her to communicate.

Kylie, ever the peacemaker, had leaned over and kissed my cheek, whispering in my ear. "She missthes you, too." Teeth had grown in and others had fallen out, but his lisp continued to melt my heart. They left shortly afterward when Renee blared her horn.

I sat there recalling the memories of the time I had spent with Emily while holding the envelope in my hands. They had been happy times. If only things could have been different. After all these years why was she the one who would make me yearn for more? We were good together. We laughed and enjoyed the same things. We connected in a way I hadn't with anyone since Isabella. Why did I have to pick a straight woman? I put the envelope in my briefcase. It could wait. Whatever she had to say couldn't be that important or she would have called.

It was after nine and time for me to head home. After two morning appointments, I would be out of the office most of the next day. I had packed my briefcase and dimmed the lights when my cell rang. "Hello."

"Mac, it's Heath. Nancy called. She's looking for Lily, but she's not available tonight. It's her mother's birthday. They've got a drunk in the ER. Did you want to handle that?"

Lily was a counselor for AA. "Yeah. I should be there in ten minutes. I was just heading out." I grabbed my briefcase and leather jacket and locked the doors behind me. Duty called. Thank God. I wasn't looking forward to going home.

"EVENING, PRETTY LADY. Whadda you got for me?"

"How you doing, hot shot?" Nancy said. "Are you losing weight? I hate you. You know that, right?"

I laughed, knowing better than to answer. Nancy was always moaning about her weight. She looked fine to me, but I wasn't the one she was trying to impress. "Yeah, yeah. So?"

She pulled a binder out of the slot and opened it. "It's a DWI. Police brought her in. She's banged up somewhat and wants to be released. Belligerent and blowing a point zero-nine-two on the breathalyzer. We're not sure if she's a victim or just drunk."

"What would Lily normally do?" I didn't really have a lot of experience with AA or their procedures.

"She tries to talk to the patient and asks if they want help. If they do she'll either set up an appointment with a counselor or give them a schedule of the meetings. I've got a copy here if you need it."

"Yeah, please." I saw a police officer, Perry Watson, waiting by the vending machines. "Are they arresting her?" I asked.

Nancy shrugged. "Not sure."

"Okay, I'm ready. Which room?"

"Two."

"Thanks, talk to you later."

I marched over to the closed door and knocked gently.

"Go away."

Hmmmm. I knocked again and slowly pushed the door open. "Hello."

"Get the fuck out."

I recognized the voice and went farther into the room. "I'm not here to annoy you. I've been asked to visit with you. See if you need any assistance. We have local AA counselors and there are weekly meetings if you're interested."

"Christ, if it isn't the damn do-gooder," Renee sneered.

I walked a little closer to the bed. She had a swollen eye and her hands were scraped and bruised. "The name is Mac Taylor. Do you need help, Renee?"

"No. Get the fuck out."

I took a deep breath and pondered the situation. "I probably should inform you there's a police officer outside. I believe his intention is to arrest you. If you have a counselor or an attorney, we can call him or her and maybe they can help you avoid that."

"Get. Out."

"Do you *want* to go to jail?"

She hurled a tissue box at me, but it hit the wall. I picked it up and tossed it back on the bed. "Have a good evening, Renee. I'll let the officer know you're ready."

Nancy glanced up as I strolled back to the desk. "So?"

"You called it. She's a mean drunk."

She signaled to Perry Watson, who entered the room I had just vacated.

"Do you need me to fill anything out?"

"Nah, Lily never does either." Nancy indicated the room with a tip of her head. "They'll probably take her into custody now."

"Really?"

"I suppose." She stared at the door.

"Hey Nancy, could I use the phone?"

"Sure." She lifted the device and placed it on the counter.

I dialed the number from memory, not sure if I should or not, but not willing to be wrong if I didn't.

"Hello?"

"Emily, it's Mac."

"Hi." A short pause ensued. "Is something wrong?"

"Well that's a matter of perception. I'm at the hospital—"

"Are you hurt, I—"

"No. It's not me. It's Renee. She was brought in after a DWI traffic stop and I think they're going to arrest her. I tried to talk with her, but she's not listening. I thought I should tell you, in case...I don't know, if you wanted to know."

"Was there an accident?"

"Not that I'm aware of. She's a little beat up, but nothing that requires medical attention. I think the officer was hoping she had a health issue. Does she?"

"No." She sighed.

"I'm sorry. I didn't mean to upset you. Do you want me to try to intercede?"

Silence hung in the air between us.

"Em?"

"No. I won't be an enabler for her. I've tried, but she's not ready to get help."

"Okay. Sorry about this. Sorry, I bothered you." I started to end the call.

"Mac?"

"Yeah?"

"Thank you."

"No problem. I'll stick around and see what happens. Don't worry about it. Good night, Emily."

"Night."

"WAKE UP, SUNSHINE." A nudge to my foot almost upended me.

I had fallen asleep in the shop. For a moment I thought I was still in town. "What the hell? What time is it?"

"Early. I come bearing gifts though."

I opened one eye and let my nose do its thing. Coffee. *Yes!* I threw the blanket off, sat up, and held my hand out.

"Large black coffee, and bacon and eggs on a toasted bagel." Michael was grinning.

"Christ, it's only five-fifteen. Either I'm in big trouble, or you need an even bigger favor. Give me two minutes." A quick trip to the bathroom let me brush my teeth and take care of morning matters.

"Are you living out here?"

The current state of the small office more than justified Michael's question. A change of clothes hung from the back of the door. My briefcase was on the desk next to my laptop and file folders were strewn about. An empty pizza box stuck out of the garbage container along with several empty water bottles. The file cabinet had a drawer open with blueprints draped across it. "I got in late and didn't have the energy to go up to the house."

"Un huh." He handed me a brown paper bag. Inside were two wrapped breakfast sandwiches. "Here."

"Thanks. Coffee?"

"Those two are yours," he said with a tip of his head.

The extra-large cups sat on the corner of my desk. "So which is it?" I asked. "Sarah driving you nuts or you need a favor?"

He grinned around the mouthful of bagel. "Both."

"Been there." I gazed at him in total commiseration.

Quiet settled over the space as we each dug into the food. I opened the lid on the second cup of coffee. "If you bring me tasty morsels like this every morning, I might have to marry you."

"Stimulating as that sounds, I thought a certain appendage of mine prevented you thinking like that."

"Oh yeah, forgot about that little issue."

"Hey, hey now."

A laugh rumbled through me and I almost spit my coffee out. "Sorry, I didn't mean that. I meant to say big problem, very big problem."

"All right then." His manhood appeased he returned to his meal.

"So you going to tell me why you're here?"

"In time. What's new?"

I heeded him suspiciously. "A couple of problems at two job sites. Other than that just busy. How about you? How's the legal business treating you?"

"I think I'm ready to come work for you."

"Sarah would love that. You're hardly home now, imagine that."

Michael laughed. "Let's play some pool."

"Can't, sorry." The hair on the back of my neck prickled at his delay tactics.

"Come on. I feel the need to beat your ass in a game of eight ball."

I glanced at him sideways. "I sold the table."

"Why?" He leaned forward.

"It just sat there, going to waste."

"Damn, Mac. We had some good times playing here."

I stood up and started to gather the garbage, last night's as well as today's. "Exactly." Thoughts of Isabella and I challenging Sarah and Michael came to mind. Never ending games until the need for sleep won out.

"Oh. Sorry."

"No problem. So you gonna tell me what's going on or should we dance some more."

Michael began to help me, and within minutes the office was back in order. "You going to a job site today?"

"It's Sunday."

He shrugged.

"It can't be that bad, whatever it is."

He ran his hands through his thinning hair. "Sarah—"

"Any sentence that starts with your wife's name can't be good."

"Sarah wants to have another baby." He stared at me.

"Shit."

"Yeah, that's about what I said." He sighed.

"What is she thinking?"

"Obviously, she's not."

"Did she talk to the doctor?"

"Not yet. She wanted to run it by me first."

I stared at him numbly. Sarah had been pregnant during Isabella and the baby's abduction and subsequent murders. The trauma and resulting shock of their deaths had caused a miscarriage. Two years later she encountered problems during Taylor's birth. Things went downhill fast and her doctor told her she'd never be able to carry again. "What did you say?"

"I told her absolutely not."

I closed my eyes and put my head back against the couch. "So I assume you're moving in with me for the foreseeable future?"

"Am I wrong?"

"You know you're not."

"Will you talk to her?"

"Yeah right." I stood up and pulled him along. "Come on, we need more coffee and that's up at the house."

"Is there scotch there, too?"

We were rounding the curve of the driveway when Emily pulled up. Michael patted my shoulder. "I'll go start that coffee. You better handle this."

"Gee thanks." I walked over to the truck and opened the door for her. "Morning."

"I'm sorry to just show up. I didn't realize you had company. This can wait."

"It's Michael and we're only having coffee. What's up?"

"I went to police headquarters this morning and they told me Renee hadn't been arrested. Then I went to the hospital and they told me she was released and left with you."

"She did."

"Why?"

"There was no accident. Her car was impounded and justice

wasn't going to be served with her sitting in jail all night. I gave her a ride home."

"Why would you do that?"

"I'm sorry. I thought that's what you would have wanted."

"No. That's not what I meant, and yes, I didn't want her in jail. She needs help."

"She has to *want* help, Emily."

Emily gazed out the windshield, the silence between us deafening.

"Would you like to come in? I'm sure the coffee's ready by now."

"No. I should go."

"Em?"

Emily stared out the windshield.

"What is it?" She turned to me and I saw the troubled look in her eye.

"Nothing," she insisted.

"Look, I know Renee doesn't have a car right now, but I'd feel better if you barred her from transporting the kids anywhere," I said. "At least until she gets her drinking under control again. I could help—"

"No. You do enough. They're my responsibility and I'll take care of it."

My chest constricted. "Of course."

She started the engine and pulled the door closed. I watched as she backed up and drove away, taking a small part of me with her.

Michael was pouring a cup of coffee when I entered through the back door. "You could have invited her in."

"I did."

"Ah."

"Yeah, she's pissed off and I can honestly say I don't know why. Fuck."

"Should I ask what you did?"

"Nothing. Now what are you going to do about your wife?"

"That's the question, isn't it?"

A COUPLE OF days later I was at the diner waiting for breakfast when Sarah and Emily strolled in. They looked right past me, sauntering to the back and took a booth.

"You okay?"

I peeked up at Maggi and shrugged. "How about making my order to go."

She glanced from me to the booth and back again. She leaned on the red laminate counter she had just wiped clean. "Or you could go back there and ask to join them."

Because she meant well I tempered my response. "Give me two large coffees with that, will you?"

Maggi shook her head. "You are a stubborn *gringa*, you know that."

"I'm not in the mood, Mags."

She grasped my hand with tears in her eyes. "I loved Isabella. We were like sisters, but she passed. She can't find peace until you do."

The statement ignited my anger and I jerked my hand back. I pulled some bills out of my pocket and threw them on the counter. "Don't tell me she's passed. I live every damned day with it. And don't ever tell me I have to let them go. She was my life." I stormed out of the diner. By the time I reached my vehicle the urge to hit something — anything — was overpowering. How dare she tell me Izzy wasn't at peace.

I hopped in my truck and turned toward the florist for flowers before going to the cemetery. It was Isabella's birthday and I wanted to spend some quiet time with her.

I parked at the edge of the walkway and gripped the flowers before exiting the truck. As I walked up the path, the ebony headstone came into view. The words etched in the marble were burned into my brain and carved into my bleeding heart. Fresh flowers and a small teddy bear at the base of the stone made me smile. As I trudged closer, tears threatened. *Sarah.* She never forgot. I kissed the stone and knelt down to place the daisies next to the other flowers, gently placing the bear in between the two arrangements. My despair filled me. I shouldn't have been visiting my family at a cemetery. I didn't want to hear that Izzy was dead. Isabella was a good person; she deserved so much more. I should have given her more. Lately I hadn't even been capable of giving her my fidelity. How could I have been interested in another woman. Another family. I heard the footsteps, but didn't bother to glance around. "I'm okay, Sarah. I don't need rescuing today."

Silence ensued. I expected an argument or retreating footsteps. Neither happened. I twisted and fell backward onto my heels.

"Maggi said she upset you. I know today's special, I — I wanted to be sure you were okay." Emily's arms were wrapped around her middle, her eyes wary.

I took in the vision of her and sighed inwardly. Her hair was down and loose the way I preferred it. She was wearing a peach silk blouse and it complemented her skin tone beautifully. Black linen slacks and pumps completed her outfit.

"Didn't know it was you, sorry." I stood and wiped my cheeks. I was done crying, done displaying my weakness. "Why are you here?"

"We're friends."

I stood there shaking my head. *Were we? Could we be?* I missed the companionship, the fun, her laughter. I didn't miss the guilt, the shame, or the self-loathing because my hormones had gotten out of control. "Are we really?"

"I thought we were." She raised her hand to shade her eyes from the sun and brushed at a wisp of hair caught on an eyelash.

My guilt and humiliation surfaced. "I don't think I'm a very good friend, Emily. In fact, I think you're better off without me around." I glanced back at the grave. It was the first time I would leave there without feeling as though my insides had been eviscerated. *Progress? Somehow I doubted it.* I turned and wandered away.

Chapter Eleven

A WEEK LATER, I was at the ball park setting things up when Emily arrived to drop the kids off. She had Sarah's two rug rats with her as well. Thankfully, I hadn't seen Renee since the incident at the hospital. The four kids ran over to their friends, happy and carefree, giggling in preparation for the game.

Emily approached me. "Can I talk to you?" She was dressed in a dove gray business suit, with a scarlet silk blouse, black pumps, and a thin gold necklace with matching earrings.

"Sure."

"I need a favor. Can you drop all of the children off at Sarah's after the game today?" Her demeanor was guarded.

I wanted to ask why. I was curious about her formal attire. I wanted...and that was the issue. "Not a problem. Is she expecting them?"

"Yes."

"I'll take care of it for you."

"Thank you." Emily hesitated. "It's because there's a book signing, I expect it to go late."

"Glad to do it."

"They miss you," she said as she studied my face. "I miss you. I miss my friend."

"*Emily.*" I shook my head and glanced away. "You don't understand."

"I'd like to."

"Look around you." I said, pointing to the various adults standing around trying hard not to appear as though they were watching us. "See what's happening? Everyone is curious what's between us. Wondering. They imagine things simply because we're talking. They believe we're *more* than friends. They assume we're *sleeping* together."

She leaned closer and touched my arm. "I don't care what they think. I only care what you think."

I pulled my ball cap out of my back pocket and punched it back into shape. "Are you really that naïve? This—" I waved my arm between us, "could hurt you, hurt your business. I don't want that to happen."

She shook her head and shuffled backward. "I don't believe you. But don't worry, I'm not going to beg. There's something you're not telling me. I don't know what happened, Mac. I don't know what I did that made you pull away, but it's not these people." She glanced around us, as if challenging someone to say something. "Goodbye Mac. I won't bother you again." She strode away.

I refused to witness her departure and instead tramped over to the bleachers and sat down with my head in my hands. My insides felt as though they were in a vice and this time it wasn't about Izzy and the baby. How could I love two women? Was that even possible?

It was the top of the second inning and Kaitlin was at bat. Though I missed it, she no longer needed my help. She had become quite the proficient player. Kylie was on third, Patrick was coaching third base, and Janice was on first. Janice could maneuver more easily with her new braces. Tommy Jenkins was up next, and edging his wheelchair closer and closer, anxious to play. I tossed the ball toward home and Kaitlin crushed it. It sailed over the first baseman's glove and rolled into right field. She squealed and took off like the wind. The joy on her face as she ran the bases made my chest swell with pride. Kylie scored. He jumped on home plate with both feet and bowed to the observers. He was such a little ham, it made me laugh out loud. He high-fived Jim, who was catching and rushed to the dugout. Everyone else was safe. But that was to be expected on Team Bella.

It was hot that afternoon and I had perspired through two shirts. It was a beautiful day for a ballgame. The sun was high in the sky, the clouds rolling, white and fluffy. A breeze coming in off the mountains kept it from being oppressive. It had rained the night before and the air smelled fresh and clean again. I loved this sport and I loved these kids. I wished for the millionth time that Isabella had lived to bring this to fruition, to see the team and the smiles on the kids' faces. Tommy wheeled to home base and turned his chair sideways. Patrick paraded up beside him, ready to assist. They were both grinning. I tossed the ball and they hit it right down the baseline toward third. Patrick pushed Tommy toward first. They were screaming as they went.

I gazed toward the bleachers and was shocked to see Emily, shading her eyes, watching me. As our eyes met, my heart expanded with an emotion that scared the hell out of me. I really and truly had fallen in love with her. This was more than infatuation, more than lust. I was in love. The admission, if only to myself, made my heart thud in my chest. I wanted her in my life. More importantly, I wanted to be a part of hers and the kids' lives. Just as quickly an image of Isabella and the baby flickered in my mind. The two of them were laughing and smiling, the way we used to, the way we never would again. The guilt of loving another had me aching for betraying what Isabella and I once shared. I wondered how Izzy would have dealt with it if our roles were reversed. Emily broke eye contact first. She strolled to her truck and drove away.

A stretch of my neck and a roll of my shoulders set me right. I turned to the next player, little Frances. She was new to the team and a sweetheart. She was born with Hutchinson-Gilford disease, the premature aging illness. Her mom was behind the fence talking to her, offering encouragement. I tossed the ball and she hit it. It rolled a few feet toward me, and she stood there clapping and squealing. I jogged into home base, picked her up and off we went. Janice hobbled in from third, Kaitlin came off second, rounded on third and ran home to score. Patrick pushed Tommy past second, heading for third and I deposited Frances on first. She was laughing as I put her down. I motioned to her mother to join us. When Mrs. Kramer arrived at first, I explained the way the game was played. "If she can't run by herself, you take her hand or pick her up and run with her, okay? We're here to make sure everyone has fun." I ruffled Frances's white blonde hair. "That's an order, young lady."

Mrs. Kramer touched my arm. "Thank you."

"Not necessary," I said with a smile. "This team is for the kids. If they're happy, everyone's happy."

The woman smiled with tears brimming in her eyes. I reset my cap on my head and walked back to the pitcher's mound. We had a ballgame to finish.

Forty minutes later as the players came off the field, the kids laughed and teased each other. I smiled, so proud of them my chest was bursting. Jim Collins approached. "So Coach, our team won."

"I think we *all* won." I grinned broadly. He knew how I felt about the games. There were no sides and everyone participated.

Jim put his arm around my shoulders. "That we do. You should be very proud. I am."

Jim and I had become friends about three years earlier. In a heartfelt conversation he had admitted he was unsure how to deal with Patrick as a youngster. It wasn't that he was ashamed, he hadn't known what to expect of a special needs child. Once he heard about our team he came out and talked with me. I explained the rules. Everyone played to the best of their ability, everyone was cheered for and everyone was a winner. Always. The kids on the team had enough crappy issues to deal with in real life. Playing ball shouldn't be one of them. Afternoons for these children were strictly about fun and trying to reach beyond their limits. They were enjoying what others took for granted.

Jim, a competitive-type personality, initially struggled with that concept. After Patrick was on the team for a few months, he conceded that his son was excelling in things now that he wouldn't attempt before. He felt sure the pride and confidence of playing was what inspired Patrick.

"I noticed Emily was here earlier," Jim commented. "She's a lovely woman."

My first impulse was to tense up. "Yeah, she came to watch her grandchildren." Jim had known Isabella and that we were a couple.

"I happened to be in her bookstore the other day with the kids. She's bright and extremely charming." He said.

Without warning, jealousy raised its ugly head. For a moment I was resentful of his time with her, ridiculous as it was. "I guess."

"Mac? You are, well, you're together right?" He looked at me, smiling.

"No. We're friends." What was he after?

"Is that what you call it now?" he chuckled. "You seem quite taken with the lady, and I can't say that I blame you."

"Jim—"

He held his hands up. "No need to explain. It's none of my business, I get that."

My flush burned the tips of my ears. I was saved from further inquiries when Kylie came over and tugged my hand. I leaned down. "Something wrong?"

"I justh miss being wifth you."

I picked him up and kissed his cheek. "I miss being with you, too." I held Kylie while Jim and I chatted some more. We discussed the schedule for the week. I kept an eye out as Mikey, Taylor, and Kaitlin got snacks for themselves. "Come on kids. I have to get you all home."

Once it became evident I would be transporting Kylie and Kaitlin, I had invested in a car and booster seats, but having four kids to transport would make things trickier. I managed to strap them all in the back seat of my truck and proceeded to drive extra cautiously.

Michael came out to greet me as I was unclipping the seatbelts. "Howdy."

"Hey, Michael. Any idea where these two rug rats belong?"

"Nope, never seen them before." He lifted a giggling Taylor into his arms and took Junior's hand. "Why don't you come in for a while?"

"Can't, but you forgot two. You're babysitting tonight."

"Really?"

"That's what Emily told me."

Kaitlin unfastened the seatbelt herself as I lifted Kylie down onto the pavement. "You two behave and have fun. I'll see you at the game tomorrow."

Kylie latched onto my leg and held it tightly.

"Hey little man, what's the matter?"

"Nuffin."

I squatted down. "You sure?"

He nodded and grinned.

"Good, go play and have fun. Grandma will pick you up later. I'm going back to work."

Michael nudged me. "Hey pal, you might want to rethink that. The odor is pretty bad."

With the kids in ear shot, my response was simply to stick out my tongue. "By the way, don't help tonight. Don't do anything to assist your lovely wife. Let her experience what it's like with two more kids to deal with."

He raised an eyebrow. "You think?"

"Can't hurt. Have a good night."

I WAS IN the office the following Thursday when Sarah dropped by. "Want to buy me lunch?" she asked. She wore a white sun dress and sandals. She had been working on her tan and the dress contrasted nicely.

"I thought you were mad at me?"

"I am, but I'm hungry."

I had missed Sarah. "Just lunch?"

"Lunch and some pleasant conversation." She batted her eyelashes and laughed.

"Okay." I picked up my keys. Mary was at the bank, so I locked the office on our way out.

"Want to walk or drive?" Sarah asked.

I gazed down at her feet. "Can you hike that far in those things?" Thin straps and flimsy soles offered no support or protection. Hell, they hardly counted as shoes.

"Want to race and find out, smart-ass?"

I grinned. "No, a leisurely stroll is fine." We trekked down the street without further conversation. In fact, there was an element of tension and I wondered if it was from earlier in the spring. "What's up?" I asked.

"Cool your jets. I want to spend some time with you. We haven't exactly been close of late." She took my arm. "I miss you. I miss the way we were." We arrived at the diner and chose a booth in the back.

I took a deep breath. "I'm sorry. I know our problems are my fault."

"Honey, I don't need your apology. I wish I knew how to reach you, especially once you get like that. You lock yourself up and you don't let anyone in. You never share the pain. You shut down and hide away, taking it all on yourself, blaming yourself."

"It *was* my fault, and you were dealing with your own grief."

She covered my hand with hers. "We could have supported each other." A couple sauntered by. I tried to withdraw my hand, but she gripped it tighter. "Stop that."

I glanced up questioningly.

"Stop worrying all the time about what others think. Stop pulling away from those who love you. I'm a big girl. I can handle it.

I blinked. "What's this really about?"

Sarah shook her head in frustration. "It's about you."

Confused I asked, "What do you mean?"

"I mean no one cares. No one's lurking around us. No one is going to storm over here and create a scene if I hold your hand or touch you."

"You know why."

"It was a long time ago, honey."

"It feels like yesterday." The vision erupted in the forefront of my mind. The boys heckling us, the fear. The bile rose in my throat with the memory of those high school jocks as they surrounded us on the way home from a movie. Their taunts still echoed in my mind. Guilt had almost paralyzed me. The fear that Sarah would get caught in the middle because of me and my proclivity had nearly debilitated me. Fortunately, my inner defense mechanism took over. I had kicked one in the nuts before he expected it. The second one caught me in the ear, but I had managed to rake his face and throat, and that was all the third one needed before he took off. A shudder ran up my spine.

Sarah gripped my hand tighter. "Times have changed, people are different. We're not in high school anymore."

"Do you honestly believe that?"

"Yes." Her blonde head nodded vigorously.

"What about the reporter?"

"He was an ass and you know it."

I sat there wondering if she was right, if things had improved that much. Oh, I knew, people actually said the word now, some even admitted to having gay friends or family members. There were marches, parades celebrating the lifestyle, and equal rights amendments. Gay Pride Day was celebrated world wide. There were also laws on the books in some states still declaring homosexual sex acts illegal, punishable with fines and imprisonment. There were countries that wanted to make homosexuality punishable by death. That part didn't sound so different to me. "I'd never forgive myself if something happened to you or anyone else because of me."

"It wouldn't be because of you. It would be that we chose you over bigotry."

"You know what I mean."

"In the meantime, you're missing out on so much. It's time to take a stand, Mac."

We finished our lunch and headed back to our lives. Strangely, Sarah had given me lots to think about.

SEVERAL DAYS LATER I was in my office checking out the final permits for the Wilson's green project. "Hey, Mary. Did Brian pick up the revised blueprints?"

"Yup and he's distributed them to each subcontractor and made them sign for the prints per your request." Mary meandered into my office.

"Good."

"Did you give him the permits to post?"

Mary flipped a page on her pad. "Sure did. He's waiting for the crane permit."

"Him and me both." I grinned.

"Henry will get to us on time. He always does."

"I know. I just wish it wasn't always at the last minute." We had already broken ground and the foundation had been poured. All the extra footings were in place and we were set to start building Monday afternoon. We needed those special permits to cover the large crane operations. The entire house had been constructed elsewhere and would be reassembled on-site. It required an oversized crane and a specially trained operator to handle the intricate assembly. The good news was all the electrical and plumbing had already been approved since they were part of the walls airtight construction. With luck and good weather, the house could be completed by the end of the month.

"Has the gravel been laid for the temporary driveway to accommodate the heavy equipment?"

"Brian said yes. He was there yesterday overseeing it."

Mary was sitting in the chair across from me making notes as I reviewed the last of the paperwork. We had been at it for hours.

"Done. That's it. What about you?"

"Did you hear about the break-in at the hardware store?"

"No, did anyone get hurt?"

"No, it took place at night. But Aaron is getting a security system. I'm curious if you want to consider one here? With the law offices downstairs we should think about it."

I sat back to do just that. "How many properties are empty at the moment?"

"I think five. The Carsons finally took possession of the house on Chester."

"He got his financing after all?"

"Yup, they closed last Wednesday."

"Good." A nagging feeling gripped me. That had been how the dickhead avoided capture for three days while he tortured Isabella and the baby. He had hidden in an empty house in plain view. "Get hold of Bob Marcos at the security company, talk with him. Work a deal, I want all the properties to have security in place by the end of the month, and if they're rentals with occupants I want the upgraded system installed this week."

"What about the two stores with apartments overhead?"

Emily and the kids sprang to mind. "Absolutely. Make it a priority."

"I'll contact the tenants and see about setting it up. What about the cost?"

"Call Heath, too. Have him do the same for the center and the safe houses."

"And."

"Huh?"

"Who's footing the bill?"

"The management company. We can afford it. Some of the business people were barely getting by, plus it should give us clout to get a better deal with the security company."

"I'll start making calls."

"Mary, tell Bob the bookstore and the apartment come first."

"Was there a problem?"

"No, but she's got two small kids and herself. I don't want them to come to any harm."

"I'll call her today."

"Get Heath to set it up with the security company. I want the center and his needs to take priority as well."

"Will do. I'll mention it to Alice, so she can have Michael start updating the contracts." She left my office to start on her list.

"Thanks." I was reviewing the schedules when Mary buzzed. "Yeah?"

"Heath is on line one."

"Hi, Heath. Did Mary tell you about the security system?"

"Yeah, we can discuss that later. There's a problem and I'm not sure how you want to handle it. A Lieutenant Patterson from Estes Park wants a representative of the center to make arrangements for a victim of his."

"Estes Park? That's gotta be a hundred miles from here."

"Sure is."

"There's a county hospital nearby that could do a hell of a lot more than we can."

"You're talking to the choir, Mac. All the lieutenant would tell me is that they'll be arriving at Mercy around one and would appreciate someone meeting them."

I glanced at the clock. It was ten to one. "When the hell did he call?"

"Ten minutes ago give or take."

"He just assumes we're going to cooperate."

"The connection was pretty bad. I had a hard time hearing him, but yeah. Obviously they were on the road. What do you want to do? Lily's still here."

"No! I'll go see him and get the full story. I want a damn good reason why we should foot the bill on this one. Thanks Heath, talk to you later." I quickly buzzed Mary and closed the files I was working on, I slipped them into my briefcase as I waited for her.

"Mac, Ms. O'Brien is here. She'd like to talk to you."

"Emily?" Mary said yes. "Send her in and call Mercy for me, please. Tell them I'm meeting a police officer there and that I'm running late.

Emily advanced into the office looking everywhere except at me. She was wearing a dress with high heels and makeup. That was the first time I'd ever seen her clad that way. She was stunning.

"Hello."

"Hi. I didn't know you were coming and I'm sorry, but I've got an emergency at the hospital—"

"Oh, okay." She turned to go.

"Emily. Wait, what did you want?"

"It's not important."

I dashed over and closed the door before she could pass through it. "Yes, it is or you wouldn't be here. Please, tell me."

"Sarah asked me to stop by. I didn't want to. I'm tied up with a book signing this evening and was hoping you could drop the children off at Sarah's after the game."

"I can do that."

"You said you're going to the hospital."

"I am and if I run late I'll get Jim to drop all the kids off. He only lives one block over from Sarah."

"No." She shook her head and reached for the door. "I'll figure something else out."

"Emily, I want to help out. You know that."

"Do I? How exactly *would* I know that?"

"Okay, I deserve that. I would very much like to help you. Please let me." I struggled not to overreact.

She glared at me. "Sarah expected to pick them up, but like you, she's been called into the hospital for some kind of emergency. Michael is in court until five, but he'll be home after that."

"I'll handle it."

"Are you sure?"

"Absolutely." I checked the clock again. "I'm sorry. I really have to go now, but I won't forget about the kids, I promise."

"All right, thank you."

"Can I walk you out? I'm going that way."

A TALL FIGURE dressed in jeans and a leather jacket was leaning on the nurses' station with his back to me, filling out paperwork. Stacey was behind the counter manning the area as I approached. "Hey, pretty lady, anyone here asking for me?"

The figure in the leather jacket turned toward me. "Ms. Taylor?"

A woman? I hadn't anticipated that. She was tall, maybe six-foot and physically imposing. There was a definite air of authority. "Yes."

"I'm Lieutenant Patterson. I'm the one who asked you to meet me here." She pulled out her badge and photo ID to confirm her identity.

"Kind of far from home aren't you, Lieutenant?"

"Please, call me Christine."

I put my hand out. "Mac."

"Thank you for being so prompt. I'm sure you don't remember me, but I attended a presentation you made in Denver back in 2008. It was horrific and enlightening all at once. I've never forgotten your story or your dedication."

"Thanks. I'm sorry. I rarely remember people I meet at those functions."

"I understand, but that's why I'm here."

"I gotta be honest. I am curious what made you make the hundred-mile trip."

Sarah stormed out of an exam room, her face tight, and charged in our direction. "That woman has first- and second-degree burns that required immediate attention. Why would you bring her here when there are better equipped facilities with a burn unit in your own back yard? Hospitals that could have handled her injuries? Do you have any idea the risk of infection you've put her under? More importantly, x-rays reveal that child's arm has been broken previously, and there's proof of other injuries. Why haven't you protected them?"

"There was no alternative, ma'am. I needed to ensure Martha

and Kim's safety first."

"Driving them across country is your idea of keeping them safe? Are you mad?"

"Sarah?" I interceded. "Why don't you tend to the patients and I'll get to the bottom of this?"

"I want her brought up on charges." Sarah pointed at the officer. "She's got to have broken some law, somewhere by transporting that poor woman and child this far, particularly since medical treatment was readily available." Sarah stormed off in a huff, dictating orders to the two nurses and an orderly outside the exam room.

I looked at Christine. "We really do need to talk."

"Once I explain, you'll understand."

I studied her. She didn't appear crazy, and she hadn't made her rank by doing stupid things. "Let's get some coffee." I pointed toward the nurses' break room for privacy.

"JoAnne, if you need either myself or Officer Patterson, we'll be inside."

"Good enough, Mac."

After pouring two coffees, we settled at a table in the far corner.

"I realize this seems bad, but something drastic was needed to save this woman and her son." Her hand and voice were steady while she talked, but her eyes glistened with unshed emotion.

"Okay, explain it to me and please start from the beginning." I took a sip of the coffee. It was awful and I wondered if there was still enamel left on my teeth.

Christine grimaced as well and put the cup down. "I need your assurance that what is said here remains off the record. The woman and her son are in grave danger."

"That much I assumed, but why can't you handle it?"

"Because the perpetrator is Martha's ex-partner, who also happens to be my chief's daughter and he'll protect *her* no matter what."

"Ouch."

"That's not the worst of it."

"Oh good, a challenge. I'm listening."

"Martha is my sister-in-law. Kim is her son. My wife, Hannah, is on the verge of committing murder if I can't protect them. We hired a lawyer, but the legal route didn't work. It didn't stop her. Paulette got drunk last night and broke into the house before dinner. As the doctor said, Martha ended up severely burned when Paulette threw a pot of boiling water at her. Kim, the boy, has a broken arm from three weeks ago, another time Paulette visited. With each incident, I go to my chief, but he tells me his daughter was home all night with him and his wife." Her knuckles were white, her jaw set. "So you can understand why I couldn't act in an official capacity and handle things through the normal channels."

"Yeah, I do. Were you careful not to be followed here?"

"I didn't make lieutenant without knowing how to handle certain situations. I left the house alone this morning after disabling the GPS system in my personal vehicle. Another car met me outside of town where Martha and Kim were transferred to my truck. We drove to the airport where I purchased one-way tickets to three different locations for the two of them. A family member swapped vehicles with me at the airport. He drove my truck back to the house wearing my hat and sunglasses. At the midway point, another family member met me and we exchanged cars again. Tom is a distant cousin and Paulette doesn't know him. Martha, Kim, and I continued the trip. Trust me I wasn't followed, I assure you."

"I guess not with those precautions."

She smiled tightly.

"You've heard my lecture, you know this is a last-chance *extreme* option. Martha and Kim get a new life, new identities, the whole package, but they can never, ever turn back. That means your wife will *never* have contact with her sister again. She'll never know their whereabouts or know their status. Is Martha prepared for that? Is your wife?"

"Yes."

I stared at the woman before me. She was strong, able, and determined. "Okay, I'm in."

"Thank you." She pulled a thick envelop out of her pocket and handed it to me. "Here."

"What's this?"

"Money. Cash, it's all we could scrape together on short notice, but it should help her get started."

"What it doesn't cover, the government agencies or the center will. I can promise you that."

"I'd like to see her before I leave, if the doctor will let me?"

I grinned at the image of an avenging Sarah trying to prevent it. "I'll see what I can do. Come on."

THE GAME WAS already coming to an end when I reached the ballpark. The kids were running off the field and waiting for refreshments.

"I got two hits today. It was so cool." Kaitlin smiled with pride.

"Excellent. What about the rest of you?"

"I missth'd." Kylie shuffled his feet in disgust.

"Well, we'll just have to practice more. How does that sound?"

He nodded vigorously and smiled at me.

"Mikey, how about you and Taylor. How'd you do?"

"Taylor missed, but I got a base hit." He was so much like his father. I picked Taylor up and hugged her close. "Some people aren't meant to be ball players. Some are meant to be astronauts, right beautiful?"

She wrapped her arms around my neck and shook her head. "Right."

"Okay gang, I have a surprise for you, we're going to the diner to eat tonight."

"Grandma said we were going to Aunt Sarah's house. She's gonna pick us up later."

"Well, Aunt Sarah is still at work and Mi...Uncle Michael is in court, so you're all stuck with me."

A chorus rang out. "Yayyyyyy."

The four of them rallied and we proceeded to dinner. Michael would meet us as soon as court allowed. Sarah was waiting for CPS to fill out paperwork pertaining to Kim. Martha would remain in the hospital for a couple of days receiving IVs to ward off infection, and to ensure the burns were healing. Sadly the boy needed to be placed in foster care in the interim.

I had called Heath earlier and advised him to start the preparation for our anticipated residents. Hopefully, we could transfer them to the safe house as soon as Martha was strong enough to travel. The sooner we could secure them, the safer they would be.

At the diner, the kids ran up the front steps with me pacing behind them. Once we were settled in a booth, they all started talking at once and I sat back and enjoyed the show. Kaitlin and Kylie seemed to be thriving since Renee's last episode had kept her away. One more reason for me to believe she was at the root of their issues.

Chapter Twelve

FORTY MINUTES LATER, Michael and Sarah entered the diner. As they came closer, I discovered Sarah was carrying a child. "Do you have room for three more?"

"Depends on who it is." I grinned at Michael.

"Mommy, who's that?" Mikey climbed out of the booth to see the boy and kiss his father.

"This is Kim, and he's going to stay with us for a couple days." Sarah sat on the edge of the seat and gently shifted the boy in her arms. He was younger than I had thought, maybe only two years old, with big almond-shaped ebony eyes, coal black hair, and an impish grin.

"Hello there, Kim." I extended a French fry from my plate and he gripped it with his chubby little hand. "I didn't realize you were going to do this," I said as I stared at Sarah. Michael climbed in next to me and lifted Junior onto his lap. The seating was tight and I lifted Kylie onto my lap to give Michael an inch more room.

"I promised Martha I would do everything possible to keep him safe. Foster care is filled and that left the CPS facility. This little guy does not belong in the system. "Do you baby?" Sarah cooed.

Michael nudged me and stole a fry. "That's why we're late. I needed to get the judge to sign off on it before they would release Kim to Sarah's care."

Kim was gnawing on the fry, drooling all over his shirt and Sarah's arm. "He's beautiful," I said, unable to help myself. He was a gorgeous little boy with a wonderful smile and his Asian features would likely produce a very handsome man in the future.

"He is, isn't he?" Sarah clasped him closer.

"How's the arm?"

"The break was set properly, but it's not his first." Sarah shook her head. "Time will tell. He's had a rough life, haven't you big guy?" She nuzzled his face and ended up with mushy potato goop in her hair when he hugged her back.

I poked Michael with my elbow. "Let me up. We're going to get out of here so you can have your dinner and talk. I need to get these two munchkins home before Emily thinks I've abducted them." She had called moments before. The kids were all saying their good-byes when I leaned down and whispered in Sarah's ear. "You always tell me not to get hurt. That goes for you too. I love you."

She smiled. "I'll call you tomorrow to let you know Martha's status."

"Enjoy dinner everyone." I dropped money on the table for our portion of the bill and tip.

Kylie was holding my hand as we walked toward the exit. Kaitlin scrambled ahead and pushed the door open. Renee was waiting on the other side.

"I've been looking for you two. Come on, I'm taking you out for the night."

Kaitlin turned to me, her eyes wide, and I put my hand on her shoulder. "Good evening Renee. They're with me tonight. It would be better if you called Emily tomorrow to make some arrangements."

"I spoke with Emily earlier. She told me I could take them for the night."

"Let's step outside," I said. "I'll call her and if she confirms—"

"They're my kids. I don't need your damn permission."

"Kaitlin, you and Kylie get in the truck while Renee and I talk." My truck was parked by the door and I hit the button to release the door locks.

"Wait a frigging minute—"

I put my hand up to stop Renee's retort. "Go ahead you two." Kaitlin took Kylie's hand and advanced toward the truck. Renee and I followed behind. I made sure they were settled inside before I addressed her.

"First, let me say I don't want to argue with you, but you're *not* much of a mother. And more importantly, I believe you lost your license recently, so why would I let them go anywhere in a car with you?"

"They're my kids, and Emily knows I'm here."

"Okay, I'm going to call her and confirm that." I pulled my cell out and hit the speed dial for the store. Renee approached the truck to open the rear door, but I engaged the locks while waiting for the call to go through.

She banged on the roof in a fit of anger. "Damn you, give me my kids."

"Don't make me call the police," I said as I advanced closer.

"Hello. Mac—what's going on there?" Emily asked when she answered. "Are the children okay?"

"Hi Emily. Yes, they're fine. Renee is here, and she wants to take the kids with her. I explained we're on our way home, but she insisted. I wanted to touch base with you."

"Please do not give her the children. I specifically told her *no*."

"Good enough. We're on our way. Thank you."

"Do you want me to come pick them up?"

"Absolutely not. We'll just be a few minutes." I closed the phone and crossed my arms over my chest.

"I've known them their whole life," Renee argued. "I helped raise them, damn it. I have rights."

"I don't know about that nor do I care. I do know the kids are afraid of you. I know you're a drunk and I know you just lied to me. So tonight they're leaving with me. Now back up."

"God, you're such a bitch."

"Good night, Renee."

"I'm gonna make you pay, you sonofabitch." She slapped the hood of the truck before bolting away.

As soon as I climbed in the vehicle, I re-engaged the locks. "Are you two okay?"

Kylie blinked furiously, holding his sister's hand.

"Kaitlin?"

"I hate her," she said as tears formed. "Please don't make me go with her."

I reached back and gently cupped her face. "You're not going with her. Grandma told me to bring you both home because she misses you."

"Honest?"

"Cross my heart, kiddo." I gave their seatbelts a tug to be sure they were snug, and started the engine. I glanced in the mirror to find Kaitlin staring at me. "I want you both to know you can talk to me about Renee or anything else that's bothering you."

There was no response, but I caught them periodically glancing at each other throughout the ride. After I parked the truck in back, I studied them. "Do you want to talk?"

They shook their heads. "Okay, but if you change your mind, you know where I am."

We climbed the stairs and knocked at the back door before entering. Emily was in the kitchen preparing coffee.

"Well, it's about time," she said. "I was ready to come kidnap you back. I've missed you guys." She held her arms out and Kylie ran into them giggling.

"Honest?" Kaitlin asked.

"Of course. What would I do without the both of you?" Emily responded.

The girl's face transformed and she launched herself into my arms, burying her face in my shirt. I leaned down and whispered, "I told you so." She grinned and ran to her grandmother.

Emily peeked over Kaitlin's head; I shook mine.

"They wanted to come home. Renee wanted to take them for the night. They got upset." This subject needed to be discussed without the kids present.

Kylie ran back to me and snatched the bag I was carrying. "We buyed you dinner Gramma."

"You did?" She mouthed thank you and I grinned.

"Are you two hungry?"

"They better not be. I broke the bank feeding them," I said and they both giggled.

"Why don't you two sit and enjoy your milk and cookies?"

That was my cue. "Okay, I'm going to head out. You guys enjoy a wonderful evening and I'll see you tomorrow."

"I'll walk you out," Emily said.

At the door, she put her hand on my arm. "Thank you for checking with me first about the kids. I'll talk with Renee."

"You should talk with the kids first. Kaitlin told me tonight she hates Renee. There's more going on than you realize."

"Kaitlin gets upset whenever Renee drinks, that's all."

"Emily, you're kidding yourself." I stole a glance once more, letting my eyes roam from head to toe and back again. "You're *beautiful*, did I mention that?"

A smile and blush were the only response as her hand pushed a stray lock of hair back.

"Gramma?"

Emily closed her eyes, and I gazed over her shoulder.

"I sthpilled my milk."

"You're being paged." I grinned. "Lock the door and set the alarm as soon as I leave." She smiled and closed the door behind me.

"CAN YOU TAKE all the kids this afternoon after the game?" Sarah asked, batting her eyes at me across my desk. "Maybe they could even stay with you afterward for a couple hours? At least until my shift ends?"

I glanced at my planner. My only appointment was with the Wilsons. "Yeah, I'll take them today."

"Sure it's okay?"

"What about Kim?"

"I'm going to take him with me. It'll be good for Martha."

"What about Emily?"

"I'll deal with Emily, you take the kids. I'm off at six so drop them off anytime afterward. Why don't you stay for dinner."

"Why aren't I dropping her two off at the bookstore?"

"Emily had to go out of town on business. She'll be back late. The kids are staying overnight."

"Okay, but you're explaining this to her."

Sarah leaned in and kissed my cheek. "Awww, you're afraid of her? That's so cute."

AFTER THE GAME I announced to the four kids that they were spending the day with me. I yanked hard hats out of the back of the truck and used a sharpie to write their names on the front of each hat. Then we tightened the plastic straps to fit their heads. Once they were properly attired, we were off.

We pulled up to the job site as the operator was off-loading the crane from the flatbed. I climbed out of the truck and helped the kids out of their seats. The children were excited and Kylie declared he wanted to drive the crane. As we approached I found my GM, Mark Phelps, arguing with Tom Wilson.

"Afternoon gentlemen." I shook hands with both and introduced my apprentices. "Something I should know about?" I asked. Mark looked upset, while Tom Wilson appeared unruffled. We observed the crane operator as he backed the unit up and swung it around to where he would start his initial drops.

Kylie and Mikey were excited at the prospect of sitting inside the operator's seat at break time. Mark had a small son and often let him sit inside the big equipment and had offered the same to the boys. I quietly mentioned that the girls should be invited as well. Mark corrected his oversight.

"Kids, you be careful. If you get hurt I'm gonna be skinned alive." I smiled at the funny face Kylie made.

Mark took the kids to the crane, while I stayed to talk with Tom, making sure he was comfortable with the progress and to figure out what he and Mark had been arguing about.

"I didn't know you had children."

"They belong to friends, actually," I said as I glanced back to watch Mark lift each child onto the bridge of the crane.

"Yes, well I had a very interesting conversation with their mother. She informed me of something quite troubling—you're a lesbian," Tom stated.

"Their mother?" I asked.

"Yes, Renee McVee."

"How do you even know her?"

"She has frequented my establishment for years. She used to come in for business lunches."

"Ahh. So you know each other well then?" I asked. He owned The Pub, in Vail. It was a seedy little place with a poor reputation which would explain a lot—about Renee.

"No," Tom said. "Not really, but she was in last week and we had a chance to talk."

I gazed at him with new eyes. "I bet she didn't mention that she's their step-mother. Their real mother was killed and they live with their grandmother now."

"Their real mother?" he asked.

"Okay, their biological mother was killed in a car accident a year ago. Renee was her partner, which makes her a lesbian as well." I watched as the homophobic bastard absorbed my words.

"Son-of-a-bitch."

"What's the matter, Tom, she forget to mention that fact?" The man was clearly seething. "I am curious how my sexuality came into your conversation?"

"She was drinking and needed a shoulder to cry on. She mentioned she was living in Malta and I told her you were building my home here," he said defensively.

"And you were only too willing to comfort her, is that it?" I was disgusted with both of them.

"But you're not denying her allegations, are you?" He smirked.

"Frankly, my being a lesbian is not exactly part of my job description and none of your business. Is that a problem?"

"Honestly yes. I don't like associating with your people."

His ignorance astounded me. A couple of weeks before, I might have let him unnerve me. But not now—not today. "Well, then I think we should cease doing business. What do you say?"

"I don't approve—"

"I don't really give a damn."

Mark returned with the kids. I whispered to Kaitlin to take the others and wait in the truck for me. I focused on Mark. "Here's the deal. Effective four o'clock, I am no longer paying your salaries. Work out a contract with Wilson directly. Understood?"

"What the hell is going on here?" Mark scowled. "I warned you, you jackass." He directed his comment to Tom.

"And I told you I won't do business with her kind of people," was Tom's pithy response.

Mark's eyes bounced from me to Tom Wilson. I shrugged. "And I told you, she's a damn expert in her field, a reliable architect, a responsible naturalist, and a dedicated planner."

"I won't deal with her deviant ways," Tom said with a glare.

"Wilson, I'll send you my bill. It's net thirty," I said. I shook hands with Mark and walked to the truck.

TWO DAYS LATER I was opening the mail Mary had left when I found the courthouse envelope. It was a subpoena. *Crap.* I'd been called to testify in the Geoffrey Allison trial on Thursday. Based on experience, I had little or no faith in the legal system. Beforehand, I was ordered to meet with the prosecutor and go over my testimony.

Randy Cartwright insisted we rehearse. He feared my temper and I couldn't exactly blame him. He insisted I keep my answers short and to the point. That I *talk* to the jury and try to make a connection with them.

The case would be simple, he assured me. The charges were assault with a deadly weapon, attempted murder, and criminal trespass which were all related to his visit to the hospital and had nothing to do with his wife's assault, since she clearly could not be a witness. I knew Randy was worried about me, more specifically my connection to the center, but I couldn't see how that would impact this case. Only time would tell.

THURSDAY MORNING I dressed for court by putting on my good gray suit with a black silk T-shirt underneath. I thought it showed respect and dignified the whole judicial process. After driving to the next town, Leadville, I checked in with the court clerk, then sat on the bench outside the courtroom waiting to be called.

Cindy Jeffries arrived shortly afterward and sat with me. "I hate this waiting," she said. "Why is it taking so long?"

"Relax, there's not a lot you can contribute," I said. "Only that he hit you and you heard him say he intended to kill Patti." I clutched her icy cold hand. Cindy didn't want to see him. She was afraid. Randy had tried to assure her, but it didn't appear to have worked. "Whatever you do, don't look at him unless you're asked to identify him. Otherwise, stare at the prosecution table or glance at the jury." I rubbed her hand between mine, trying to warm it.

A bailiff came to the door. "Mackenzie Taylor. Hey, Mac, you're up."

The courtroom was packed as I made my way inside. I was curious as to who would be interested in this trial and why. Other than Mr. Patchlouge, the owner of the *Chronicle*, the local paper, I couldn't imagine. Randy Cartwright sat at the prosecution table sifting through some paperwork. Across the aisle was the dandy defending Geoffrey Allison. He had a be an outsider or I would have recognized him. They were chuckling between themselves, arrogant and cocky. Judge Williams and I made eye contact and I saw a pained expression cross his features. He shook his head and glanced away, not wanting to appear sympathetic. I walked up to the front and waited to take the witness chair and be sworn in. The jury was made up of acquaintances and friends, people who valued life and understood loss. My oath taken, I sat but remained alert.

Randy Cartwright, the prosecutor, started off slowly, I assumed to set the scene. "On the evening in question, you received a call from Heath Bachman, of the crisis center, that Mercy wanted a counselor for a patient, is that correct?"

"Yes."

"Is this unusual?"

"No."

"Without getting into specifics did you meet with the patient."

"Yes."

"Can you tell us what time that was?"

"Approximately midnight, give or take a bit."

"What happened next?"

"Objection, Your Honor, the witness can not provide details about a patient that we are not privy to cross-examine, and to date we have not been able to locate said patient." Davis was tapping his pen against the top of the table.

"Your Honor, Ms. Taylor is strictly going to detail her actions and exchanges with the defendant." Randy calmly replied.

"I'll allow it, but be careful Counselor." Judge Williams said. "Overruled."

Randy walked to the front of the prosecution table, closer to the jury. "What happened next?"

"The patient I was seeing had been admitted, and was going to be monitored overnight because of her medical condition." I looked at the jury. "She was pregnant and the doctors were concerned for the safety of her child." The story had been in all the papers. It was my fervent hope that the jurors would be able to put two and two together.

"Why did you stay with her?" Randy walked back to his desk.

"Objection, prejudicial?"

"Sustained." The Judge responded. "Rephrase the question."

"Ms. Taylor, without getting into privileged details, can you tell us why you were still at the hospital almost two hours later?"

"The woman had some concerns, so her brother and I agreed to stay with her until the doctors released her the next day." I said.

"Objection. Unless her brother intends to be a witness, this testimony is unsubstantiated." Davis said.

"Mr. Chester, the brother, is on our new witness list, Your Honor," Randy confirmed.

Davis objected again, there was a sidebar with both sides heatedly presenting arguments, then the Judge had them step back. "Overruled."

"What happened next?"

"We all dozed off in the room. I was awakened to a loud commotion out in the hallway. I woke the patient's brother and walked to the door." I turned to the jury. "There was a lot of noise and yelling going on, then some screams and a loud crash. I instructed the patient and her brother to hide. I called the operator and told her to get security and the police to the ER as soon as possible. Then I climbed in the patient's bed and waited."

Randy walked around the prosecution desk. "What happened next?"

"There were still some loud noises and yelling going on, but then someone tried to open the door to the room I was in. The door handle was rattled repeatedly. I had locked it earlier that evening. Shortly afterward, Mr. Allison, the defendant, kicked it in and waved a gun at me."

"Did he say anything to you?"

"He asked me," I turned to the Judge first, then the jury and started again. "He asked who the fuck I was."

"What did you say?"

"I told him my name and asked his."

"What happened next?"

"Well he had this pistol, a semi-automatic, and he kept wielding it around the room. He stepped further into the room, apparently searching for something or someone. He walked to the bed and grabbed my wrist, the next thing I knew the security guards were there and he was on the ground, secured."

"Are you telling me you have no knowledge of how Mr. Allison was injured?"

"No, I'm saying I'm not sure. And I'm not sure he *was* hurt." I swung back toward the jury. "It happened very quickly. His gun was pointed at me and he was angry, yelling. I was afraid he was going to shoot me. I don't remember much beyond that. Security showed up, there *was* a short scuffle, and they apprehended him. The end happened very swiftly."

"What happened next?"

"The security guards took possession of the gun Mr. Allison was brandishing and secured his hands with plastic ties. The patient's brother stayed with her while I went to the nurses' station. I wanted someone to examine her after all the commotion."

"And?"

"I couldn't find anyone. Mr. Allison had locked them in the medicine closet. One of the doctors, Cindy Jeffries, had been knocked unconscious during her confrontation with him."

"Objection hearsay, Your Honor." Davis said.

"Sustained."

"Just tell us what you saw." Randy stated.

"There was no-one at the nurses' station. I heard voices coming from down the hall. I found the key and opened the medicine closet. Three nurses, Dr. Jeffries. and a candy striper were all inside. Dr. Jeffries was unconscious on the floor and bleeding. She was subsequently moved to an exam room, just *one* of the victims of Mr. Allison's assault that night. Doctor Downs was called in to treat her."

"Objection, misleading." Davis popped up.

"Your Honor, the answers are regarding the assault at the hospital, and there was more than one." Randy said.

"Overruled." Judge Williams responded.

"No further questions." Randy Cartwright returned to the prosecution table.

"Good afternoon, Ms. Taylor," the defense attorney began.

The asswipe introduced himself as Harrison Davis, like I gave a fuck.

"Did you know my client before the night in question?"

"No."

"Yet, you dislike him, correct?"

"I dislike any person who abuses those weaker than themselves."

Davis turned to the Judge. "Your Honor, move to strike. This requires a yes or no response."

"Please restrict your answers to yes or no." Judge Williams advised.

"Did you witness my client threatening any nurses?"

"No."

"Did you witness the alleged attack on Doctor Jeffries?"

My stomach tightened. "No."

"Ms. Taylor, did my client threaten you?" Davis was standing behind the defense table.

"No—unless you count the gun he pointed at me?"

"Your Honor, please." Davis was losing his temper.

"You opened the door counselor. I'll allow it," the judge responded.

"Objection, Your Honor, the witness was specifically instructed to give yes and no responses."

"Rephrase the question then." Judge Williams was losing his patience.

"Ms. Taylor, did my client attack you, physically?"

"Yes."

"Yes? You mean you were injured that night?"

"He grabbed my arm and twisted it without my permission."

That threw the bastard off his stride. He glared at me and returned to the desk and started shuffling papers. "Ms. Taylor, are you saying—" Davis looked up, then came around the desk to sit on the corner. "Let me begin again. You didn't actually witness any of the *alleged* abuse on hospital staff, did you?" Davis asked.

"I saw him kick a hospital door in and wield a gun. That's not alleged and it's certainly assault."

"Your Honor, permission to treat the witness as hostile."

The Judge looked at me, then Randy, who never blinked. "Granted."

"Ms. Taylor, did my client threaten you directly?"

"Yes."

"You've already testified you did not know my client before the night in question, is that right?"

"Yes."

"Then he would have no reason to attack you, correct."

"Yes, but he did."

"You didn't actually witness anything untoward against the hospital staff that evening, did you?"

I raised my voice slightly. "I witnessed the result of his attack."

"Your Honor, please remind the witness to answer yes or no."

"Just answer the questions." Judge Williams admonished.

The defense attorney took a step closer. "I'll repeat the question, did you observe the alleged attacks?"

"I discovered Doctor Jeffries—"

"Just yes or no, Ms. Taylor." Davies interrupted.

"Doctor Jeffries was on the floor of the medicine room, unconscious and being attended by the head nurse and two others—"

"Objection, Your Honor. Please—"

"They were locked inside. We needed a key to open the door. They didn't do that to themselves." I was talking to the jury and ignoring everyone else.

"Move to strike." Davis was losing his temper and so was I.

"Objection, Your Honor, the response was on point." Randy responded.

"Sidebar, Your Honor." Davis stormed to the bench, Randy followed. After a short conference, the Judge ruled. "Objection sustained."

Davis returned to the defense table and opened a file. He was flipping papers and finally leaned back in the chair. "Who is Heath Bachman?"

"He works for the crisis center." I sat up more alert.

"Your crisis center, isn't that right?"

"The crisis center is for any woman in need."

"Ms. Taylor, you have a direct connection with the crisis center, isn't that true?"

I felt my temper flare. "I beg your pardon?"

"Objection, what does this have to do with the evidence presented?" Randy was on his feet and staring at me.

"Counselor?" The Judge asked.

"I intend to show that this witness is prejudiced, and therefore, her testimony will unfairly taint the evidence." Davis had remained seated.

"I'll allow it." Judge Williams was not happy. "Be very sure you don't go beyond the scope or the court won't be so agreeable the next time."

"Do you need me to repeat the question?" It was clear the asswipe was feeling cocky.

"Yes." I said.

"It's a simple question. Are you affiliated with the crisis center? You're a successful architect. I'm sure it's not about the money."

"I don't see how that's relevant to your client attacking hospital personnel."

"Your Honor, please advise the witness she's under oath."

Judge Williams stared at me. We knew each other well, and I could see the compassion in his eyes, but his voice belied that. "Answer the question, Ms. Taylor."

"Yes."

"In what capacity?" Davis was after something, Randy had been right regarding his concern about my connection with the crisis center.

"I *volunteer* there."

"How very nice," Davis said as he studied the paperwork. "Any other reason?" He sat back in his chair, a smug expression plastered on his face.

"Nope."

"Ms. Taylor, that would be the Isabella and Bella Sanchez Women's Crisis Center, correct?" Davis asked.

"Objection." Randy Cartwright jumped up from his seat. "What's the relevance, Your Honor?"

"Your Honor, I intend to prove this witness is biased and detrimentally representing the facts." Davis was on his feet as well.

"Overruled." Judge Williams glared at Davis. "Remember Counselor, you reap what you sow. Be careful."

I glared at the jackass.

"Ms. Taylor do you need me to repeat the question?" Davis asked.

Fuck. "That's correct." *I hated this prick.*

"And isn't it true that the center was named after your dead lesbian," he drew the word out for full effect, "lover, Ms. Sanchez, and her child, who was killed some years ago, by her ex-husband?"

I stared at him, refusing to engage the asshole.

"Objection," Randy Cartwright said as he stood again.

"What grounds?" Judge Williams asked.

"Relevance, Your Honor. This has nothing to do with the

evidence." Randy blinked rapidly.

"Your Honor, I'm trying to show the jury that there's a personal issue at stake for this witness. That she's prejudiced against my client." Davis sat back gloating.

"Overruled. You may answer the question."

I remained mute.

"Your Honor, please," Davis said.

Judge Williams stared at me. He wasn't happy. "Answer the question."

"No sir."

"Your Honor," Davis called from his chair.

"Ms. Taylor, answer the question or I'll hold you in contempt." Judge Williams was a gentleman from the old school and played by the rules.

"I'm sorry, Your Honor, but I'm not going to discuss a personal tragedy so that Mr. Davis can paint a tainted picture of the events the night Mr. Allison attacked and threatened the staff at the hospital—"

Davis was on his feet. "Objection. Move to strike."

"He brandished a gun, assaulted a doctor, threatened a nurse and myself with it," I continued over the objection. My voice rose, I wanted to make my point to the jury and I wanted them to understand the facts, not some idiot attorney's misrepresentation of them.

Davis strode to the bench. "Objection. Your Honor."

"He hit Doctor Jeffries with the butt of his pistol and she sustained a concussion. He threatened a couple of nurses, he broke into a patient's room, he pointed the gun at me." I said. I was on my feet yelling directly to the jury so I could be heard over the defense counsel's objections.

"Your Honor, I want this entire testimony stricken from the record." Davis was furious.

Randy Cartwright was also on his feet and had objected to the entire line of questioning.

The pounding of the gavel echoed off the walls. "Order. I want order. Sit down all of you," the judge commanded. "Mac, answer the question or I'll hold you in contempt."

I studied him. "With all due respect, sir, I will not discuss my family."

Judge Williams knew the history. He knew what had happened to Isabella and the baby. He felt a certain amount of guilt because he had refused us a restraining order, claiming there were no grounds. Three days later, my family was dead.

He rapped the gavel. "Ms. Taylor, answer the question."

"There's no relevance, sir. That man used a gun to scare and injure a doctor and three nurses, and to threaten me. That's what this case is about. *Not* my family."

"Your Honor, this is beyond contemptible." Attorney Davis was livid.

"I will have you taken into custody." Judge Williams implored.

"I can't."

"Bailiff, arrest Ms. Taylor."

I rose with my wrists out. John Marshall cuffed me and I was escorted from the courtroom through a side entrance.

The bailiff and I were old friends. "Mac, why didn't you answer the damn question?"

I shrugged, but he knew why. They all knew the facts of the case. It had been the big story for about a month after it happened. News people, photographers, TV cameras, the incident with me punching the news anchor. *I felt like it had happened yesterday.*

The reporter had stuck his damn microphone in my face and asked me how I felt about everything. *How the fuck did he think I felt?* I had just buried my wife and daughter. I had tried to walk away, fought to ignore him, but he wouldn't let it go. He pushed for the *big* story. He had asked if I thought Izzy and Bella were being punished because of our lifestyle. I broke his jaw.

After my story took a back seat to another family's tragedy, everyone went back to their lives. I, on the other hand, went home to an empty house and my memories.

John took me to the only holding cell in the courthouse, opened the door and un-cuffed me. I took a seat on the cot. "Can I call anyone for you?" he asked.

Who to call? It wasn't the money, but the nuisance. "How long do you think he'll keep me?"

"Hard to say."

"Any chance I can use my phone?"

He gave me a thumbs up and strolled out of the cell without locking the door. They hadn't processed me and I wasn't sure whether they would. My phone was in my pocket. I should call Emily. She would need to make arrangements for the kids. I thought of calling Sarah, but she would only raise hell. She had never forgiven the judge or the system for refusing the RO to Isabella in the first place. I feared this could be the last straw for her. I dropped the phone back into my pocket. There was no sense upsetting everyone and I'd slept in worse places.

I sat back on the cot and rested against the brick wall, recalling the week leading up to Isabella's death.

It had been such a crazy time. The business had won a new contract. Personally, we were happy and Isabella and the baby were thriving. Then one morning Izzy made the mistake of going into town for groceries, something she had done a thousand times before without consequence. The local store had gotten a delivery from a giant food chain. The tractor-trailer was parked out front while the driver had waited patiently in the cab for the foodstuffs to be unloaded by the store's employees. Izzy hadn't seen him when she arrived at the store, but he had seen her. They had been married previously, a bad situation made worse once she got pregnant. He had beaten her and she lost their child. Two months later she left him, but not before he had brutalized her, promising to kill her. She relocated across country from Philadelphia, Pennsylvania to Leadville, Colorado, a town located seven miles from Malta, and my home. We had met about thirteen months after her escape. The attraction between us had been mutual and instantaneous.

Juan Sanchez accosted Isabella outside the store as she exited. She had managed to pull free and drive to my office. We had tried everything to get him arrested, but he had done nothing to warrant it. Judge Williams told us to relax, he'd have the police talk to Juan. The judge had been adamant that Juan was most likely surprised to see Izzy again after all this time. *No one* had believed she was in danger. Things like that didn't happen here.

I was pulled from my memories by Sarah's big mouth. I heard her yelling, and shortly afterward, she was shown to my cell. "Hi." I smiled ruefully.

"I can't freakin' believe he had you arrested. Is he out of his goddamned mind?"

"He didn't have a choice." Sarah was dressed in her blue scrubs and white lab coat. "How did you find out anyway?" I asked. "I didn't make any calls."

She flushed crimson and I realized her father, Judge Williams, had called her. There were tears in her eyes.

"I didn't give him an option." I gathered her in my arms to comfort her. "Don't be mad."

"He's keeping you until witness statements are complete or you rethink your testimony."

She knew better. I wouldn't change my mind. Discussing Isabella was a rare event. Discussing her death was out of the question. "I'm fine. Go home, Sarah."

"I've posted bond for you, but he won't renege on the order. I'm sorry. He said it wouldn't look right."

"Go home. I'm fine." I pulled her closer. I loved her with all my heart and I respected her father. "I'll pay you back as soon as I get out of here."

"Do you need anything? Should I call Emily?"

"No! Don't tell her, please. The kids are going to need a ride home from the ball field though."

"I'll pick them up."

"Thank you, and don't worry about me. I love you."

JUDGE WILLIAMS ENTERED the cell that evening and sat beside me. I didn't bother to look up. I already knew he was disappointed. He had been like a father to me all those years and I knew he was hurting.

"I'm disappointed," he said.

"I'm sorry, sir."

"You tied my hands, young lady."

I could see he was struggling. "I'm not upset, sir. I knew what would happen if I refused, and we both knew I would."

He sighed.

"What happened after I left?"

"I can't discuss the case."

"Can you at least tell me if Cindy was okay?"

"Cynthia was fine as were the other witnesses."

"Good."

"Will you be all right here?"

"Yes sir. I'm fine." I smiled at him. He was a good man. It wasn't his fault. He was only one cog in the wheel of the misbegotten legal system. I refused to blame him.

"Well I'm going to visit my daughter and beg for mercy. She's not quite as forgiving as you are."

I laughed out loud. "Do you know when I'm getting out, sir?"

"Yes. With no further witnesses, closing arguments begin first thing tomorrow morning. How's nine o'clock, after the shift change?"

"That's fine, sir. Thank you. You have a good evening."

After he left, I sat and thought about how good he had been to me. He had always accepted me and my sexuality without question. Even though he was of the old school, he never made me feel uncomfortable or odd. I spent the majority of my teen years living in his house. He taught me the finesse of woodworking, for which I would always be indebted to him. After Izzy and the baby had been killed, his guilt had been palpable. He almost resigned from the bench. It hadn't helped that Sarah blamed him. It would have been so easy to blame him or blame the police, but the bottom line was it was my job to protect my family. I was the one who failed Izzy and Bella. No one else.

THE NEXT MORNING the judge himself strolled into the cell to tell me I was free to leave. I saw the circles under his eyes. Sarah must have given him a hard time. "She'll calm down, sir, she always does. She's too protective of me."

"She's pretty irate, even asked me not to come to the barbeque tomorrow." The judge appeared older than his years.

"I'm sorry, sir. I'll talk to her."

I STEPPED OUT into bright sunshine when I left the courthouse. It had been a long night. I was tired and needed a shower. The guard on duty had brought me a burger and fries for dinner. Later we'd watched TV on his little six-inch portable. They had done everything possible to make sure I was comfortable. I pulled my cell out and dialed Sarah.

"Are you all right?" she asked.

"I'm fine, and stop treating your father like he's the bad guy. You know better."

"He makes me so mad. There's never any gray area for him. It's either black or white."

"And that's what makes him a good judge. Now call him and apologize."

"You know I'm right."

"Sarah."

"All right."

"How's Martha? Can I transfer her and Kim yet?"

"She's receiving the last of the IV antibiotics today. She'll be ready for release Sunday as long as her fever doesn't come back, but I'll need to see her in ten days to remove the bandages and check the burns."

"Thanks. I'll plan on transferring her Sunday morning. Kim, too."

"You're picking her up?"

"Yeah. Heath has the weekend off so I'm in charge."

"She could come and stay with me."

"No. She *can't* and you know why. Now go call your dad and make nice."

"Are you coming over tomorrow?"

"I can't Sarah. I'm really backed up and after yesterday it will be worse. I'm on my way to the office now."

"Stop by if you want, even if it's only to get a burger."

"KNOCK, KNOCK."

I saw Emily in the doorway. "Hi, how are you?"

"Good. I was wondering if we could talk, but you're busy," she said.

"Sit. I just got here really. Other than a shower nothing is urgent."

"Are you just getting in from last night?" She took a seat in front of the desk, and I sat beside her in the other arm chair.

"In a manner of speaking, yeah. What can I do for you?"

"Nothing, this was a mistake." Emily leaped up and I did the same.

"Damn it, Emily. Okay, so you heard about me being in jail. The least you could do is listen to why. I thought you knew me better."

Emily spun back around. "Jail?"

"You didn't know?"

"No."

"Why are you here?"

"You first," she said.

"What?"

"*Why* were you in jail?"

I sighed. "I had to testify in court yesterday."

"Go on."

I shoved my hands in my pockets. Tears rushed up out of my depths and I brushed at them with the sleeve of my suit jacket.

Emily came to me, took my hand, and pulled me toward the couch. We sat side by side with her holding my hand between hers. "Go slow. Take your time."

I couldn't look at her. "This was the guy who beat his pregnant wife. Later he showed up at the hospital with a gun and hit the doctor, if you recall. His asswipe defense lawyer tried to make it an issue that I run the crisis center." I picked at a thread on my pant leg. "The Isabella and Bella Sanchez Women's Crisis Center to be exact. That my lesbian lover and her daughter were victims years ago."

Emily gasped. "Oh Mac."

"Yeah, he was a real friggin' hero. I guess he thought if he took the onus off his client and questioned my integrity, the jury would forget the real issue, which was attempted murder and assault with a deadly weapon on the staff at the hospital." My voice rose as my temper climbed.

"Wait a minute. You run the center? I thought you were a volunteer." Emily seemed perplexed.

"My management company runs it, and I do volunteer."

"Management com—never mind." She shook her head. "What happened next?"

I shrugged my shoulders and gave her a weak smile. "I refused to discuss it. I don't talk about Isabella or the baby. Very few people know the details regarding the abduction and their murder and I wasn't going to let him use them as pawns to help his fuc-, ahhh client."

She brushed the hair out of my eyes. "And?"

"You know how these court things are. Prosecution objects, asswipe counters and the judge rules. In this case, he told me to answer the questions. I refused," I said.

"What did the judge do?"

"He warned me I would be in contempt. I told him I would not discuss my wife and baby." I glanced at Emily. "They took me into custody."

"That son-of-a-bitch. What did any of that have to do with this case?"

I grinned. I had never seen her temper before.

"Why didn't you call me?" she asked.

"I thought about it. I even started to dial the phone, but I didn't want to upset you." She seemed hurt. "I didn't know when they'd release me."

"That's ridiculous. He had no right, no right at all." Her eyes were stormy. "Mac, I'm so sorry."

"Are you mad at me?"

"No," Emily sighed.

"Why are you here?"

"I wanted to talk to you about the other night."

"Ahhh. I guess I shouldn't have said what I said to you."

"What?"

"That I find you beautiful."

"No." Emily shook her head as her cheeks colored. "That's not it at all. I thought we should discuss Renee."

"Then let me be honest, I don't like her."

"She wants to be a bigger part of the children's lives. She—"

I sighed inwardly. "Emily, that woman is scaring the crap out of your grandchildren and whether you admit it or not, they don't like her."

She turned to face me. "She was Melanie's partner. My daughter would never have stayed in the relationship if Renee endangered those children."

"But Melanie's not here anymore. And there's a reason she appointed you *sole* guardian. Think about it."

Emily sighed.

"Does this bigger role include paying support? Does she even work? Seriously Emily, Renee is a drunk, and those kids hate her."

"She lost her job shortly after Melanie died. The drinking had gotten out of hand again." Emily said. "That's why she followed me here from Vail. She lost everything there. Melanie, her job, their house. The kids."

"That's tough and part of me sympathizes, but it doesn't change the fact the kids are afraid of her.

"I need to think." She rubbed her forehead.

I waited.

"Mac — will you ever tell me about your family?"

"The details are horrific. Are you up to that?" I gazed directly at her.

"No, but I'd like to understand you better."

"Okay." I took her hand in mine. "But not today. It's too beautiful out to think about that or talk of such things. We will though, I promise."

"Thank you."

Chapter Thirteen

I RAPPED SOFTLY on the door of room three-fourteen and slowly pushed inward with my foot. "Hello. Martha? Are you up for some company?"

"Yes, totally."

"Mama!"

Little Kim opened his arms, stretching forward trying to get to this mother. I held my squirming little package tighter. "Are you allowed to hold him yet?"

"Yes, my arms are healing. It's only my left thigh that's still blistered."

I gently placed Kim in his mother's arms. "Ohhh baby boy, I've missed you so much." She nuzzled his neck and clasped him tightly.

Martha stared at me. "These last eight days were the longest of my life. I was so worried about him until Doctor Downs told me she obtained temporary custody pending my discharge."

"Speaking of your release, I understand today's the big day?"

"I'm waiting for the nurse to give me the homecare instructions. Doctor Downs has already been in and said I need to see her in a week."

"Good, I'm glad."

"Am I allowed to ask you if preparations have been made for us yet? I haven't heard from the gentleman—Heath, is it?"

Kim tugged his mother's auburn hair, shoving the ends into his mouth. I quickly handed her his pacifier. "Yes, you can ask. That's why I'm here. You're coming with me today and staying temporarily at my house. It's equipped with a top-of-the-line security system and far enough away that no one bothers to visit."

"That's so sad."

I chuckled unexpectedly. "No, it's fine and I was mostly teasing you."

"Oh, sorry. I'd be lost without my friends and family."

"Martha, that could be a real problem. You do realize that is exactly what's going to happen. You can never contact any of them again if you want to remain safe."

"Yes." She blinked away tears that were beginning to form. "I know, but I have to keep my baby boy safe, no matter what."

"Good."

"Unfortunately when Christine came up with this plan, there

was no time for me to gather clothes or supplies for him or myself. I—"

My hand shot out. "Don't worry. It's all been taken care of. There's a week's worth of supplies in my truck for Kim along with clothing and a couple of packages for you at the house. If there's anything we've forgotten, make a list, we can always get it for you later."

"Also my money is tied up in the bank. I'm afraid to access it for fear my ex will find me. Christine did tell you about Paulette's father right?"

"Yes."

"Paulette always displayed a temper, but this past year I think she's had some kind of psychotic break. She's become aggressive. I know this is an extreme step, running away, but I don't know what else to do."

"It is a drastic act, but if you know my history you understand the alternative could result in dire consequences. Christine told me how close you and your sister are. I imagine this will be hard on the both of you."

"Hannah, that's my sister, is furious. She's been very supportive throughout the breakup. She's almost as frightened of Paulette as I am."

"That's perfectly normal."

"I—"

"Okay Martha, we're all set," the young nurse, Stacey, said as she entered the room. "Here's a prescription for pain medicine." She laid it on the table. "Doctor Downs had it filled downstairs in the pharmacy for you." Stacey pulled two sheets of paper off her clipboard. "These are your home care instructions and here is a phone number if you should experience any unusual seepage or bleeding." Stacey placed the instructions with the prescription. "I need you to sign here, here, and initial there. Then hop in the wheelchair and we can get you the heck out of here."

"Stacey, we're going to take the service elevator downstairs and leave out the back." I interjected. "My truck is parked at the loading dock."

"Okay." She didn't ask, but the question dangled in the air.

Martha handed Kim to me and signed the appropriate lines on the documents.

"Stacey, please make sure that binder is put in Doctor Downs office and the door locked. The formalities will be handled through the center."

"Gotcha. I'll do it personally." It was clearly a light bulb moment. "You take care of yourself and this adorable little guy." She took Kim's hand in hers and shook it gently. "If you need anything, don't hesitate to call the number on the sheet."

"YOU WEREN'T KIDDING about living remotely," Martha said, "I'm not sure I'd ever find my way home in the dark." Martha was surveying the landscape as we traveled up the mountain.

"Told ya." I grinned. "Wait until we get closer. I've planted so many shrubs and trees that if you don't already know where the driveway is, you'd never find the house."

"Christine told me about your family. I'm very sorry."

"Don't be, but don't allow yourself to become a victim." I swerved onto the dirt path that, at a glance, seemed to be a deer track. The native shale did an impressive job of hiding any tire tracks, and the overgrown vegetation further obliterated the narrow corridor through the woods.

"I don't know how to thank you," Martha said. "This is very kind of you to take us into your home."

"Currently the safe house is empty, but more importantly there's no security system there. That's about to be changed, but in the meantime I felt this was the best alternative."

"Whatever you think. You're the expert and we're relying on you."

A shudder viscerally torqued my insides and I found myself driving white-knuckled. Isabella had relied on me, too. That failure could not be repeated. "Here we are."

After climbing out of the truck, I collected Kim and the bags Sarah had packed for him from the back seat.

"I can take him."

"After we get inside," I said. "I've got him for now." She limped slightly and I didn't want to stress her leg any more than we already had. "Once we get you settled, I'll make us some lunch. I'm not much of a cook, but if you don't mind omelets and toast, I can whip that up easily."

"Hey, I'm a great cook." She grinned. "I'd be more than happy to help out with that while I'm here."

"My stomach will be eternally grateful." I opened the door and let Martha enter first.

"This is gorgeous. I love the post and beam architecture."

"Thanks. We bought the property because the barn out back was already there. We fell in love with the rustic openness of it and the exposed beams and we decided to utilize that design in the house. Isabella loved the end result."

"You still miss her."

"She was my soul mate in every sense of the word." We wandered through the great room to the other end of the house.

"Right down this hall is the guest room. It's got its own bath, and I've set up a crib for this little guy."

"This is incredible. I may never want to leave." I glanced around trying to see my home through her eyes. A queen-size bed was against the wall. It was hand-crafted from logs and stained dark walnut, like the rest of the furniture in the room. Isabella had created a seating area near the small fireplace and windows so guests would be comfortable. She spent months searching for the perfect side chairs and placed them opposite each other facing the fireplace.

I put Kim on the area rug with a few toys from the bag Sarah had provided. "The floors have radiant heat, so he'll be fine playing there." I pointed to the wall just inside the doorway. "There's the thermostat for this room if you get cold," I pointed to the next unit. "Here's the intercom if you need me, but remember it can be heard throughout the house, so if you're frightened, use caution with it." Next I showed her the largest controller, hanging immediately above the light switch. "This is the panel for the security system. This button here will set off the alarm and alert police. If anything frightens you hit it and lock yourself in. There's a panel in every room, just in case."

"May I ask you something?"

"Of course."

"With this type of security, how did your family get abducted?"

"Malta is a small town. You know your neighbors. You know who drinks, who cheats, and who gambles. We didn't know there was danger lurking. After Juan approached my wife, we knew we had to take precautionary steps. We ordered the security system the same day, but it wasn't installed until a week after her death."

"I'm so sorry."

I shook my head, unable to respond.

"This room is amazing, I can feel myself starting to relax already. Thank you so much."

"I'll leave you to freshen up and get settled. Those bags on the bed are for you. I'll be in the den, which is off the kitchen." I started to leave the room, then remembered. "The baby monitor is set up and, with your permission, I'll take the hand-held with me in case you need help. I could even watch Kim for you if you wanted to take a nap?"

"Absolutely." Martha handed me the remote for the monitor. "Take this, but I think you're right. I'm a little tired and it's past time for Kim's nap. I'll settle him down and lie down myself. Have I said thank you?"

"Yes, you did. Rest well."

MONDAY MORNING I was up before the sun and rolled out
of bed to a definite nip in the air. A surprising frost had hit the
mountain during the night and high winds were driving the
dampness through the house. I pulled on the jeans I'd worn the day
before and a T-shirt and proceeded to the great room to start a fire.
Coffee would have to wait. An hour later I was sipping my first cup
and enjoying the warmth from the fireplace.

"Good morning."

I spun on the stool at the breakfast counter. "Hi, how'd you
sleep?"

"Like a rock. I didn't even dream last night." Martha said.

"Here let me take him." I reached out for Kim.

"Thank you." Martha looked rested, but it was clear she needed
more.

I tilted my head in the direction of the kitchen. "Coffee is fresh.
Get yourself some and I'll get him some juice."

"What would you like for breakfast?"

I glanced at Martha and grinned. "You're not required to cook
for me."

"I want to. It's the least I can do."

"In that case, the chef gets to decide."

"Let me check and see what's here. I'll let you know what our
options are." She drifted to the cabinets and fridge to explore while
I poured juice for Kim.

He settled on my lap with his juice. "Can I ask you a question?"
I inquired.

Martha was pouring her cup of coffee and looked up at me. "I
think that's fair considering the circumstances."

"Is your partner Kim's other parent?"

She smirked. "Unless you know something I don't, Paulette
truly is a woman."

"Walked right into that one, didn't I?" I chuckled. "I meant
legally?"

"No." She shook her head. "I started the adoption process for
Kim three years ago after I visited an orphanage in China. Paulette
and I met a year ago, after everything was finalized in the courts
and about a month after I had brought him home."

"Good."

"Why?"

"Well, this way she can't try to charge you with abduction. He's
your son, not hers."

"I never thought of that."

"It's one less thing you'll need to worry about."

Martha reached in a cabinet. "How does chocolate chip pancakes sound."

"Like heaven, but are you sure? I do make a mean omelet."

"Please, I cook because I love it. It's relaxing."

I wiped Kim's chin with a napkin. "Woodworking is like that for me. I get so totally involved that I block out everything else."

"I'll make his breakfast first, if that's okay."

"That's fine, isn't it little guy?" I held the cup for him while he drank more of his juice. "Later I need to run to the workshop out back to get my laptop. I'll be working from here this week."

Martha mixed the ingredients for oatmeal and set it on the stove to cook. She was busy mixing the pancake batter and folding in the chips when she said. "You don't need to stay with us. I can't imagine Paulette has sobered up long enough to discover I'm even gone. With the precautions Christine took, I doubt she can trace me here."

"Nah, getting my laptop and files will take all of five minutes. After that I'm here for the long haul." Kim was carrying on an entire conversation, waving his arms and banging a spoon on the granite countertop. I chortled at his antics. "Besides, Kim and I are going to play cars later, right little guy?"

"Kim will enjoy that, won't you sweetie?"

The boy gurgled at his mother's use of his name, a big grin stretching across his beautiful little face. "So what was your occupation before all this happened?"

"I'm a CPA."

"Good. That's general enough for you to continue that profession if you choose to do so."

"But all my certifications have my name on them."

"We can work around—" A knock at the front door surprised us. Martha's eyes went wide and I put my hand up. "No one knows you're here. It's perfectly safe." I slid off the stool ready to hand Kim to his mother, when he called out. "Kele." He stretched with his arms open. My eyes shifted to where he was looking. "Told you. It's a friend and her grandson."

Emily was on the front porch with Kylie. I grasped the handle and pulled the door open. "What a nice surprise."

"Kele." Kim was struggling to get down.

"Kim. Hi." Kylie laughed at the boy.

Emily's eyes flitted from Kim to me. "I'm sorry, I didn't realize you had company. I should have called."

"No. It's all right."

"Grandma, can I play with Kim?"

"I—" Emily hesitated.

"Come on in. We were about to have breakfast."

Kylie ran through the door and I put Kim down. They entered the great room and started to play with Kim's toys. "Please?" I pulled the door wider. Emily entered.

"Where's Kaitlin?"

"She has a play date with Janice."

Martha was flipping pancakes as we approached. "Martha, this is my friend Emily, and that's her grandson Kylie, or Kele as Kim calls him. Emily, this is Martha she's —"

"Martha, why on earth are you cooking with those injuries?" Emily addressed Martha, but glared at me.

"I offered —" Both women ignored me.

"It looks worse than it is and I wanted to do this. You'll stay won't you?"

Emily strode around the breakfast bar and began opening cupboards. "I'll set the table."

"I'll make more coffee," I said, feeling as if I should be doing something.

Martha was stacking pancakes and draining bacon. "I'm going to feed Kim in here. He can't sit in a chair so I need to be able to hold him."

"Wait, wait one minute." As I aimed for the basement, Kylie sidetracked me.

"Can I come wifth you?"

"Of course you can. I need a helper." He grinned and I called over my shoulder, "Can you ladies keep an eye on Kim?"

Emily went into the great room and picked him up as we started down the stairs.

In the far corner of the basement, I spied what I was searching for. "Come on, little man, what we need is over there."

"Is Kim living wifth you now?"

I pulled some boxes out of the way. "For a little while."

"Do you like him better than usth?"

I turned to Kylie. "I could never like anyone better than you and Kaitlin. I love you two."

He smiled, but it didn't reach his eyes.

"Hey," I said as I cupped his face in my hand. "Are you okay?"

I squatted down in front of him. "You remember what I said. I'm always here for you, and if you need help all you have to do is ask."

Kylie wrapped his arms around my neck and squeezed.

"Okay now?"

"Yesth."

"Okay, let's get this upstairs."

Kylie took the tray, while I carried the highchair.

"Here we go ladies."

"Mac. That needs to be wiped down first." Emily shook her head in disgust. Kylie shrugged as his grandmother found a kitchen towel and the dishrag.

"At least I remembered there was one."

Kylie giggled.

"Thank you." Martha placed Kim in the chair. "Come on, let's eat everyone."

THE MEAL WAS relaxed, with friendly conversation. Kylie sat next to me and I helped cut his pancakes while he told me about a new video game. I sensed his unease, but he wasn't ready to talk. Emily sat across from us and Martha was on Kylie's other side. They discussed recipes and politics. Kim maintained his nonsensical litany throughout the meal, making me grin. Sitting quietly, watching, I was reminded of the many meals shared here with good friends. Back then Isabella did the cooking and provided the animated conversation. Sadness engulfed me.

"Mac?"

I glanced up and into Emily's compassionate eyes. "Sorry, I spaced out for a moment."

She grinned and shook her head. "I suggested we clean up and then maybe we could talk somewhere?"

"Let's put everything in the kitchen. I'll do the dishes later." I glanced at Martha. "Will you be okay here with the boys? We'll only be out at the shop."

"We'll be fine," Martha said with a smile. "Kele here is a huge help with Kim."

The compliment drew a glowing grin from Kylie. I held the front door for Emily and flipped the lock behind us.

"If you're concerned about her safety, we could talk inside," Emily suggested.

"It's complicated, but she should be fine. We're only going to the shop. The doors are locked and she knows to hit the alarm button."

We strolled along the path to the shop without further conversation.

"Mac?"

"Hmmm?" We had entered the office.

"Are you sleeping out here?" A blanket was thrown carelessly across the couch. Dirty clothes lay on the floor, two pair of shoes next to the pile.

"No. Well—not since Martha and Kim arrived."

"I presume there's a bed inside, right?"

Words escaped me.

She shook her head. "I have something to tell you. I've made a decision."

"Should I be scared?" I raised my eyebrow.

"Maybe. I've decided I'm not going to let you pull away from us. Not unless you can give me a better reason."

I handed her a bottle of water. "I told you why."

"Yes, but I don't believe that's the real motive."

"Emily, I've already explained. People think we're sleeping together."

"Maybe I should kiss you in public, give them something to talk about." Her eyes were bright and mischievous.

I glanced at her lips, wondering how they would taste. An image of her willingly in my arms, kissing me, sent ripples of desire through me. I felt the tingling in the pit of my stomach, a dampness between my thighs. "Oh yeah, that would really solve the problem." My voice cracked. I was hard.

"Why are you so concerned about this? Is it me?"

"You're being ridiculous."

"Then why do you care?"

"Why don't *you*? You're a beautiful, straight, single lady. Why would you want potential dates to be confused?"

"If they're that perplexed I wouldn't be interested in the first place."

I stared incredulously. "I swear if I live to be a hundred, I will never understand women."

Emily grasped my sweaty hand. "Is it so hard to understand I've come to care about you? The friendship we've built is very important to me and I don't want to lose that."

I shook my head. "Please don't do this." A tremor of need shot through me. "I don't ever want to hurt you or the kids. I believe that is what would happen if we — well if — you know what I mean."

"Mac, do I embarrass you?"

"No. Never."

"Are you involved with another woman? Are you afraid she'll misunderstand?"

"No."

"Then who are you protecting?"

Me. I was trying to protect me. "I don't want you to regret this."

"I won't."

I stepped back and started to pack up my laptop and place the open files into my briefcase. "We better get back to the house."

"Yes, I agree. I need to pick up Kaitlin soon."

"Hey Em. Don't think I've forgotten that I owe you the explanation about Isabella and the baby."

"I assumed you were biding your time."

"Maybe. But I gave you my word. I'd prefer if it could be a night when neither of us has other plans and the kids are asleep."

Emily patted my hand. "Agreed."

A WEEK LATER, Heath was back from vacation, the alarm systems had been installed, and Martha and Kim had relocated to begin their orientation. Without Martha to cook, I was at the diner early the following Monday for breakfast. Cindy Jeffries strolled in and I invited her to join me. "How are you, gorgeous?"

"Take me out and find out for yourself?" Her grin was sexy and provocative.

"I'm afraid you'd kill me."

"Good answer." She cocked her head. "I heard rumors there's a new lady in your life."

"Don't believe everything you hear. Especially from Sarah."

Cindy laughed. "So true."

Before the conversation went any further, Emily entered the diner. I called her over. "Cindy, this is Emily O'Brien, my friend. Emily this is Cindy Jeffries. She's a doctor at the hospital." Emily looked great. Her hair was down and loose and her skin glowed. I invited her to join us, but after the initial hellos, she chose to leave.

"She's attractive, and you are so obviously smitten," Cindy observed with a smile.

"I am not."

"I know that look. I've seen it before."

"She's straight."

Cindy placed her hand on mine. "Tell her. She may surprise you." She squeezed my hand. "Either way, it will work out the way it's meant to. I believe that."

Cindy was beeped and left for the hospital. I paid the bill and proceeded to my first appointment. I kept recalling Emily's abrupt departure. It seemed a bit odd. There was no time to really think about it. I had meetings all morning. My cell rang as I was headed to the office.

I read Heath's name on the display. "We received a call from Mercy. There's a woman at the emergency room. They'd like someone to talk to her. See JoAnne. She's the one that called it in."

"Okay. I'm in the truck. I'll head right over. Let 'em know I'm five minutes out."

JoAnne was at the nurse's desk when I arrived. "Hi, pretty lady."

"Charmer."

"Guilty. So what've you got for me?"

"Most likely nothing. The husband showed up ten minutes ago, put on an act like he's all concerned, and now she's getting ready to go home with him." JoAnne rolled her eyes.

"Give me the specifics quickly. Maybe I can talk to her before she leaves."

JoAnne pulled the binder from the slot as a loud ruckus broke out in exam room five.

"Crap, I'll go see what happened," I said.

"Don't bother, that's not our room. Your lady, Annette, is in room three, other side of the hall. She's beat up pretty good. Broken nose, split lip and bruising. She's from Alamosa. She traveled a good distance to get here."

"Yeah, but remember we're the only women's center for a hundred-mile radius, and that tells me she trekked here in the hope of getting help. I'll see if I can talk to her."

"Do you want security with you?"

"Nah, if it's only me, the husband will be less likely to feel threatened."

Forty-five minutes later Annette, or Nettie to her friends, strolled out of the hospital with her husband, Barney, who was sincerely sorry for the misunderstanding and unfortunate incident. Annette apologized for bothering us and making such a fuss. They started home arm in arm.

JoAnne and I watched them leave. "Would it be wrong to make bets on how long it will take him to do it again?" she asked.

"Yeah, it would, but I agree." Loud voices coming from room five drew my attention. "What the hell is going on in there?"

"Female victim brought in unconscious with minor injuries after an MVA. She was under the influence. When she woke up, she became cantankerous."

A feeling of unease crawled up my spine. "Do we have a name?"

JoAnne pulled the binder for me. "Renee McVee."

At almost the same moment, a police officer, Daniel O'Leary, exited the room with Mommy Renee in cuffs. She was mouthing off and I cringed as he escorted her out and placed her in the back of his patrol car. *Crap.*

AS SOON AS I left the hospital I headed back to my office. The first five miles of the ride I argued with myself regarding Renee and what should be done about her. In the end I hit the center's speed dial on my cell. Lily picked up on the second ring.

"Hey, lovely lady, how goes it?"

"Mac. Good, what's up?"

"I was at Mercy on a separate issue and Renee McVee was there. She's drunk again. They arrested her upon medical release. Do you know if she's been to any meetings or sought any help?"

"She doesn't want help. Believe me, I've tried."

I pulled into my parking space and shut the engine off. "Could you try one more time? As a favor to me?"

"Do you know her?"

"It's complicated, but I'd like to walk away clean."

"I'll go see her after work and try to talk to her. I can't promise anything though. She's pretty difficult."

"So I've been told. Thanks Lily. I owe you big time."

"Oh goody. I love it when you owe me." The smile in her voice echoed through the line.

"Bye, gorgeous. Let me know how it goes."

"Will do. Have a good day. Bye Mac."

I convinced myself that I had done all that I could and there was no need to involve Emily. Hopefully it was the right decision.

I waved to Alice, Michael's secretary, on the way up the stairs. Mary was at her desk. "Hi, doll face. Anything important happen this morning?"

Mary glanced over the top of her glasses. "You're late."

"Couldn't be avoided. Mercy needed a counselor. I even had to reschedule the two morning appointments."

She tilted her head. "Are you okay?"

"Yes, ma'am." I flashed her my best grin.

"Mail's on your desk, messages, too. It was quiet. You lucked out."

"Good enough. Thanks."

Hours later, I had initialed the last of the pending documents, separated the mail, written out supply orders, and returned all my calls. Mary left at six, after discreetly leaving half a roast beef on rye on my desk, where it remained. Finally, I could get down to working on the three design projects that were pending. Two were standard low-cost housing structures, boring but the nuts and bolts of the business, and the last was for a garden center. I was halfway through the second set of plans when my cell rang. "Hello."

"I've got a deep-dish apple pie in the oven, fresh coffee brewing, and the kids are in bed. Are you available?"

Desire bloomed at the sound of Emily's melodic voice. "Is there ice cream for that pie?"

"You do have a sweet tooth, don't you?"

"It's not like I asked for chocolate syrup, too."

"So....?"

A low energy built in the pit of my stomach, spreading out through every nerve ending. The option to spend a night designing cookie-cutter homes or an evening in Emily's company was a no-brainer. "I'm leaving now."

"Good. The pie should be out of the oven when you get here."

Chapter Fourteen

EMILY GREETED ME at the back door. "Hi."

"Hi yourself," I said as I slipped past her.

She closed the door and set the alarm. "I have to force myself to use this. It was installed recently and I find myself forgetting to set it."

"How's it working out?"

"At first I thought it was extravagant, but honestly now that it's here I find I'm not listening for every noise at night, only the children. I'm sleeping better."

"Good. That's what I was hoping."

"You were hoping?"

She didn't know. "The management company owns the building."

"*Your* management company?"

"Yes."

"You never said anything."

"It's not important."

She stared at me for long moments. "Coffee?"

"Absolutely."

"Sit."

I did.

Emily had set the table for us and the pie was sitting in the middle on some sort of rack. "I'm glad you could make it." She poured the hot liquid.

"I gave you my word."

"I don't want this to be a responsibility you feel obligated about. I'd like to know the truth about everything and not the gossip."

"It's not. It's okay."

"Let's start easy. Tell me something about yourself as if I haven't learned something already. Why did you never mention that you're my landlord?"

"I don't look at it that way. Mary handles everything with Michael. I stay pretty much hands free."

"You're rich."

"Not really, most of the money from the management company goes to the women's center and then to Team Bella." She gave me a look. "Okay, I'm comfortable."

"Right." Her eyes twinkled.

My smile was sardonic. "So, what do you want to know that Sarah hasn't already told you?"

"Now see, that's not true. Sarah is very judicious when talking about you."

"Good to know. Okay, what would *you* like to know?"

"Mother, father, siblings, favorite color, blood type, bank balances, pin numbers." She grinned as she put the coffee pot back on the hotplate.

I lifted a shoulder noncommittally "I don't really know, Em. I grew up in foster care. The Abingtons took me in at the age of six. They were good to me for the most part. They were killed in a car accident the year I turned thirteen."

She tugged my hand and linked our fingers. "I didn't know. I'm sorry."

"Luck of the draw."

"What happened to you after that?"

That recollection brought back warm memories. "Judge Williams sat me down for a talk. He knew about my proclivity for girls and correctly suspected his daughter was on my radar. He read me the facts of life, according to him. I would be moving in with them effective immediately. He would house me, feed me, and educate me. In return, I would respect him and his family." I smirked at Emily. "In judgespeak that meant keep my hands to myself."

"Still, you seem to admire him."

"I do. He's a wonderful man. He introduced me to woodworking long before I was living with him. Let me use his workshop whenever I wanted. He loves me freely. I think he was the first adult who did without being paid to." A blush suffused my face as I realized what I'd said.

"Were you and Sarah ever involved?"

"No, never."

"So tell me about your first girlfriend." She rubbed her hands together with glee, her eyes glowing with mischief.

Laughter bubbled out of me. "Well, there's not much to tell really. It was high school, my senior year. There was a girl who kept giving me signals. One night we ended up in my car, parked."

"And?"

"And I had no clue what to do. I knew what I wanted, but I was too terrified to try." I grinned thinking about it.

"Wow. I always imagined you as a bit of a lesbian Lothario," she chuckled.

"Hardly." I took a sip of my coffee. It was hot and strong. "Why do you say that?"

"I'm not sure. Maybe it's how attentive you are. Or the way you try to take care of people, women especially. When you're talking to a woman, she gets your entire attention as if she was the only one in your universe. You're always complimenting them or flirting." She gave me a grin. "Maybe it's the way women seem to fawn over you."

"That's an exaggeration."

Emily laughed. "You don't see it, but it's true. Everyone's attracted to you. Some more than others."

"Who?"

"Never mind who. Tell me about this young sexpot."

"Well, like I said we were parked, talking. Robin kissed me. I mean *really* kissed me. I had no idea what to do so I let her take the lead. After a while I was beyond aroused. I wasn't sure how to go about it. I mean, was I supposed to touch her?" I raised my hands, palms out.

Emily laughed out loud. "Tell me you didn't do that?"

"No."

"My whole image of you is eroding. What happened?"

"Nothing. A cop pulled up behind us and put his lights on. Back then that was the signal to move along or get taken in."

"What did you do?"

"I took her home. I didn't want to get in trouble. Jeeze, I lived with the damn judge. Can you imagine what he would've said?" An image of me in his library trying to explain to him what I had been doing flashed before my eyes. The fear of making him regret taking me into his home, or disappointing him, was always utmost in my mind. He had been nothing but kind and generous. How could I have explained my lustful fumblings to him?

"So you never got to first base with her?"

"Nope."

"No second dates?"

"I was too afraid."

"And your next attempt?"

"Not for a couple years."

"A couple years?"

"Well, this is a small town. We're not exactly the lesbian Mecca of the Midwest."

"I know, but years?"

Her line of questioning was a bit unnerving, and I stalled by casting a glance out the window. A full moon was rising in the sky. *Lothario? Where the hell had that come from?* "Yeah." I shrugged sheepishly.

"Tell me?"

My attention was focused on Emily and I wondered why she cared. Was this merely idle curiosity? What was she learning from it? It felt good talking to her, so I forged ahead. "It took place my third year of college. I lived in the dorm at the time. It was a holiday weekend, but I stayed behind for extra credits. I wanted to graduate early and get a job so I could pay the Judge back." I gave Emily my most lecherous grin. "She was an older woman, a senior."

"Oh, do tell."

"College for me was all about learning, and making the Judge proud. I was in my room studying. Most of the dorms were empty. Everyone had gone home for the holiday. Kelly knocked on the door Friday night." A sip of my coffee helped to fortify me. "I had seen her around school. She was pretty, athletic, and a total flirt. She came into my room and sat on the bed. We talked for a long time that evening. You have to understand. I *never* assume someone is gay. And even after I know they are, I can't imagine they'd be interested in me."

"You've never approached a woman on your own?"

"No."

"I don't understand. Why?"

"I'm sure you're familiar with the saying, failure is not an option?" An empty feeling filled me. Knowing how I felt about Emily had me breaking out in a cold sweat.

"Well, what happened with Kelly?"

I grinned lasciviously. "She made the first advance. *She* kissed me. She was the first girl I French kissed." The memory still brought a little thrill to my senses. "She was hot. Totally dominant. I was like putty in her hands. We explored every fantasy I had ever had. Kelly showed me, and showed me, and showed me."

"Oh my."

"Oh, yeah. She totally educated me on the finer things lesbian for the next two weeks." I should have been embarrassed admitting that, I wasn't. "I was in heaven."

Emily shook her head. "Two weeks? My goodness. That was quick."

"It turned out Kelly was as innocent as I had been, but much more curious. Once she gained her confidence with me, she was free to go after the woman of her dreams, her roommate."

"That's awful."

"Nah. I was fine, really. I knew it wasn't love. Hell, I was thrilled to get to third base. More importantly, I learned that casual sex wasn't for me."

Emily got up to pour more coffee. She reached toward the pie and cut big slices, putting them on our plates. "Seriously?" She covered my hand with her own and there was sadness in her eyes. "So who was next in line now that you possessed all this newfound experience?" She dropped a dollop of ice cream on each piece of pie.

I took a deep breath. "Isabella."

"That...was years later." Emily blinked.

"Yes."

"Why?"

"I abhor rejection. I never set myself up for it. The attraction to Izzy didn't change that. She made the first move. I was shocked. She was beautiful, intelligent, funny, and kind." An image of Isabella's face as she howled at my bashfulness peppered my brain.

"And since Izzy?"

I shook my head, picked my cup up, and sipped my coffee.

"Because you're still married?" Emily asked softly.

I gazed into her eyes. "No—yes—no." They say confession is good for the soul, but I was a coward. "At first yes. It didn't seem right. It felt like I was still married. It felt like I was cheating. Later it was a matter of keeping our vows. Now I've come to accept that she's gone. Recently I discovered I want more, so no."

"Are you dating Cindy?"

Confusion filled me. "No. Never."

"It had all the earmarks of romance when I saw you two at the diner."

I touched the top of Emily's hand, trying to capture her eyes. "I was there for breakfast. She came in afterward, alone. I invited her to sit with me and catch up. We've never dated. I swear it."

"It's none of my business."

"Em, I'm telling you the truth. We're friends, that's all."

"It looked like more, intimate even."

"Cindy was on duty the night Izzy and Bella were brought in. She's the one who told me they were dead."

Emily picked up her cup and I saw her hand was trembling. "I'm sorry," she breathed.

"We're close, but only as friends." Emily's posture was rigid. She sat pensively for long moments.

"Em?"

Her eyes seemed pained as she raised them. "Richard cheated almost from the beginning."

"Why?" The admission shocked me.

"That's the question, isn't it? It started right after the honeymoon. I always wondered what was lacking in me that made him search elsewhere."

"Richard was an ass. Didn't he know how damned lucky he was?" It came out heated and there was an undeniable jealousy fueling my reaction.

"See, that's what I mean about you." She smiled at me warmly. "You're always attentive. You *always* say the right thing."

"You deserved better, Emily. You deserved someone who

would appreciate you for the exceptional woman you are."

This time she blushed. "You haven't dated at all since Izzy?"

"No." *Not unless I can count you,* I thought.

"Goodness, you surprise me." Emily smiled

"Why?"

"You really are timid."

"Well—I guess. A quick dalliance is merely sex. I want to know the woman I'm with. I want to care about her." I shrugged.

"That's an admirable trait."

"Which brings us full circle, right?"

Emily squeezed my hand. "Only if you're comfortable telling me."

Was I? Would it serve any purpose? I gazed at Emily and realized it might. "Yeah, I'm ready."

"Thank you."

I stood and walked to the window. I thought better on my feet. For the past five years, I'd never talked about it, had never expressed what I felt, the devastation that had ripped me apart. But this was Emily. A woman who somehow removed all my defenses.

I shoved my hands into my pockets and stared out at the black night, finding refuge in the inky darkness, which helped me to speak of the horror. "You should know, I've never talked about the murder of my family," I started. "Especially once the facts came to light." Normally by now, I would be crying, but not tonight. *Strange.* I felt as though I needed to do this, to cleanse myself of the nightmare once and for all. Maybe, I finally could. I took a deep breath. "You already know about how he found her outside the market. That it was a fluke." I shifted toward Emily. She watched me intently. "After the Judge refused us a restraining order, I tried to stay around the house. I wanted to protect them. I knew he was violent, but not fuckin' crazy." I turned back toward the window and stared out into the blackness, the moon offering the only light on an otherwise hidden landscape.

"You need to understand, Izzy helped me build my business up to what it is today. We sank every penny back into it for the future. About three months before her death, I submitted a set of designs for a big townhouse project on the golf course over in Pueblo. They awarded the contract to me and it was finally going to be Isabella's chance. We were going to use the money to fund her dreams, the crisis center and the ball field. *She* was the brainchild behind each of them. She spent years researching and planning the best way to construct and organize each facility. She volunteered at Rocky Mountain Hospital for Children in downtown Denver, and it was her idea to organize a ball team for special needs kids. She met with women's organizations throughout the United States trying to build a network, discovering ways to legally help victims of domestic violence. She worked for Michael part-time and in return, he helped her with the legal aspects of the center. Isabella was a good and caring person who wanted to make a difference and I'm not saying that just because I loved her."

"I didn't know." Emily dabbed at her eyes. "I'm so sorry."

"Anyway, Juan must've hidden in the hills back behind the house or down below in the flats and waited for me to leave. I'm not sure which, and there was no proof either way. No witnesses or evidence of the actual abduction."

I returned to sit beside Emily. She took my hand in hers, holding on tightly. "Sometime after I left for work, early Thursday morning and before ten, he came and snatched Isabella and the baby. All the evidence pointed to a violent struggle. Blood, furniture overturned, Bella's baby bottle broken on the floor."

The need for control had me up and pacing. This was the part that always did me in—the uncertainty, the unknown, those gaps in time and evidence that my mind filled with ghastly imaginings. The horror Izzy must have felt all because I needed to go to a meeting that morning for the damn condo project. "The police put out an APB on his truck, Juan and my family as soon as I discovered them missing. I was only gone three hours, but that was three hours for him to get away without discovery. The crime lab came out and processed the scene to start the investigation. Other than fingerprints there were no clues. We knew who took her and the baby, but not where. The truck turned up in Leadville, and the possible crime scene suddenly grew larger." A long moment passed.

"Mac?"

"Do you stock anything stronger than coffee here?"

She pointed. "There's beer or wine?"

A trip to the fridge offered cold beer. "Want one?" At her nod, I retrieved two bottles. I opened them and went back to the table, handing one to Emily and drinking from the other. I pressed the cold bottle to my forehead and closed my eyes, trying to think of the best way to tell the rest. "The police discovered the bodies of Isabella and Bella in an abandoned house over on what was once Whitley Drive three days later. The hot line received a tip about a strange car parked in the driveway of an unoccupied home. Juan was in the process of making his escape when police pulled up to the site. He shot himself before they could call for backup."

I took another pull on my beer and a deep breath. Fury had me wanting to smash everything in sight. In contrast, Emily soothed my inner beast. The terror of the ordeal was churning in her eyes and was somehow comforting. "The police called the house and told me to meet them at the hospital. I raced there, hoping, praying that Isabella and the baby were okay. Cindy—she told me. They were dead—they'd been shot."

I bowed my head as I cried, embarrassed as I recalled the details. It still hurt so much. I ran my hands through my hair, trying to make the images disappear. The vision of their broken bodies would haunt me until the day I died. "I demanded to see them. I wanted to see for myself. I needed to know there wasn't a mistake."

I drew a breath. "Cindy and the police tried to talk me out of it. Said I didn't need to. Friends could identify the bodies. They didn't get it. They were *my* family."

After downing my beer, I placed the bottle on the table, every nerve in my body vibrating. Silent tears coursed down my cheeks. "The rest came from the autopsy reports. I fought with Judge Williams for copies. He didn't want them released to me. He claimed I didn't need to know those particulars." I peered at Emily hoping she understood. "I needed to know. It was *my* wife, *my* child. It was my responsibility."

I stood in front of Emily, searching her eyes. "Are you sure you want to know this part? It's—grisly."

She wiped the tears from her face. "Yes. Please, go on."

I returned to the glass doors that led to the deck. The moon had shifted and was shining on the backyard. It illuminated some rose bushes recently purchased, but as yet unplanted. The black skies and moonlight reminded me of other nights like this at our house. The moon shining on the pond out back and the water reflecting the light in the darkness of night. Izzy and I used to skinny dip there before Bella was born, swimming to cool off on hot evenings. Izzy had loved the water and I had loved watching her. I faced Emily again, prepared to continue. "Everything else we know is based on science, the evidence, and Juan's arrest history. You see, unbeknownst to Izzy or myself, he had a long list of arrests for molestation, rape, and domestic violence. He did time for nearly killing a girl when he was twenty. He had been sentenced to twenty-five years, but only served eight. He convinced the psychiatrist and the parole board he was cured. From the forensic evidence, we know that at some point he tied Isabella up. There were ligatures on her wrists and legs. He presumably forced her to witness the—he—he—tortured," a sob escaped my throat, "and shot Bella."

Emily gasped.

I rushed on. I had to. "The evidence confirms the baby was shot in the head." I pointed to the frontal lobe where the bullet had entered, only to explode out the back scattering brain matter about the room. I didn't mention that part to Emily. There was only so much the human psyche could absorb. I didn't mention the vaginal tearing, the baby brutalized simply because Juan was a sick, sadistic bastard who should have been stopped years earlier. Emily was mewling, but I needed to finish this. "The medical evidence further showed that Isabella was beaten repeatedly. Tortured. Raped. He murdered her after three days of what had to have been sheer agony. Bella was dead at least one day when the bodies were found. They believe Izzy died mere hours before having been discovered. It means she witnessed our daughter's death and most likely everything else. She was killed the same way as Bella, the same results. Both dead of gunshot wounds. I believe that's how it was described by the ME. He also noted that Isab—that—Isabella was six weeks pregnant when she died."

Emily was sobbing softly. I pulled her into my arms and we stood there clinging to each other. Crying.

"Oh, my god, Mac. I had no idea. I don't have words."

"There's something else."

"Christ. What?" She shuddered.

Embarrassed, I confessed. "I have nightmares, often wake up screaming. In the beginning I hadn't slept at all for fear of the dreams, but I was dead inside. Later I had found comfort in the nightly visits, because at least I was feeling something. Even pain had become welcome. Lately, I've dreaded the dreams because I couldn't get the images out of my mind afterward. All I could remember was Izzy and the baby with bullet holes. I wished I could remember the good times without the pain and carnage."

"Jesus, Mac." Emily caressed my cheek and pulled me close. "Thank you." She buried her face in my neck as she continued to sob.

"I've never shared this, Em. Not even with Sarah." I held her, relishing the comfort of her arms. Relief flooded through me, the baring of my soul washing away some of my torment. I felt raw inside but settled, too, in a strange way.

"You never told Sarah?" Emily asked.

"No."

"Why?"

"Lots of reasons. This pain was mine. I was afraid to share it, afraid I would be giving away parts of Isabella, Bella, and our unborn child. Sarah was seven months pregnant back then. It was a difficult time for her. She loved Izzy and Bella. The events ended up causing her to lose her unborn child. Mostly because it was all my fault. I'll carry that guilt the rest of my life. I never should have left the house."

"You can't believe that?"

"Of course I believe that. I failed my family." I pulled out of her arms. "I'm sorry. I gotta get outta here."

"Mac, please don't go, please."

I shook my head. Holding Emily in my arms, accepting her solace had made me crazy. It was more than my need for human contact, it was Emily. "I can't, Em, sorry. I'm no good to anyone like this." I took a deep breath. "Lock the door and set the alarm behind me."

She kissed my cheek. "Please be careful. Call me tomorrow."

BACK AT THE office I reopened the CAD program and got back to the design I had left half finished earlier. My head was throbbing. I reached for the fridge door and opened it. A cold beer called my name.

Memories of the week I had turned to alcohol sprang to my mind. I had spent the entire time drunk. Our house had almost been destroyed by the damage generated by my anger. There had been bottles everywhere when Michael showed up and took me to task. Afterward, he held me in his arms and cried with me. He had loved Isabella and our daughter as much as his own child. Later after our tears were spent, he put me in the shower and cleaned me up before tucking me into bed. The next morning most of the destruction had been cleaned up, as well as the bottles, and my need for them. I redirected my efforts to work and Izzy's projects. I never looked back.

I shook myself and made a decision. I opened the cap on the bottle and took a deep swig of water.

Hours later I hit the save button. The designs were completed and could be sent to the printers. Mary would mail them out and we'd wait to see if they were accepted.

"Morning."

I glanced between the clock and Mary. "Hi."

"How old is this coffee?"

I grinned. "How's the enamel on your teeth?"

"That old, huh? I'll make fresh."

"I'm gonna hop in the shower." I closed the office door and did just that. When I walked out twenty minutes later, Sarah was sitting at my desk, sipping coffee and eating Danish. "Comfy?" I asked.

"Yup." A bright smile spread across her face.

I sauntered over and pinched off a piece of her pastry and popped it in my mouth, before strolling out to get some coffee. "Do you need a refresher?" I held the carafe up in Sarah's direction.

"No. I'm good, thanks."

I sat opposite her and grinned. "Well?"

"Nothing. I wanted to drop by."

"Uh huh." I sat and waited. Sarah would spill the beans sooner or later.

"There's a new case worker at the hospital," she finally said.

"What happened to Margaret?"

"She retired."

"Good for her." I sipped my coffee and let it flow through my system.

"The woman plays for your team."

"You mean Team Bella?"

"Smart ass."

"What are you up to?"

"Leah is attractive and since Emily is straight —"

"You thought Leah and I would meet and live happily ever after, did ya?"

"I'd settle for a date. Don't worry, I haven't contacted the wedding planner yet," she smirked.

"Why not? What's wrong with her?"

"Nothing. She's a lovely person and very attractive."

"Uh huh."

"Knock, knock."

Emily stood in the doorway. "Am I interrupting?"

I surged up. *"Mercifully, yes."*

"Mac, we're not done." Sarah was indignant.

"Why do I feel like I should leave?" Emily glanced from me to Sarah.

"Sarah is busy playing match maker and I'm ignoring her," I said.

"Interesting. Who's the victim?" Emily asked.

"Her name is Leah. She's the new CPS caseworker and she's very pretty, plus she plays for Mac's team." Sarah had perked up.

Emily pulled a chair up. "So what's the problem?"

"Mac is being Mac, as usual," Sarah responded.

"Ah, that makes sense." Emily said sagely.

"Helloooo, I'm sitting right here," I reminded them.

"Do I rate coffee?" Emily leaned back in her chair, a mischievous grin on her face.

"Not if you're going to take her side." I got up and filled a cup, adding two spoons of sugar and a bit of cream.

Emily took the cup. "Thank you. So why don't you want to date, Leah is it?"

"I've never even met the woman."

Sarah leaned forward. "I can remedy that. I'm hosting a barbeque at the house on the twenty-ninth. She'll be there and you're invited."

"Good for her."

"I'd like to meet her," Emily said.

I spun toward Emily. "Wait. Why are you interested in meeting her?"

"To see whether she's your type or not." She grinned. "Give my approval."

"Oh, as if you'd even know my type."

"I think I do."

"Yeah, right."

"We're talking about Leah here." Sarah interrupted. "All you have to do is show up. If you don't like her, nothing's lost."

"I'll pass."

"Chicken," Emily said, sipping her coffee and appearing smug.

"Why not?" Sarah pushed. "You don't even have to take her out. Just meet her at the party."

"Sarah, you know why," I said.

Emily leaned forward. "It's because she's shy."

"Exactly." Sarah slapped her hand on the armrest. "Did you know she's never initiated a date?" she asked.

"Inhibited I'm telling you." Emily grinned.

"Will you two knock it off?"

Emily started laughing. "Can I come? I want to see this."

"Absolutely. Bring the kids; the pool is heated."

"Out, both of you, there's work to do. And I'm not interested in getting fixed up."

Sarah stood. "I should get to work. Thanks for the coffee. I expect you at the festivities, so don't disappoint me."

"Don't expect me and you won't be disappointed."

Emily remained seated while Sarah hugged me. "Love you."

"I love you, too, but I'm still not coming to your little soirée."

After Sarah left I sat down next to Emily. "So Ms. O'Brien, to what do I owe the pleasure of this visit?"

"I was worried about you. Now I see that was unnecessary."

"I'm okay."

"Thank you for explaining to me about your family. I know it was difficult."

I shrugged. "You made it easy."

"You should meet this friend of Sarah's."

"Why?"

"Because you're a wonderful person and any woman would be lucky to fall in love with you."

If only *you* felt that way — if only I wasn't spoken for. "I hate blind dates."

"But this isn't a blind date."

"Emily, I know you mean well, but I really, truly am not interested. Now, as much as I enjoy your company, I need to work."

"Think about it. You might like her."

"Good day, Ms. O'Brien." I escorted her out and poured more coffee. It had already been a long day and it was only eight-thirty in the morning.

Chapter Fifteen

THE AFTERNOON MEETING ended quicker than I had anticipated and I drove to the ballpark early. I had already begun unloading the truck and setting up the infield when Sarah, her kids and Emily and her grandchildren pulled up next to each other in the parking lot. A third car pulled in next to them, a small red compact with a parking sticker for the hospital on the bumper. There was a blonde driving. *Crap.*

Kaitlin was the first to exit the truck and she ran over and hopped into my arms.

"Hey, beautiful, how are you?"

"Good." A pleased blush tinged her cheeks. I held her tightly, and kissed her, laughing out loud when she kissed me back.

"You make sure you have fun today, hear me?"

"I will, I promise." She was giggling as I let her down. Kylie approached and after a hello hug from him, Mikey, and Taylor, the kids took over the chore of hauling the remaining equipment out to home plate and the bench area.

"Afternoon, Coach." Sarah beamed. At least Emily had the decency to appear ill-at-ease. "I'd like you to meet a new friend and co-worker. This is Leah Mikowitz. Leah, the coach, Mackenzie Taylor."

I extended my hand. "It's Mac and it's nice to meet you. I've heard a great deal about you."

She took my hand. Her grip was firm without being over the top. "Nice to finally put a face with the name. They both talk about you all the time." Her smile was pleasant, her eyes full of mirth.

"Understandable since they're already planning the wedding. I hope you want children because I'm sure they've already named the first two."

"Mac!" Sarah shrieked. "Behave yourself!"

"Admit it. You've already booked a hall for the reception."

"You're incorrigible. Leah don't listen to her." I knew I had hit a nerve judging from the red blush Sarah was sporting.

"I'm going to go help with refreshments," Emily said before she bolted away.

"Don't let her deceive you, Leah. She's as guilty as her partner here. They've been planning this union since you hit town."

Leah's laughter was heartfelt. I was relieved to see she had a sense of humor.

Sarah stood with her hands on her hips. "Are you done yet?"

I put my finger on my chin to think. "One question, Leah. Can I coach the game or should we go get the U-Haul now?"

"That's enough." Sarah linked arms with Leah. "Ignore that rude person. We're going to enjoy the game and afterward I'll introduce you to my *real* friends."

I laughed long and hard at the indignation on Sarah's face. Poor Leah had no idea what she was in for.

The weather was exceptional, with blue skies, light breezes, and plenty of sunshine without being oppressively hot, and I was eagerly anticipating the game. The batter, Tracey, struggled to contain herself, waiting for me to throw the pitch. She was keen for her chance to run the bases. I glanced toward first where Patrick was ready to push Tommy to second. Kaitlin was on third and inching her way toward home. As I made a show of tossing the ball, the girl leaned into the pitch. The bat connected and the ball blasted down the baseline this side of fair. Kaitlin scored, Patrick pushed Tommy to third as Tracey landed on first.

An hour later, Andy, the first baseman, tossed the ball to Jim who was catching for us. Jim lobbed the ball to me and I threw the last pitch of the day.

After six innings all the kids had at least three turns at bat and had run the bases as many times. They were enjoying some refreshments and joking with each other.

I strolled over to the refreshment stand. "Hi. Noreen, can I get a water when you get a chance?"

She smiled and finished the requests from the kids before handing me my drink. "How you doing, Mac?"

"Good. How's the big guy?"

"Sleeping at the moment. We'll wake him when we get back."

"He's home? Terrific. Tell him I said hi."

"Mac?"

I shifted to find Emily behind me. "Yes?"

"Did you have to be so rude? Leah seems like a nice person."

Contrition was definitely called for, but the looks on Sarah and Emily's faces had made my bad behavior worthwhile. "I believe I made myself very clear on this subject. I am not interested in dating."

"You didn't even give her a chance."

"Emily, I'm not interested. What do you want me to do?"

"How do you know? Give her a chance. Get to know her."

"Why is this so damn important to you?"

"Because we're friends and I want to see you happy. Sarah thinks Leah would be good for you"

There were so many responses, but none I was capable of

sharing with her.

"Mac? Gramma?" Kaitlin and Kylie approached hesitantly.

"That was some game today, you two," I praised. "You were both spectacular. I'm proud of you."

"Are you fighting with Gramma?"

I squatted down and took Kaitlin's hand in mine. "No, sweetie, I'm not fighting with your grandmother. We're discussing something, but we're not mad at each other. I promise you."

She glanced at Emily for confirmation, and visibly relaxed when her grandmother agreed. "Okay, good."

"Did you get your snacks?"

"I havfe two."

I tickled Kylie's belly. "You're gonna get fat, little man."

Taylor ran over. "Hi kiddo, you okay?"

She raised her arms for me to lift her and I did, nuzzling her close.

Emily laid her hand on my arm. "Please go apologize to Leah and give her a chance."

"Emily, I'm not available. Why is that so hard to understand?"

"Because you need more in your life than your job, the center, and this. You need to actually *have* a life." She crossed her arms.

My temper began to simmer. Rather than make a scene, I strolled away with Taylor still in my arms. "You did good today, little one. Did you have fun?"

She gave me a sleepy nod. I stopped to talk with various parents while slowly making my way back to Sarah, Emily, and Leah. "Well, have you ladies finished crucifying me yet, or should I take another stroll around the field?"

"Give me my daughter. I don't care what you do." Sarah scowled at me.

Emily called out for the kids. "I'm going to get these two home. I'm glad you could make it, Leah, and I'm sorry about this one's behavior." Emily indicated me before striding away with Kaitlin and Kylie in tow. "Sarah, I'll call you tomorrow." She called over her shoulder.

I leaned in conspiratorially. "Leah, if you're not ready to marry me, would you consider dinner sometime?"

"Wha —" Sarah stopped short.

"I don't know. I kinda had my heart set on moving right in. That way I wouldn't need to finish my unpacking first," Leah responded.

We both laughed. "Why don't I escort you to your car. Bye Sarah." I kissed the kids and fell in step with Leah.

"You really gave the two of them a hard time," Leah smirked. "Did you enjoy it as much as I did?"

I glanced up. "I'm sorry. It's not you. I specifically told them I did not want to be set up, but as you can see, they don't listen." I grinned. "Thank you for being a good sport."

"Hey, I feel the same way. I'm just glad it wasn't a guy they were trying to force on me."

We both chuckled. "So, would you consider dinner?"

"Are you expecting benefits?"

"Absolutely not. A friendly meal."

"I'd like that."

"Friday?"

"It's a date." She said.

Before leaving, Leah provided me with her number and address. We made plans for me to pick her up at seven on Friday evening.

LEAH OPENED THE door. "Mac, come in. I'll only be a minute."

"That's fine."

Her apartment was the entire second floor of an old Victorian structure built in the early part of the previous century. Renovations opened the floor plan, making it airy while still maintaining the integrity of the time period. Leah closed the door behind me.

"Nice place."

"Thank you. I'm really so sorry about the delay. There was a last-minute emergency with one of my cases that took a while to resolve. I would understand if you wanted to postpone dinner."

"No problem. We missed our reservations in Bailey, but we both need to eat."

"Thank you for understanding," Leah glanced at her watch. "I'll get a jacket. It's a little cool this evening."

While Leah was gone I took a minute to examine the living room. It was a good sized space, probably fifteen by ten feet, with lots of natural wood trim and built-ins which made the area appear even bigger. The furniture was a mix of colors and styles that screamed college dorm and brought a smile to my face. I leaned closer to one of three niches that were built between the studs, a perfect use of dead space, and peeked at a selection of photos on display.

"Ready," Leah said when she returned.

"Is this you rock climbing?"

"Yes, do you climb?"

"No, but I always wanted to try it."

"Maybe we'll go some time."

"Maybe. All set?"

Once we were securely ensconced in the truck and en route, I glanced at my companion. "Since the Canyon Grill is no longer viable, we'll have to deal with the diner in town and most of the townspeople tonight."

"It couldn't be avoided and besides I've heard good things about the food at the diner." Leah frowned. "Isn't that true?"

"The food is great. Unfortunately, as soon as you're seen with me you'll be outed. If that's a problem we should head out of town."

Leah grinned. "I would've thought Sarah and Emily took care of that by now."

"You're probably right."

"Will we create a scandal?" she laughed.

"Only if Mrs. Parker hasn't snuck into Mr. Jackson's room again at the old folks home. That's always good for a week's worth of innuendo. We'll find out soon enough." I pulled into the lot and parked. "You ready to be placed under the microscope?" I asked.

"This is the side of small town life I forgot about." Leah gripped my hand. "Come on, let's give them a show."

I held the door for her and waited for the hostess to seat us. Teresa grabbed two menus. "You want a booth, right Mac?" At my signal she wove her way down the aisle and settled us at one of the front booths. "Enjoy your meal, ladies." She winked, before hurrying on.

"So, what do you recommend?"

"Everything is pretty good. It's simply a matter of what your taste buds are clamoring for."

"Evening Mac, and who's your pretty friend?" Maggi was grinning like a fool.

"Leah meet Maggi, waitress extraordinaire and a good friend. Leah works for CPS. She took Margaret's place.

"It's nice to meet you. Can I get you ladies anything to drink?"

"Leah?"

"Coke with lemon please."

"Coffee, Mags, and thanks."

Maggi strolled away after taking our food orders. "One, two, three—" I counted.

"What?" Leah asked.

"I figure by the count of ten Maggi will be on the phone with Sarah and Emily letting them know we're here."

"Seriously?"

"Hell yes, this is a big deal for all of them."

Leah's pleasant expression seemed to falter for a moment.

"What?" I asked.

"I don't want to cross a line, but is that because of what happened to your family?"

"Yeah. Probably." I should have expected that, but it took me by surprise nevertheless.

"I'm sorry — about what happened."

"Thanks." I took a deep breath. "Not exactly first date conversation, huh?"

"One of the nurses was concerned that I not stick my foot in my mouth. She meant well."

"See what I mean? Nothing is private in a small town."

Maggi arrived with our meals. "Enjoy you two." Her grin split her face.

"And there's the proof."

Leah chuckled. "So you've been friends with Sarah and Emily since childhood?"

"Not exactly." I dipped a fry into some ketchup. "I'd already been placed here when Sarah relocated next door. Emily only recently moved here with her grandchildren."

"Wow, the way you all interact, I assumed you grew up together. Wait, placed? You were in the system?"

"They transferred me here from Grand Junction when I was about six."

Leah appeared stunned. "I didn't realize. I'm sorry. Guess I put my foot in my mouth anyway."

"It's not a problem, believe me."

"How long were you in the system?"

"From birth until about thirteen. Then Sarah's dad took me in and that was my last placement."

"I'm impressed. You seem sane."

I laughed out loud. "Don't tell Sarah or Emily that."

"Tell me about them."

"Emily is wonderful, as you've probably already figured out. Smart, beautiful and very witty. Her grandchildren are terrific and she's great with them."

"And Sarah?"

"Sarah's my best friend."

"Hmmm." Leah took a bite of her turkey club.

The rest of the evening we got to know each other. Later she invited me in. After more coffee and talk, I took my leave around midnight.

OVER THE COURSE of the next few weeks, Leah and I managed to see each other a couple of times. She came to two games, we shared dinner at a wonderful Mexican restaurant in

Pueblo, and a movie night at her place the previous Tuesday. That was when she confronted me.

"So Mac, what is this?"

I sat in an armchair, sipping my first beer. "I'm sorry?" I asked as I gazed up at her.

"You, me. What do you see for the future?"

"Are you asking if I'm ready to set the wedding date?"

Leah leaned forward. "I'm being serious."

"Sorry." I sat up straight. "I—don't know what you're asking. We've only started seeing each other."

Her smile was wistful. "I wonder if you realize how strong your feelings for Emily are?"

"I—Leah, I never promised you anything. I thought you understood that."

"I'm pointing out the obvious here. We have never had a conversation or spent time together when you didn't regale me with stories about Emily or her many attributes. You don't feel the same compulsion when it comes to Sarah."

"I'm sorry."

"Have you told her?"

"What? A—who?"

"Emily."

I closed my eyes tightly. "No."

"You really should."

"I can't."

"Why not, for heaven's sake?"

"She's straight."

"Ahhh. So by dating me the pressure is off, right?"

"I—"

"No, it's okay. I wasn't sure at first, but the more time we spent together the more it became clear you're enamored with her."

"I'm sorry." I stood up. "I should go."

"Don't be sorry. As you said, you were truthful from the start. I misunderstood."

"Leah, I never—"

She smiled and shook her head. "Cindy Jeffries has asked me out. I think I'm going to see if she's still interested."

I grasped Leah's hand. "Cindy is a lot smarter than I am. She knows a good thing when she sees it. Good night."

THURSDAY MORNING I was in the office clearing my desk, preparing for a site visit scheduled for early afternoon.

"Morning, boss."

"Hey Mary. The coffee is fresh. I just made it."

"Thank you."

"After you settle I've got some correspondence we need to go over."

"Okay."

"Morning, handsome."

I glanced up to find Sarah in the doorway. She was carrying a bag with Stella's Diner embossed on it. "I come bearing gifts."

"Yeah, but what's it going to cost me?"

She was dressed in scrubs and sneakers and slipped in to plop down opposite me. "I brought you food. Stop complaining."

Mary approached with two cups of coffee and placed them on the desk, one for me and one in front of Sarah. "Thank you, Mary."

"Let me know when you want to do the paperwork." She left quietly and pulled the door, leaving it slightly ajar.

"So?" Sarah stretched the word out, emphasizing the question.

"Give me the food."

She chuckled and handed me an egg and cheese on a raisin bagel, one of my favorites. "How's Leah?"

"Ask her." I tore the wrapping off and took a bite of the sandwich, a low moan escaping as the flavors flooded my palette.

"Well, I know you've been seen together multiple times."

"Then you're caught up."

She stuck her tongue out at me and took a sip of coffee. "Come on, spill it."

"There's nothing to spill. We dated a couple times."

Sarah leaned forward and placed her hand on mine. "I want you to be happy. Does Leah make you happy?" She lifted her coffee to her lips and stopped. "Wait a minute—dated? As in past tense? What did you do?"

"Hello ladies." Michael strolled in carrying a folder. "Hello, sweetheart." He bent down and kissed his wife. *Thoroughly.*

"Should I leave you two alone?" I asked.

He tossed the folder on my desk. "This is ready for your signature. It's the contract for the Pueblo Canyon project."

"Thanks." With no room at my desk I took the documents over to the couch to review them and sign where appropriate.

"So what are you two up to?" Michael sat on the arm of Sarah's chair and took a bite of her sandwich.

I glanced up from the contract. "Your wife is being a pain in the ass, as usual."

"Sarah?" The smile he bestowed on her was telling.

"Mac is the one who's being a brute. I simply asked how things are between her and Leah. Now I find out they're not dating any longer." She was pouting.

"I thought you were going to stay out of that?" Michael chuckled.

"Mac?" Mary called from the doorway, unable to see me on the couch.

"Over here, Mary."

"I'm going to run to the bank and make the deposit. I'll be back in a bit."

"Okay, thanks." I glanced up. "Michael, how soon can we close on this?"

"Should be end of next week."

"Good."

"Honey, tell Mac what a sweetheart Leah is," Sarah said. "How good she is with the kids."

His eyes shifted between me and his wife. "I don't think so. I'm staying out of this one and you should, too."

"Good thinking, big guy," I said.

"Can you give me one good reason why you don't want to see her again?" Sarah asked.

"*Yes* I can."

"Mac," Michael shook his head.

I stalked over to Sarah's chair, my eyes boring into hers. "As I explained, I'm not interested in the damn woman."

Michael put his hand on my arm. "Ahh, Mac?"

"It's fucking simple, Sarah," I said, ignoring him. "I don't want to lead her on—"

"Mac!"

"No, Michael, Sarah needs to hear this. Leah's a good person who deserves better, and even she's figured out I'm in love with someone else."

The sound was small but enough to make me glance around. Emily was standing in the doorway. *Fuck.*

"I think that's our cue to leave," Sarah said, patting Michael's arm. She pulled me into a hug. "Tell her. I love you. Call me later." She mouthed "Tell her" again, as if I hadn't heard her the first time. Michael patted my shoulder in commiseration and followed his wife.

"I'll see you tonight at the book signing," Sarah said as she kissed Emily's cheek.

As they left the office Michael quietly closed the door behind them.

"Did I interrupt something?" Emily asked.

"No, just Sarah driving me nuts as usual." I shoved my fingers through my hair in frustration. "Come in, sit, and tell me how I got so lucky today."

"Flatterer. I was wondering if you could babysit tonight? The book club is hosting another reading and I'll be closing late again."

"Absolutely. I'll take them to the diner or maybe for pizza. Maybe we'll do some miniature golf."

"You don't have to do that. I made a roast yesterday. There are plenty of leftovers and you can watch a video or play one of the games Kylie insists on beating you at." Her smile radiated warmth, soothing my inner turmoil.

"Whichever you think best."

"Thank you. Sarah's coming, as you heard, or I'd have asked her."

"I like spending time with the kids. We have fun together. Can I get you something to drink? Coffee, water?"

"No thanks."

I sat in the chair next to her grinning, happy to see her.

"Are you going to tell me who the mystery woman is?"

I picked at a loose thread of my cuff. "Sarah was irritating me, so I said the first thing I could think of to shut her up."

"If that were true she would have come back at you. She believed you. So did I for that matter."

"She's pissed because Leah and I agreed not to see each other."

"Why? Sarah was so sure you two were perfect together."

Humph. "Not hardly."

Emily reached out and covered my hand with hers. "Are you okay?"

"I'm great. Leah's good, it's fine."

"So?"

"So nothing."

"Why do you insist on shielding me? I don't need you to do that."

I glanced up. "I'm not."

"I thought we got past this. Did you forget I've dealt with bigotry before with Melanie and Renee?" Emily took a deep breath. "My daughter was one of the bravest women I know. I would hope she got some of that from me. I promise I won't be shocked, no matter who this mystery woman is."

"There's no one, Em. Really."

"Dammit, I thought you trusted me."

My heart thudded in my chest.

"What's wrong with her? Is she younger? Is she older? Is she married?"

I shook my head, unable to utter a response.

"Fine. Don't tell me. I'm leaving. I need to open the store and I'm tired of this same old crap from you. You're either going to trust me or you're not."

"No." I bounced up and reached the door before her. "Don't

go." The hurt reflected in her eyes shattered my common sense. My hands gently cupped her face. Any words she might have uttered were smothered as my mouth covered hers. Her lips were soft and tasted so much better than I could have imagined. When she didn't push me away, I deepened the kiss and Emily groaned. Emboldened by the sound, our kiss continued, our lips moving together sensually. The tip of my tongue peeked out, searching, tasting. Tendrils of heat spread from my lower stomach outward, burning through every cell and nerve ending. My heart fluttered with joy. Months of dreaming, wishing, had led to this one moment, this one kiss from the woman who had crashed into my life and crumbled my walls.

As quickly as it began, Emily reached between us and pushed. I leaned back, but the closed door halted my retreat. The kiss had muddled my brain and my senses were numb as I struggled to understand the sudden separation.

Her cheeks were flushed red. "Why did you do that?" She appeared stunned.

I clasped her hand in mine and met her eyes. "I was making the first move," I said.

"First move? First—what did I do to indicate that I wanted you to kiss me? That I—that I, I don't even know what to say to you." She pulled away from me.

"Please don't be upset. I *tried* to back away from you, Emily. I *tried* keeping my distance, but you insisted we remain friends."

"Friends yes, but not this."

I shook my head. "I never wanted to betray you, but—"

"But what? Say it."

"I've fallen in love with you." I took a deep breath. "You're my mystery woman."

Emily stared at me. "What about Izzy?"

"This isn't about Isabella. When I began to want more, it was you I wanted."

Emily stood there, arms crossed.

I shoved my hands in my pockets. "Allow me to apologize. I'm sorry."

"Sorry? Sorry?" She touched her lips. "I don't understand what just happened."

I stepped around her and walked to the window, her anger washing over me like a mist covered mountain, smothering my momentary elation. "It's simple. I crossed the line. I'm sorry I upset you. I'm sorry I kissed you, and I'm sorry—I'm—sorry."

Emily slipped out the door without a word. Her footsteps echoed as she ran down the stairs. The front door slammed behind her. I leaned my head against the windowpane, aching inside as she crossed the street and climbed into her truck. I watched her pull away from the curb, pain nearly doubling me over. Tears tracked down my face, dripping onto the windowsill as I watched her taillights drift from view. A painful tearing in my chest left me hollow and gasping as I succumbed to her rejection. I pressed my palm against the glass and whispered, "I love you, Emily. I'm sorry."

Chapter Sixteen

THE SMOKE DETECTOR blared as I reached into the oven, grappled the dish that was bubbling over and spewing black smoke. I pushed the button for the exhaust fan as the mess in my hand continued to smolder. My eyes watered from the acrid smoke.

"Should I call the fire department?" I spun around to find Sarah removing batteries from the offensive alarm.

"Ha, ha."

"What are you doing?"

"What does it look like?" My glare did nothing to unnerve her.

"Well, if I didn't know better I'd think you were preparing dinner, but I know you can't cook."

"I can cook."

Sarah went to the fridge and removed two beers, handing one to me. "Being able to break eggs and throw them into a pan with leftovers is *not* cooking. Boiling water to prepare boxed noodles and drowning them in a cheap jarred sauce is *not* cooking."

"How did you get in here?"

"The door was open." A broad grin filled her face. "I brought dinner," she said. "It's a good thing, too."

A glance at the burned concoction on the counter top forced me to concur. With a sigh I dumped it in the garbage. "What'd you bring?"

"Pizza and wings, your favorite."

I grabbed two plates, napkins and utensils and placed them at the breakfast bar. "What's this gonna cost me?"

"Nothing. I'm doing it out of the goodness of my heart," she said, sticking her tongue out at me. "Charity is good for the soul, doncha know."

"Yeah, right." The pizza box sat between us, but the wings were in the middle of my plate. Sarah didn't like them, so I didn't need to share.

After she wolfed down three slices of pizza and was finishing her second beer, she asked, "Want to tell me why you weren't coaching the team the other day?"

"Work is crazy and there were problems at various sites that needed my attention."

"Uh huh."

I shrugged. "Honestly, the team was Isabella's dream, not mine. You know that's the truth. I've decided to pull back."

"Bullshit. You love coaching those kids and they love you. Try again."

"Sarah, I don't—"

"Okay. Okay. Tell me what happened between you and Emily."

"You see her every day, I'm sure you know exactly what happened." At the fridge I pulled out two waters. Sarah still needed to drive home.

"Honey, you should know better. I care about Emily and we've become good friends, but I told her that I wouldn't discuss you and whatever transpired." She wiped her mouth with the napkin. "I would never betray you."

"Sorry. I know you wouldn't."

"Why haven't you returned my calls? It's been almost two weeks."

"And say what?"

Sarah leaned back against the counter. "I gather she didn't take it well when you told her you had feelings for her."

"You could say that."

"What'd you tell her?"

"I didn't exactly tell her anything."

Sarah arched her brow.

"I kissed her."

"Holy Mother of God."

"Yeah."

"What happened?"

"She pushed me away, told me she's not interested." I placed the leftover pizza on a dish and put it in the fridge.

"I'm sorry. I—I wish I could offer some words of encouragement." Sarah drew me into a tight embrace.

"At least she didn't slap me, right?"

"This still doesn't explain why you're not at the ball field coaching."

"Because I didn't want Emily to pull the kids off the team. Without me participating, there's no reason to."

"Did she threaten to do that?"

"No."

"So you abandoned the kids because Emily's not interested in you." Sarah asked.

"No. I would do anything for those kids. I love them, for god's sake."

"Then why aren't you making yourself available to them? When was the last time you actually saw Kaitlin and Kylie? Did you explain this to them?"

"Two days ago. And no."

"Have you even thought about how they're feeling?"

I marched to the door and stared out at the landscape. "I think about them all the time, and about Emily. I don't know how to fix things."

"You need to talk to Emily and find out where the relationship stands. You need to let the kids know you love them no matter what."

I walked back to her. "Is there something wrong? Something specific?"

Sarah took my hand in hers and looked me in the eye. "I can't betray Emily any more than I would betray you. Please understand."

"I do."

"Talk to Emily. Both of you need to figure this out."

"There's nothing to figure. She hates me."

"No, she doesn't hate you. She's confused."

"She didn't act confused. She was adamant."

"Go see her. At least try to save the friendship."

"I'll think about it."

"I love you, honey. I wish it had gone differently."

I shoved my hands in my pockets. "Yup, me too."

"You still look like crap."

"Love you, too, Sarah."

"MAC, HEATH IS on line three."

"Thanks, Mary."

I picked up the receiver. "Hey big guy, what's up?"

"Hi. Something a little unusual and under the circumstances I assumed you'd want to handle it."

"Okay?"

"Martha's sister-in-law, the cop, is going to be at Mercy this afternoon and would like you to meet her there."

"Any idea why?"

"None. Martha hasn't made any calls except to me for supplies, and she hasn't left the house, so she didn't initiate this."

"Interesting. What time am I supposed to meet her?"

"At your convenience after three."

"Okay, thanks. I'll make sure I'm there." After hanging up, I thought about the lieutenant and all the precautions she took to keep Martha safe. It was highly unlikely she would endanger that without good reason. A glance at the clock told me I'd have the answer within hours.

THE EMERGENCY ROOM was hopping, and Nancy was talking on the phone. I waved to her as I strolled past toward the waiting area. "Lieutenant, how are you?" She stood as I approached and I noticed another woman with her. She stood as well.

"Mac, thank you for meeting us. This is my wife, Hannah."

The strong resemblance reminded me of Martha. "It's nice to meet you, but I'm sure you didn't come all this way to meet me," I said.

"No. We didn't." The lieutenant glanced around. "Is there somewhere we could get a cup of coffee and maybe something to eat?"

I checked the clock on the wall. The cafeteria stopped serving at two, and the crap in the machines was just that, crap. "We could go to the diner up the street if you like."

"Is their coffee better than what we had last time?"

I howled with laughter. "Yes, I promise. So's the food."

"Let's go, it's our treat."

We turned to leave, but Nancy called and waved me over. "Excuse me, I'll be right back."

She hung the phone up and motioned for me to step closer.

"What's up, doll face?"

"Hey. Do you carry home phone numbers for the kids on your ball team?"

I reached in my pocket and pulled out my Blackberry. "Absolutely. Why?"

"I've got two MVA victims coming in. The EMT, Sammi, is pretty sure she's coached them with you."

"Do you have names?" As one of my regular volunteers Sammi would know.

Nancy shook her head. "One is unconscious, the other inconsolable."

"How far out are they?" My answer was the wail of the siren as the ambulance pulled up to the bay doors.

"We'll know in a minute." Nancy rounded the desk and hurried to the door to meet the attendants.

I returned to Christine and Hannah. "I'm sorry, but they're bringing in two kids who may play on my ball team and they need names and numbers for the families. It shouldn't be long."

"We're in no rush. Take your time."

"Thanks." I went back to the door as they brought in the first stretcher with a child whose head was swathed in bloody bandages. Cindy Jeffries was listening to the stats as they rushed past me into room six. That's when I saw the child's face and fear paralyzed me. The second patient was rolled in and Kylie was screaming hysterically. My knees trembled as I followed behind his stretcher into the same room as his sister.

My heart thundered. "What happened?" I asked as I gazed

around. "Somebody, please tell me what happened."

Cindy removed the bandage as Kaitlin opened her eyes. Blood was running down the side of her face.

My vision blurred. "Is she?"

"Mac." The warning in Cindy's voice stopped me cold.

I took a deep breath and straightened my spine. "Is she okay?"

Cindy continued her exam. She had Kaitlin follow her finger and shined a light into the child's eyes. She touched Kaitlin's forehead, palpating the spot and around her eye socket, before working her hands down each side of Kaitlin's head, neck and shoulder area. "Do you know our pretty little patient?" Cindy asked.

"Yes. Her name is Kaitlin. Kaitlin O'Brien. She's seven. And that's her brother, Kylie. He's five." I stepped closer to him and took his hand in mine. "I'm here, little man. It's okay."

"Ms. Kaitlin, you've got a pretty nasty bump on your head, but we're going to fix that for you," Cindy said. "We'll run some tests to be sure, but I think you're going to be fine." Tears slid from the corners of Kaitlin's eyes, but she remained unresponsive.

Cindy resumed the examination while Nancy cleaned the wound on Kaitlin's temple. An intern worked on Kylie. So far, he had confirmed a broken arm.

Cindy motioned for me to follow her outside. I patted Kylie's hand and told him I'd be right back and kissed Kaitlin's cheek. Neither child had spoken and I was getting scared.

JoAnne blocked the doorway. "Nancy, the driver of the MVA is coming in. Her injuries are extensive and they want us to get her stable before they medivac her out to St. Luke's. Should I contact the pilot now?"

"I'm coming." Nancy pushed through the door and I followed behind her, a sick feeling settling in the pit of my stomach.

Emily. "Emily must be the driver. Oh my God." *Stabilize her.* I couldn't lose her. The kids, they needed her. Dear Lord, don't let anything happen. My chest tightened and I felt light-headed.

Cindy gripped my arm. "Mac?"

"It's Emily, their grandmother. You can't let her die." I clutched Cindy's arms. "You have to save her. The kids need her. I need her, *please.*"

An EMT pushed a stretcher through the double doors of the ambulance bay while a second one straddled the unconscious form, administering CPR. The patient was covered in blood and wires dangled from various pieces of equipment. I started to push against Cindy's arms, but she blocked my way.

"Mac." Nancy's voice startled me. "The cops ID'd her, it's Renee McVee."

I sagged against the wall. Emily was safe. Then my temper kicked in. "I'll kill her," I growled. Renee would pay for endangering the children. My vision wavered and my legs threatened to go out from under me.

"Mac?" Cindy eased my head down by my knees. "Breathe deeply. I've gotta go help the patient. You need to contact the grandmother for us. Can you do that?"

I took another breath. "Sorry, I thought—I was afraid it might be—"

Cindy patted my arm. "I hope she knows how lucky she is," she said as she entered Renee's room.

"Mac, can we help?"

I gazed up to see Christine and Hannah's concerned faces. I had forgotten all about them. The wall supported me as I bent at the waist trying to clear my head. "I'm sorry. I'm going to be tied up for a while. Where are you staying?"

"I hadn't thought that far ahead." Christine answered.

I took a deep breath. "Is there a working GPS system in your vehicle?"

"Yes."

I pulled my wallet out, withdrew a business card, and wrote a series of numbers on the back. "Here." I pulled my house key off my ring. "This opens the deadbolt on my back door. The coordinates are on the back of my card, and the security code's there, too. Go to the diner, have dinner, then go stay at my house. I'll meet you there as soon as I can. The guest room is straight down the hall on the left. Drive slow. It's tricky."

"You don't have to do this."

"It'll be easier for me, if I know where you are and that you're both safe."

"We'll see you later." Christine said.

Officer O'Leary strolled in the front door with Randy Cartwright, the prosecutor. They walked up to the desk as I attempted to place a call to Emily.

"Gentlemen, can I help you?" JoAnne flashed her loveliest smile.

"We've got an arrest warrant for the driver of the MVA. We need a blood alcohol test done and I want to be sure she remains in custody while undergoing any medical treatment." Randy handed a document to JoAnne.

"Let me get the doctor for you. She's in with the patient now." JoAnne appeared flummoxed. "Please take a seat."

There was no answer at the bookstore or the apartment and Emily's cell was going direct to voicemail. I dialed Sarah in desperation.

"Hi, handsome," she answered.

"Sarah, is Emily with you?"

"Yes. Why? Do you want to drop the kids off—"

"Sarah—" My voice cracked.

"Honey, what's wrong?"

"I need—" Icy tentacles of fear constricted my chest.

"You're scaring me."

"I—I need your help." A sob escaped. "There's been an accident."

"What kind of accident?"

"Motor vehicle. You need to come down to the hospital. And Sarah—bring Emily with you."

"We're on our way. We'll be there in twenty minutes." The connection ended abruptly.

"WHAT THE HELL are you doing?" Officer O'Leary was questioning the children when I entered the room.

"I'm trying to determine how they were hurt."

"Isn't it obvious? Renee most likely got drunk and drove them into a ditch or a tree or whatever the hell she hit. She almost killed them—again. Now get out and leave them alone."

"I can't do that, Mac. You're right, there was an open bottle of Jack Daniels on the front seat. But the rear of the car sustained *no* damage. When we arrived at the scene they were securely strapped into their safety seats. The car accident is not the reason for their injuries."

"What?" My eyes darted from Kylie to Kaitlin and back to Daniel. I went to Kylie and clasped his hand in mine. "I love you, but you have to tell the truth. What happened to your arm? How did Kaitlin get hurt?"

"Sthe hurth me." He was trembling. "Sthe did it."

"Who, baby? Who did this?"

Kylie whimpered. "Mommy Renee. Sthe locked uths in the closthet again. Sthe wasth gone a long time. I wet mysthelf and sthe got real mad and twisthted my arm, and sthe hit Kaitlin causthe Kaitlin tried to make her sthtop. Kaitlin falled and hit her head. Sthe was mad and yelled at usth."

"Okay, one more time, slowly. Renee hurt your arm?"

He nodded his head. "She twisthted it."

"How did Kaitlin get hurt?"

"Mommy Renee hit her. She falled. She was bleeding bad. She always locksth usth in. Then sthe yellsth at usth."

I walked to Kaitlin's side. "Honey, tell the truth. Did Mommy Renee do this to you?"

She gestured with her head as tears ran down her cheeks. I kissed her forehead gently. "Thank you."

I hugged Kylie. "You did good, little man. I'm proud of you."

I turned to Daniel. "Can you go to the apartment and investigate this? Document your findings and take pictures?"

"Absolutely." He started to walk away, but stopped. "Mac, I need to notify CPS, too."

Rage pounded in my veins. "I'm way ahead of you. I'll place the call right now."

LEAH WAS IN the exam room talking with the kids. She had asked me to step outside so I wouldn't be an influence.

"Mac?" Nancy touched my arm.

"Tell me she's dead. Otherwise I'm gonna fuckin' kill her."

"It doesn't look good." She shoved her hands into her pockets. "How are the children?"

"Mostly okay, thank God. Kylie's arm is busted, and I believe Kaitlin's only injury is the head wound and some bruising."

"She's probably got a concussion. She was unconscious."

I stood up straighter. "That should be okay, though, right?"

"I'm sure it'll be fine, but we can't ignore it."

"Okay."

Nancy patted my shoulder. "Did you reach the grandmother?"

"Yeah, and Sarah is coming in, too. I need her to examine the kids."

Nancy bristled.

"It's not about Cindy. I want Sarah's professional expertise to document the abuse and injuries."

"Abuse? You think the driver hurt them?"

"She's the step-mother. And that's what they tell us."

"Does the grandmother know?"

"It's complicated."

"Good luck with that one." Nancy went back to the desk.

The emergency room doors opened and Sarah and Emily rushed into the ER. Sarah was in doctor mode. Emily was falling apart. "Where are they? What happened? Are they okay? Tell me."

"Sarah, Leah wants you to examine the kids." I indicated the room. "She's inside with them." Sarah's brow arched and she strode through the door.

Emily tried to follow her, but I put my arm out. "You can't go in there just yet."

"And who's going to stop me?"

"I am."

Her face paled. "Are they—how bad—how bad is it?"

I tried to grasp her hand and struggled to ignore the hurt as she jerked it away. "It's not life threatening. Let's go into the nurses' lounge."

"I'm not leaving here. I want to see them. What's happened? How did they get hurt and not you?"

I blocked the door. "They weren't with me. I was here on other business when they were brought in."

"I don't understand. I dropped them off at the ballfield myself."

"Kylie said Renee picked them up there."

"That can't be. I want to see them. Now."

"Emily, it's going to be a little while before you can see them and we need to talk first."

The door to exam room eight opened and two orderlies pushed the stretcher carrying Renee through, heading for the elevator.

"Was that Renee?"

"Yes."

"Where are they taking her?"

"She's being medivaced to the Trauma Center in Denver."

"Why?"

"She has serious internal injuries from the accident."

Emily stopped pacing. "Renee? The kids were with her? How?"

"I'm not sure. Come on, let's get coffee." In the lounge I poured two cups and placed one in Emily's hands. "Drink that. It's bloody awful, but you're going to need it. Look, Kylie told me Renee showed up shortly after they arrived at the ballfield and told them they had to go with her. Since I wasn't there to stop it, they went with her."

"How bad are they hurt, and please tell me the truth?"

"I'm going to tell you the truth. It's not about their injuries so much as *how* they were injured. Renee will most likely be charged with child abuse upon completion of this investigation. Kaitlin has a couple bruises and an ugly gash to her head. Possibly a concussion. Kylie's arm is broken. He told us she locked them in a closet."

I explained about the car accident and the likelihood of Renee being drunk. I described the scene and the condition of the vehicle as Daniel had relayed it to me, and finally I related the details as Kylie did to the officer and myself. "Kaitlin verified it all, Emily. Renee's been abusing them since Melanie died. And I think there's more to it."

"But why were they with her today? I specifically told her no."

"It didn't stop her that night at the diner."

"I don't believe this." Emily picked the coffee up and put it back down. "How did I miss this?"

"You were too busy trying to do what Melanie asked of you. She took the coward's way out by not telling you the truth."

Anger flashed in Emily's eyes.

"*She* made you promise something that you would never have done if you had known the facts."

"What's taking so long? I want to see the children."

"They know we're in here. You need to let Sarah do her thing first and talk to them."

Thirty minutes passed before Leah found us at the table. "I assume you've explained things?" she asked me.

I stood to let Leah sit. "I told her what I knew about how they were injured and what I understood to be the extent of their injuries."

"Emily, I need to be clear." Leah looked at her. "I'm here in a professional capacity not as your friend."

Emily glanced from Leah to me. "I don't understand."

"Anytime a child is brought into the emergency room with injuries that can't be properly explained, CPS is called in to investigate."

"Did you know about this?" Emily addressed me.

"I'm the one who called Leah."

Emily jumped up. "You son-of-a-bitch. I refuse your advances and you call CPS on me!"

"That's *not* what happened."

"I would never hurt those children—"

Leah tugged on Emily's hand. "We're not investigating *you*. It's Renee McVee who's being charged with neglect and abuse. The children will remain in your custody as long as you ensure Renee has no further contact with them."

"I'll do whatever you say." Emily sat rigidly.

"There were no prior indications?"

Emily shook her head. "No."

"If I had known I would have killed her," I said.

"It's unlikely you'll get the chance, Mac. I've been told her injuries are life threatening."

"Good." The two of them glared at me, but I felt no sorrow for the bitch.

"Would you like to see the children now? Sarah's about finished with her exam."

Emily stood up eagerly. "Yes, please."

Leah tapped on the door before opening it. Daniel was conferring with Sarah.

"Gramma." Kylie began to cry.

"Oh sweetie, are you okay? Gramma's here now. I've got you." She embraced Kylie first, then Kaitlin.

Kaitlin was sitting up, yet other than watch she hadn't reacted. Fear gripped me.

"Hey you, how are you?" Kaitlin slid into my arms. I held her tightly against me. "Honey, it's okay, Grandma's right here and I am, too." I wrapped my arms tighter to quell her shaking. "I won't let anyone hurt you." I kissed the top of her head and pushed hair out of her eyes, eyes she had so clearly inherited from her mother and grandmother. "You're gonna be okay."

Kaitlin's tears kept flowing and I glanced at Sarah.

"Kaitlin has a concussion. It's mild and she'll need to be monitored for the next twenty-four hours, but I don't see any reason you can't do that at home," Sarah explained. "This little guy—" Sarah tugged on Kylie's foot "—has a fractured radius, x-rays confirmed it. I put a hard cast on it. Everything's been documented, pictures taken, statements recorded, and best of all, we're waiting for their ice cream before I release them."

I murmured in Kaitlin's ear, "Mommy Renee's never going to hurt you again. I promise you."

Kaitlin raised soulful eyes. "But what about Gramma?"

AN HOUR AND a half later the kids and Emily were ready to leave the hospital. Sarah had been called upstairs for another emergency, leaving them stranded. "I can give you a ride."

"I think you've done enough for us already." Emily pointed the kids to the waiting room and told them to sit.

I remained still, frustrated and angry. When Emily went to the nurse's desk, I approached her. "Look dammit, I was out of line in my office, but you have no right to question my concern or integrity with regard to the kids. I love them and you know it."

"Fine." She motioned to JoAnne. "May I use the phone?"

"Give me the keys to your truck."

"What?"

"Give me the damn keys to your truck," I snapped.

Emily pulled her key ring out and unclipped the truck's key. "Why do you want these?"

I pushed my keys into her hands. "Take my truck and get the kids home. Leave the key under the mat. I'll go get your truck and make the switch later."

"You don't need to do that. I can call Mrs. Tompkins."

Fury made me jerk her away from prying ears. "What did I ever do that was so horrible? I don't deserve this bullshit because of a simple kiss."

"All right." Emily jerked her arm back. "Come on, you two, Mac is lending us her truck so we can go home."

I watched them leave the hospital and started off myself. The forty-minute walk to Sarah's did little to ease my hurt and anger. As I pulled into the lot behind the bookstore I refrained from glancing up. I knew there would be no welcoming beacon, no friendship being dangled in front of me. I pushed the keys for Emily's truck through the mail slot in the front door, then hopped into mine and drove away.

WHEN I PULLED into my driveway, I saw a U-Haul and a truck parked next to it. The lieutenant and her wife. I had forgotten about them for the second time that day. The following morning, coffee was brewing when Christine moseyed into the kitchen. "Morning."

"Hi." I turned to her. "I'm really sorry about yesterday."

"Are the children okay?"

"Yes, for the most part. Thank you."

"You're close to them."

"Yeah, I am."

"I'm glad it worked out."

"Me too." I poured two cups and placed one on the counter for her.

"Thanks."

After providing sugar and milk for her use, I got down to it. "So what's this about, Lieutenant?"

"First off, I'm not a lieutenant anymore." She stirred sugar into her cup and grinned. "I put my papers in."

"Is that a good thing?"

"Yes. Hannah and I agreed."

"Then congratulations. I'm happy for you."

"But still confused, right?"

I climbed up on the stool next to her. "Yeah, I am."

"We'd like to relocate with Martha and Kim."

"Don't you own a house back home?"

"My parents bought it from us, cash. They'll handle selling it."

"What about your family?"

"We held a big meeting between my family and Hannah's. This is the right thing for us."

"Morning."

Christine turned to Hannah. "How'd you sleep, sweetie?"

"Good, thanks." She leaned over and kissed Chris on the cheek.

I got up and poured another cup of coffee. "Enjoy."

"Thank you. I guess Chris told you what we want by now?"

"Yes."

"Is it possible? Please tell me it is."

I grinned. "There're no hard and fast rules about this. Chris, what about your pension? It can't get mailed to a PO box."

"I went to a lawyer. My sister has my power of attorney. She will receive my pension and forward it on to me."

"No checks, no bank transfers. It's got to be money orders."

"I understand."

"No contact from home."

They looked at each other. "We know."

"Well, if you two are sure about this, there's no reason not to arrange it. I'll transfer funds to the center and —"

"No need. We've plenty of money from the house and we managed to get Martha's money, too."

"You're determined to make this easy on me, aren't you?" I grinned as I picked up my cell to call Heath.

The U-Haul remained in my driveway until the final plans could be made, but the sisters, Kim and Chris were reunited within hours at the safe house. Heath took the title to the truck and would work on that along with the new identities for Chris and Hannah.

TWO WEEKS LATER, on Wednesday afternoon, I arrived back at the office an hour before game time. Mary needed paperwork for two different projects, which required a visit to the reprographers. Afterward I intended to clear up some bills before driving to the ballpark. Mary met me on the stairs.

Kaitlin and Kylie were in my office sitting on the sofa, playing Go Fish. "Hey guys, what's up?" I'd seen them almost daily since the accident. Kaitlin's stitches had been removed leaving a slight scar that would heal in time. Kylie had another couple of weeks before his cast came off and was dealing with it well. Still, I couldn't penetrate the sadness that seemed to surround them. Emily remained aloof.

Kaitlin peeked at Kylie, then me. She had been crying. I walked to my desk and dropped my briefcase and jacket before sitting down between them. "Want to tell me why you were crying?"

Kaitlin's tears started anew. I pulled her into my arms and held her. Kylie watched us. I dried her cheeks and wiped her eyes with a tissue. "If you tell me, I might be able to help."

She buried her head in my shoulder. "No one can help."

I turned to Kylie. "How about it, Bub?"

He averted his eyes and appeared ready to cry himself. He watched his sister.

"Sweetie, you can trust me."

I grasped Kaitlin and turned her on my lap. "Honey, talk to me. I'll protect you."

She glanced at me through her tears. "Like the day you hit Mommy Renee?"

"Well—yes," I responded sheepishly. "That's probably not a good example, but like that day, yes."

They both stared at me.

"Mommy Renee won't hurt you ever again."

Kaitlin hid her head on my chest.

"Honey, what are you not telling me?" I rubbed her back gently. "Please sweetie, talk to me."

She whimpered softly.

"Is it about Mommy Renee?"

She nodded and Kylie joined her, but more vigorously.

I pulled her closer and held her tighter. "Okay. Remember when Aunt Sarah and Leah were taking pictures and talking to you at the hospital?"

"I wasth in my underroos." Kylie giggled.

"Yeah, you were." I grinned at his remark. "That doesn't matter though. What matters is that Aunt Sarah wrote a report and sent it to the court along with the pictures. That's so Mommy Renee can never hurt you again."

"How?"

"Well, the judge read the report about what Mommy Renee did to you and now she's not allowed near you anymore."

"He can do that?" Kaitlin asked.

"Yes, he can." *And if he can't I will.*

"Sthe hatesth usth," Kylie whispered.

"What?"

"Sthe sthaid we killed Momma," he said.

"Listen. You two *did not kill your mother*. It was a terrible accident, but it wasn't your fault." My temper was about to explode.

Kylie rested his head on my chest next to his sister.

"Did you tell Grandma about this?"

"We can't."

I pondered that. "Why not?"

"'Cause she'll make us leave."

"Okay, I'm confused." Frustration was making me nuts. "Why would Grandma make you leave?"

"Because she hates us, too."

"Why would you think that?"

"Mommy Renee told us Gramma wanted to give us away because we made Momma die." Kaitlin buried her face in my shirt.

"That's not true. Your mother died because a bad man got drunk and drove. You didn't have anything to do with that."

"But Mommy Renee said—"

"I don't give a damn what she said, she lied to you. Do you trust me?"

They both bobbed their heads.

"Then listen to me. Mommy Renee is wrong. You did not cause your mother's death and Grandma loves you with all her heart."

"How do you know?"

"I just do. I think we should go get a pizza, take it home to grandma, and have a long talk with her. Whadda ya say?"

"What about the ball game?"

"I think it's more important we talk to Gramma." Kaitlin wiped her tears.

"What if sthe sthays we hafe to go?" Kylie asked, he lower lip tremulous.

"She won't." *She wouldn't.*

"Can we live with you if Gramma doesn't want usth?"

I kissed Kaitlin and hugged Kylie to me. "It's not going to happen, but yes, I promise you can live with me." *Even if we needed to leave town.*

Ms. O'Brien and I were going to have a long talk. Renee was never going to hurt these kids again, either physically or with her viral mouth. "So pizza, yes?"

They both agreed. I kissed Kaitlin's cheek. "It's going to be okay, baby. I know Gramma loves you very much."

"I hope so." She clung to me.

Chapter Seventeen

THE KIDS RAN up the stairs ahead of me while I carried the pizza.

Emily opened the door and it was abundantly clear she wasn't happy to see me. "What's going on?"

I leaned in and whispered, "We need to talk and like it or not, we're going to."

She glanced at the kids' eager faces and finally let me in.

"We brought dinner," I said.

"I see that. Go wash up, you two. Mac and I will set the table."

As soon as the kids left the room, she glared at me.

"Look, this is important or I wouldn't be here," I said.

"We have nothing to say to each other."

"This isn't about you and me. It's about them."

Emily opened the cupboard and started removing dishes, as well as a couple glasses. Her body language told me all I needed to know with respect to us. It hurt, more than I ever imagined. After the impromptu meal was done and the mess cleaned up, Emily put a movie in for the kids before we convened in the kitchen.

"What's this about?" she asked.

"They were waiting for me when I got back this afternoon."

"They were supposed to be at the Tomlinson's."

"What can I say, they were in my office."

"And?" she asked impatiently.

"And Kaitlin was crying. Kylie wasn't far behind."

"Why?" That got her attention. "What happened?"

"They're scared."

"They're never going to be around Renee again. I already told them that," Emily retorted.

"They're not afraid of Renee."

"Who then?"

"You."

She bounded up, anger oozing from every pore. "I've never hurt those children and I never would. How dare you—"

I put my hand up. "That's not what they're afraid of." I motioned for her to lower her voice and to sit. "Renee told them it's their fault Melanie died and, most importantly, that you hate them for it."

Her eyes reflected it all. Shock, sadness, anger.

"She really did a job on them," I said.

"It's not true."

"I. Know. That. But they're frightened kids who've been battered by a sick, malicious bitch, and they believe her."

Emily appeared bewildered. She sprang up and dashed into the living room. Kaitlin was sitting on the couch reading. Kylie was playing with his Matchbox cars close by. Emily shut the TV off and approached them. "Children, we need to talk."

Kaitlin glanced fearfully from me to Emily.

"It's okay," I said. "Tell Gramma the truth."

Emily began. "I want you to tell me exactly what Renee has been telling you."

Kylie shifted closer to his sister, grasping her hand. Emily's anger was clear, but they didn't realize it wasn't aimed at them.

"Kaitlin, Kylie, tell me what she said."

Kaitlin's lower lip trembled and Kylie confronted Emily. "We're gonna run away." His jaw was set, his shoulders hunched. I smiled behind Emily's back, proud of his determination to safeguard his sister.

Emily got down on her knees, grasping each child's hand. "You are not going to run away. You're going to stay right here. I need you."

Kaitlin looked up at Emily. "But you hate us."

"Honey, why would you say that?"

Kylie explained. "Sthe sthaid you hate usth. That we killed Momma. Sthe sthaid ith's our faulth." He launched himself at his grandmother. "I'm sthorry."

Kylie was crying and tears gathered in Emily's eyes as she hugged him. "That's not true," she said. "I love you both. It's no one's fault Momma is gone. Most importantly, not yours."

Kaitlin glanced at me and whispered, "She said Grandma hates us for ruining her life. We didn't mean to." Tears ran down her face.

Emily pulled Kaitlin close. "Listen to me. You two are the best thing in my life. I love you very much. I don't blame you. I love you. I'm thankful every day that you're with me. You have to believe that."

"But she said —"

"I don't care what she said. I'm telling you, I love you. Both of you."

"Kaitlin, honey, think about this." I waited for her to look at me. "Does Grandma treat you mean? Does she hurt you? Has she ever made you feel bad?"

Kaitlin immediately shook her head.

"Does she hurt your brother, or treat him mean?"

They both shook their heads.

"Then you have to trust that Grandma loves you both and

wants you with her always."

Emily shook her head as tears flowed. "I love you so very much. I would die if you left me."

Kaitlin threw her arms around Emily, and Kylie joined them. It was a family moment, one that didn't require an audience. I slipped out of the room.

The coffee cups and pot were cleaned and the counter wiped by the time Emily returned to the kitchen. "Why didn't they tell me?" she asked.

The guilt and pain etched on her face broke me. "They were afraid."

"Why?"

I held my hands out. "They've had a hard year. They're still trying to cope with the loss of Melanie. The move. Renee." I put the towel on the rack to dry. "Did you — was Renee violent with your daughter?"

Emily seemed bewildered. "I didn't think so, but honestly, I have no idea."

"Did she even want the kids?"

Emily rubbed her forehead. "They both were excited about Kaitlin's birth, I really thought it would make them a family." She took breath. "Right before Kylie was born things seemed to erode. I'm not sure why, but that's when Renee started drinking too much. She went from a social drinker to constantly inebriated in a flash."

"What did Melanie say about that?"

"She loved Renee, but she hated the drinking. They started spending time apart. I think that's when Renee got out of control. They were arguing all the time." Emily looked up. "I don't know if she was violent, I never suspected though."

"Leah said CPS was getting an RO. Have you been provided with your copy?"

"Yes." Emily gazed into the living room where the kids were sitting huddled together on the couch whispering. She whirled back to me. "Why did they tell you and not me?"

"They wanted to know if they could live with me, if you made them leave."

Emily fell onto a kitchen chair, her head in her arms, crying. I waited her out as she dealt with the grief.

Her tears continued and I asked, "Can I do anything?"

She raised her tear-stained face and my resolve crumpled. I pulled her up into my arms and held her, murmuring, "This is not me making a pass at you. This is your friend offering comfort. I promise." She cried harder and held on tightly for long minutes.

Emily appeared staggered, the shock of the situation just starting to sink in. "I had seen some bruises before, you know. Any time I asked, Kaitlin said it happened in gym, or school, or at the ballpark. I mean kids get bruises, right? Do you think it's worse than they're telling us?"

"I'm not sure, but you might want to think about letting them see someone."

"Do you really think that's necessary?"

"No, I don't. Maybe talk to Sarah and get her opinion."

"I'll call her right away."

"Good, I'm gonna say good night to the kids and get out of your hair."

Emily stepped back. The separation was more than mere inches. "Yes, that's probably a good idea."

"I do love them, Emily. I hope you know that."

"I do."

"Okay."

We walked into the living room area. "Well, since it seems Grandma is not willing to part with either of you, I'm going to say goodnight." I leaned down and kissed both of them. Kaitlin wrapped her arms around me and whispered, "I love you, Mac."

"You be good and I'll see you tomorrow at the game." I glanced at Emily quickly. "If Grandma says it's okay."

"They'll be there."

In the kitchen there was an awkward silence and desperation engulfed me. "Emily I'm sorry about—"

She shook her head. "I think it's best if you don't come around, at least for a while. You can see the children at the games, but as far as we're concerned, there's no future."

"I knew that." I forced a grin.

Emily followed me to the door. "Good night, if you need anything—"

The stiffness returned. "We'll be fine, thank you."

"Right." She closed the door and I waited as she set the alarm, then climbed into my truck to head up the mountain. All hope of saving the friendship was gone. Tears flowed freely as the pain filled me.

THE FOLLOWING WEEK I was in Denver picking up a set of prints. Saint Luke's Trauma Center was three blocks away and I drove directly there. I had kept in contact with the staff since the accident. They told me Renee was improving daily and I thought it was time she and I had a talk.

The hospital was huge and the buildings were spread out over a massive compound. The reception desk was large and round and there were three volunteers working behind it. I approached a woman whose name tag identified her as Gladys. "May I help you?"

"Hi, I'm here to visit Renee McVee."

"One moment." While the woman entered some information into the computer, I took a look around. The floors and walls were white Italian marble, the real stuff, imported years ago and still standing to demonstrate its quality. A small florist was located off to the side, right next to a row of elevators. Different colored lines on the floor with matching color-coded signs overhead directed patients and visitors to the various specialty floors and treatment areas. Oncology was yellow, maternity green, dialysis purple, bones, joints and muscles gray, and so on and so forth. Even with the lines, it was easy to get lost within those walls. I'd been there before and I knew.

"Ms. McVee is in room six-sixteen on the sixth floor. Take the elevator over on the right."

"Thank you." She handed me a pass and I started in the direction she had indicated. Unbeknownst to her, though, I searched out the stairwell around the corner. A mild case of claustrophobia kept me out of elevators whenever possible. The free exercise was a bonus.

The nurses' station was empty when I came through the door on the sixth floor. A small sign on the opposite wall indicated two series of room numbers and their location, left or right down the hall. Room six-sixteen was to the left.

The door was ajar as I approached. The TV hanging from the wall was on, but the volume was muted. I knocked softly.

"Yeah." The voice was gravelly and low.

I strolled in. The blinds were closed tight, the TV the only illumination within the darkened space. Shock settled in at the vision before me. Renee appeared shrunken and half-dead.

"What do *you* want?"

"Just checking up on you."

"More likely wishing I was dead."

"Initially yeah, I did. I even wanted to speed you along."

That brought what I thought was a genuine smile to her face.

"How are you really?"

She glared. "Well, if you don't count the fact that my liver is shot, my kidneys got damaged in the accident, and the violent shaking from severe DT's, I'm doing great, thanks."

"You could have killed the kids. They're fine, by the way, good of you to ask."

Renee squinted at me. "You really care about them, don't you?"

"More importantly, why the fuck don't you? Melanie left you a gift and you threw it away. Do you have any idea how fucking selfish that is?"

Renee stared at me and it shocked me when tears leaked from her eyes. The fight had gone out of her. Her lips trembled. "I hate them." She averted her glance, leaving me with my mouth hanging open. I knew, of course, but hearing it made me want to bash her head in.

Renee continued. "It's their fault Melanie's dead. She was rushing to their daycare when the accident occurred. If it wasn't for them, she'd be alive today." Her eyes were flinty hard.

I thought back, trying to remember everything Emily had told me about the accident. A drunk driver leaving an office party had slammed head-on into Melanie two blocks from the school. The saving grace was it had been quick. I thought about all the platitudes people forced on me after Isabella and Bella died. How everyone assured me time would heal all wounds. Yes, mine were healing, but it was because of my interest in Emily. Not that she would be happy to hear that. My love for the children helped for sure, but time never factored into it. Emily was my redemption. I couldn't imagine what Renee's would be. I glanced up to return her gaze. Is that what this was about? She was hurting? She missed Melanie? Had that driven her to drink even more? I took a minute trying to see beyond my prejudice and anger. A sigh escaped.

"Aren't you going to tell me what an evil person I am?" She seemed defeated.

"No, I'm not. I understand your pain—"

"*You* understand jack shit. How could you?" Renee fisted her hand.

I seized the chair in the corner and dragged it back to the bedside. "I'm going to tell you a little tale, and you're going to shut the fuck up and listen."

Minutes went by. "Do you hear me?"

Renee remained defiant. "Not like I have a fucking choice."

"Let me start by saying I don't normally talk about this. You're only the second person I've ever told, but, you see, I really do understand what you're going through. I have my own hell." I told her about Isabella, our relationship, our love, the home we shared, the life we built. Then I told about the miracle of Bella and how our happiness was complete. I explained about Juan, the things we knew, and those we didn't. I related to her in full, gruesome detail the circumstances surrounding their deaths, and the fact that all I had to show for it was a grave marker to symbolize our life together. When I finished we were both crying.

"Sorry," Renee managed.

"I don't need an apology. I want your word you'll leave the kids alone and never, ever bother them again."

"Whadda you care?"

"I care. I care about the kids and I care about Emily, and I'm not going to let you hurt them anymore."

"Are you in love with Emily?" Renee asked.

"Yes."

"Does she love you?" she whispered.

"No." I shook my head. "At the moment she doesn't even like me."

She laid back against the pillows. "Do you love the kids?"

"With all my heart."

"Good, that's good," she sighed. "Melanie would be pleased to know that." She turned on her side. I wondered if it was that simple, really.

Moments later I heard her. "Do you really love them?"

"Yes."

"How come?"

"I don't understand?"

"Melanie did, too. They *were* everything to her. She was a good mother. She loved them more than anything or anyone in the world. Even me." Tears ran down Renee's face unchecked.

"She must have loved you, she stayed with you."

"Everything went to hell once Kaitlin was born." Renee rubbed her eyes. "Our relationship was in trouble, I kept telling her I needed more attention, but the baby came first. Later she even convinced me Kaitlin needed a sibling."

"You could have said no."

"Could you have said no to your wife?"

"No."

"Exactly. Once Kylie was born, she had no time for me at all, or any love left over."

It was clear Renee believed that.

"She chose you for a life partner."

"Aren't you listening?" Renee's eyes shot daggers. "She loved them with all her heart. Everything was about them. I hate them. I will always blame them for Melanie's death. I remind them every chance I get."

I sat stunned by her further admission. The hateful words chilling me.

"Go on tell me what a bastard I am?" Renee asked.

"No." I shook my head sadly. I ached for the kids, but I understood Renee's heartache, if not her handling of it.

She frowned and rolled away from me. "I yell at them, or make them stay in their room when they're with me. If I need to get away from them, I lock them in and go to the bar. I hate spending time with them. It hurts too much." Tears were streaming down her face. "I lost everything when Melanie died."

"Why do it? Why take them?"

"Because—it's what's expected. Emily expects it. Melanie would have expected it." Renee closed her eyes and leaned her head against the pillow. "Because they expect it."

"Not anymore. It's over. There's a restraining order in place. They don't deserve this abuse."

"I don't beat them. Maybe a slap here or there."

"Verbal abuse is still abuse. Kaitlin had a concussion from the last slap you gave her and Kylie has a broken arm, and that defines abuse."

"Okay."

"Okay?"

"Yeah—I hated hurting them. It made me drink even more. Especially Kaitlin. She's so much like Mellie—it's—it's like I was hurting her. You have to believe me, I loved Mellie—with all my heart." Renee was sobbing now.

"Okay."

She didn't even notice the tears dripping off her chin.

"What's next, Renee?"

"I want to stop hurting. I want Melanie to be alive and to love me. I want our life back. I hate that I hate the kids."

I closed myself to her pain. "What about your future?"

She closed her eyes and tilted her head back. I wondered if she would even answer.

She rolled onto her back and pinned me with her stare. "Was it easy to—you know, fall in love again?" Renee glanced away, as if embarrassed.

"Let's say I didn't expect to. Isabella's been gone almost six years and I was not searching for love, trust me. Emily kind of slipped under my radar. I think it's because I knew she was straight and not a threat. Unfortunately, I forgot to tell my heart that."

Long after I thought she was ever going to respond, she whispered, "Melanie was my reason for living. I don't know how to go on without her."

I waited silently.

Minutes passed and she sobbed. "I need to go into rehab. I need help."

"Yeah, you do." I touched her arm. "First you need to get well, then you need to deal with your legal issues. After that, if you want, I'll ask Lily to make arrangements for rehab."

Renee glowered, anger simmering below the surface. "Why do you even care?"

"Because Melanie loved you, I have to believe you have some redeeming qualities that I haven't discovered."

"She did you know, love me."

"All the more reason to find that person and help her get her life back."

KAITLIN AND KYLIE were in the backseat of my truck. "Are you mad at us?"

I glanced in the rearview mirror and caught Kaitlin studying me with a serious expression. "Absolutely not. I love you."

"Why don't you come to the house anymore?"

Fuck. "It's complicated, honey. I did something to upset your grandmother and she's annoyed at me."

"Justh sthay your sthorry. It worksth for usth." Kylie grinned.

"I tried, but I really made her mad. She needs some time to calm down and besides we get to see each other every day, right?"

"I guess. But I liked when you came to dinner. It was..." Kaitlin stared out the window.

"What, honey? What were you going to say?"

"It was like when Momma was alive. Gramma was happy and laughing and we would all talk. She's not happy anymore."

Not happy? "Well, that's my fault not yours and she'll be better soon. She loves you both. Be patient."

"Okay."

"Good, and remember we both love you. Even if she's mad at me, that has nothing to do with you. I promise."

"Can we come to visit you sometime?"

"If Grandma says yes, absolutely. But—why don't you wait a little while to ask her. Let her stop being angry first."

"Okay."

"Here we are. I love you, have a good night."

"Bye." They scooted out of the truck and into the bookstore. I saw Emily glance up and wondered why she was unhappy?

I STOPPED BY the office to grab two files I wanted to work on at home. Mary had a few things that needed my attention. Everything was organized as usual. She'd left sticky notes on the pertinent issues. I was reviewing the latest permits on two projects when I heard Tom Wilson's voice in the hall. Hopefully he was there to make payment.

A small stack of folders placed in my inbox needed a signature. Once I got through them I could leave.

Thoughts of Emily swirled in my mind. Why was she unhappy? It had to be big if the kids noticed. Should I try to talk to her? Did I dare?

THE NEXT WEEKEND with the onset of Fall fast approaching,
I decided to get some chores at the house done on Sunday.
THWACK. The impact of the axe started at my fingertips and
resonated up to my forearms, making its way past my biceps and
finally to my shoulders. They acted as shock absorbers before it
transferred to my entire upper body. THWACK. The only sound
was the concussion of axe to wood. Even the animals had stopped
scurrying about, instead taking refuge from my intrusive
reverberations.

The block of wood was set atop the old tree stump. THWACK.
I swung the axe down hard and split it in half, then repeated the
process. THWACK. THWACK. THWACK. I had been chopping
wood for hours, frustration and anger filling me, building instead
of diminishing. Laborious chores usually helped me cope, helped
me deal with my problems, but now all I was accomplishing was a
mindless task.

"I would think there's enough wood there for the next three
winters."

I didn't bother turning around. THWACK. "Never know. It
could be a bad one."

"I brought food."

That was the impetus to make me look since I couldn't smell
anything. Sarah hovered nearby, bundled in a heavy coat and
gloves. "Don't you think you're a bit overdressed for September?" I
asked.

"I'm cold. I stoked the fire and there are chicken wings and
hoagies inside."

I closed the distance between us and hugged her. "It's not that
cold, but thank you. Come on, before Michael kills me because
you've caught a chill and he gets stuck with all the chores."

She slipped her arm in mine and we strolled toward the house
in silence.

"Soda or beer?"

Sarah was setting plates on the counter. "Soda."

"So what's this about?"

"I haven't seen you and I worry when you're in hiding."

"I'm not sure why you're my friend, but I'm thankful every day
that you are." I pulled her into my arms and held her tight. "I love
you."

"Damn, don't get all mushy on me. I'm married you know."

I laughed loudly. "Trust me, I know. Tall guy, bulky and
capable of killing me with one swipe."

"That would be the one. Don't forget cute, too."

Sarah unwrapped her hoagie and dug in. I remembered a bag
of chips I had picked up a couple of weeks earlier and retrieved it

from the cabinet. "Here, they're old, but unopened."

She grinned. "Thank you." She loved junk food.

"So?"

"I told you, I'm worried about you." She picked up a chip and popped it into her mouth.

"I'm fine."

"You don't look fine. In fact, you look like crap."

"Thanks."

"There's a rumor going round." Sarah looked up. "Word has it you helped Renee get into rehab."

The silence was deafening. "What if I did?"

"Why?"

"Does it matter?"

"I'm surprised, that's all. So is Emily."

Fuck. "Who the hell told Emily?"

"Renee did."

"What?"

"Part of her twelve-step program. Making amends to those she's hurt."

"Did she fuckin' go over there?" I leapt up, furious. "Jesus fucking Christ, she knows there's a restraining order against her. I'll kill her."

"Relax." Sarah wore a silly grin. "She called Emily at the bookstore, not the house."

"She didn't scare the kids, did she?"

"No, she never even asked to speak to them. Only to Emily."

I climbed back on the stool next to her. "And what the hell is so funny?"

"You are."

"Nice, forget what I said about us being friends."

"You're desperately in love with her."

I got up and took a beer out of the fridge. "Of course I'm in love with her. Did you think all this was for the ha ha's?"

Sarah took my hand in hers. "Have you talked to her lately?"

I shook my head.

"Why?"

"She asked me to stay away." I peeled the label off the bottle, not really in the mood after all. "I guess I'm just lucky she let's the kids spend time with me."

"Did she say that, or is that you again?"

"Me."

"So?"

I glanced up quizzically.

"Why did you help Renee?"

I let out a long sigh. "Because I *am* Renee, Sarah."

"Honey, that's not true and you know it."

"Really?" I ticked the similarities off on my fingers. "Renee is shattered over the loss of her partner. She hates everyone and everything that is keeping them apart. She's angry at herself and at the world. She hurts in every fiber of her being and still the booze can't numb her pain. She's a lost soul. You don't think that sounds like me?"

"Wow." Sarah stole a chip from my plate. "She told you all that?"

"Yes."

"When?"

"I went to see her a couple of weeks ago."

"Are you the one that posted her bail?"

The shrug was becoming habitual. "She didn't have any money." The truth was she'd lost everything; all her possessions, her apartment, if that's what you could call it, her job, her car—everything since Melanie's death.

Sarah stole another chip, but stopped midway to her mouth. "You're the one who wrote the letter to the courts."

"It's not a big deal."

"Mac, it's a very big deal. You wanted to kill her and instead you end up her savior."

"Don't get carried away. I'm merely giving her a chance to get it together."

"Why?"

I pondered her question for a moment, and told her the same thing I told Renee. "For the kids, because Melanie loved Renee, and I'd like that person to return and make the kids whole again."

"You want her in their lives?"

"No, not at all." I shook my head decisively. "But I think the kids need to see her whole without their mother to better understand it was a sickness and not the real Renee."

Tears filled Sarah eyes.

"*Now* why are you crying?"

"It's like you're growing up before my eyes. I almost don't recognize you."

"Smart ass." I got up and dumped the beer down the drain and replaced it with a bottle of water. "Is Emily okay? I mean after talking with Renee."

"She's fine." Sarah sipped her soda. "She was surprised by the call and even more after Renee told her you were helping her, but she handled it well."

"Good."

A silence developed. It was comfortable and Sarah finished eating.

"So what's new with you and the big guy?" I asked.

A sly smile spread across Sarah face, her eyes were shining. "Michael and I are adding to the family."

I struggled for words as icy dread filled my veins. "How—how did this happen?"

"We applied and have been approved."

"Huh?"

"We're adopting, silly."

"That's wonderful, Sarah, absolutely wonderful. You must be so excited." I pulled her to me and squeezed gently. "You are, right? I mean adopting isn't a problem for you?"

"No, adoption is not a problem. I want more children. Michael agreed as long as it wasn't from my womb. We're both thrilled."

A grin spread across my face, and inside I felt happiness spreading. "I am very happy for you."

"Good, 'cause you're going to be godmother."

"When?"

"As soon as a child is available."

"It could take a long time, Sarah. You need to be patient."

"I know. But I have hope now."

"So, give me the details. How did this all come about?"

"Remember when Michael and I flew out of town a couple months ago?"

"You never said anything. How could you keep this to yourself?"

"We weren't exactly talking and I was afraid."

"What were you scared of?"

"That they'd turn us down."

"And?"

"We've been working with an agency and we've been approved. All the paperwork's been signed. Now we just need a baby." Sarah was bursting with joy.

"Excellent. The baby is going to be very lucky to get you and Michael."

"Thank you." Sarah was sniffling.

"There are thousands of babies that need good homes, you know that."

"Which is why we decided to adopt."

"This is really exciting. I'm psyched for you both, really."

This time she embraced me. "I want this, Mac. I still mourn the baby I lost, and you know Michael and I always wanted a big family."

"I know, sweetie. I totally understand. After I realized Izzy was—"

"Was what?"

"Nothing, it's not important. Do you want a boy or a girl?"

"Mac, what was Izzy?"

I took her hand in mine. "This is a time for celebration, not sadness."

"Please don't do that. Don't shut me out."

Tears gathered in my eyes. "Isabella was six weeks pregnant when she died."

"Oh my god. Oh, Mac. Did you know?"

"No. I mean yes." I held her hand tightly. "We had done the whole in vitro thing, but, no, I had no idea it had taken."

"Oh honey, I'm so sorry." Tears ran down Sarah's face.

"Come on, talk to me about the adoption, tell me, boy or girl?"

She grinned and wiped her face with a napkin. "We don't care. We want a healthy baby."

"Amen to that."

Chapter Eighteen

SATURDAY AFTERNOON, A week later a knock at the office door disrupted my concentration. With my back to the entrance I called out, "It's okay, Alice. Flip the lock on the way out and have a good evening."

Long seconds elapsed. "This place looks like a tornado hit it."

At that moment I felt like it had hit me as well. I slowly turned around. "What are you doing here?" I asked.

"I thought we could talk, but if you prefer, I can leave." Emily said.

"*No.*" I yanked some plans off the couch and placed them on the floor in the corner. "Sit, please."

"This place is a mess. What the heck happened?"

It was a balancing act as I treaded over folders and around another set of plans tossed carefully on the floor. "Mary has the flu. I sent her home Monday."

Emily gazed around. "She deserves a raise if this is what happens when you're left on your own." She tip-toed toward the couch. "Are you living here?" She indicated my laundry in the corner. She was dressed in jeans, a scoop necked T-shirt and a bomber jacket, an alluring enticement for sure.

"Work's been crazy."

She slipped out of the coat and the shirt spanned her chest. I caught myself ogling the soft swell of her breasts as they peeked out above the ribbed neckline. I quickly diverted my eyes lest I be caught. "Would you like something to drink?" I stumbled to the fridge. "We have beer, OJ, water, and sip-its."

A smile lit her face. "Sip-its?"

"The kids like knowing they can help themselves when they're here. It makes them feel important. You don't approve of soda, so I don't stock it."

"Beer. And thank you, that was thoughtful about the soda."

I was dumb-struck. Emily filled my every waking thought, at night she monopolized my dreams, and now she was in my office in the flesh. *No. Don't think about flesh, especially not Emily's flesh.* The question was, why was she here? "What—I'm sorry, what did you say?"

She was waiting by the couch and flopped down on the cushions. "I'd like a beer, please."

"Where are the kids?"

"Home with a babysitter."

I grabbed her beer and a water for myself, placing the bottle on the coffee table. "I'm sorry about—"

She waved her hand and shook her head. "No, I'm not here for another apology." She picked up the bottle and opened it. "You apologized when it happened. I received the flowers the next morning with your request for forgiveness. You repeated your act of contrition when the kids were hurt. Now *I* want to talk to you about everything. I think I'm finally ready." She shrugged "At least I hope I am."

My butt came to rest on the edge of my desk. "All right."

"I've missed you." She stared at the floor. "I've missed our relationship."

My guilt for ruining that bathed my face. "I'm so sorry, Emily. I wish I could take the kiss back."

She peeked up through her lashes. "Do you regret the kiss?"

"I—"

She smiled ruefully. "Why did you *never* respond to my letter?"

"Huh? What letter?"

"I sent you one weeks ago."

Then I remembered it. The envelope I had stuck in the back of my briefcase. I dug into the leather pouch, finding it crushed down beneath some files and pulled it out. "I'm sorry." I glanced up. "When it first came I was sure it spelled rejection and I couldn't bear to read those words." I clasped it tightly thinking I still couldn't.

"Come, sit down. You're making me nervous over there." She patted the cushion next to her. "I want to talk—about everything. I'd like us to be honest with each other."

A couple of empty storage tubes that normally held architectural plans were the only items on a side chair. I dumped them on the floor and sat. Keeping a safe distance from Emily was my only hope of getting through this dialogue.

She reclined against the cushion, her arm spread across the back of the couch, her shirt spanning her chest while I struggled not to stare. "Do you miss me?" she asked.

"*Yes*," I croaked.

"So the really important question is, do you miss me as a friend or as a potential lover?" Emily leaned forward, her elbows resting on her knees, her hands clasped, watching as if my answer was the most important thing in the world.

"I..." My inner voice screamed, *Lie to her.* It would be so easy, a quick resolution to a painful disconnection. I shook my head. "I can't separate the two, believe me I have tried. You're my friend and I miss you, but—I'm drawn to everything about you. I love your smile, your kindness, your sense of humor, the way you approach life, your logic of right and wrong, your loyalty, your beauty. I—"

"Beauty? Please, I'm a grandmother, for god's sake."

"I think you're exquisite."

"And thirty pounds overweight."

"Womanly in every way, including your curves. Sorry, I didn't mean—"

"No, you answered the question. Don't say anything else." Emily took a long swig of her beer and put the bottle down. "I need to explain a couple of things." She hesitated. "I think a small part of me knew you were attracted to me right from the beginning. When it became obvious you wanted a real relationship, I was flattered. I wasn't 'darlin' or 'gorgeous' or 'pretty lady' like all the other women in your life. Any time you addressed me, it was personal and your eyes shone with everything you were feeling. You don't really hide things very well, you know." She took a sip of her beer. "The way you treated me, the way you listened to me, the way you dealt with the kids. The few times you accidentally touched me, I sensed you wanted more and a part of me was thrilled."

— Emily rose and walked to the window. I followed her with my eyes, wondering what the hell she meant.

"At first I thought it was about the kids. That you were kind to me because we were a package. Later I knew it was more. You were interested in *me*, wanted *me*, and what's more, I *liked* it. In fact, I felt pretty cocky."

"I—"

"No, don't. I want to finish." She kept her back to me. "Richard cheated on our honeymoon. Did I tell you that?"

"No, but I told you, Richard was a fucking idiot."

Emily's face was reflected in the window. Our eyes met and she smiled warmly. "What you don't know is we were separated for the last five years of our marriage. I'd had it with his cheating. Melanie was a grown woman with a family of her own and I was tired of being treated like a laundry service. We slept in separate bedrooms for years before I moved out, before I realized I deserved better. Once we separated and before he died, I dated a couple of times, but I was never going to let someone hurt me or use me like that again. After Richard passed, it was Melanie who suggested I bury him here with his grandparents. Especially since I had no intention of sharing eternity with the bastard."

Confusion fogged my brain. "Wait. Richard is buried here?"

"Yes."

"Is that why you relocated here?"

"No. By that I mean Richard had nothing to do with it. I liked the small town atmosphere. I love the mountains and I have fond memories of when Melanie was small and we would visit her paternal grandparents. I wanted her children to be raised here."

"I always wondered about you being at the cemetery."

"That's how I came to be there the afternoon I learned of Isabella and Bella. Now be quiet and listen, this is difficult." Emily glided closer and took my briefcase off the matching chair and sat opposite me. "Ever since the night you kissed me, I've thought of nothing else. I came to realize that I led you on in so many ways even though it wasn't my intention. As I said, I enjoyed the interest you showered on me. I felt like a princess and what made it even nicer was you didn't expect anything in return." She grinned at me. "Or so I thought."

The comment made me flinch.

"You've got a way of making a woman feel very special, like she's the only person in your world. As if she is the most important woman you've ever met or ever will meet. I had never experienced that before and found it very alluring. You were always so concerned whenever we were out together, worried about my reputation, about me, and I loved you for it." Emily got up and retrieved her beer bottle from the table. "I have a confession, Mac. I enjoyed our kiss. More than I ever expected I could. Maybe even more than I ever had before."

She stared at me, a small smile tugging the corner of her mouth. It reminded me of Kylie's impish grin.

"I'll tell you something else. To my knowledge, I've never been attracted to another woman. I've had friends yes, dear ones, but never that way, physically, you know. You told me often enough that Isabella was your soul mate, that you loved her and missed her. I felt safe flirting because you weren't interested, but I still benefited from your innate thoughtfulness. All at once everything changed. You still loved Isabella, but you wanted more and I was secretly envious of who would fill that need." Emily chuckled softly. "Of course, I didn't admit to myself that I was jealous. I explained it away as being concerned about you, wanting only the best for you. That is until you started dating Leah. That was when it became real. I wanted it to end, I knew she wasn't right for you. I knew she couldn't make you happy." Emily took another pull on the bottle of beer, finishing it.

"Would you like another?" I asked. She inclined her head and I got it for her.

"Thank you." Emily rolled the cold bottle between her hands and glanced up at me. "That infamous morning I walked in here and you were yelling at Sarah that you had already fallen in love with someone nearly broke my heart. I was so afraid of losing you to this unknown woman. Then Sarah left so abruptly, it was like she knew and was pushing me—pushing us."

Emily's words were bouncing around in my head and I couldn't make sense of their meaning.

"Lastly, if I want to be honest, I need to accept a lot of the responsibility for that kiss and for your declaration of love. If I hadn't pushed you during that exchange, you would never have made the move, and I think I knew that, too. The day you brought me flowers, my heart tumbled and I knew I was in danger of losing it to you. You're so damned gallant, always giving of yourself and your time. You wanted to make me happy and I wanted to let you." Emily wrapped her arms around her middle.

"I did. I tried." I said.

"Yes, you did. The problem was I was afraid."

"Because I'm a woman."

"No." She leaned over and placed her hand on my knee. "Because I was sure you would change the minute I opened myself to you. The same way Richard had."

"Emily, I love you."

"So I've been told." A warm smile reached her eyes. "Repeatedly, I might add."

"I don't understand."

"Sarah's been urging me to admit what was happening between us. She loves you very much, I hope you know that. But she's honest and will gladly list your faults, all of them. She also said when you love someone it's completely and singularly."

I had no words for that.

"So, I guess that's it. I wanted you to know the truth." She leaned back into the chair. "Oh, and I'm sorry. I needed time to come to grips with everything. Time to get my courage up."

My hand instinctively reached out, but I pulled it back quickly. "All of this is a lot to take in. Are you saying you want to be friends, after everything that's happened?"

She tilted her head at me. "*Do* you want to be friends?" Emily watched me, a smile curling the corner of her lip.

"I've missed you, but—I'm not sure I can separate friend from lover.

She climbed onto my lap and wrapped her arms around my shoulders. "Good. Cause I'm not easy you know—you'll need to take me on a couple of dates. Court me, spend adult time alone, prove to me I can trust you."

"Do you mean it?"

She answered by lowering her lips to mine.

Chapter Nineteen

"YOU'RE SURE ABOUT this, right?" I asked.

"Yes, as long as you remember your promise to take things slowly. The children are my first priority."

"I do, and I will. I give you my word."

She grinned and took my hand. "Come on, they're going to be so excited to see you. They keep asking why you don't come over to visit any more."

"I know, they asked me, too. I told them I had made you mad and you needed time to forgive me."

Emily stopped short and turned in front of me. She gripped the lapels of my jacket and pulled me closer. "There was nothing to forgive. I needed to trust you." She kissed me, right there on the street.

"I won't hurt you, Em. I promise."

"We'll talk later. Right now we're going to make my grandchildren happy."

Emily opened the back door. The babysitter was in the kitchen getting a drink from the fridge. "Hi, Mrs. O'Brien."

"Hello, Marcy, is everything okay?"

"Yes, ma'am. Kaitlin is reading and Kylie is playing a video game."

Emily pulled some bills from her wallet and handed them to the girl. "Thank you. I really appreciate your help on such short notice."

The girl glanced at the money in her hand. "*Thank you*. Call me anytime." Marcy lifted her coat from the hook at the door and called goodbye as she left.

"Kids, come see. I have a surprise for you." Emily called out.

They came running and it reminded me of the first time all those months ago. This time Kaitlin bounded into my arms gladly. "Hello, beautiful. How are you?"

"Good." She kissed my cheek and hugged my neck. "Are you staying for dinner?"

I glanced at Emily and she nodded. Kaitlin jumped down and ran to her.

"Me, too."

I lifted Kylie into my arms and kissed him hello. "How's it going, little man?"

"Good. Will you play wiff me?" This time we both turned to Emily.

"Go on, but only until dinner's ready."

Kylie bolted from my arms and ran to get the game and controllers set up.

"I could stay and help you," I offered. "I really do enjoy watching you in the kitchen."

Emily shook her head. "You like *leering* at me in the kitchen."

"Watching, leering — as long as it's you." I grinned.

"Go entertain my grandson. I'll call you soon. If you're good, I'll let you help me with the dishes."

My eyes grew big at that thought, but I quickly contained myself. "Call me if you need help. Seriously."

She pulled me to her and kissed my cheek. "Go."

"Yes, ma'am."

"How did you get so good at this?" Kylie and I were engaged in a Nascar racing game.

He grinned and passed my car for the third time. "Pwactice."

Kaitlin sat behind us on the couch. She was supposed to be reading, but she kept snickering.

"Hey you, if you can do better, get over here."

She scooted down onto the floor and took the controller. She slowly gained back one of my lost laps. I tickled her ribs. "You've been practicing, too, haven't you?"

She squirmed and laughed as she completed another lap, gaining back more lost ground. The game continued until Emily called us to dinner.

At the table Emily asked if we had fun.

"It's not fair," I grumbled. "They cheated."

She glared disapprovingly. "My grandchildren don't cheat, they're simply better at these things than we are."

Both kids giggled.

"I'm going for a rematch and I'm going to win," I threatened.

An hour later the sink was filled with hot water and I was adding dish detergent, while Emily put the kids to bed.

"Well, I can certainly see the appeal. Watching someone do dishes *is* sexy." She came up behind me and wrapped her arms around my middle. I could feel her breasts against my spine, her thighs along the back of my legs, and desire pulsed to life.

"Careful, or I'll drop a damn dish."

She dried as I washed, completing the task in a short amount of time. "Would you like coffee?"

"No, thanks. I already know I'm not sleeping tonight. No sense being wired on caffeine."

Emily blushed crimson.

"I didn't mean it like that. I never —"

"I know, I — maybe I did." She took my hand and tugged me

into the living room. I sat on the couch and she reached for the remote, then sat next to me.

I poured us some wine. A white zinfandel, light, because I wanted both of us in complete control of our faculties. I handed one to her. "We probably should talk." I looked at her expectantly.

She took my glass and placed it on the coffee table. "I know everything I need to know. Right now I want you to kiss me."

I groaned out loud. She pushed me backward on the couch. I pulled her with me and gently tugged her head lower as our lips met. *Jesus, God.* I let her lead. She needed to control what we did or didn't do. She was lying on top of me, settled between my thighs. My hands glided down and over her hips. Our kisses grew more urgent and she started to thrust against me. My hands dropped lower. I cupped her full cheeks, pulling her closer, tighter against where I needed her. I loved the fullness of her butt, and squeezed as she drove her hips in time with mine. The contact was stimulating, creating a flood of arousal.

She wiggled her ass from my grasp. "You can't keep doing that," she said. "It's doing wickedly sinful things to me." She kissed my neck and whispered in my ear, "Don't stop. I haven't felt this good in a long, long time."

My lips continued to explore hers. I was on fire. My hands slid beneath the back of her T-shirt. Her skin was hot to my touch. Her nipples were stiff against my chest and her flesh quivered with each stroke of my hand.

She pulled away and gazed into my eyes. "Mac. What do I do?"

Sweet Jesus. I slid a little to the left and pulled her over and under me. "I love you, Em, very much." I kissed her lips, brushing them softly. "We don't *have* to do anything unless you're sure." I kissed her again, soft, light kisses across her lips, running my tongue along the edges, eliciting a moan from her.

She wrapped her arms around me, pulling me closer. She shifted her legs and opened her mouth to me.

My tongue skimmed her lips, tasting her. My head felt like it would explode when I slid my thigh between her legs and pushed against her gently. She arched upward, whimpering. I pulled away from her lips and nuzzled her neck, licking and kissing the area right below her jaw, down to her collarbone, where her pulse was beating rapidly. I brought my lips back to hers to kiss her again, more deeply this time, thrusting my tongue exactly as I wanted to drive my fingers deep inside her. I explored every inch of her mouth as we kissed. "I love you," I breathed. My hand slipped beneath her T-shirt, stroking the skin of her ribs and stomach, moving higher with each sweep of my hand. The muscles of her stomach contracted with every touch. A low growl rattled through

me as I made contact with her breast. It felt wonderful in my palm.
I had dreamed of this moment for months. I touched her lovingly,
gently teasing the cloth-covered nipple between my fingers. It
wasn't enough. I wanted to feel skin. As I reached around to
unhook her bra, I paused to look into her eyes. "Okay?"

Blushing, she nodded and pulled me back down for another
kiss.

She thrust her tongue and hips in rhythm as I released the
clasp. My desire exploded and I could barely contain myself. I
slipped my hand back to Emily's breast and lifted the silk garment
out of the way. As I lowered my palm to her soft skin, a growl
rumbled within me. Her need was pulsating against my leg and I
felt the beginning shudder of my own orgasm. I pulled my lower
body back, trying to quell its response as I lowered my mouth to
Emily's neck, licking her skin, working my way lower toward my
target. I lifted her T-shirt and placed kisses across her chest.
"Beautiful, you are absolutely breathtaking," I said. I played with
her nipples, teasing them into hard little nubs. I lowered my mouth
and sucked one between my lips. Loving it gently, I moaned at the
sweet, sweet taste of her. She arched against me, clutching my head
tightly to her breasts. I licked and suckled first one breast, then the
other until my head was spinning. I returned to Emily's lips,
pushing my tongue into her mouth, claiming it and her as my own.
She clung to me desperately as my hand moved down her stomach
and across her hip. I heard her whimper. The lower my hand
traveled, the more she thrust to meet it. When my palm slid lower
still she surged up, gasping. I pulled back immediately, breaking
the kiss and looked into her eyes. "Okay?"

"No. Not at all." Her face was flushed with desire, her eyes
glazed. "We have to shift this to the bedroom, now."

"We don't *have* to, we—"

"Oh *yes*, we do. You are not leaving me like this." She
shimmied out from under me and stood, holding out her hand. "I
want you to make love to me, Mac Taylor. It's time."

A shudder rolled through me. I quickly rose and took her
hand, following her toward the bedroom, toward our future, our
haven, and *my* deliverance.

FIVE WEEKS LATER, on a beautiful Indian summer day in
autumn we arrived at the ballpark a little later than normal. Jim
Collins had already set things up. Connie and Sarah had the
refreshments stacked and Michael was coaching Patrick as he
practiced throwing. Today was Patrick's debut as the full time
pitcher, and he was excited.

Kaitlin spotted us and bounced into my arms. I swung her up and kissed her cheek. "So how's it going, doll face?"

"We waited for you to start."

"Where's Kylie?" Emily shaded her eyes as she searched for him on the field. There was an edge to her voice.

Kaitlin giggled as she pointed to home base. Jim was catching and was attempting to show Kylie the finer aspects of that position. Jim was also a mountain of a man and Kylie was practically hidden between his legs, squatting down, ready to catch the pitch coming at them.

Emily laughed out loud with relief. I put Kaitlin down and she advanced into the on-deck circle.

"I'm supposed to help Patrick today. I better get out there," I said with a smile to Emily.

She pulled me close and kissed me on the lips. "I'll be here watching, so make sure we win today, Coach."

"Yes, ma'am." I grinned. It was time to play ball.

For a fall day it was absolutely gorgeous. The sun was warm even with the breezes coming off the mountains. The sky was cloudless, an endless blue on the horizon. Patrick started his wind up, released the ball, and it sailed right across home base to be slammed into left field by Kaitlin. Patrick grinned, pride evident on his face. Kaitlin raced around first and headed for second, getting a double.

"Excellent Patrick. I couldn't have done it better myself," I praised.

He grinned at me and awaited the next player. It was Tracey and she was smiling in anticipation. She'd come a long way in the last six months. She still had moments, but between her mother and counseling she was starting to forget the horrors her father had inflicted upon her. Patrick threw the ball. Tracey bunted it midway into the infield and raced for first. Kaitlin slid into third and everyone was safe. Tracey waved to her mother in the bleachers. Andrea was sitting next to Emily and they were both clapping for the girl.

Tommy was up next. Patrick gave him a thumbs up, wanting him to do good. The kids cared about each other. Sportsmanship was alive and well on Team Bella because they genuinely rooted for one other. They cared about their teammates because they were friends. That was why Isabella wanted to start this team in the first place and that was why it would continue as long as there were kids who needed and wanted to play. For these children it wasn't about winning or losing, it was about unity of triumph. It was about sharing and friendship and living normal everyday lives to the fullest.

I waited and observed as player after player took their turn at bat, each eager for the chance to play, each cheering for their teammates.

After the game I sat in the bleachers talking with Michael and Jim while the kids got their refreshments. "So Mac, how's that *friendship thing* with Emily going?" Michael asked and slapped me on the back as Jim Collins chuckled.

My head dropped between my shoulders and I took a deep breath. "Who knew she could actually care for me?" I shrugged.

Michael bumped shoulders with me. "With some women there's no accounting for taste. She'll wise up in oh — about twenty or thirty years." He laughed.

The ladies approached. "What's going on here?" Sarah flicked her eyes from one to the other of us. "And don't say nothing. I can see the guilt on your faces."

I glanced at Michael. He winked, but kept laughing. Jim put his hands up. "We were talking, that's all."

"Uh huh." Sarah grinned as she sat next to her husband. "We're gonna take all the kids with us while these two do some food shopping. I've given Emily a very long list of supplies we'll need." Sarah winked at me.

"Didn't you just do the shopping?" Michael asked.

Emily shook her head, laughing. "I don't think we can find all that Sarah asked for at the market, but we'll give it a shot." She tugged my hand and pulled me up. "Come on, we have our assignment."

"For what?"

Emily laughed. "Sarah's having a barbeque."

I glanced from Sarah to Emily. "That's great, when?"

"This afternoon — at your place." Sarah burst out laughing.

"Huh?"

"Sarah invited the entire team and their parents to your house this afternoon for a barbeque." Emily seemed thrilled while I felt sick to my stomach.

"There's no food in the house, you know that."

"I'll explain in the car. Come on, we have lots to do."

We said our goodbyes then started off. "You're excited. How can you be excited? I don't have anything to feed these people."

Emily took my arm and pulled me closer. "I'm happy. Is that okay? Besides that's why we're going shopping."

"Of course it's okay." I opened the door of the truck for her. "I'm glad you're happy. But damn, she could have given us a little warning."

Emily climbed up on the rail and kissed me before sliding into the cab. "She came up with the idea and I agreed. I hope you don't mind?" I closed her door as she fastened her seatbelt.

"I don't mind."

After we were on the road, I turned to Emily. "You're really enjoying this, aren't you?"

She was grinning from ear to ear. "Michael and Sarah adopting a baby makes me happy. Makes me believe in tomorrows. *We* make me happy, and suddenly I'm looking forward to the future. This barbeque is a good way for everyone to realize we're a family."

My heart skipped a beat. I gripped Emily's hand and kissed her palm. "Are you sure about this?"

"I am."

"Aren't the kids going to ask questions? You wanted to go slow."

Emily kissed my cheek. "You've been great about that, even making sure they don't realize you've been sleeping over. But you know what? They already figured it out. They're not stupid." She took my hand, holding it tightly. "It's time."

"Does this mean you've thought about us moving in together?" I tried to see her peripherally, while keeping my eyes on the road at the same time.

"Yes. I'm thinking about it. A lot actually."

I swerved to the side of the road and put my flashers on. "Are you serious?"

"This was a big decision and you've been really patient. Now it's time I stepped up. I love you, the kids love you, so why wait? If you still want us, we're ready to be a family." She grinned.

I slid across the seat, took her in my arms, and kissed her.

"Okay, okay." She yanked the hair on the back of my head and tugged hard. "That's enough or we're going to miss our first barbeque as a family."

"I wouldn't mind if we were a little late." I had worked the buttons on her sweater loose and had my hand under her shirt. Her nipple was hard and begging to be suckled.

She smiled and pushed my hand away. "Later Romeo. We have a party to host and an announcement to make."

Other Regal Crest books you may enjoy:

Re: Building Sasha
by S. Renee Bess

Sasha Lewis, the uber-competent manager of Whittingham Builders, finds herself drowning in a riptide of distrust as she struggles to maintain her relationship with Lee Simpson. A genius at balancing details, Sasha commits a career-derailing error while being distracted by Lee's threat to burn down their house and its contents.

Lee's flagrant sexual liaisons with a business client, Angela Jackman, and her escalating deeds of emotional cruelty rip apart Sasha. In self-imposed exile from most of her friends, Sasha recalls a brief encounter with Avery Sloan; an encounter destined to become more meaningful when Avery's social service agency hires Whittingham Builders to rehab an old Victorian house.

What hateful acts will Lee perform in an effort to degrade Sasha? How much damage will Sasha endure before she begins to rebuild her spirit? Will Sasha grab Avery's outstretched hand and accept the gentle yet exciting offer of love she sees in this woman?

ISBN: 978-1-935053-07-1

Faithful Service, Silent Hearts
by Lynette Mae

Faithful Service, Silent Hearts is the story of Devon James, a bright young military officer, dedicated to serving her country. She soon learns that finding love under any circumstances is difficult, but when your love is forbidden by military regulations and a relentless zealot pursues you, it can seem impossible. Following an investigation that destroyed her first lover's career and their relationship, Devon hopes her new assignment will allow her a fresh start.

She is reunited with an old college friend, and together, they form an impressive intelligence team and red-hot couple. When their assignments take them to the war-torn Middle East in the early days of terrorists targeting Americans, then things really get interesting. She returns home a decorated veteran with numerous physical and emotional scars. Devon soon discovers that the battle for her own integrity and faithful service has only begun.

ISBN: 978-1-935053-49-1

OTHER REGAL CREST TITLES

Be sure to check out our other imprints,
Yellow Rose Books and Quest Books.

About the Author

Her short stories include, "Who's In Charge" and "Silent Journey" in Khimairal Ink, (Bedazzled Ink) October 2008, "Bareback"—Lesbian Cowboys Erotic Adventures (Cleis) 2009, "Silent Journey"—Year's Best Lesbian Fiction 2008, "Nuance" (Bedazzled Ink) 2009, and "Never Too Old"—Lesbian Lust Erotic Stories (Cleis) 2010. Novels include *Redemption* (Regal Crest Enterprises, LLC) 2011, and *Strangers* (Regal Crest Enterprises, LLC) 2012.

Visit her Webpage: www.dejaynovl.org

Find her on Facebook: www.facebook.com/dejaynovl
She can be contacted at: dejaynovl@gmail.com

Information about Domestic Violence

Nearly 3.2 million people, both men and women, called a domestic violence crisis center or hot line in 2009 to escape violent situations, don't be afraid to seek for advice, or assist someone that might be a victim. (National Network to End Domestic Violence)

It's said that if there's a gathering of one hundred men and women, at least 70% will know someone who's been a victim of Domestic Violence, even if they don't realize it. To take this a step further 44% will have a close relative who's been a victim. Up to 33% will have been victims themselves. These are shocking numbers, but there is help available, you need only avail yourself of it.

Studies show that access to shelter services leads to a 60-70% reduction in incidence and severity of re-assault during the 3-12 month follow-up period compared to women who did not access shelter. In fact shelter services led to greater reduction in severe re-assault than did seeking court or law enforcement protection.

If you need help, go to this website:
http://www.thehotline.org/resources/

If you don't have access to a computer, call this toll free phone number: 1-800-799-SAFE

Most importantly get help, or help someone in need.

The author has stated she will donate a portion of her royalties to the above site.